A WIZARD'S
WHAT A WIZARD

"So you have a new wizard
to the king in a high and rather nasal voice. I hope I
would never have one. I'd been hoping that when
your old one retired you'd have the sense not to get
another."

Since I had just finished bowing to him, and my
predecessor was standing only a few feet away, this
struck me as unusually rude, even for a member of the
aristocracy, but he kept on talking about us as though
we weren't there. "My father kept a wizard—or he *said*
he was a wizard, someone I think my father had picked
up at a carnival somewhere—but as soon as I inherited,
I sent him packing right away, you can be sure."

"We've always been very happy with our wizards,"
said the king stiffly.

"Is there anything in particular you object to about
wizards?" asked my predecessor with a calmness that
he was having trouble maintaining.

"Everything about them is so, well, on the surface!" said the young count, waving his beautiful
white hands. "Once you've seen an illusion or two,
you have nothing left but vague talk about the powers of darkness and light, which someone like me sees
through at once."

"I think you're underestimating real wizardry," continued my predecessor, with an evenness of tone I
admired.

"You're the wizard who used to be here, aren't you?
My father told me about your illusions over dessert,
back when he used to visit the king. But really, when
you go beyond illusions, what do you have?"

I turned him into a frog.

A Bad Spell In Yurt

C. Dale Brittain

A BAD SPELL IN YURT

A Baen Books Original

Baen Publishing Enterprises
P.O. Box 1403
Riverdale, N.Y. 10471

ISBN: 0-671-72075-9

Cover art by Tom Kidd

First printing, August 1991

Distributed by
SIMON & SCHUSTER
1230 Avenue of the Americas
New York, N.Y. 10020

Printed in the United States of America

Dedication

To R.A.B.
Who made me do it.

CONTENTS

PART ONE

Yurt

I

I was not a very good wizard. But it was not a very big kingdom. I assumed I was the only person to answer their ad, for in a short time I had a letter back from the king's constable, saying the job was mine if I still wanted it, and that I should report to take up the post of Royal Wizard in six weeks.

It took most of the six weeks to grow in my beard, and then I dyed it gray to make myself look older. Two days before leaving for my kingdom, I went down to the emporium to buy a suitable wardrobe.

Of course at the emporium they knew all about us young wizards from the wizards' school. They looked at us dubiously, took our money into the next room to make sure it stayed money even when we weren't there, and tended to count the items on the display racks in a rather conspicuous way. But I knew the manager of the clothing department—he'd even helped me once to pick out a Christmas present for my grandmother, which I think endeared me to him as much as to her.

He was on the phone when I came in. "What do you mean, you won't take it back? But our buyer never ordered it!" While waiting for him, I picked out some black velvet trousers; just the thing, I thought, to give me a wizardly flair.

The manager slammed down the phone. "So what am I supposed to do with this?" he demanded of no one in particular. "This" was a shapeless red velvet pullover, with some rather tattered white fur at the neck. It might have been intended to be part of a Father Noel costume.

I was entranced. "I'll take it!"

"Are you sure? But what will you do with it?"

"I'm going to be a Royal Wizard. It will help me strike the right note of authority and mystery."

"Speaking of mystery, what's all the fuzzy stuff on your chin?"

I was proud of my beard, but since he gave me the pullover for almost nothing, I couldn't be irritated. When I left for my kingdom, I felt resplendent in velvet, red for blood and black for the powers of darkness.

It was only two hundred miles, and probably most of the young wizards would have flown themselves, but I insisted on the air cart. "I need to make the proper impression of grandeur when I arrive," I said. Besides—and they all knew it even though I didn't say it—I wasn't sure I could fly that far.

The air cart was the skin of a purple beast that had been born flying. Long after the beast was dead, its skin continued to fly, and it could be guided by magic commands. It brought me steeply up from the wizards' complex at the center of the City, and I looked back as the white city spires fell away. It had been a good eight years, but I felt ready for new challenges. We soared across plains, forests, and hills all the long afternoon, before finally banking steeply over what I had been calling "my" kingdom for the last six weeks.

From above, there scarcely seemed to be more to the kingdom than a castle, for beyond the castle walls there was barely room for the royal fields and pastures before thick green woods closed in. A bright garden lay just outside the castle walls, and pennants snapped from all the turrets. The air cart dipped, folded its wings, and set me down with a bump in the courtyard.

I looked around and loved it at once. It was a perfect child's toy of a castle, the stone walls freshly whitewashed and the green shutters newly painted. The courtyard was a combination of clean-swept cobbles, manicured flower beds, and tidy gravel paths. On the far side of the courtyard, a well-groomed horse put his head over a white half-door and whinnied at me.

A man and woman came toward me, both dressed in starched blue and white. "Welcome to the Kingdom of Yurt. I am the king's constable, and this is my wife." They both bowed deeply, which flustered me, but I covered it by striking a pose of dignity.

"Thank you," I said in my deepest voice. "I'm sure I will find much here to interest me." The air cart was twitching, eager to be flying again. "If you could just help me with my luggage—"

The constable helped me unload the boxes, while his wife ran to open the door to my chambers. The door opened directly onto the courtyard. I had somehow expected either a tower or a dungeon and wondered if this was suitably dignified, but at least it meant we didn't have far to carry the boxes. They were heavy, too, and I had not had enough practice with the spell for lifting more than one heavy thing at a time to want to try it in front of an audience.

The air cart took off again as soon as it was empty. I watched it soar away, my last direct link with the City, then turned to start unpacking. Both the constable and his wife stayed with me, eager to talk. I was just as eager to have them, because I wanted to find out more about Yurt.

"The kingdom's never had a wizard from the wizards' school before," said the constable. I was unpacking my certificate for completing the eight years' program. Although, naturally, it didn't say anything about honors or special merit or even areas of distinction, it really was impressive. That was why I had packed it on top. It was a magic certificate, of course, nearly six feet long when unrolled. My name, Daimbert, was written in letters of fire that flickered as you watched. Stars twinkled around the edges, and the deep blue and maroon flourishes turned to gold when you touched them. It came with its own spell to adhere to walls, so I hung it up in the outer of my two chambers, the one I would use as my study.

"Our old wizard's just retired," the constable continued. "He must be well past two hundred years old, and when he was young you had to serve an apprenticeship to become a wizard. They didn't have all the training you have now."

I ostentatiously opened my first box of books.

"He's moved down to a little house at the edge of the forest. That's why we had to hire a new wizard. I'm sure he'd be delighted to meet you if you ever had time to visit him."

"Oh, good," I thought with more relief than was easy to admit, even to myself. "Someone who may actually know some magic if I get into trouble."

I took my books out one by one and arranged them on the shelves: the *Ancient and Modern Necromancy*, all five volumes of *Thaumaturgy A to Z*, the *Index to Spell Key Words*, and the rest, most barely thumbed. As I tried to decide whether to put the *Elements of Transmogrification* next to *Basic Metamorphosis*, which would make sense thematically but not aesthetically, since they were such different sizes, I thought I should have plenty of quiet evenings here, away from the distractions of the City, and might even get a chance to read them. If I had done more than skim those two volumes, I might have avoided all that embarrassment with the frogs in the practical exam.

"You'll meet the king this evening, but he's authorized me to tell you some of our hopes. We've never had a telephone system, but now that you're here we're sure we'll be able to get one."

I was flabbergasted. In the City telephones were so common that you tended to forget how complicated was the magic by which they ran. It was new magic, too, not more than forty years old, something that Yurt's old wizard would never have learned but which was indeed taught at the wizards' school. How was I going to explain I had managed to avoid that whole sequence of courses?

He saw my hesitation. "We realize we're rather remote, and that the magic is not easy. No one is expecting anything for at least a few weeks. But everyone was so excited when you answered our ad! We'd been afraid we might have to settle for a magician, but instead we have a fully trained and qualified wizard!"

"Don't worry the boy with his duties so soon," the constable's wife said to him, but smiling as she scolded. "He'll have plenty of time to get started tomorrow."

"Tomorrow! A few weeks!" I thought, but had the sense not to say anything. I didn't even have the right books. If I did nothing else, I might be able to derive the proper magic from basic principles in four or five years. I was too upset even to resent being called "the boy"—so much for the gray beard!

"We'll leave you alone now," said the constable. "But dinner's in an hour, and then you can meet some of the rest."

I had seen faces peeping out of windows as we went back and forth with the luggage, but no one else had come to meet me. While I unpacked my clothes, I tried gloomily to think of plausible excuses why Yurt could not possibly have a telephone system. Nearby anti-telephonic demonic influences and the importance of maintaining a rustic, unspoiled lifestyle seemed the most promising.

II

Dinner was formal. Freshly washed and brushed but still wearing my red and black velvet, I was led by the constable out across the courtyard and to the castle's great hall. On the way out, I stopped to put a magic lock on the door to my chambers, a lock that would recognize only my own palm print. It took me only a second, even though it's fairly complex magic; I had needed it on more than one occasion in the City, living among an unruly group of other wizardry students. The constable was impressed, as I knew he would be; that's why I had waited to do it until he came back.

We walked under a tall archway, through studded doors that looked as though they stood permanently open in the summer, into a hall whose high roof was four stories above us. The walls were hung with brightly colored pennants, and a cheerful fire burned in the great fireplace at the opposite end, in spite of the warmth of a summer evening. The room was well-lit by a series of suspended globes. I peeked at them surreptitiously as we advanced across the flagstones, and my opinion of my predecessor went up; I didn't think I could make magic lamps that burned so well.

A group of people waited at the far end of the hall, made to seem almost insignificant by the height of the room. Their talking faded away as we approached. My attention went of course to the throne, pulled close to the fire, where a stoop-shouldered, white-haired man watched me coming with surprisingly sharp eyes. The velvet of his ermine-decorated robes was even more brilliantly red than my pullover.

"His majesty, King Haimeric of Yurt!" announced the constable. "Sire, I wish to present the new Royal Wizard."

I did the full bow in the proper stages, first the dipping of the head, then the wide-spreading of the arms, then the drop to both knees with my head still lowered. They had taught us etiquette in the first few weeks after we arrived at the wizards' school, while I was still attending all classes.

"Rise, Wizard, and advance to the throne." The voice was thin and quavery, but the eyes regarded me shrewdly as I lifted my head. I came toward him, holding out my hands palm up. He placed his hands on top of mine; they were dry and so light I almost didn't feel them. "Welcome to Yurt."

This seemed to end the more ceremonial part of the introductions. The constable now came forward and began introducing the rest of the party. There were a number of knights and ladies and two boys. The queen, it turned out, was not there, having gone to visit her parents. "I wonder how old *they* can be!" I thought.

The most important person there, after the king, was Dominic, the king's nephew and, I presumed, the royal heir. He didn't look like someone you'd want for an enemy. His golden hair had gone sandy with the first streaks of gray, and his doubtless once heavily muscled body was pushing out his tunic in places where muscle didn't grow. But there was a hard look about the eyes and a twist to the lips that made me glad he didn't seem to resent me.

After Dominic came an assortment of other knights, ladies, and more distant royal relatives, none of whose names I caught. The boys, it seemed, were there to be trained in knighthood. I did the formal half-bow to each of the men and the full bow to the ladies. "He looks, so . . . young!" I heard one of the ladies whispering to another. She was very young herself, but I feared it was not a compliment.

Last came the chaplain. Even though he was young, probably no older than me, he had a maturity about him that made my own one-inch beard seem rather trivial. He had a gaunt face, enormous black eyes, and a mouth that looked as though it rarely smiled. In short, he looked like a good chaplain should look.

I wrung his hand with enthusiasm. His was the only hand that was offered for me to shake. His responding squeeze was both stronger than I had expected and much stronger than my own. "I'm delighted to meet you," I said, and meant it. Calculating quickly, I decided he was the only person in the court I would be able to talk to, really talk to, about interesting topics. I was used to a social life in the City and had no intention of spending *every* evening with my books if I could help it. Priests and wizards traditionally do not have cordial relationships, but I never let something like that stop me. "I hope we can become closest friends."

He looked a little taken aback, which I thought of as a good sign; at least he was paying attention to me. But he only said gravely, "I hope so. I regret that I never enjoyed a particularly amiable friendship with your predecessor."

While I was being introduced, servants in blue and white livery had been setting up the two long tables. The king now rose from his throne, leaned on Dominic's arm, and led the rest of us to dinner. As he reached the table, a brass quartet, on a balcony above us, began to play. I thoroughly approved. Several of the other young wizards had left to take their posts at about the same time as I, and although all of them had bigger kingdoms, I was sure none was as charming.

The king's party, consisting of his relatives, the other knights and ladies, the chaplain, and me, sat at one table, with the king at our head, while the constable and his wife took the head and foot of the other table. The brass quartet changed to a different, even livelier, tune, and through the arch at the far end of the hall came more servants in procession, carrying huge steaming platters. They served the king a portion from each, placed the platters on the table, and stood back. He took a bite of the fowl, looked up, and nodded. The music came to a close with an abrupt flourish, the servants all rushed, smiling, to sit down at the constable's table, and in a moment the trumpeters joined us, laughing and wiping off their instruments. The platters were passed up and down. I took much bigger helpings than anyone else.

Conversation at our table tended to be rather refined, but at the other table the constable and his wife, the servants, and the trumpeters were talking and joking. I tried to keep my attention both on my neighbors at table and on what the servants were saying. They were talking about the day's events, work done, fields almost ready for haying, news from the forest, gossip about someone they all knew who had been away but might be back soon. It was insider conversation, where each only had to make a passing reference to something before the others all knew what he or she meant. I wondered how soon it would be before I too knew without even thinking what they were talking about. This was, after all, *my* kingdom.

At my own table, of course, everyone was well-schooled in manners and was explaining things for the benefit of the outsider, me. "One becomes so aware of the agricultural cycle out here," the lady at my right was saying. I dragged my attention back to her from a pretty servant girl at the next table who had given me a saucy look over her shoulder, while chewing enthusiastically on a drumstick. Wizards, like priests, never marry, but unlike priests we're allowed to look at girls.

"All our food, or almost all, is produced right on the castle estates. At this time of year they're winnowing the cockerels out of the young fowl, so we'll have chicken very regularly. I hope you don't miss the greater choice of the City."

"Well, this is delicious," I answered, wiping my lips and wondering if I could reach the platter or if I would have to interrupt Dominic in his conversation with the lady on his far side to get him to pass it.

"I spent three seasons in the City myself when I was younger, *much* younger."

"Then you must have been an infant," I said gallantly. I slid my hand nonchalantly to the left along the table, calculating the distance. I guessed her as perhaps half again my age, in spite of the big pink ribbons with which her braids were looped and the myriad flowers and flourishes of lace on her gown.

"On, no," she said with a tinkling laugh. "I'm *so* much older and wiser than you might think. I may have kept my youthful looks, but they conceal a *wealth* of experience. You may not realize it, but it can be a serious disadvantage to still have golden curls when one has passed twenty summers. It's so hard to be taken seriously!"

Although my curls were not golden, I actually realized it quite well, having the same problem—except that I didn't have the wealth of experience either. Dominic's wine glass was unfortunately placed; I was afraid I'd catch it with my elbow. I wondered if I dared use a lifting spell on the platter.

"Go ahead, see if you can guess my age," she continued. I was tired of this topic, but she was just warming to it. "Come on, everybody, guess!"

"Twenty-five?" I said judiciously.

"My goodness, you're getting close, but you're still too low." She laughed again. "Anyone else?" looking around the table.

Dominic looked toward us. "Pass the chicken, please," I said quickly.

The chaplain, sitting across the table from me, had been following our conversation in silence. "Forty-eight," he said, just as everyone else had stopped talking.

My companion blushed up to the roots of her hair (if she dyed her hair, she was careful; the roots were as golden as the rest). The chaplain resumed eating, and, after a brief embarrassed pause, so did everyone else. I reloaded my plate with more clattering of spoons than was strictly necessary.

"While you were in the City," I said, "did you ever go on the tour of the wizards' school? Did they show you the dragon in the basement?"

Conversation resumed around us. I glanced over again at the chaplain. I was afraid he didn't have a sense of humor, which could be a problem for him if he was going to be friends with me, but on the other hand he didn't seem to have any tact either, which could have advantages.

I don't know why I kept expecting Dominic to be my enemy, but the burly royal heir was trying to be friendly. "There's a story we've heard even out here," he said, "that if you go far enough north, thousands and thousands of miles, you come to a land that's nothing but dragons and other magic creatures. Is this true? A wizard came through once, to visit our old wizard, and he said he'd been there."

"Oh, it's real enough," I said. "The magic is wild up there." Other people were turning toward us, and I was enjoying the audience. "It's the same magic we use, because it too grows out of the power that shaped the earth." I caught the chaplain's eye across the table and winked. He made no response.

"But the magic there is more primitive," I continued, "not formed into the deep channels that generations of wizards have made for it down here. It's a land of dragons, of giants, of unspeakable monsters. The air cart you saw me arrive in today"—I knew some of them must have been peeping at me from the windows—"is the skin of a beast from the land of dragons. Anything could happen there; it can be a highly dangerous place, even for those most experienced in wizardry."

"Have you been there yourself?"

I had been hoping Dominic wouldn't ask that. Of course I hadn't been there. There had been a field trip from the wizards' school, but only the best students were invited to go.

"I am not yet worthy of the voyage," I said in what I hoped would be a mysterious voice. Surprisingly, the chaplain sat up straighter and fixed me with his enormous eyes at that. Several ladies further down the table smiled as though they saw right through me. "Has your old wizard ever been?" I said disingenuously, knowing the answer from what Dominic had said but wanting to make it clear that I at any rate had company.

"Not that he ever told us," said the lady on my right, but much more uncertainly than I had expected. Several things several people had said about the old wizard made him seem like a more distant and more shadowy figure than someone should be who had lived in the court for years, and even now, apparently, lived just outside the castle. I was both going to have to work on my own aura of shadowy mystery and visit him.

There was a clearing of a throat at the upper end of the table. Everyone fell silent at once. "Wizard!" said the king. "How are you finding Yurt? Do we have company to make up for the pleasures of the City?"

The chaplain might have said "No." I instead answered only the first but not the second question. "I like it very much!" I said with perfect honesty.

"But already you're worrying that the evenings will

be quiet," said the King with a smile. How had he known that? "This will be an incentive for you to work on our telephone system, so you can talk to your friends again."

The disadvantage to studying wizardry, instead of religion, is that you don't learn good curses. Everything you learn is in the powerful language of magic and will have an effect if you say it, even if the effect is not the intended one. I really didn't want to propel King Haimeric and his talk of telephones across the hall and into the fire, so I couldn't even think it. "The constable's already mentioned that to me!" I said with cheerful noncommittal. If I already *had* a telephone, maybe I could call up some of my teachers, the ones who still liked me even at the end, and ask them how to put one in. But this line of thinking clearly was not going to get me anywhere. "Do the neighboring kingdoms already have their systems?"

"Ours will be the first in the region," said the king proudly.

III

Dessert came at that point, providing a welcome distraction. A few minutes later, the king rose, and everyone rose with him. He left the hall, again on Dominic's arm, presumably bound for bed. Some people stood talking, and others started to disperse. I touched the chaplain on the shoulder. "Would you like to go to my chambers for a last glass of wine?"

He looked slightly surprised but nodded, and we walked together back out into the cobbled courtyard. The long summer evening was still lingering, and the air was like a caress on the skin. My magic lock was glowing softly. I pressed with my palm to open the door, then threw the casements open to let in the air.

The chaplain took a seat by the window, eyeing my

diploma and books. I opened one of the bottles of wine I had brought with me. Tomorrow I would have to ask the constable about getting some of the local wine for my chambers; it was better than what I had been able to afford in the City on a student stipend.

"You seemed surprised that I asked you in," I said as I handed him a glass. "Why was that? Were you and the old wizard enemies?" I knew at least that he would give me a direct answer.

"No, not enemies," and he held the glass up to the light. "I trust this isn't *magic* wine," he said and smiled for the first time since I'd met him. He took a sip without waiting for the answer to what was obviously meant to be a joke. "But your predecessor resented religion. I don't know whether he thought there shouldn't be a court chaplain at all, or whether he thought that the fact that religion demands a higher standard of human behavior than does magic put him at a disadvantage. I have only been here three years myself, and clearly something happened between the old wizard and my own predecessor. I have never heard what it was; I had too much Christian tact to ask."

"You didn't have too much Christian tact to guess the lady's age tonight!" I said with a laugh. If he could make a joke, so could I.

"The Lady Maria?" He considered for a moment. "Maybe it wasn't tactful at that." I began to wonder if he would be as good a person to talk to as I had hoped.

"Did the old wizard have these same chambers?" I said to change the subject.

"These chambers? No. In fact, I was rather surprised when I heard the constable was putting you here. The queen's old nurse lived here until she died last year; the rooms were then shut up until last week. The old wizard had his chambers in the north tower."

I knew it. They weren't taking me seriously. I could

be ten times more powerful and mysterious in the north tower than in the old nurse's chambers!

As though reading my thoughts and wanting to contradict them, the chaplain said, "Everyone was enormously impressed when a wizard trained in the great school answered the constable's ad. The queen started talking at once about a telephone system."

"Why a telephone, in the name of the saints?" I cried, using an exclamation I trusted he would understand.

He lifted his eyebrows at me. "The queen has found telephones extremely convenient the times she has been in the City. She thought that if we had a system here, she could phone here and talk to the king wherever she is, in the City or visiting her parents, rather than having to rely on carrier pigeons."

The queen was clearly an important presence here in Yurt. I wondered if she could possibly be as old and bent as the king, and, since she seemed to take frequent trips, when she would be returning.

The chaplain hesitated for a moment before speaking again, taking unnecessarily long over a sip of wine. It was probably Christian tact failing again to control his words. "I don't like this talk of telephones," he said brusquely.

"Neither do I," I said cheerfully, but he didn't hear me.

"The queen herself tried to persuade me that it's only white magic, that it involves no dealings with the devil, but I can't be sure. There must be black magic in being able to hear someone else's voice over hundreds of miles."

Since it could have been pink or purple magic for all I knew about telephones, I responded to a different aspect of his comment. "If you had been more friendly with my predecessor, surely he would have persuaded you there s no such thing as either white magic or black magic. That's only a popular perception. Didn't they teach you that at seminary? Magic is neither good or evil in itself, only natural, part of the same forces as the world and mankind. The only good or evil is in the people who practice it."

"And you don't practice magic with evil intent?"

"Of course not," I said self-righteously. A few student pranks hardly counted.

"Then why do you have a well-thumbed copy of the *Diplomatica Diabolica* if you don't converse with demons?"

He was looking at my shelf. The volume's spine was cracked; it *did* look well-thumbed. But that was from the time I had been reading it late at night, the night before the demonstration, and had become so terrified I had slammed it shut and it had fallen on the floor. That book gave me the willies.

"One prefers not to talk with demons," I said. It didn't seem appropriate somehow to tell him about that demonstration, about how two other wizards were there to help our instructor if they had to, and how when a very tiny demon, maybe a foot tall, had appeared in the pentagram, the room had gone totally dark and some of the students (not me!) had fainted in fear. "But one meets them occasionally," I continued airily, "and if one does one had better know exactly what to say and how to say it. Otherwise, as you know yourself, one's immortal soul is in danger."

"But why practice magic at all?" he cried, his black eyes burning. "You put your souls in danger, and for what? Your predecessor used to entertain us with illusions during dessert, but that's the only magic I ever saw him do."

Illusions! Clearly I was falling down already. It hadn't even occurred to me to produce special entertainment at dinner; I had enjoyed the brass quartet and the food too much to think anything else was needed.

"There's lots of magic besides illusions," I said. "You saw the magic lock I have on my door."

"My door locks with a key. It works just as well."

He had emptied his wine glass and was spinning it in his fingers. I said two quick words in the Hidden Language and the glass spun away from him, rose majestically, and slid across the air to my own hand. I refilled it and sent it sliding back without spilling a drop.

He had to smile at that. "Very deft," he said. "But you could also have gotten up."

"But wizards have known about magic since the beginning of human history," I protested, feeling that I was not the person who should be having this discussion. I was also rapidly running low on the spells that I knew always worked. "You can't turn away from knowledge." He opened his mouth to speak, and I knew he was going to say something about Eden and the Tree of Knowledge. One thing they taught these priests in seminary was how to have quick answers to everything. "And magic *works*!"

"Every single time? You've never had a spell that didn't work perfectly?"

Maybe they taught them to read minds too at seminary. "Well, maybe just once, or twice, or a few times . . ." But I realized that, if I was going to have him for a friend, I was going to have to be honest. "Don't tell anyone else, but a lot of the time things don't work out exactly as I expected. But that's not a problem with magic. That's a problem with *me*. If you do it right, magic always works."

"You're implying religion doesn't?"

"You *know* it doesn't!" I protested. "Lots of people pray to the saints all the time and never get anywhere, whereas if they consulted a competent wizard they'd always get results."

"The saints don't listen to formulae. The saints listen to pure and contrite hearts. You spoke at dinner of a voyage you thought you were not yet worthy to take. Doesn't even magic make absolute demands on your mind and your soul?"

I felt I was being backed into a corner instead of sitting comfortably in my own study in my own kingdom, with the stars coming out through the window. "So what would *you* do if you met a demon and you didn't know how to speak to him? Have you ever had to do an exorcism?" I paused briefly before continuing, taking his silence as a negative answer. "You can't very well practice and study ahead of time to make sure you have a pure and contrite heart when the time comes. Suppose you meet a demon and you've had an impure thought a few minutes ago and, never having studied the *Diplomatica*, don't know the words to say to keep the demon from being annoyed?"

"We have the liturgy and the ritual of exorcism."

"See?" I said triumphantly. "You have to learn magic words too, even if you don't call them that."

He changed the topic abruptly away from demons. I was just as glad. I didn't like talking about demons with it now full dark, even though one of my predecessor's excellent magic globes was shedding a soft light in the room—I hoped the chaplain didn't consider *that* an illusion.

"You say that magic always works," he said. "But they must have taught you at the very beginning of your studies that there are only limited areas in which magic works at all." For someone who claimed to have no knowledge of or interest in magic, he seemed to be able to guess remarkably well. "Since magic is part of the earth's natural forces, it can modify them but never alter them irrevocably."

I nodded ruefully. "The cycle of birth and death, sickness and health. We can lengthen life, but not indefinitely. We can't cause someone to be born, and we can't bring them back when they're dead."

He smiled for the third time that evening. "For

twinkling lights and fairy gold, see a wizard. For a miracle, see a priest." That must be something else they had taught them at seminary, a handy phrase to confound wizards.

"Would you like more wine?" I stood up this time to get his glass.

IV

Bells were ringing out in the courtyard. Snuggled down in my pillows, I opened one eye. Early morning light was coming in the window, too early, I decided, to make it worth thinking about yet. I closed the eye again.

My door handle rattled, then the door swung open. I wished again for a good curse to use, this time against myself. I remembered now forgetting to lock the door when I let the chaplain out, well past midnight. I sat up straight, both eyes wide open.

I was, however, somewhat mollified when I saw it was the pretty servant girl who had given me a saucy look at dinner the night before, and that she was carrying a steaming tray. "Good morning, sir. Are you ready for your tea and crullers?"

I pulled on my robe and tried to push my hair into line with one hand.

She set the tray on my table. "The crullers are still warm; I just finished making them."

I took a drink of scalding tea and a bite of cruller. They were just the way I liked them, with lots of cinnamon. "These are wonderful."

"Thank you, sir. As well as bringing you your breakfast, the constable's wife said I should explain to you how to get to the chapel for service. You go back through the great hall—"

"Church service!" I cried. "That's why they're ringing the bells. I'm going to be late."

"You have plenty of time. They always ring the bells half an hour early, to give slack-a-beds time to get up and dressed."

"I forgot it was Sunday," I said somewhat sheepishly.

"We have service in the chapel *every* morning," she said primly. "Anyway, you go through the great hall, and at the far right-hand corner there's a door into a stairway. Go up to the third landing, and there's the chapel. You shouldn't get lost; just about everyone else should be going there too." But though she spoke formally and correctly, as a servant should address even someone who was fully dressed and combed, she gave me a wink as she left me to finish my breakfast and get dressed.

Twenty minutes later, dressed and reasonably tidy, though I was still licking crumbs from my lips, I walked through the great hall and joined a large group of people going upstairs. The stairs were dark and badly lit—no magic globes here—so it was with surprise and pleasure that I emerged into a very tall chapel, whose walls were made almost entirely of stained glass. The eastern light illuminated the Bible stories and the saints, and blue and green shadows were cast across us.

The chaplain was already at the front. The white and black linen of his vestments was immaculate. He looked sober and shaved, not at all like someone still feeling shaggy from being up half the night. And he had not even had the benefit of excellent fresh-made crullers; priests are not supposed to have breakfast before service.

The king was already seated in the first row, surrounded by his knights and ladies, but I sat down with the servants and attendants. They kindly passed me a copy of the hymnal and gave me no odd looks when I didn't know the tune and discovered that my ability to sight-read music was even worse than I remembered. Everyone else's singing, however, was lovely.

As the service ended, I wondered why they had assumed that I would go, and if my predecessor had ever come to chapel.

The constable fell into step beside me as we filed out. He asked, "So how are you finding Yurt so far?"

"I like it very much. I'll have to see how well I can do once I really take up my duties; so far I've been a guest on vacation." This was to forestall any remarks about telephone systems.

We groped our way down the stairs, our eyes almost blind after the brilliance of the chapel's colored light. He chuckled and said over his shoulder, "Maybe you could get some lights put in here. Your predecessor made our lights for the great hall, but he never wanted anything to do with the chapel. The roof here is too low to hang regular lamps, so we've always had to stumble as best we could."

Magic lights were something I was fairly sure I could make, though it might be tricky making them bright enough while also making them small enough to fit in the restricted space. "I'll try to manage something in the next few days," I said cheerfully.

We emerged at the bottom of the stairs. "I must say," said the constable in a low voice, "that I was delighted to see you inviting the chaplain to your chambers last night." He glanced about quickly to make sure we were not overheard. "I hadn't wanted to say anything at first, but there had been a certain ... *tension* between him and your predecessor, and when we hired a new wizard one of the things I had been hoping was that that might be resolved. Your predecessor really was an excellent wizard, and I wouldn't want to be thought to speak ill of him, but in a small kingdom one doesn't need these petty enmities. That's why I knew you wouldn't mind being brought breakfast in plenty of time to get to service."

"Of course not," I said noncommittally. I really was going to have to meet the old wizard.

The constable started to turn away. "Oh, just one thing," I said, and he turned back at once. "Where do you get the Sunday paper around here?"

He looked surprised. "We don't get the Sunday paper. We don't get papers at all in Yurt."

"But your ad for a wizard was in the Sunday paper."

"Yes, that. The queen had brought a copy back from her last trip to the City, so we had the address to which to write. Now, if you'll excuse me."

He walked briskly away. "Well," I said determinedly to myself, "if I'm not going to waste half the morning reading the color supplements, maybe I can see if there's anything in any of my books about telephones."

With my casements wide open, and red and white climbing roses peeking in, I settled myself in the most comfortable chair in my study and put my feet up. *Thaumaturgy A to Z* had nothing to offer, but the first volume of *Ancient and Modern Necromancy*, the volume I had never looked at because most of it was just a history of wizards and wizardry, gave a brief description of the discovery of telephones. "The person's voice actually enters the flow of magic. The spells attached to each telephone find the voice's way through magic's four dimensions, so that even a person without magic skills can operate it. All he has to do is to speak the name attached to the telephone instrument with which he wishes to communicate, and that instrument's bell will ring, summoning someone to answer."

Well, I had vaguely known that already. The part this historical snippet seemed to pass over was *how* one created spells and attached them to the telephone, to localize the instrument in both space and time, and then set up the permanent channels through the flow of magic for the voice to travel. I closed the book and would have frowned if the summer breeze hadn't been so soft on my cheek.

Clearly I was going to have to try something different. The thought of going back to the City and stealing an instrument occurred to me briefly, but it would never work. The instrument would have to have all its spells redone or it wouldn't function. The times I had seen a new telephone installed, it had always seemed to take several days and require several wizards—usually of the serious, pale-faced sort with whom I had not associated much at school. A kingdom didn't hire a new Royal Wizard and then pay enormous sums to import other wizards who might know more than he did about telephones.

I stood up and yawned. Maybe Yurt didn't need a complete telephone system. Maybe it would be possible just to work out a way to communicate with the City and with wherever the queen's parents lived. I stopped in mid-yawn and thought about this. It seemed to have possibilities.

I found a piece of string that had been used to tie up my luggage and strung it between my bedroom and study. I already knew how to communicate, without speaking, to another wizard, at least if he was next to me and willing to listen to the thoughts I sent him. Therefore it should be possible to attach a communications spell to a string. An object with a spell attached became a magic object, and anyone could operate it.

"It's like invisibility," I said to myself cheerfully. A ring of invisibility will always work, even though invisibility is one of the harder spells. For some reason, even though it is straightforward to make the empty air take on solidity in illusions, it is very hard to make solidity look empty. There is probably a good theoretical explanation, but I have never paid much attention to theory, preferring the practical.

I paused to see how well I could make myself invisible. I had been working on the spells intermittently for almost a year now. Concentrating hard, breaking off pieces of the flow of magic and controlling them with the Hidden Language, I watched my feet disappear, first the left one, then the right one. At this point, however, things stopped. My knees remained obstinately visible. I snapped my fingers in disgust and my feet came back. Just last week I had made it almost all the way up my thighs.

"But I'm not trying to make a ring of invisibility anyway," I told myself firmly. "I'm making a communications string." I put both hands on the string and concentrated on it, thinking of how one reaches out, slides just the corner of one's mind into the stream of magic while leaving most of it firmly anchored to one's body (one of the most dangerous moments for young wizards is discovering how to slip one's mind out without losing oneself forever). I alternated the spells that seek another mind with attachment spells, and suddenly the string stiffened and glowed pink.

I rushed out into the courtyard. Since it was Sunday, the servants were only doing necessary chores, and a number of them were now playing volleyball while the others watched and cheered. I found my own saucy servant girl, flushed and laughing after having just been replaced at the net.

"Come on," I said, "I need your help with a magic spell."

She looked over her shoulder at the others, said, "I'll be back in just a minute!" and came with me, straightening her skirt. "What sort of magic spell? You're not going to turn me into a frog or anything!"

Ever since that practical exam, I had tried to avoid mention of things being turned into frogs, but she wouldn't know that. "No," I said, "I think I've invented a new kind of telephone, and I want to test it."

In my chambers, I stationed her in the study, at one end of the string, and went into the bedroom. "You listen," I said, "and see if you can hear me." Then, with my mouth close to the other end of the string, I said in my deepest voice, "All powers of earth and air must obey the spells of wizardry."

To my surprise, she burst into peals of laughter. "You're the funniest person I've ever met!" she said when she had caught her breath. "Are you sure you're really a wizard?"

"Did it work?" I said with irritation. "Could you hear me?"

"Of course I could hear you. You were only standing ten feet away! All powers of earth and air!" Still laughing, she went back out to rejoin the game.

I looked at my piece of string in disgust. It was still glowing. I snapped my fingers and said the words to break the spell, but nothing happened. I seemed to have a piece of string permanently able to convey words over the same distance one could hear them anyway.

"Except that it may not even do that," I thought. "All I know for sure is that it's pink now." Besides, the more I thought about it, the more strings seemed like an impractical idea. One couldn't run a string two hundred miles to the City. It was with relief that I heard the gong for dinner.

My good humor was restored by another excellent meal. At the end, King Haimeric said, "Come with me. I want to show you my rose garden."

He walked on his nephew's arm out of the great hall, through the courtyard, and out through the great gates of the castle. Since I had arrived in the courtyard by air cart, I had not before been through the gates. The portcullis was up and looked as though it had not been lowered for years. Swans were swimming peacefully in the moat.

A red brick road ran down the hill from the castle gates toward the forest below. Next to the road was a walled garden, with roses creeping over the tops of the walls. Dominic swung the barred gate open, and we went in.

I had thought the roses in the castle courtyard were good, but these were spectacular. "You can leave us, Dominic," said the king. "I'm sure this young man can see me back safely."

His burly nephew gave me a slightly sour look, but left. The king seated himself on a bench while I wandered up and down the rows, admiring the different colors, the enormous blooms, the vibrant green of the foliage.

"I'm too stiff to work on them much anymore, but I planted every bush you see," said the king. "Most of them are hybrids I developed myself, though I've also picked up a few cuttings over the years. The newest one is that white bush; I planted it the day I married the queen."

It was smaller than the other bushes but growing vigorously. The white blooms faded to pink in the shadows of the petals. When I bent to smell it, the sweetness was almost overwhelming.

"I'm looking forward to meeting the queen," I said, realizing that she must be substantially younger than the king and wondering why I had ever thought otherwise.

"I've been king of Yurt a long, long time. It's been a good run of years, but in many ways the last four years have been the best, even though I can't crawl around with a trowel anymore."

So they'd only been married four years. I had to readjust several of my assumptions. It seemed most likely that the king had found a pliant young princess to marry, someone to adore him and do his bidding and fulfill the adolescent fantasies he had never been able to fulfill in his years in the rose garden. The only difficulty with this picture was that it was hard to see the king as the old goat. "You may think me silly," I said, "but when I heard the queen was visiting her parents, I'd somehow thought of them as extremely old."

"Old?" he said and smiled. "No, they're not old. The Lady Maria, who lives here with us, is the sister of the queen's father. And you know from a remark at table last night how old *she* is." He laughed. "Give me your arm; I want to look across my kingdom."

Though he needed my help to rise, he walked unaided back out of the walled garden. I swung the gate back into place, and we stood looking down the hill toward the plowed fields and the variegated green of the woods beyond.

He stood without speaking for several minutes. Somewhere down there, I thought, was the old wizard. I was startled out of conjectures about him when the king said suddenly, "Can you transport me by magic?"

"Transport you?" I said with some alarm. This was worse than telephones.

"Lift me off the ground so I don't have to walk. I've always wanted to try it."

"I think so," I said, and "I hope so," I thought. "Lifting spells become more difficult the larger the object one is lifting," I explained. I didn't tell him that he was a lot larger than a wine glass. Inwardly I was wondering how, if I hadn't been sure I could magically pick up a heavy box or an awkwardly placed platter of meat, I was going to manage my liege lord. "We'll take it slowly. I'll just lift you a little way, and I'll walk right next to you so you can take my arm if you're feeling unsteady. Or," I added silently, "if I start to drop you."

The king, I decided as I started pulling the spells together in my mind, was actually not much heavier than a box of books. He stood looking at me with a faint smile as I concentrated, feeling my way into the magic, making sure each word of the Hidden Language was right. Slowly and gracefully, as though he were thistledown blown by the wind, he rose four inches, so that his toes just brushed the grass.

We started toward the castle gates. I walked immediately next to him, just barely not touching him. Fortunately he was silent and let me concentrate. When we reached the drawbridge I had a sudden panic, picturing myself dropping him into the moat, and with my wavering in concentration he started to slip. I found the words just in time to set him down as gently as he had been lifted up.

We walked together across the bridge and under the portcullis. Dominic was waiting for us just inside. "That was extremely enjoyable," said the king. "Could you teach me to do that myself? Not today, but soon?"

This earned him an odd look from Dominic, who had no idea what we were talking about. "I've never taught anyone," I said honestly, "but I could try."

Back in my chambers, I spent the rest of the afternoon practicing lifting things.

V

After two days of loving my kingdom, I woke up the next morning hating it. Bells awakened me again. When I lifted my head I could hear hard rain on the cobblestones outside. The windows were streaked with water. My door handle rattled and didn't open, since I *had* remembered to lock it last night, but there was immediately a loud and persistent knocking.

When I opened the door, the servant maid stood there, trying without great success to shield both herself and a tray with an umbrella. I took the tray and half pulled her inside. "You're going to get soaked!" I said.

Her umbrella streamed water on my clean flagstone floor. My tea seemed to have been diluted with rain, and the napkin on the basket was damp. When I pulled back the napkin, I found not crullers but cake donuts, which I don't like nearly as well. They weren't even warm.

"I just wanted to make sure you were up in time for chapel," she said without a smile or any sign of friendliness. She put the umbrella back up and started out again.

"Thank you very much!" I said quickly, wondering if everyone went to chapel every single day. "You know, I don't even know your name."

"Gwen, sir," she said and was gone. I wondered as I ate if she didn't want to associate with someone as foolish as I must have seemed after the incident with the string. The donuts tasted as though they had been made several days before.

My mood was not improved when I banged my head on the dark stair going up to the chapel and then found, when I reached the top, that the king and the chaplain were the only other two people there. I rubbed my head surreptitiously all during service. At the end, I offered the king my arm, but he shook his head.

"A prerogative of being king is that I don't have to use those stairs." A small door which I should have noticed before opened halfway down the inner wall of the chapel, presumably into the royal chambers. He went through it and left me alone with the chaplain.

The chaplain fixed me with his dark eyes. "Don't think I don't welcome you in the chapel," he said. "But don't come because you think you have to. I hold service every morning for anyone who needs spiritual refreshment, and the king usually comes, but the rest of the castle mostly come on Sunday." He turned away without waiting for a response.

"In that case," I thought, "maybe I can start sleeping later." I would have to tell Gwen, if she was still speaking to me. I wished I could talk to some of my friends at the wizards' school. The chaplain still seemed like the only person at the castle I could hold a conversation with, and at the moment he was to me profoundly strange and distant.

"There's incentive for me," I thought bitterly, groping back down the stairs. "All I need to do to talk to them is get the telephone working."

Back in my room, I was looking glumly at the backs of my books, wondering which ones I should try next, when there was a knock. I hoped it was Gwen, come to apologize for the dry donuts, but to my surprise it was Dominic, the royal heir.

He lowered his umbrella and pulled off his coat. He looked around my study for a moment in silence, paused for a longer look at my diploma, and closed the door behind him. "May I sit down?"

"Please do," I said, wondering what he could want.

He planted his solid body in a chair by the window, set his elbow firmly on the arm, and leaned his chin on a massive fist. "I've come to talk to you about your duties."

This was it. I knew my problem wasn't the rain or the lack of crullers. I had spent two days on vacation, but now I was going to have to start work on projects I didn't think I could do. I tried to look intelligent and alert.

Surprisingly, he hesitated for a moment before beginning. "You're an outsider," he said at last—something I already knew!—"and maybe I shouldn't prejudice your mind with too many details. But you have to know one thing now. The king is under a spell."

This was not at all what I had expected. "Under a spell? What sort? I talked to him in the rose garden yesterday afternoon, and he never said anything about it."

"He wouldn't have, of course. He doesn't realize it himself. But the spell was one of the major reasons *we* decided to hire you."

He didn't say who *we* were. He looked at me from

under heavy lids, waiting for my answer. "But what sort of spell? Do you know the source?"

"The king is growing old and feeble. This can only be the result of enchantment. We don't know the source of the spell, but we want you to overcome it."

"But that's silly!" I protested. "Of course he's getting weaker as he gets older. And besides," thinking that the chaplain should hear me now, "wizardry can't reverse natural aging."

"The king isn't as old as you may think. When he married the queen, only four years ago, no one thought of them as an extremely ill-matched couple."

A sudden vision flashed into my mind of a girl married to a much older man, excited at first at the power of being queen, but soon made irritable when she discovered she was not supposed to have a mind of her own, but only be the king's pliant companion. It shouldn't be hard for her, on one of her trips to the City, to find an unscrupulous wizard willing to sell her a powder or spell to sicken her husband.

"It must be the queen, then," I said. "She has bewitched him somehow."

A low rumble began somewhere in his barrel chest and emerged in an angry, "No! It's not the queen. It couldn't be anyone at court. It must be a malignant influence from outside."

I modified my vision to have the queen and the royal heir secretly in love, plotting to have the king die so that they could rule together. But I stopped myself. This made no sense. If Dominic were partially responsible for putting an evil spell on the king, he certainly wouldn't tell me about it.

"Thank you for this warning," I said in a deep voice. "The power of magic to conceal itself is often great, but the skill of the forewarned wizard is potent indeed."

To my surprise, he treated this statement perfectly

seriously. "Good. I knew we had done well to hire you." He started to rise.

"But how about my other duties? The king's talked to me about a telephone system, the constable's said you need more magic lights—"

He waved these away with his broad hand. I was fascinated by the ruby ring on his second finger. Its setting was a gold snake supporting the jewel on its coils. It looked like a perfect ring for a wizard, and I coveted it for myself. "Those are a façade for your real work." He pulled his coat back on, picked up his umbrella, and left without saying good-bye.

I stood by the open door, looking across the rain-drenched courtyard. The paint and the flowers were bright in spite of the dark sky. Could there actually be dark powers at work here in such a perfect little castle?

I closed my eyes, probing past the closed doors and shuttered windows. There were plenty of minds there, most of which I did not know well enough to recognize, though I could tell the king and Gwen. Oddly, I didn't find the chaplain. I stayed well outside their minds, slipping by so lightly they wouldn't even feel me there. I found no powerful evil presence.

But when I opened my eyes a sense of foreboding lingered. Dominic might be right. If not the queen, then who wanted the king dead, and how were they doing it? Was the constable, with his talk of lights and telephones, deliberately trying to mislead me? Had Gwen been warned against me?

I shook my head. This would get me nowhere. Maybe while everyone else was sheltering from the rain I should take the opportunity to explore the castle; so far I had seen very little of it. I remembered a spell I had seen once, and reached for my shelves. I found it in only the second book I consulted, the spell to keep dry in the rain. "Why didn't I learn this one before?" I asked myself. It was only a variation of the lifting spell, creating a diversion for all the raindrops before they hit one's head.

I set the spell in place and stepped outside. It worked perfectly, although I immediately stepped in a puddle and got water in my socks. But this was not the fault of the magic. My good humor restored, I turned back to lock the door to my chambers, then started across the courtyard.

I stopped in the stables, where the horses whickered at me and the cats came to rub against my legs. It was warm and dusty with the smell of hay. The sound of rain seemed faint and faraway in the comfort and dim light. I stroked the horses on their noses and laughed when they tried to nuzzle my pockets. "No carrots," I told them. Also no malignant influences. I readjusted my spell and stepped back into the courtyard.

This time I walked to the north end of the courtyard, where a massive tower rose. The stones of the tower, unlike the stones of the rest of the castle, were not whitewashed, but were so dark they were almost black. There were no windows for the first thirty feet. It was in this tower, according to the chaplain, that my predecessor had had his study.

A heavy oak door was the only way in. I tested the handle, but it wouldn't open. With my eye to the crack along the doorjamb, I thought I saw a bolt on the inside. Delicately I tried a lifting spell on the bolt, or rather a sliding spell, to push it back in its track. Although I had to abandon the spell against the rain to give all my concentration to the bolt, my sliding spell actually worked. With only the slighest squeak, the bolt slid back, and I was able to pull the door open. Damp but delighted, I went in and closed the door behind me.

Inside it was completely black, except for tiny streaks of light around the door frame. I needed a light; I wondered if maybe I should start carrying a wizard's staff. I could make a light, at least temporarily, but I needed something to attach it to. I found a piece of hay sticking to my trousers and tried that, but it made only a faint firefly glow. So I took off my belt and used the buckle. It was still not very bright, but it was serviceable, and since the design of the buckle was the moon and stars, it was rather dramatic. I wondered why I had not thought of making the buckle glow earlier and wondered if it would be possible to attach the light permanently.

Pleased with myself, I started up steep, uneven steps. It wasn't until I had spiraled up at least halfway, I estimated, to the first window, that a sudden thought brought me to a halt. If the tower was empty, why had the door been bolted on the *inside*?

I listened for a moment, hearing nothing but my own heartbeat, and probed with my mind, without finding another intelligence in the tower. I shrugged, telling myself that there was perhaps a connection to the rest of the castle from an upper level, but I had again the goose-bump feeling of evil.

Shortly I reached the first window and looked out across the wet courtyard. Except for the smoke from the chimneys and a distant sound of voices and laughter, the castle looked deserted. From here on up there seemed to be windows enough that the stairs were never black. I had been walking with my belt held out ahead of me to watch for uneven places in the stairs, but now I put it back around my waist. To my disappointment, the moon and stars of the buckle slowly faded once I turned my attention from keeping them bright.

My legs were just starting to ache when I reached another oak door. I admired my predecessor if he had walked up and down from here for every meal. "But he probably flew," I thought. "And that's why the door was bolted on the inside; the last time he was here, he closed it down below and then left through a window."

For some reason I had never liked flying. I could

do it if I had to, at least for short distances, but I preferred my own feet on the ground. The king with his aching joints might prefer to skim above the grass, but I liked to feel my shoes among the blades. I was *quite* sure my dislike for flying had nothing to do with my experiences that first day our instructor had tried to teach us.

This door was not locked. It opened smoothly, letting me into a large and airy room. There were cupboards, desks, benches, and boxes, but all the cupboard doors were open, and there was nothing inside.

"So he took it all when he left," I thought, and then wondered what *it* might be. The room was almost disappointing. After the dark climb and the length of the stairs, it seemed as though there ought to be something significant here, rather than a room from which someone had removed his possessions and which he had swept thoroughly before leaving for the final time. I realized I did not know how long the old wizard had been gone; I had been acting and thinking as though it were a very long time, but in fact it might only have been a few days.

There was nothing else to see. One of the casement windows had had the glass broken out, but the rest were closed. I looked out the southern window toward the second highest tower in the castle, on the opposite end of the courtyard. It had a dovecote on the roof and was doubtless where the carrier pigeons came in. I opened the casement and climbed up on the sill, hesitated a moment, and stepped out into the air.

The rain had let up, but the damp cool air swirled around me. Although I would not have joined the king in characterizing flying as "extremely enjoyable," there was a certain sense of power in holding oneself up against the tug of gravity, of letting oneself drift slowly down, so that the ground sometimes came too soon. This time, however, I was glad to be back on the ground. I rebolted the outer door to the tower from the outside, as I had unbolted it, and started back toward my chambers.

With my door in sight, I stopped abruptly. The handle should have been glowing softly from my magic lock, but it was not glowing at all. I was certain I had locked it. I stepped forward, tried the door, and it opened at once. Someone had taken off my lock.

I stepped inside cautiously, but all seemed undisturbed. My books were as I had left them, and my clothes seemed untouched. I probed for a trap, both with magic and by lying down and looking under the bed.

Finding nothing, I sat back on my heels. Although it was impossible to say where it was coming from, and although it disappeared if one tried to sense it directly, the dark touch I had been feeling all day was here in my room. It was like trying to see something that could only be glimpsed from the corner of the eye.

To remove my lock, someone would not only have to know magic, but a lot more magic than I did. It was probably possible to break a magic lock, but a lot of the young wizards, including me, had tried to find the spell and never done so. I tried to dispel the chill that came from more than the rain. "Maybe I should be glad he or she left it unlocked; they couldn't have duplicated my palm print, which would mean that if they relocked my door it would only open to them." But who in the castle besides me knew magic?

PART TWO
The Queen
I

It took me a week to figure out how to do the lights. During that week, Gwen continued to bring me breakfast every morning, though not quite so early. I had told her that, in spite of my friendship for the chaplain (or maybe, I thought, in order to preserve that friendship), I would not be attending chapel every morning. Once or twice she brought me crullers, but usually it was cake donuts.

Although she was perfectly cordial, I got no more winks or saucy looks. I wondered if she had been warned against me, and if so by who. The constable, who oversaw the castle staff, seemed the most likely person, except that I couldn't picture him doing it. I preferred to think that she had found out that wizards are not supposed to marry and was trying to rein in her affections before she developed a broken heart.

My initial problem with the lights for the stairs was finding something suitable to which to attach the magic. The headroom was so limited that I decided to use a flat surface rather than the more normal globes. My first thought was to do something with glass.

The constable introduced me to the young man who blew glass for the castle. I recognized him as one of the trumpeters who played at dinner. Once he had his livery off and his leather smock on, however, I would never have known him.

When he had his fire burning so hot that his glass was liquid and I had to stand back at the far side of the room, he dipped a long tube into the molten glass and began to blow. I was fascinated; I had never seen glass being made before.

He blew a large, thin bubble, brilliantly red, then laid it down and rolled it flat before it could cool. He stepped back, wiped his forehead with the back of his arm, and waited for comments from me.

It was exactly what I had asked for, an oval piece of glass a little thicker than a window pane. But I had had an awful thought. I had knocked my head on the ceiling going up the stairs to the chapel, and I was not the tallest person in the castle. I didn't want my magic lights shattered into shards of glowing glass the first time Dominic raised his head too quickly.

"I'd like to try something a little different," I said. "Maybe this time could you make something hollow, like a flat-bottomed bottle that tapers toward the top—" I waved my hands in the air, sketching the shape. I was describing the base of a telephone.

"These are going to be strange-looking lights," he said with a grin when he had blown it. "How many do you want?"

"Just one more, I think," I said, looking at my telephone; it was still glowing hot. "And then I'll want some more parts in different shapes." For the next hour, he blew different shapes to my specification. The mouthpiece was the trickiest part. At the end, I had a glass oval and two very lovely though very unusual glass telephone instruments.

"These actually aren't all going to be lights," I told the young man. "Have you ever seen a telephone?"

"Those are telephones?" he said with interest. "And I made them? Can I make a call and tell my mother?"

"Does she have a telephone?" I said quickly, hoping that she didn't and wanting to forestall explaining that these were far from operational.

"No," he said and frowned. "I hadn't thought of that. You need two of them, don't you, one for each person. I expect that's why you made two. She lives in the next kingdom, about fifty miles from here; maybe I'll send her a message by the pigeons."

"You do wonderful glassblowing," I said. "And I also very much like your playing at dinner." I hurried back to my room with my prizes.

The telephones I set carefully on a high shelf, but I sat down with the oval of glass to try to make it glow. This piece, I thought, I could use for just inside the door from the great hall, where the ceiling was still high. Once I had been able to attach magic light permanently to it, I would talk to the armorer about getting some pieces of steel made in the same shape, for farther up the stairs.

At first I was no more able to make my piece of glass shine permanently than I had been able to do with my belt buckle. I had been spending much of the day with my books of spells when, in the middle of the week, Joachim, the chaplain, invited me to his room after dinner.

I think I was the only person who called him Joachim. I had in fact known him for some time before even learning he had a name. Almost everyone else in Yurt called him Father, which I resisted doing, both because he wasn't my father and because I was afraid that to do so would let down the dignity of wizardry. He didn't seem to mind.

As I sipped the wine he poured me, I looked around his room. It was lit with candles, no magic globes here. He had only the one room, rather than the two I had, and his bed looked hard. The walls were unadorned, except for the crucifix over the bed, and all the books on his shelf seemed well-thumbed.

"Have you started feeling comfortable with your duties yet?" he asked, setting down the bottle and sitting on another hard chair opposite mine. The air from the window made the candle flames dance and his shadow move grotesquely behind him.

"I keep on hoping I'll find out what my duties *are*," I said. I was wondering if I could trust him with my climb up the north tower and the sense of evil I had first felt there. "They hired me as Royal Wizard, and they've given me some tasks, but these aren't going to keep me busy forever—or I hope not. Do *you* know exactly what your duties are?"

"A chaplain's are a little clearer. I perform the service in the chapel every day, or oftener if needed, I encourage the sick, give solace to the dying, write treatises if treatises need writing, and am here whenever I'm wanted. But maybe a Royal Wizard's duties are not much different; I would think your principal responsibility is to be at hand whenever magic is needed."

"Is that what our predecessors did, perform useful tasks if called upon and spend the rest of the time waiting to be needed?" I had a vision of spending the next two hundred years of my life trying to make glass glow, and I didn't like the picture.

"I think that's what *your* predecessor did, at least part of the time, though he spent much of his time alone up in his tower. He sometimes wouldn't emerge for days. He always said he was trying to gain new knowledge. Certainly his illusions at supper were livelier when he'd been gone for a few days. As for my predecessor, I don't know; he was dead when I came."

"He was dead? I hadn't realized that."

"He's buried in the cemetery out beyond the gate. I think he was very old. But as I told you before, there had clearly been some sort of disagreement between him and the old wizard, and though it colored the wizard's attitude toward me, I never found out what it was."

I slowly drained my glass, giving myself time to think. I had a vague recollection of hearing that young priests were rarely sent out to their first positions alone. Usually they went where older priests could guide them for a few years before retiring themselves. Everyone knows that we wizards fight with each other all the time, which is why a new Royal Wizard only takes up his post when the old one is well out of the way, but priests are supposed to show each other Christian charity and support.

The shadows from the candle made my companion's eye sockets enormous and so dark that his eyes were invisible. I shivered involuntarily, not liking what I was thinking. Four years ago, the king had married, and, according to Dominic, had still been strong and vigorous. Three years ago, probably after their old chaplain had died unexpectedly, the kingdom had had to send for a new one. Not long afterwards, the king began to grow weaker.

It was a small kingdom. When they wanted a wizard, the best they could do was me. When they wanted a chaplain, they got a young man, who perhaps had a dark stain they had already suspected at the seminary, and who took up his duties without all the fatherly guidance and assistance that was normally considered necessary. I liked to give the impression that wizards were familiar with the powers of darkness; priests had to deal with them every day.

Joachim seemed content to let the silence stretch out. "The other day I came back to my chambers," I said suddenly, "and the magic lock on my door had been broken."

He didn't seem as shocked as I thought he should have, but then he wouldn't know how hard they are to break. He didn't look guilty either, but I found it hard to read his face. "It doesn't sound as though a magic lock has any advantage over cold iron, then."

This, I realized, was supposed to be another one of his jokes. "You don't understand. Someone would have to know a tremendous amount of magic to break it. It can't be done with brute force."

He leaned forward, and his eyes reemerged from darkness. "But I didn't think there was anyone else in the castle who knew magic."

I looked into my empty glass. "Neither did I."

He had no ideas about who might have known such a powerful spell, and I went back to my own chambers not much later. The bright glow of the magic lamp left by my predecessor was very reassuring. I sat up for several more hours, reading about such lamps, and by the time I went to bed I thought I had worked out the spells, though I was too exhausted to do them then.

I set to work on the spells in the morning. I had known how to make something shine before, but the attachment spells and especially the spells to make the magic respond to the voice were much harder than I had imagined. After one more glance at my books, I closed the windows, pulled the drapes, and put the volume away. It takes too much concentration for the complicated spells to be able to look at anything else, even a book of magic.

I started with my belt buckle, not daring to risk my oval of glass. First I started it shining, then slowly, in the heavy syllables of the Hidden Language, I pronounced the words to keep the spell attached. The moon and stars shone brilliantly, and I closed my eyes against them. I was alone in a deep tunnel where magic flowed, but as long as I kept on saying the words and saying them correctly the flow obeyed me. This was the most difficult part of all, to set up the translation between the Hidden Language and the language of men. "On. Out," I said aloud, and my words were so loud that they startled me into opening my eyes.

My chambers were dark, and the buckle in my hands was lifeless. "On," I said, and the full moonlight shone. "Out," and all was again night.

I jumped up and pulled open my curtains. I wanted to tell someone about my triumph. But when I looked out the only people I saw were the stable boys, currying the horses. I thought of telling them but didn't want to interrupt them. While putting my belt back on, I also decided against interrupting the chaplain just to show him my buckle; after all, since I had told him magic always worked, it would be silly to be this elated over having it work once.

I pulled the curtains shut and started on my oval of glass. I knew the spells now, and everything went smoothly. As I stood at the edge of the river of magic, I knew exactly what to say, to have my mind control the spells without ever endangering myself.

At the end I opened my eyes. "On. Out." The piece of glass obediently shone out with a brilliance far beyond what I had expected, then darkened again. This, I thought, would make a remarkable improvement in the chapel stairs. I hoped Joachim would be suitably grateful.

"On," I said again, reaching for the curtains. My belt buckle lit up, but the glass stayed dark. I tried again, changing the modulation of my voice, but nothing happened. I tried probing the spell attached to the glass with my mind, but there was no magic there at all.

I sat down. Somehow I must not have attached the

spell properly, so that it had withered and returned to the deep channels of magic as most spells do. But I could not see where I had gone wrong. Magic really should work all the time if the wizard does it correctly.

I shook my head, then shook my shoulders as well, dispelling the chilling unease that suddenly gripped me. I would try again.

This time there was no problem at all. I threw open the windows and opened the door to my bedroom, where I had taken my predecessor's magic lights so they wouldn't come on and break my concentration.

The spells had taken all morning. I tucked the oval of glass under my arm, planning to show the constable at lunch. I would let him find a way to attach it to the ceiling in the staircase. My predecessor might have been able to make his lamps hang suspended in the air, but at this point I thought glue would work just as well.

As I pulled my door shut and attached the lock, I wondered again why my spell had not worked at first. Had I just said one of the many words wrong in setting up the spell, or had an outside magical force broken it for me?

The seating arrangement at dinner the first night was maintained, and I ate every noon and evening between Dominic and the Lady Maria. Occasionally Dominic would be away in the middle of the day, but she and her golden curls were always at my right. The Lady Maria seemed, if possible, to be growing younger. She liked to engage me in lively conversation, punctuated with girlish laughter. If I tired of her laughter, I had only to look across the table to meet the chaplain's completely sober eyes.

But in fact I started to like the Lady Maria. As long as I could keep her off the topic of how young and charming she still was, she had a lively mind that was hungry for new ideas and information. She repeatedly pressed me for details on the dragon in the wizards' school cellars. I decided to have her help me with the telephones.

During the two days that the armorer was making steel plates for my lights, I set to work trying to derive the right spells. I decided that the first step would be to make it possible for two telephones in the castle to talk to each other; if that worked, then maybe I could start on the much more complicated task of starting communication with telephones elsewhere.

The king seemed stiff and said nothing more about learning to fly, and Dominic asked no questions about malignant spells, so I devoted full time to the telephones. It occurred to me that I was becoming obsessed with them, but at least at every meal the others all asked me interested questions about how I was coming and seemed, I thought, to be drawing comparisons between the old wizard and myself with the comparison favorable to me. I tried not to think what they would say when I gave up the project in despair.

At first nothing worked at all. With one telephone in my study, I put the other out in the courtyard and had the Lady Maria listen while I tried to communicate. The knights and ladies, the boys who were being trained as knights, and the servants tended to flock from all over the castle to watch my latest attempt. At least they weren't laughing at me, yet.

"Did you hear anything?" I'd yell from the door of my chambers.

"Nothing that time," she would call back in what were meant to be encouraging tones.

Then my steel ovals were ready, and I had an excuse to put the glass telephones back up on the shelf while I worked the spells of light. Since I had to do each individually, it took all day, and it took another day for the servants to attach them inside to the ceiling of the stairway. But on Sunday, in time for service, they were ready.

I had Gwen wake me early and was at the bottom of the stairs before anyone else. "On," I said in my deepest voice, and all the lights blazed on. The glass light inside the door was the brightest of all, but the steel plates gave a rich and somber light that I thought most appropriate. I stood modestly outside the stairwell, letting everyone else precede me, smiling in spite of myself when I heard their admiring comments.

But the telephones continued to elude me. After two more days of studying my books, I thought I had found the spell, and again set the Lady Maria in the courtyard with one instrument while I talked into the other. "All powers of earth and air must obey the spells of wizardry," I said into my own telephone. Gwen had laughed at that until she could hardly stand up, but it seemed safe to say, since no one seemed able to hear me anyway.

I hurried out into the courtyard. "Could you hear that?"

The Lady Maria didn't answer at first. The people with her were smiling, either in amusement or encouragement, but she looked both puzzled and somewhat concerned. She came toward me, carrying the glass telephone.

"It's very strange," she said. "Nobody else could hear you, but I could."

"You could? You mean it *worked*? You know that, with a telephone, you have to hold the receiver to your ear, and other people don't hear what's being said." I almost laughed with excitement. At last, I thought, I was making real progress.

But she shook her head. "I didn't hear you through the receiver. I don't think I even heard you with my ears. It was as though you were talking inside my brain."

"Bring the telephone into my study," I said in

despondency. I put both instruments back up on the top shelf. While I thought I was attaching communications spells to the instruments, I was instead discovering that, even though the Lady Maria was not trained in wizardry, it was still possible for me to communicate with her, mind to mind. While I had begun to like her, I didn't want to do it again. Anyone else's mind is always acutely strange if met directly.

She started to leave, then hesitated. "Is it true that all powers of earth and air must obey the spells of wizardry?"

At least she had heard what I'd said, rather than whatever random thoughts I may have been having. "Yes, if the wizardry is done right," I said.

"So a wizard can, if he knows his spells, exercise ultimate control over every being on earth?" It would have been more flattering if she had not still looked so puzzled.

"No," I said honestly, "not ultimate control. Wizardry is a natural power. Like anything else on earth, it can be overcome by the supernatural."

"You mean by the saints?"

"Or by demons."

"But who controls the saints and demons?"

I shook my head and tried to smile. When I was at school, I had known I wasn't a very good wizard, but at least I had believed in wizardry. Here in Yurt everyone seemed to want to remind me of wizardry's limitations. "You'll have to ask the chaplain about that. But no one really controls saints and demons. At best the priests learn how to ask them favors."

At dinner that night I told the constable that I was going to have to pause in my work on the telephone system for a while, until I had discovered the source of the anti-telephonic demonic influence.

48   *C. Dale Brittain*

II

I rode out of the castle on an old white mare. Although I had only been in Yurt a little over two weeks, my life in the City had begun to fade into the distant past. Life in the castle had settled into a comfortable pattern once I abandoned work on the telephones. The queen was spoken of every day, but she was still gone, and I found it hard to imagine what the castle would be like when she returned. To me, to whom two weeks seemed like a year, she had been gone forever, had indeed never been in Yurt, but to the others she was just a little over halfway through the month-long visit to her parents that she took every summer.

Some of the knights and the boys were riding out at the same time. Their horses were much livelier than mine, but as I had not ridden in a long time I was happy with my mount. She walked steadily and placidly down the brick road that led from the castle gates. While the knights turned off to the field where they were teaching the boys jousting, my mare and I continued past the little cemetery, dotted with crosses, where the chaplain's predecessor and presumably all former kings and queens and chaplains and servants were buried, and down the hill toward the woods. I was going to visit the old wizard.

Although the "anti-telephonic demonic influences" I had used as an excuse to the constable had been my own invention, I didn't like the cold touch that was never there when I looked but might surface, unexpectedly and fleetingly, while I was thinking of something entirely different. My predecessor should have some ideas.

The green of the leaves in the forest below me had gone dusty in the heat of late summer, and the breeze across the hill made silver ripples in the grass. I was enjoying being out near fields and forest, and real forest, too, not the manicured parks I was used to near the City. I hadn't told anyone where I was going, only that I was out for a ride. As my horse and I reached the edge of the woods, I was wondering again how I should address the old wizard.

Casual conversation with the constable's wife had informed me where his house was, but protocol was still a problem. I, now, was Royal Wizard, and he was only an old retired spell-caster. But he was two hundred years older than me and certainly knew a lot more about Yurt than I did. I had dressed formally in my red and black velvet but decided to address him with deference and respect.

In the cool shade of the woods, birds sang in the treetops far above us and insects hummed closer to hand. The mare shook her head, making all the bells on her bridle jingle. I whistled as I rode, a little tune in minor that the trumpeters had played at dinner the night before. We were going parallel to the edge of the forest, and occasionally I could see the fields through a gap in the trees. The long summer's day stretched before me, leisurely and lingering, with no thought of the night.

After half an hour's easy riding, I found the trail mark I had been looking for, a little pile of white stones. Just beyond, a narrow grassy track wandered away from the road, off between the beeches, and disappeared over a rise. I would never have spotted it except for the stones.

The branches here were low enough that I dismounted and led the mare. We should be almost there. I stopped at the top of the rise, looking down into a valley with a stream at the bottom. Even the sound of the water on stones was sparkling. The grass was richly green on either hand, and the trees that surrounded the little valley cast dancing shadows.

My horse snorted and made for the grass. I pulled

her nose up and continued toward a little bridge. We passed a branch that had half-shielded my view of the bridge, and sitting on the far side was the most beautiful woman I had ever seen in my life.

She had thick golden hair that made the Lady Maria's seem thin and lifeless, and it rolled in rich waves down her back and ten feet out behind her. She was wearing a dress of brilliant sky-blue, and when she lifted her head and looked toward me, her eyes were the same color. And most marvelous of all, an alabaster-white unicorn was kneeling beside her, with his muzzle in her lap.

I dropped the reins and approached slowly, not daring to take my eyes from her. She lowered her gaze again but did not speak. "Um, hello," I said. Gently she lifted the unicorn's muzzle from her lap, rose to her feet, and began to walk away, her arm around the creature's neck. Her hair floated in a weightless cloud behind her.

"Wait," I told myself sharply, resisting the initial impulse to run after her. I put my hand over my eyes, said two magic words, and looked again. She was gone.

I recovered my horse and started forward again. As we crossed the bridge, I told the mare, "If that's a typical sample of his illusions, the old wizard must really have impressed the castle over dessert." The mare seemed uninterested, but I took a deep breath and wondered how abjectly it would be appropriate to address the wizard.

The grassy valley continued to follow the stream. Within a hundred yards it turned and descended a steep hill, where the water foamed white. I was easing the mare's steps down the hillside when I heard a twanging noise. The sound was repeated, and then again.

I looked forward. Flying across the width of the valley in front of us, one after the other, was a series of golden arrows. I finished getting the mare off the hill, dropped the reins to let her graze, and walked a little closer. I probed them gently with my mind. Unlike the lady with the unicorn, these arrows were real.

No one was shooting them, however. They were being propelled by magic. Our scrambling on the hillside must have triggered a magic trap.

I thought about this for several minutes, waiting to see if the supply of arrows would become exhausted. When the steady twanging of an invisible bow and the whirr of each arrow continued, I decided that the arrows must be circling around somehow and coming back. The mare grazed unconcernedly.

I carefully put in place what I hoped was a protective spell against arrows, a variation of the spell that had kept me dry in the rain but needing twice as much concentration. Leaving the mare behind, I went slowly forward, going down on my hands and knees to crawl under the flight of the arrows. Ten yards farther down the valley, I heard the twanging cease.

I stood up, brushing the grass off my velvet trousers, and looked back. The valley was quiet and peaceful. For a moment I hesitated, wondering if I should go back for my mare, and then decided she would be fine where she was; she was unlikely to retreat back up the steep hill, and if she came forward she would be following me. If I went back, I was afraid I would set off the arrows again.

The valley took another twist and suddenly widened into a clearing. On the far side, half tucked under the drooping branches of an enormous oak, was a small green house, and sitting in front of the door was an old man with a white beard down to his knees.

I came three-quarters of the way across the clearing and then did the full bow, ending with my head down and my arms widespread.

"Welcome, Wizard," said a rasping voice.

"Greetings, Master," I answered.

I surprised myself by calling him Master. At the wizards' school, the only wizard who had that title was the oldest wizard of all, the one in whose castle the school was held, who was reputed to have been in the City since the City was founded.

He accepted the title. "So you weren't taken in by the Lady and weren't frightened by my Arrows," he said. His voice was rough, as though he had not used it for weeks. "I know who you are. You're the new Royal Wizard of Yurt, and probably think you're pretty fancy."

I rose and came toward him. "I have come to seek the guidance of my predecessor."

"You aren't going to find much help from me if you're after what I think you are. I can tell from your clothes—and especially that ostentatious belt buckle—that you fancy yourself to have authority over the powers of darkness." I guiltily turned off the glow of the moon and stars. "I may not have studied in the City, but *I* am a wizard of air and light."

I sat down at his feet, determined not to be insulted.

"Or is that pullover supposed to be a Father Noel costume?"

I was mortified. I had of course taken the tattered white fur off the collar as soon as I bought the pullover and had hoped all suggestions of someone fat and jolly were long gone. But I was going to have to be polite to this crotchety old wizard who clearly knew ten times as much magic as I did. I took a deep breath. "I've greatly admired your magic lamps in the castle."

"Of course you have. I'll bet *you* couldn't make anything that nice."

"I made some very nice magic lamps for the chapel stair!" I said, stung into a reply.

"And the chaplain didn't tell you to mind your own business?" he said, apparently surprised.

"The chaplain and I are friends," I said stiffly, then wondered why I was defending him when one of the reasons I had come was to find out if my predecessor had ever thought the chaplain was turning toward evil.

"Young whippersnapper," pronounced the old wizard, which was probably his opinion of me as well.

There was a pause while I tried to find something diplomatic to say. "Do they miss me up at the castle?" the old wizard said suddenly.

"They always speak well of you," I said with my best effort at Christian tact. "They've told me many times how much they admired your work and your illusions. The Lady down in the valley is certainly the finest example I've ever seen, even in the City."

I probably shouldn't have mentioned the City, because it made him snort. "Illusions!" he said. "Things were different when King Haimeric's grandfather was king. Then a Royal Wizard had *real* responsibilities. The harvest spells were just the start of it."

"Harvest spells!" I said in panic. I knew I didn't know anything that could be considered a harvest spell. In an urban setting, we learned urban spells.

"And now they don't even want harvest spells anymore," continued the old wizard, paying no attention to me. "They say that hybrid seed is more effective. The closest I've come for years is the weather spells when they're cutting the wheat."

This was a relief. Weather spells I could probably manage. I had even gone to the lectures. I tried a different approach. "Have you ever taught anyone how to fly?"

"Fly? You mean someone who isn't a wizard? Who wants to learn magic *now*?"

"The king mentioned it," I said, but I was struck by the suggestion that someone else had apparently wanted to learn magic.

"Well, he never mentioned it to *me*. And with good reason. He knew what *I'd* say. Haimeric's not half the man his grandfather was, or his father either. Never marrying all those years, and then marrying late. If he expected an heir, he's certainly disappointed. But I must say, I don't think he married in the hope of having a baby. I think he married because he was just besotted."

I tried to return the topic to the question of who in the castle, besides me, might know magic. "So some of the others had asked you to teach them magic?"

"Well, Dominic and Maria did," he said shortly. After a somewhat long pause, he added, "Never got anywhere with it."

"Prince Dominic and the Lady Maria?" Somehow I would not have expected it.

"There was talk of *them* making a match four years ago," continued the old wizard, in a more pleasant tone. "Maria's the queen's aunt, you know."

I nodded, waiting for him to go on.

"When the king got married four years ago, the queen brought her old maiden aunt to live with her—probably thought she needed a change. And then Dominic's only a few years younger than she is. He's been heir presumptive for years; the king's younger brother, at least, had the sense to get married when *he* was young. But he's gone now too, and Dominic's not half the man his father was."

Apparently I had reached Yurt in a decadent time.

"But she was too flighty for someone that phlegmatic. If the queen was waiting for a match, I think she gave up waiting some time ago."

While these insights into the people in the castle were extremely interesting, I could not help but notice that he had again deftly turned the topic away from the question of to whom he had taught magic.

III

While we had been talking, the brilliant blue of the sky was darkening. An abrupt clap of thunder, apparently coming from just behind the wizard's house, startled me so much that I jumped to my feet. "It looks like rain," said the old wizard complacently. "You'd better get your horse; it will stay dry enough under the oak here. And don't worry about my Arrows!" he called after me as I hurried back up the valley. "You won't be shot this time."

It certainly wouldn't be hard for him to guess that I *had* been wondering if I could bring my mare safely past that shower of arrows. And I didn't think it could have been much harder for him to bring on a thunderstorm to demonstrate his power.

My mare had her head up, waiting for me. Chill little breezes flicked her mane, and there was a steady low rumbling from the sky. I led her by the bridle back down the valley, past the place where the arrows had been shooting, and around the final twist to the clearing where the wizard's house stood under the sheltering branches of its oak. The first drops pattered on the leaves above us as I led the mare under the branches. The old wizard was no longer sitting in front of his house, but the green door was open.

I took off the saddle and bridle and rubbed the mare down. Being under the tree was like being under a tent. I could hear the drum of drops on the leaves, and the air became damp, but we were safe in a bubble made of branches. I finished with the horse, tapped at the door, and went into the house.

I had been expecting shelves of books; after all, every wizard I had ever known had books on his shelves, books piled on his desk, even books in heaps on the floor. But there were very few books in the old wizard's house.

Instead there were cones of light, gently swirling masses of stars, forms that changed from tree to man to beast and back to tree as one watched. I ignored them all assiduously and concentrated on the old wizard, who had just lit a fire in the small fireplace. Bolts of lightning flashed outside the window, and thunder rumbled continuously. But inside all was peaceful. "Come sit by my fire," said the old wizard in the friendliest tone he had used to me yet.

I sat down on the hearth, thankful for the warmth; the summer's day had grown cold. We sat in silence, except for the thunder, for several minutes while I tried to decide how to ask him what I had come to find out.

"We heard a lot about the old magic at the wizards' school," I began. I had considered saying that we had been taught to respect the old magic, but decided it would sound as though I were being condescending to someone more than seven times my age. "And I grew more and more convinced that there is magic that wizards all used to know that has never been put in our books."

"Well, you're right," he said almost reluctantly, as though not wanting to admit that I was right about anything.

"And yet the old magic is the basis for all the new magic of the last hundred and fifty years," I continued. "The wizards who learned by experimentation and apprenticeship channeled the power of magic, made it possible for magic to be organized, to be written down in books, made it less wild, made it something that could actually be taught in a classroom."

I had been going to go on from this brief history of modern wizardry—nearly everything I remembered from a whole course!—to explain that I needed his special and ancient magic talents to help me find out what was happening in Yurt, but he interrupted me.

"And look what's happened!" he cried in his rasping

voice. "With all you young wizards and magic workers, the channels of magic have been worn so deeply in some areas that any fool can work a simple spell. You say you've made magic less wild, but all you've done is make it easier for the wild magic of the north to come in!"

I was horrified. I would normally never have thought that the wizardry that tamed magic also invited wild magic into the land of men, but in the old wizard's dimly lit room it seemed most probable.

"Or didn't you ever think of that?" he said with a sneer. I decided no answer was best. "You and your books! You think you've made magic easier for the simple-minded who shouldn't be doing magic anyway, but by cutting deep ruts in the channels of human magic you've just made it easier for wild magic to come pouring in. How would you like to see a dragon in Yurt?"

I considered and rejected the possibility that there was a dragon in the castle cellars already.

"And now you can't go anywhere without some fool claiming he or she knows magic."

"*Does* anyone in the castle know magic?" I said quickly, trying to get in at least one of the questions I had.

"Of course not," he said brusquely. "Unless you'd consider counting yourself!"

I wondered if his brusqueness was concealing a lie, but between his manner and the insult it was impossible to ask him again. Instead I tried to be conciliatory. "I was just wondering because a strange thing happened when I first arrived. I'd put a magic lock on the door to my chambers, and when I came back it was gone."

Unlike the chaplain, the old wizard would surely know how hard it is to break a properly constituted magic lock. But he just snorted at me. "Did the spells wrong, I reckon," he said. His insults scarcely even strung anymore.

"But while you're speaking of locks," he added abruptly, "you haven't tried to get through the locked door of the north tower, have you?"

"The north tower?" I said ingenuously.

"Don't play the fool with me. I used to have my study in the north tower, as they must certainly have told you. The constable seemed to think you'd have your study there, too, but I straightened him out fast enough."

"They gave me a very nice set of chambers," I said cheerfully.

"When I left I locked the door and windows to the tower with both magic and iron."

I sat up straighter but managed to cover my surprise with a fit of coughing; tiny tendrils of smoke from the fire were whirling into the room, and I was sitting very close to the hearth. There had certainly been no magic lock on the tower door when I pulled back the bolt, and all the windows had also been unlocked.

"That sounds pretty secure, then," I said blandly, then fell to coughing again. The smoke really was getting in my nose, and it had an unusual, almost spicy quality.

"No one shall go in that tower again while Yurt survives," the old wizard said grimly. "Did you notice that I even ordered them not to whitewash it? I don't want any young men on scaffolding peeping in the windows."

"I noticed that the tower walls are dead black while the rest of the castle is white," I responded, wild with curiosity in spite of the headache the smoke was beginning to bring on. "But Master," I continued tentatively, "as long as I'm living in the castle, don't you think it might be better if I knew why you locked up your old study? That way, in case any—"

"NO!" he interrupted, leaving it quite impossible for me to ask again what he thought he had locked up. "I've taken care that no problems shall ever arise, for reasons of my own, and by methods of my own. Why should anyone else ask me about it?" He glared at me so fiercely that I retreated to the far side of the room, where I finished coughing as quietly as I could. The air was better farther from the fire.

After a moment I caught my breath and looked at the table next to me. As well as a constant cascade of ice-blue stars, it contained piles of leaves and roots, some in earthenware bowls, some loose on the table. There were also mortars and pestles, fire-blackened pots, and bits of stone rubbed into dust. In spite of his boast about being a wizard of light and air, I thought, the old wizard was not too proud to be a wizard of earth as well.

Modern wizardry uses very few herbs and roots. We keep our magic technical, straightforward, capable of being attached to such simple substances as steel and glass and of being reduced to written spells. But all wizards know, even those, like me, who tended to skip the lectures on the history of wizardry, that there is a natural affinity to magic in some growing things. In the days when books were few and apprenticeships long, young wizards learned how to recognize and gather plants with magical properties, even discover new ones. It occurred to me that, since I hadn't exactly been a huge success as a wizard taught from books, maybe I should give apprenticeship a try.

That is, of course, if the old wizard would be willing to teach me. So far everything I had said seemed to infuriate him. I looked across the room to where he sat rocking by his hearth. The room had darkened, but the fire's glow reddened his face. The rain's beat fell steadily on the oak leaves above the roof.

"Master," I began, and he whirled toward me abruptly, as though, deep in thought, he had almost forgotten my presence. "Master, I was glad to see that you had brought at least some of your apparatus from the castle to be able to continue your research into magic properties."

"What do you mean, at least *some?* I brought everything I had and swept out my study when I was done. If you're trying to find out by hints and insinuations what might be in my study, you must not have been listening to what I said. There is *nothing* left in my study, but for reasons of my own I want it locked while the kingdom remains! Can I make it any clearer than that?"

He stirred the fire vigorously, and the smoke found me again. The old wizard coughed a few times as well. I realized I had almost been hoping he had left something in his study that it had escaped, but now I just felt disappointed. It was likely only an old man's pride that had made him not want any other wizard ever to use the room where he had studied and done his research for so many years. If he had put a magic lock on the door, well, even City-trained wizards like me didn't always get the spells just right.

We sat and listened to the rain for several more minutes. Time seemed to stretch out endlessly in the dark room. I wasn't even hungry, even though it must have been long past dinner time. A small calico cat appeared suddenly from behind a chair, startling me for a second into thinking it was a large rat, rubbed against me, then crossed the room to hop up on the old wizard's lap. He stroked it absently, staring into the fire.

I tried again. "Master, in spite of my degree from the wizards' school, which seemed to impress them up at the castle, I'm really not a very good wizard."

"You didn't need to tell me *that.*"

"But I want to learn! If I came here regularly, could you teach me about the magic of air and herbs?"

He glared at me so fixedly that I was sure he would refuse. The cat in his lap, unconcerned, gave a wide pink yawn and settled itself more comfortably. But then the old wizard's shoulders seemed to relax a little. He rocked in silence for a moment while I held my breath, then answered at last. "Maybe. Just maybe. After the *last* time, I'd determined I'd never teach anyone again."

This must be the time that Dominic and the Lady Maria had tried to learn magic, I thought, but did not dare speak.

"But I don't think you're as stupid as you seem at first." This was apparently a compliment. "I'll have to consider it. I haven't had an apprentice for many years, maybe for a century."

If he was trying to pretend an old man's forgetfulness, he wasn't fooling me; I was sure he knew exactly who his last apprentice had been and when he had taught him.

"No one wanted to be an apprentice anymore after that wizards' school started." This thought roused him into a new glare. "But the old magic cannot be forgotten. You young whippersnappers are going to need it when your 'modern' magic gets into trouble. I'll think about it for a while."

I was delighted but dared not show it. This was virtually a promise. During his "while," as he thought about it, I could teach myself a lot of the magic I was supposed to know already if I spent every evening with my books. Then if I started coming down here regularly, maybe I could actually become a competent wizard. I imagined myself going back to the City for a visit and showing off all my new skills.

He interrupted my imaginings with almost a shout. "But would you then go back and tell everything I taught you to that chaplain friend of yours?"

This had never occurred to me as a possibility. "No, of course not! Why should I do that? He doesn't even really approve of magic."

"But you said he was your friend," said the wizard with a grunt.

"Just because he's the most intelligent person my age in the castle. It's nice to have someone to talk to over wine in the evening."

"And you like your wine, don't you?" If I wasn't careful, he was going to rescind his offer to think for a while about teaching me the old herbal magic.

"He seems to think even ordinary magic is black magic. I might have a glass of wine with him, but I certainly wouldn't tell him anything I'd learned."

This seemed to irritate the old wizard, but I realized it was not something I had said but something I reminded him of. "His predecessor was just the same. Accusing honest wizards of pacts with the devil. As though I didn't know better than to deal rashly in black magic!"

In spite of what I had told the chaplain, wizards do in fact talk among themselves of "black magic." There is no evil in magic itself, only in the intention of those who practice it, but in the few cases (*very* few, I hope) where a wizard has summoned a demon to add supernatural ability to his evil intentions, we refer to him as practicing black magic.

It is of course always difficult to draw the line. No one at the wizards' school would call it black magic to summon a demon (and a very small one at that) to demonstrate to the class what to do if you meet one, but I hardly found it appropriate to discuss this with the old wizard any more than I had with the chaplain.

"Interfering old busybody! Frustrated old maid!" The old wizard sank back in his chair with a snort. He was apparently referring to the old chaplain.

I tried to think of something to say to change the subject and decided silence was best. Besides, my head was starting to ache fiercely. There are magic spells to minimize pain, and I decided to try one, very delicately and surreptitiously, hoping that he wouldn't notice.

But I couldn't help but wonder why the old chaplain

had thought the wizard had been practicing black magic, and in what he had tried to interfere.

The old wizard went back to rocking, the cat asleep in his lap. What seemed like several hours passed. The fire kept on burning steadily, though he added no more wood. If he noticed that the smoke from his hearth had given his guest a headache, and that the guest had had the poor taste to practice magic in his face, he didn't deign to mention it.

I roused from a reverie to notice the rain had stopped. My head felt fine. I stood up from next to the table where I had been sitting, stiff in all my joints. Horizontal rays from the sun came through the narrow window, lighting up the piles of herbs and making the swirls of light and illusion seem rather insignificant.

Almost sunset, I thought, suddenly ravenously hungry. The old wizard was looking up at me, a half smile on his dry lips. The cat was no longer on his lap.

Then I realized what was wrong. The sunlight was coming from the wrong direction. Even a city boy like me knows that the sun rises and sets on opposite sides of the sky. I wasn't seeing the sunset but the sunrise. I had passed all night in the old wizard's house without even realizing it.

"I'd better get back to the castle," I said, hoping I'd be able to make it back in time for breakfast. "I was very glad to be able to meet you, and I'm sorry if I overstayed my welcome."

"You think you passed the night here, don't you?" said the old wizard with a chuckle. "In fact, you spent two. Maybe your friend the chaplain will be worried about you."

Two nights! Whatever magic powder he had put on his fire must be powerful indeed. "Good-bye, Master," I said and rushed out the door. My mare, cropping grass contentedly, seemed no worse for having spent two nights under the wizard's tree. I saddled her without looking back. As I led her out into the grassy clearing and mounted, the calico cat came bounding after us, dropped down to lurk behind a clump of grass, and lashed its tail. "Good-bye, cat," I said gravely, and rode as quickly as the mare would go back up the valley.

At first I was worried that I would have upset them at the castle by being gone for so long, but then I decided it was probably time anyway that I started seeming mysterious in my movements. I was more concerned about the old wizard's motives, and what I might find when I got back. Was he just showing off his power to me again, or had he had some reason for keeping me away from the castle?

IV

The queen was coming home.

I looked at myself critically in the mirror. In the month I had been at the castle, my beard had grown out enough that I didn't think the clothing department manager at the emporium would laugh at it anymore, but it was no longer uniformly gray. The roots were definitely chestnut brown. I would have to touch it up before the queen arrived.

Being gone for two days without explanation had, as I had hoped, actually made me seem rather powerful and mysterious. Even the chaplain had had the tact not to ask me directly where I had been, but he did raise his eyebrows at me most markedly at dinner.

Now, two weeks after my visit to the old wizard, I wondered, as I got out my bottle of gray dye, if it was too soon to ask him to start teaching me his form of magic. In the last few days, I had started trying to teach the king how to fly, and I had new respect for the teaching process. So far, in spite of the king's hopes to impress the queen with his new ability when she arrived, he had managed to lift himself from a chair about one inch for about one second. I, on the other hand, had become *much* better at flying than I had ever been. It hardly even bothered me anymore.

As I rubbed the dye, which stung, into my beard, I absently wondered if the Lady Maria had to do this every day. In all the meals sitting next to her, I had yet to see a gray hair or root.

There was a sharp knock on my door. "Just a minute!" I called, finished rubbing in the dye, rinsed it out, and went to answer the door with my chin in a towel.

It was Dominic. He always seemed to be crouching to fit into my chambers, even though there was plenty of headroom. "Please have a seat," I said brusquely and retreated into my inner chamber to finish drying my beard, trying to retain some of my dignity.

When I emerged again a few minutes later, I was amazed to see that he had taken my copy of the *Diplomatica Diabolica* down from the shelf. It was still closed, but he was holding it in his huge hands and staring at it.

I whisked it away from him and returned it to its place. "Don't you know how dangerous it is for those not trained in wizardry to look at magic's spells?" I said, trying to hide my fear behind anger.

He dropped his head in almost comical embarrassment at being found out. The old wizard, I thought, must have caught him doing something similar, and that was why he had been so reluctant to want to teach his form of magic to anyone else.

"Have you still not learned your lesson, Prince Dominic?" I said very gravely. "You first tried to interfere with the forces of magic four years ago, and in spite of the warning you received then you have begun again."

This speech had a much better effect than I had hoped. Dominic, who was shorter than I when sitting down, looked up with what seemed genuine terror in his eyes.

"If you value the kingdom of Yurt," I continued, seizing the advantage while I had it, even though I wasn't sure why I did, "or even your own life, you won't try to interfere in magic processes again."

"All right," he said, almost grudgingly. He shot me a look that was part fear and part resentment of my authority over him. I decided to leave the topic.

"So what can I do for you?" I said in a more normal voice.

He leaned back, as though casually. "Since the queen is coming home today, I wanted to find out what progress you've made in your duties, finding out who's put a spell on the king. Or haven't you gotten anywhere yet?"

This last, though said in the same light, conversational tone as the rest, was clearly meant to be a jab.

"Actually I have made significant progress," I said, wondering how much I dared say to him; I still hadn't ruled out an illicit love-pact between him and the queen. I hurried on because he looked dubious. "There is definitely an evil influence here in the castle, but it's not tied to any one person. I'm going to need a complete list of all visitors to the castle in the last four years. It's possible a spell was put in place by someone who's now gone."

For a moment he looked as though he were going to object. But then he nodded slowly. "That's a very good idea. You should ask the constable; I'm sure he can provide it for you. Since it's clear that no one in the castle wishes to harm the king, it must be someone from outside. Although," and here he paused for a look at me, "if you found it too *difficult* to examine four years of guests, maybe it would be easier just to get rid of the evil spell, without worrying where it came from." He lurched to his feet. "Well, I won't keep you any longer from your *special* preparations to meet the queen.'

With this last jab, he opened my door and was gone. I stared thoughtfully for several minutes at the inside of the door. I hoped I would not in fact have to go through a long list of visitors to the castle; I had suggested it primarily to see how Dominic would react. He clearly believed that this evil influence, which I was quite willing to accept as real, came from those now at the castle—if one included the queen. If he believed it, so did I.

But in the meantime, the fact that I had been able to frighten him, even momentarily, made him resent me. I had felt all along that he would not be comfortable to have as an enemy, and I feared that now I was going to find out just how uncomfortable that could be.

Later that morning, I stood outside the castle gate with everyone else. A chair had been brought for the king, but the rest of us stood on tiptoe, walked around, peered into the distance, and tried to listen through the sounds of conversation and the whisper of the wind for the sound of distant hooves.

One of the boys who was training for knighthood had the sharpest eyes. "There she comes!" he shouted. There was a surge forward, and several of the younger servants made as though to run down the brick road, but the constable motioned them back. In a moment all of us could see the little procession, emerging from the woods and starting up the hill toward the castle.

There was a crowd of white horses, with one black horse in the middle. White pennants, emblazoned with a bright pink rose, fluttered above them. As the horses ascended, a trumpeter with a long silver trumpet came to the fore and blew a swirl of notes. The riders kicked their horses into a run for the last hundred yards, and then they had arrived.

They were all around us, knights and ladies on

horseback, servants leading the pack animals, everyone swinging down from their mounts and laughing and shouting at the people from the castle, who were laughing and shouting back at them.

I spotted the one I thought was the queen, a delicate, pale blonde, with a beatific smile. But as she pulled up her white mare, one of the knights from the castle took the bridle with a smile of delight all over his face, and she slid from the saddle and into his welcoming arms.

And then I did see the queen, and wondered how I could have been so mistaken.

Based on the features of the Lady Maria, her aunt, and on the white rosebush which the king had planted on their wedding day, I had expected someone blushing and fragile. But she looked no more like the Lady Maria than she looked like the old woman I had thought her to be when I first arrived in Yurt.

She was riding a black stallion, and her hair was the same midnight black. Her eyes were a brilliant and startling emerald beneath dark lashes. A crimson cloak swirled around her as she tossed the reins to one of the servants and leaped off. She and the king met with outstretched hands, much too dignified to kiss in front of all their subjects, but looked into each other's eyes with joy.

I had been wrong in the old wizard's valley. *This* was the most beautiful woman I had ever seen. She made the illusory unicorn lady seem rather insipid in comparison. As she leaped from her stallion, I had for a moment thought her a hard woman, but her face when smiling was the sweetest thing I had ever experienced.

She turned that smile toward me. "The new wizard!" she cried in what seemed genuine delight. "I'm so sorry I wasn't here to greet you when you arrived! My parents had been counting on my coming ever since last summer, and the old wizard retired so abruptly that it was too late to change my plans. Has everyone been treating you well? If I know them, and I do, I'm sure they have! Are you happy in Yurt?"

I stammered that I was very happy in Yurt. I was in love at once.

While I stood staring at her—besotted, the old wizard would have said—I thought that here truly was a creature of fire and air, finer than anything illusion or imagination could create. She was beautiful, energetic, and loving-hearted. She took the king's arm; I was relieved to see that he showed no intention of trying to fly for her benefit, being too happy to see her to think about anything else.

We all started up the last slope to the moat and the castle gates. The king and queen, arm and arm, were beside me. "The king has been telling me in his letters that you're developing a telephone system for us!" she said, the perfect hostess, complimenting her guest on his accomplishments.

This brought me back somewhat to reality. "I've been working, but it's proving more difficult than I expected," I said, realizing it had been some time since I had had my glass telephones down from the shelf, and resolving to start with them again tomorrow, or even today.

The royal pair kept moving, as she spoke a few words to first one person, than another. I found myself near the back of the group, walking with Joachim, as we entered the castle courtyard.

"Why didn't you warn me?" I said.

"Warn you against what?"

"The queen!"

"But there is no evil in her."

I gave him up. "It's a good thing you're a priest," I said, left him wondering what I meant, and went into my chambers.

I pulled down one of the books I had not tried yet, because it was all advanced spells that assumed you already understood the basics without having to think about them. This seemed like the best place to start anew on the problem of the telephones.

But I had trouble concentrating on the pages. I kept thinking about those emerald eyes. Since I wasn't such a wonderful wizard anyway, maybe I could give up magic altogether when the king died, and then she and I—

This was clearly an unprofitable line of thought. I wished I had had the sense to watch Dominic, to try to judge his reaction to her homecoming. But I had been too busy staring at her, doubtless open-mouthed, to pay attention to anyone else.

Neither the king nor queen was present at the table at noon nor again in the evening. The queen, we were told, was resting from the fatigues of her journey, although she had appeared to me to have too much energy ever to be fatigued. I didn't want to think what the king might be resting from.

Instead I talked animatedly to the Lady Maria. Everyone at both tables was delighted to have the queen home, so she was the chief topic of conversation, except for the couple farther down my table who were just delighted to see each other again.

Lady Maria was happy to discuss her niece. "That's right, she and I came to Yurt together when she was a bride, a mere child really. Her mother is a cousin to the duchess, or maybe they're second cousins. Haven't you met the duchess? You will, I'm sure. Yurt has two counts and the duchess. Anyway, the king was visiting his subjects, and he came to the duchess's castle at the same time as the queen's family was visiting, including me. Of course she wasn't the queen then. But as soon as the king met her he started making his plans, you can be sure!"

There was a sort of grunt from behind me where Dominic was sitting. He had not spoken to me again all day.

"Dominic remembers," the Lady Maria said in a teasing voice. "I think my brother, that's the queen's father, of course, had some hope of marrying his daughter to the royal heir, when he first heard the royal party would be visiting the duchess's castle at the same time we were. Did the royal heir have some plans that way himself, Dominic?"

She laughed, a light, tinkling laugh. I turned my head just in time to catch an extremely surly look from Dominic. I felt much more affectionate toward the Lady Maria than I ever had before.

"But imagine our surprise," she continued, "when it turned out the king's plans were quite different! Everything worked out so beautifully. Except," she paused, looked around, and dropped her voice. "Except," so low that only I could hear her, and I thought for a moment that she was going to say, except that she had never been able to make the hoped-for match with Dominic herself, "except that the queen has so hoped to provide the king a little prince, and she hasn't been able to."

"What are you two whispering about?" one of the ladies called to us from down the table. I realized that we had our heads bent together as though engaged in intimate secrets, certainly more secret than what everyone else must long have guessed about the king and queen. I sat up almost guiltily and caught the chaplain's dark, sober eyes on me.

"We're talking about the telephones!" I said gaily. "Now that the queen's back, I'm sure she's eager to be able to telephone her parents, and I have some ideas for the next step to try. The Lady Maria has graciously agreed to assist me again." If anyone giggled, they were polite enough to turn it into a cough.

V

I stayed up late that night with my books and was up again after only a few hours' sleep, and was almost too engrossed in the spells to hear Gwen's knock. But I heard it the second time and went to answer. This morning the breakfast tray held hot cinnamon crullers as well as my tea.

"Sir, could I speak with you?" she said somewhat timidly.

"Of course!" I said, motioning her to a chair. Gwen hadn't seemed to want to talk to me since the first days I had been in Yurt. She now seemed subdued, not at all inclined to laugh at me. Maybe seeing me gaping at the queen had had the salutary effect of making her jealous.

Her first words destroyed any hope I might have had in that direction. "Sir, do wizards make love potions?"

"Love potions! My dear, why would anyone so charming as yourself need a love potion?" I realized I sounded as though I were her uncle and about forty years older than she was, but I couldn't think of what else to say.

She ignored the compliment if she even noticed it. "No, I don't need a love potion myself. But I'm afraid Jon is going to use one on me."

"Jon?"

"You know him. He's one of the trumpeters, and he also does the glassblowing. He made you your glass telephones."

"He does very good work, too," I said, wondering why she would need a love potion used on her. "He seems a very nice young man." Now I was sounding like an uncle again, trying to persuade the coy niece to accept her gallant suitor.

"I like him, sir, I really like him a lot. But he wants

to get married, and I'm not sure I'm ready. Maybe not ready to marry anybody, and certainly not to marry him. He gets so jealous! Can you imagine, when you first came he even was jealous of you? He made me promise not to speak more to you than absolutely necessary."

This, of course, was devastating. At first I had thought someone had warned her against me, and had speculated whether this might have something to do with the strangely distant yet evil touch I felt in the castle. Then I had decided she had had to restrain her affections before her heart broke. And now it seemed it was all due to a jealous glassblower, who she thought should have known better than possibly to be jealous of me!

"I guess I'm breaking my promise talking to you now, but I really do feel I have to."

"If you're worried he'll use a love potion to make you marry him," I said with as much dignity as I could, "where do you think he'll get it?"

"At first, of course, I was worried he'd get it from you, that he might even have asked you for it the day he blew that glass for you. But a month has gone by, and I know he hasn't tried to slip me a potion yet, and I haven't seen him talking to you again, except a few words in front of a lot of other people."

"I don't make love potions," I said honestly. "That's not something they teach us in the wizards' school. That's more something for magic-workers at carnivals than real wizards."

"I think the old wizard, your predecessor, might have made love potions."

This was entirely possible, but I didn't say so. "I don't, at any rate, so you need fear nothing from me."

"But he might get it somewhere else, then, at a carnival, or even from the old wizard. How can I tell if he's put it in my food?"

A good question, and the same question I was wondering about the king. A wizard can recognize another wizard at once, but since magic is a natural force, someone simply carrying a magic potion is not particularly obvious. If someone could poison the king, then Jon could try to make Gwen love him.

"Don't ever eat or drink alone with him," I said, which was not a particularly useful answer, but was all I could think of. "He wouldn't mind taking the love potion himself, since he's already in love with you, but I don't think he'd dare have anyone else fall in love with him." Gwen looked at me skeptically, as though disappointed that such obvious advice was all I could give. "And smell your food," I said. "Love potions are made of herbs and roots and usually smell rather nasty."

"Thank you, sir," she said, rising and taking my now-empty tray.

"Thank you for the crullers!" I called after her. "They were delicious."

A little later that morning, I sat with the Lady Maria in my outer chamber, the curtains drawn, and the telephone instruments before us. I didn't really need her for what I was trying, but after what I had said at dinner I felt I ought to include her. Besides, she had been talking to Dominic in the great hall when I went to find her, and he had given me an almost furious look when I interrupted and asked her to join me. If Dominic had turned against me, I wanted him as uncomfortable as possible.

"Now keep perfectly silent while I work this spell," I said. "I'm trying something different this time. It's a far-seeing spell, and extremely difficult. They never even taught it to us at the wizards' school." They might have taught some of the other students, but they most certainly had never taught me. "I'm going to try to attach it to the telephone."

The Lady Maria did as she was bid, even breathing

virtually without a sound, as I checked the spell one last time in the book, put it away, and closed my eyes to begin. The heavy syllables of the Hidden Language rolled from my tongue. It was a long spell.

I opened my eyes and looked at my glass telephone in the dim light of the room. It looked exactly the same. I was about to try speaking a name to it, to see if it might respond, when I was almost knocked from my chair by the surprise of another voice speaking the Hidden Language.

It was the Lady Maria. Her eyes closed, she was resting her hands on the telephone instrument in front of her and repeating the long spell I had just given, word for word.

In ten minutes, at the last syllable, she opened her eyes and gave me a saucy look that Gwen could not have equaled. "There! You probably didn't think I could work magic."

"But can you?" I cried, flabbergasted. I hadn't thought anyone could say a spell, except one of the very simple ones, without actually learning the Hidden Language, knowing what the words meant as well as how they were pronounced. And I was quite sure there was no way to learn the Language other than a lengthy apprenticeship or years in the wizards' school.

"If your spell works, mine should too," she said complacently. "I just said everything you said, the same way you said it."

"Let's try yours, then," I said and pulled the curtain open. I picked up the receiver and spoke the name attached to the telephone at the wizards' school in the City.

Very faintly, from the receiver, I could hear a distant ringing. "Triumph at last!" I thought, but dared say nothing. I held the receiver so Maria could hear as well. She leaned close to me, her hair brushing my cheek.

"Look!" she said with indrawn breath. The glass

base of the telephone had lit up. Inside was a miniature but very real scene, a room at the wizards' school, a telephone sitting on a table, and one of the young wizards, one I knew but not well, picking up the receiver.

"Hello?"

"Hello!" I cried. "Can you hear me?"

"Hello?" somewhat more dubiously. "Is anyone there?"

The tiny figure inside the telephone base turned his head, as though talking to someone else. "No, I can't hear anyone. It's just silent."

"We're here! We're here! Hello?" I shouted.

"Maybe someone's idea of a joke." We watched his hand move to replace the receiver, and then our telephone went blank.

"We did it!" said Maria, giving me a hard hug that startled me so much that I couldn't answer at once. "We made the telephones work!"

"In fact, we didn't," I said, trying to catch my breath.

"Let me try this time." Before I could say anything she had picked up the receiver and spoken another name. Again I could hear the faint sound of ringing. Then, once again, the telephone base lit up with a miniature scene within it. This time, it was a liveried servant picking up the receiver.

"That's a servant in my brother's castle," she said. "We can tell them the queen got home safely. Hello? Hello? Can you hear me?"

As I expected, the servant could not hear us and replaced the receiver in a moment. "We don't need to tell them," I said. "The queen sent a message by the pigeons when she got home yesterday."

"But why can't they hear us?"

"I was trying to tell you," I said, drawing my chair away from hers. "A telephone, if it's working, is a communications instrument. Our telephones don't communicate at all. I've taken the far-seeing spell and attached it to the instruments, but it's not working right. Now it only means that someone using our telephones can *see* a distant telephone, not that he or she can talk to anyone far away."

"But couldn't you still use our phones for communication? You could send a message by the pigeons that you were going to telephone, and then when the phone rang and they couldn't hear anyone, they could just say whatever they wanted to say, knowing *you* could hear *them*."

This was too elaborate for me. "No; all it means is that I'm not closer to the telephone system they wanted. On the other hand," feeling more cheerful, "I don't think anyone's ever attached the far-seeing spell to an object before. This means someone, even if not trained in magic, *could* see far away, as long as he only wanted to see a distant telephone room."

But this brought me back to an earlier concern. "Lady Maria, how do you happen to know magic? Usually women don't know any. Have you been trained?"

"Of course not; all you male wizards refuse to teach women magic. Are there really no women wizards?"

"Not really."

"But why not? I've heard of witches; aren't they women wizards?"

This was going to be difficult to explain. "Of course there are witches in the world. They're women who've learned magic on their own, for the most part, or from other witches. But there have never been women in the wizards' school."

"Is there a real reason, or just a silly tradition?"

"Tradition's not silly," I told her. "Anything that has functioned well for centuries must have some validity. But you're right, it *is* a tradition, rather than a written law, such as that barring women from the priesthood."

I didn't want to be distracted from my original question of where she had learned magic, but she kept on pushing me about women wizards. "But what validity can a tradition have that keeps women from learning magic?"

"You're not the first to ask this. It's actually a question that's being raised by some of the wizards of the City. The real reason, the original reason, is that women already have a creative power that men don't have, the power to create life within their wombs." If I hoped to embarrass her by my frankness, I should have known better; this was the same woman who had been whispering to me at dinner about the queen's attempts to have a baby. "It would be too dangerous to link wizardry with that kind of creation. Witches are always teetering, about to go over into black magic, unless they know so little magic at all that their spells are useless. If you've heard of witches, you must have heard that some of them are said to create magic monsters in the womb."

Maria paused for a moment; she clearly *had* heard something of the sort. "But that wouldn't apply—" She broke off. That wouldn't apply, she had been starting to say, to someone already forty-eight, but she wasn't going to say it. Instead she said, "In that case, wouldn't it be better to train the women properly, so they would know how magic *should* be used? Isn't that training why the wizards' school was started originally? That's what we were told when we started looking for a new wizard."

This argument too I had heard in the City. But instead of answering I changed the subject back to my question. "So how did you learn the Hidden Language?"

"Is that what it's called? When I first came to Yurt, I was terribly excited at the opportunity to learn magic, when I found there was a Royal Wizard here; there was no wizard in my brother's castle. And then, at *most*, he let me be there while he worked some spells! But I found out I had the ability to say spells myself, if I'd heard them even once, and then I started making requests of my own!"

"Requests?" This sounded dubious. "What were you requesting?"

"Don't ask a girl all her secrets!" she said with a smile which was indeed positively girlish.

She seemed, I thought, to be one of the rare persons born with a flair for magic. This was why, weeks earlier, she had been able to hear my voice speaking within her mind.

"The old wizard wouldn't teach me anything. Could you, might you, teach me wizardry?"

There was actually no reason why I shouldn't. But I hesitated. Magic was a powerful tool, and the old wizard had been right in calling her flighty. But no one would have called me sober and stable either when I first came to the wizards' school.

"You'd have to learn the Hidden Language first," I said at last. "You can do a few spells by saying the words, but to create your own spells you need to understand them thoroughly." I reached for the first-grammar from my shelf. It was heavy, and the cloth binding was starting to fray badly. "Take this if you want, but I will need it back again. Start studying, and if you're still interested I can help you further."

She took the volume eagerly, but her face fell as she leafed through it. "But it doesn't tell how to do spells."

"As I said, you can't create your own spells unless you understand the Language first. But tell me," as a thought struck me, "how you've been able to make magic 'requests' without knowing magic."

There was no doubt now that she didn't want to answer me. She stood up rapidly, clutching the first-grammar. "I'll try to work through this," she said. "I'd better go now. But wasn't it fun that it was *my* telephone that worked?" She rushed across my room and was gone before I could answer.

I sat down again and leaned my face on my fists. I had imagined being a Royal Wizard was exciting, mysterious, and awe-inspiring. So far, I had actually promised to teach wizardry to a woman, one who was positively flirting with me; another woman, who came to ask my wizardly advice, left thinking of me as a rather dim-witted uncle; and I was in love with a third woman, this one married already.

PART THREE

Carnival

I

I came up the hill toward the castle on the white mare, exhausted and exhilarated. It was midmorning, and I had again spent the night at the old wizard's house without intending to do so when I arrived. But this time I had known the night was passing (and it *was* only one night, not two) and had stayed because I decided to, not because the old wizard had used his magic herbal smoke to put me to sleep.

The harvest was over, now, although the turnips still lay in the ground, awaiting the first real frost. For two weeks I had stood out in the fields with the harvesters, wearing a wide-brimmed hat against the sun and doubtless looking much more like a farmer than a wizard. I had kept my eye open for thunderstorms, or the hailstorms that could destroy the ripe grain, but for the most part the weather had stayed clear, and the weather spells I had assiduously reviewed were only needed once. With my harvest responsibilities over, I had gone back to the old wizard's house under the giant oak.

Yesterday he had begun to teach me herbal magic. I smiled ruefully at myself, arriving yesterday morning, doubtless very like the Lady Maria expecting the first-grammar of the Hidden Language to be a tidy list of useful spells. I had expected a quick listing of different herbs and their properties. Instead he had begun teaching me to *know* the herbs, as well as I already knew the Language, to recognize the possible properties in each and to determine how to combine them and how to find the words that would reveal their potency.

It was only twenty-four hours ago that I had naïvely said, "You mean that you have to *do* something with magic herbs? Anyone can't just pick them and use them?" The old wizard had snorted and looked at me as though he were going to send me back to the castle at once, but he hadn't.

The exhilaration had come just before I left, while the old wizard was slicing me some coarse bread and vegetables for breakfast. I stood next to the table where he had different herbs laid out, trying to picture what each might do, while the calico cat rubbed against my ankles.

"You didn't tell me you had a stickfast weed," I said.

"I don't," he said from the other table without turning around.

"This one," I said, holding it out until he did look back over his shoulder.

"That isn't anything," he said, returning to the vegetables. "It got into my basket with a lot of other herbs."

This, I decided, was a test. "But look!" I said. I squeezed the sap from the stem onto my palm, said two words, and reached down to pat the cat. When I stood up, it was firmly attached to my hand.

The cat didn't like being suspended from my open palm. It yowled and extended its claws. I said two more words and it was free. It dropped the short distance to the floor, gave a short hiss, and disappeared under the old wizard's chair.

Then I realized it hadn't been a test. The old wizard stared at me, the knife forgotten in his hand, without speaking. After a long minute, as though he had finally won the struggle to avoid praising me, he said, "Stickfast weed," and grunted.

He put the bread and vegetables on a plate and handed it to me without another word. But I knew. I had discovered an herbal property he had not known. While I ate, I kept tossing little crumbs toward the cat until it emerged. Then I scooped it up and settled it on my lap, where in a minute it settled down to purr to show we were friends again.

"Maybe I'll be able to teach you some real magic after all," said the old wizard as I saddled my mare. "Even if you did get some fancy notions at that City school." The excitement lasted all the ride back through the woods, even though the exhaustion of staying up all night hit me as soon as I left the wizard's valley. I had even learned a simple spell that someone not trained in magic could say, to detect magic potions in food. I couldn't wait to tell Gwen.

I wondered again, as the castle came in sight, what had happened during the day I had passed in a trance in the wizard's house last month. Yesterday, as I ducked under the volley of magic arrows to reach him, I had been wondering if he had used the time as an opportunity to come back up to the castle without my knowledge. But if so, no one had seen him, and he had said nothing about it, either then or now. If he *had* come to the castle, I now thought, he would have seen at once that his magic locks were gone from the north tower and would most certainly have held me to blame. That his manner now sometimes verged on friendly showed he did not yet know what had happened there. But sometime I was going to have to tell him.

As I started across the drawbridge over the moat, I almost collided with the queen coming out.

"I'm so pleased you're back!" she cried with the smile that made my heart turn over. "The king told me to meet him in five minutes in the rose garden. I'm sure he'd like you to be there as well. He said it was a magic surprise! The five minutes are almost up."

I dismounted to walk with her. She was wearing a long white dress with a standing crimson collar that framed her face, and her eyes flashed with delight at me from under an errant wave of hair.

We stopped at the garden gate. "I'm here!" the queen called. "And I've brought the Royal Wizard with me!"

"Come on in!" came a faint call, and we entered.

Coming toward us between the rosebushes, his toes just brushing the grass, was King Haimeric. His face was so tight with concentration that he seemed not to see us. I could tell he wasn't even breathing. When he was within three feet of the queen, he lifted his eyes, took a sudden breath, and dropped to the ground. She steadied him with her strong young arms.

"You were flying!" she cried. "When did you learn to fly? I know you said it would be a magic surprise, but I hadn't imagined it could be anything so wonderful!"

The king winked at me over her head, a wink of triumph.

He leaned on her arm as they walked toward the bench, and I followed behind.

"I've been having the wizard teach me," he said.

"And you've clearly been practicing on your own!" I added. "You've made *much* better progress than I would have expected. But you do have to remember to breathe."

"I noticed that," he said, sitting down and breathing hard now. "But it seems to interrupt my concentration."

"All it needs is a little more practice."

"I'd had no idea you were learning to fly," said the queen in admiration, and for one bad moment I was afraid she was going to ask me to teach her too. "When did you start learning?"

"It was while you were at your parents'. Originally I was hoping to show you when you first got back, but I wasn't as quick a pupil as I'd hoped. Not that our wizard isn't a good teacher!" They both turned wide smiles on me. "One of the many, many things I like about having you here is that it makes me less dependent on Dominic. As you know, since my legs started to get weak I haven't always been able to walk as well as I'd like, and he'd baby me unmercifully. I thought that if I learned to fly, I'd be able to move around as I liked without him always hovering. The boy means well, but . . ."

He didn't finish the sentence. I was very pleased to see that I was not the only person in the castle referred to as a boy—especially since Dominic was half again my age.

I was also pleased to see how much more cheerful the king had seemed since the queen came home. When I first arrived, he was looking back over his years as king as though they would shortly be coming to an end. Now he acted as though he were only in the middle of them. I began to wonder if the mysterious ailment that Dominic thought someone had given the king was nothing more than some stiffness in the knees combined with loneliness. If she had been *my* queen, I would certainly have been lonely when she was gone.

We looked at the roses while the king finished catching his breath. Some of the bushes had already finished blooming for the season, though late roses still bloomed defiantly on others.

"You know," said the king, "it's been several years

since I've been to the harvest carnival. Would you like
to go?"

"Oh, could we?" said the queen with that smile.

"I'd be delighted," I said, since the question seemed
to include me as well, and suddenly had to stifle a
yawn.

"The carnival starts in two days," said the king.
"We'll leave first thing in the morning." With the tact
I was pleased to see even a sometimes incompetent
wizard deserved, he added, "You'll have plenty of time
before then to recover your strength after your magic
activities."

While I napped that afternoon with my curtains
drawn, the rest of the castle must have buzzed with
activity, for in the morning all was ready. The constable and his wife were staying behind with a few servants, but the rest of us rode out just after dawn: the
knights first, led by Dominic, then the king and queen,
surrounded by the ladies of the court, then the boys,
the chaplain, and me, all followed by the servants, who
led pack horses loaded with food, supplies, and the
tents.

The queen rode her black stallion, but the rest of
us were on the white or bay mares and geldings of
the royal stables. Bells on our harnesses jingled as we
waved good-bye to those staying behind and rode
down the brick road toward the forest. The air was
crisp, with a faint haze, and there were spots of orange
leaves among the green before us.

"Have you been to this harvest carnival before?" I
asked the chaplain. He was riding beside me, his horse
the only one without bells.

"Not since I came to Yurt," he said. "The carnival
was already past the fall I arrived, and the king has
not felt well enough since then to go. But of course
I know the city well where it is held."

Clearly I was missing something. Since I didn't even

know where we were going, I kept on with my questions. "Why do you know it well?"

Joachim looked at me in surprise, then nodded. "That's right, you wouldn't know. It's my cathedral city, the city of the bishop. Yurt isn't big enough for its own bishop, or for that matter its own harvest carnival, so for both the kingdom must rely on the nearest city of the next kingdom over. That's where we're going."

"Then you'll get to see your old friends at the bishop's school," I said, thinking I would like to see some of my friends from the wizards' school. But this small city where we were going was still a long, long way from the City by the sea, where the wizards trained, and I knew that most of my best friends were by now off in various parts of the western kingdoms in their own posts as wizards.

Joachim looked at me a moment in silence, then smiled. "I still don't always recognize it when you're making a joke," he said. As I hadn't been making a joke, this naturally surprised me. "I'd been about to say, you must not know very much about the way the Church is organized to think that a priest would take up his first post in the same diocese as his seminary."

Since I had no idea what he was talking about, I decided to say nothing.

"But I *am* going to see the bishop. It would soon be time for my annual visit anyway, so it seemed easiest to come with the party from Yurt. I sent him a message by the pigeons yesterday so that he would expect me."

"That will be nice to see him, if it's been a year," I said to keep the conversation going.

" 'Nice,' " said Joachim, as though testing the word. "You know, I don't always understand you. Are you still joking? Or is it really 'nice' for you to explain to the old wizard of the wizards' school your progress in the last year in combating evil?"

"Oh," I said, understanding at last. "I'm sorry, I don't think I'd realized that you had to undergo an annual assessment."

"How else would the bishops of the western kingdoms be able to be sure that the priests under them had kept the pure faith?"

We reached the edge of the forest and passed into the cool shade. The early morning light was dim, but I could see Joachim's dark eyes glaring at me.

"Don't you wizards from the wizards' school have to do something similar?"

If so, no one had ever told me, or at least I hadn't heard. I missed my friends and I missed the City, but I certainly hoped I would never have to explain to the Master of the wizards that I had spent the past year adeptly aiding mankind with benign wizardry. "Maybe it's because wizards tend to fight all the time," I said, "but they leave us alone once we've left the school."

"Maybe it's because the worst you can do is endanger your own souls," said Joachim with a snort that would have done credit to my predecessor in Yurt.

We would soon be reaching the little pile of white stones that marked the turnoff for the old wizard's hidden valley. I decided not to point it out.

We rode in silence for a few minutes. What he said seemed to dismiss the theory I had once had that a young, untried and unsupervised priest had somehow let evil loose in Yurt. I was happy to see the theory go. Although Joachim seemed short on tact, even for him, this morning, I could not be irritated. He was not only going to have to explain why everything he had done was good, but make it clear that he had done it with a pure heart. Whatever wizardry demanded, a pure heart didn't seem absolutely necessary.

Reflecting on the lack of purity in my own heart made me think of Gwen. I hadn't yet had a chance to tell her I had a spell against love potions. I excused myself, reined in my mare so that others could pass me, and dropped into line again as Gwen came even.

"Hello, sir," she said in evident surprise.

"I'd like to talk to you a minute," I said. "Privately, if we could."

She had been riding next to Jon. Although the young trumpeter and glassblower had always been perfectly friendly to me, he now shot me a brief but unmistakable look of jealousy. "Don't worry," I said with a grin. "We can't possibly get into trouble on horseback."

This did not improve his expression, but Gwen laughed and reined in her own horse, so that the two of us fell to the back of the procession.

"You were asking me about love potions," I said as soon as I thought no one else would hear us. Jon was riding a short distance ahead, but his back was turned toward us stiffly, as though to say that he would not deign to turn around. "I've learned a spell you can say to detect one."

As I'd hoped, Gwen was delighted at this helpful advice from her elderly uncle. As we rode, I taught her the three simple words of the Hidden Language that would reveal such a potion and made her repeat them until I was sure she knew them. "Say them over any drink or dish you suspect," I said, "and if there's a love potion it will turn bright red."

"That should make the danger clear, then," she said with a smile.

"Very clear. And remember: I know the spell too, so don't try slipping anything in my crullers!"

This attempt at flirtation was met with highly amused laughter. The elderly uncle was clearly cute and quaint. She kicked her horse and hurried forward to rejoin Jon.

We rode on all that day, stopping for lunch at the border where we left the kingdom of Yurt. In late afternoon, when the king was clearly exhausted, Dominic called a halt at a meadow next to a stream. The servants unloaded the horses and set up the tents with the knights' assistance, then started fires to cook supper. The ride had made me ravenously hungry, and the smoked sausage they were grilling smelled delicious long before it was ready. The king and queen retired to their tent even before supper was ready, but the rest of us strolled around the meadow, glad to be on our own feet again after a day on horseback. Even the more reserved ladies of the court were talking and laughing about the events of the harvest carnival, which we would reach tomorrow, and the Lady Maria was positively giddy.

II

The first sight we had of the city was the spire of the cathedral, seeming to rise out of the golden stubble of the wheat fields. The forests of Yurt were far behind, and all afternoon we had been riding past wide fields. As we came closer, we could see that the cathedral spire was surrounded in turn by a small walled city, and that the city was surrounded with the colorful striped tents of other people who had come to the carnival. As we approached, I could see crenellated towers rising on the opposite side of the city from the cathedral, directly against the walls. The city gates stood wide open, and a crowd hurried in and out. Distant sounds of shouting, of laughter, and of song reached us on the wind.

We rode through the encampments, through the city gates, and were plunged into narrow streets bustling with humanity. We had to ride carefully to be sure our horses did not bump into anyone or knock over tables set out with everything from fresh vegetables to tooled harnesses to bales of fabric. I had expected that we would be camping again, but instead we proceeded through the streets toward the small castle whose towers I had seen from outside the walls.

"This castle belongs to Yurt," explained the Lady Maria, riding beside me. "Our king's grandfather, I think it was, bought the land outside the old city walls, built the castle, and rebuilt the walls to go around it. He wanted to have a place to stay when he came for one of the carnivals or to visit the cathedral. Now even the king of this kingdom has to ask our king's permission if he wants to stay here!"

Before reaching the castle, we had to pass the wide open square in front of the cathedral. Here, in the long shadow of the spire, the market tables were thickest, and the music was the loudest. Ahead of us, I saw the chaplain speak for a moment to the king, then pull his horse out of line.

"I'm leaving you now," he said as I came even. "But I'll be with you when you go." He dismounted before I could say anything and led his horse through the tangle of tables to the cathedral steps, where I saw him talking to a boy and handing him both the reins and a coin. I looked over my shoulder before we left the square to see him going, straight-backed, up the cathedral stairs and in the tall door.

"The king and queen were married in the cathedral," said the Lady Maria. "It was the sweetest ceremony, with roses brought from the king's own garden, and the queen just radiant. I always like to visit the cathedral when we come here."

In a few more twists of the street, we had reached the gateway which led into the courtyard of the king's little castle. The constable of this castle and his wife were at the gate waiting for us, wearing the same blue and white livery as the constable back home in Yurt. There were only a few chambers besides the royal chambers, so my little bundle of clean clothes ended up in the same room with Dominic and the knights. But none of us wanted to stay in the castle's narrow rooms when the sounds of carnival were right outside the windows. Within a few minutes, everyone but the king and queen was out in the city streets.

Most of them went in groups of three or four, but I went alone. At a booth just down the street from the castle I discovered something I had not expected to see but which I had to buy at once: a newspaper. I had not seen a newspaper since arriving in Yurt.

"This is dated five days ago," I said, leafing through it excitedly. In fact it didn't matter when it was dated, because I hadn't heard any news for two months anyway.

"That's when it left the City," said the man at the booth. "It came up here on a pack train, and they hurried, too, to get it here so quickly. You don't expect the pigeons to be able to carry a newspaper!"

"Of course not," I said absently, moving away, avidly turning the pages. But in a moment I paused, thinking something was wrong. When I had been at the wizards' school, I had always read at least the Sunday paper, and often the paper during the week as well. It had always been full of interesting news, ads, and information, whereas this paper was all full of the doings of some rather uninteresting people far away. Then I realized what the problem was. There was nothing in the paper about Yurt.

I laughed and folded it up. At this rate, soon I wouldn't be able to think of myself as a city boy any longer.

I had only a rather vague idea of how newspapers were produced, except that the presses that covered piles of newsprint with black ink were powered by wizardry. But I hadn't thought before how localized newspapers were, all produced in the City, by wizards trained in the school, carrying ads for the City emporia or sometimes ads sent in from distant kingdoms, like Yurt, that were aimed at people in the City, like young wizards. I opened the paper again, and saw that on the inner pages there was some news of political events in some of the western kingdoms, but for the most part the paper was devoted exclusively to topics that would interest people of the City. When I stopped at a stall to buy a bun topped with spices and melting cheese, I held the newspaper under my chin to catch the drips before they reached my clothes.

If I belonged anywhere, I thought, I now belonged to Yurt, not the City. Both my parents had died when I was very young, and the grandmother who had brought me up and operated their wholesale warehouse for a few more years had died my fifth year in the wizards' school. I had made some good friends at the school, but now that we were scattered over the western kingdoms we would not see each other very frequently, and probably not in the City at all.

Even if I wasn't a city boy anymore, I was exhilarated to be back in busy streets, where people on foot and horseback jostled with carts and booths. Competing music rose from every corner. I tossed coins to the best musicians, or at least the ones I enjoyed the most. As the afternoon dimmed toward evening, lamps were hung above the shop doors, and the shadows danced over faces that in many cases now were painted and decorated. Men, and a few women, with glasses in their hands spilled out of tavern doors. Although this was a small city, we were certainly not the only ones to have come to the carnival from far away. This, I thought, compared favorably to the harvest carnival in the City itself.

The relief after a long summer's worry and the work of harvest, of knowing food was stored away for the next year, made people giddy. Or at least I could imagine myself saying that to Joachim, to show him I often thought deeply about human nature, not just magic. On consideration, it didn't appear as deep or unusual a conclusion as I hoped. For that matter, the chaplain wasn't spending the carnival being giddy; he was doubtless at this moment describing the purity of his heart to the bishop.

But I was enjoying myself. I tried all the different kinds of food being served, from sausages to sweet hot pastries. I stopped briefly at a tavern, though the air inside was so thick and hot that I moved back out to the street after a single glass of wine. I admired and tossed coins to a girl doing a fairly provocative dance. I was startled and had to leap back against a wall as six people collectively wearing a dragon costume came running around the corner. For one horrible moment, I was afraid it actually was a dragon.

They certainly made a spectacular beast. Seeing they had startled me, they paused in their progress and did a dance for my benefit and that of several people near me. The dragon's fringed ears whirled around its head, its twelve legs stamped and weaved, and its eyes glowed red, not, as I realized in a moment, from fire but from magic.

I threw down a few coins, and a hand emerged from beneath the dragon's chest to scoop them up before the dragon continued down the street, roaring convincingly. I felt somehow inadequate. My great triumph at Yurt so far had been making lamps for the chapel stair, and yet a group of people in a dragon costume, who most probably had access to nothing as exalted as a Royal Wizard, were apparently able to make glowing dragon eyes without difficulty.

My steps took me back to the square in front of the cathedral. Since I had been there an hour before, the scene had changed. With the coming of evening, the merchants selling leather and bolts of cloth and the farmers selling loads of vegetables were all gone. The musicians and dancers were thicker, however, and at least half the people in the square were wearing some kind of costume. I saw no priests, even though we were next to the church; I guessed they stayed well inside during carnival.

And then I saw the most startling thing I had seen all day. Floating toward me, just over the heads of the crowd, was a glowing red bubble. As it came closer, I could see into it, and there, looking right back at me, was a grinning demon.

I was too struck with panic to think and therefore reacted out of instinct. I said the two words of the Hidden Language that would break an illusion, and the red bubble and the demon with it dissolved first into red dust and then into nothing.

And then I saw the magician. He was wearing a long, flowing robe, covered with every symbol imaginable, from the zodiac to a crucifix to a gleaming sun. On his head was a tall, pointed hat, and in his hand a heavy oak staff.

"What did you do that for?" he demanded. "Those take a long time to make, you know!"

I recognized him at once—not him personally, because I had never seen him before, but as a type. He was a magician, the sort of fellow who might have, in the youth of Yurt's old wizard, picked up a little magic in an abortive apprenticeship. Nowadays he most likely had studied for a year or two at the wizards' school. He was appreciably older than I; he would have left there before I arrived.

"I'm sorry," I said. "I know they're hard to make. But it was so convincing you scared me."

He smiled at that, a slightly gap-toothed grin over a scraggly beard in which the gray was real. "Not bad to be able to scare a real wizard," he said with a chuckle.

He would have known of course that I was a wizard. I had tried to explain once to the manager in the emporium how wizards can always recognize each other. He had thought it was some magic impress put on us at the same time we received our diplomas, but I had argued that that couldn't be the case, as many young wizards appeared to be wizards long before the eight years were up, and old wizards who had never gone to the school were always recognizable.

"Shall I help you make a replacement?" I said to the magician, then realized it was tactless as soon as I said it. I had been spending too much time with the chaplain.

The grin disappeared. "This is *my* corner. If you want to do some illusions of your own, go somewhere else, but don't interfere with my business."

I stepped back without saying anything, watching as he set to work on a new magic bubble. This one he made green, and instead of a demon he put a dragon inside. He was good, I had to admit. In a few moments he had it finished and launched it into the air. A crowd started to gather, and several people tossed him coins, which he snatched up while continuing to concentrate on the next bubble.

"Did you make the eyes for those people in the dragon costume?" I asked.

"Yes," he said with a quick glance in my direction, as though doubting my motives for asking.

"I just wanted to say that they're excellent dragon eyes."

"Well, *thanks* for your exalted opinion."

I wandered off through the crowd without saying anything more. I should have known better than to risk appearing to be condescending. Wizards fight all the time with one another anyway, and it's even worse with magicians, who are constantly imagining an insult or a joke at their expense.

I was walking more or less in the direction of the castle when I was surprised but highly pleased to see two familiar forms coming toward me: the king and queen. I was delighted not to be a carnival magician. There was nothing I could imagine better than being the Royal Wizard of Yurt. I would have to ask the chaplain to teach me a proper prayer of gratitude.

The king seemed rested from the journey and was

looking around with enjoyment, while the queen's emerald eyes sparkled with excitement. "I'm sorry I haven't been to the harvest carnival for a few years," the king said as we met. "It's even more fun than I remembered. The king of this kingdom never comes, preferring to go to the big carnival at the City by the sea, but I think he's missing something. You must have seen them both—what do you think?"

"I think this is a marvelous carnival," I said. "But it's getting late, and the crowd will be getting wild soon. Do you think it's quite, well, safe to be out?"

They both laughed. "No one will bother the King of Yurt," he said. "Not knowing the swift retribution that would follow from both my nephew and my Royal Wizard! And besides," to the queen, "you know a few tricks, don't you, my dear?"

She laughed in agreement. I was sure she did.

"We're going to see some of the costumes and maybe have something to eat," she said. "Do you want to join us?"

"I've already eaten quite a bit," I said. "Go ahead— I may go back to the castle and rest a little myself." I watched them as they proceeded down the street, arm in arm, both pointing and laughing as they went. When they disappeared around the corner, I continued to the castle.

None of the knights was back, though I could hear the voices of several of the ladies down the hall from the chamber where I was staying. I was delighted to see the king so well. What I couldn't decide was whether he was just improved by the pleasure of the queen's company—something I had already seen happening—or whether he was further helped by leaving Yurt. I hoped it was not the latter. Yurt was his kingdom, and I didn't see how I could tell him there was a malignant influence there that I couldn't find, but that meant he would have to leave.

The carnival continued all the next day, but I surprised myself by becoming bored. Maybe it was because I was there for pleasure alone, and pleasure seemed to pall faster than I remembered. The lords and ladies were busy buying supplies, new saddles and harnesses, shoes and boots, bolts of cloth for winter outfits, decorative tapestries, jewelry and chests. The servants too were busy at the merchants' tables. The constable had sent a purse and a long list with them, and they were comparing, pricing, and buying everything from fabric for new curtains, to tea and spices, to flagons, to bed linens, to pots and pans, to a new volleyball net. The pack horses, I thought, would be heavily laden when we started for home.

I myself bought a new red velvet jacket. I had originally planned to wear my red pullover to the carnival, but after looking at it critically in the light of my predecessor's magic lamps, I had decided it really did look like an old Father Noel outfit. I also searched for, but did not see, anyone selling books that would interest me.

The king and queen didn't seem at all bored, even though they made no purchases. But they had each other, and that seemed to keep them happily occupied.

I didn't see the magician again, though I was sure he was still at the carnival; one time I thought I saw a cascade of glistening stars rising from farther down the street, and turned and went another way. I kept thinking about him, however. If I had done only a little worse in my studies, if Zahlfast had not given me a passing grade on the transformation practical in spite of my problem with the frogs (and I still did not know why he had), then I too would be working the corner for coins at carnivals.

The next morning, after the carnival was over, Joachim came to the castle very early, as the servants were packing the horses. I saw him from my window, walking down the narrow street with a much older priest, who paused, his hand on the younger man's shoulder, to give him what appeared to be last-minute advice, before turning back toward the cathedral. Joachim came in looking serious, as always, but did not look like I imagined someone would who had been accused of evil.

I wanted to talk to him about the magician, but was not sure he would understand. He, for his part, seemed unwilling to say anything about the last two days. As we mounted and rode through the empty and littered city streets toward the gates, I thought that I might send Zahlfast a letter.

III

The king was ill. He took to his bed the night we got back to Yurt, saying he was exhausted, and he did not get up again, not for chapel service, not for meals, not to work in his rose garden.

The queen seemed driven to new levels of energy. She was constantly in motion, and from the windows of my chambers I kept seeing her cross the courtyard, from the king's room to the kitchen, where she herself tried to concoct a soup that would tempt him, back to his room again and then to the chapel to pray, to his room and then out to confer privately with the doctors she had sent for from the next kingdom. Although she did not say anything, I knew she was thinking that the doctors would have come more quickly if she had been able to telephone rather than relying on the pigeons. The pigeons were rapid, being able to carry a message to any of the nearby kingdoms in an afternoon, but not as fast as a telephone.

I mostly stayed out of the way. I did not know how serious the king's condition was, but since I doubted the queen was someone who panicked easily, I feared the worst. The rest of the castle seemed gripped with a similar fear. No one came to my chambers, not even the Lady Maria for her lessons in the first-grammar, and meals tended to be hurried and silent. At this point, the dank autumn rains began.

With little to do, I set myself the goal of reviewing everything I had supposedly learned at the wizards' school. Within a week, I had finished all the assignments from the first year. I was both pleased to see that I really had progressed in my eight years at the school, from an audacious but (in retrospect) shockingly ignorant young man from a merchant family in the City to someone recognizable as a real wizard, at least to an illusion-weaver at a carnival; and embarrassed to see what truly basic information I had managed not to learn. At the end of the week, I sat down to write Zahlfast a letter.

It was hard thinking what to write, out of all that had happened to me since leaving the City. It would in fact have been easier to write a twenty-page letter, but I was restricted by the size of message the pigeons could carry. Unless one was willing to wait to send one's letter by someone from Yurt, or someone stopping by Yurt, who was traveling to the City, the only alternative was to write one's letter on one of the tiny, lightweight pieces of paper the pigeons could carry. There were postal stations spread in a semicircle, fifty miles from the City, where carrier pigeons from all the western kingdoms brought messages and dropped them into the greater urban postal system. The postal system itself could handle almost any size letter, but only if mailed within fifty miles of the City.

"I am enjoying being Royal Wizard," I finally wrote, "and at last I may be learning some of the magic you tried to teach me. So far I've made a series of magic lights. I am even learning some of the old herbal magic as well. My king is sick now, however, so I don't know what will happen. If you are ever near Yurt, it would be nice to see you."

The last line surprised me, as I had not intended to write it. Just getting lonely for company, I said to myself, but I let the sentence stay. I folded the tiny piece of paper I was allowed, wrote the address on the outside, rolled it up and slipped it into the cylinder that would be attached to the pigeon's leg, and took it across the slick courtyard and up to the south tower. The pigeon keeper assured me my letter would be delivered in the City the next day—or certainly within two days.

Back in my chambers, I found the book in the front of which I had written the schedule of courses and readings at the beginning of my second year at the school. Some of the courses I had no recollection of, and I was quite sure I did not own all the books.

I was sitting, frowning at the list, when I heard running feet outside. My door swung open without even a knock, and Gwen burst in. "Sir, oh sir, excuse me, but you must come at once!"

The book fell from my hands unheeded as I leapt up. My heart fell with as heavy a thump, for I was sure the king was dead.

"Someone's trying to poison the king with magic! You must find out who it is!"

At least it sounded as though the king was not dead yet. "But how do you know?"

"Please come!" she cried, tugging at my hand. "The others don't believe me—they say I don't know any magic."

We hurried across the rainy courtyard to the kitchens. I was too confused and upset even to try a spell to stay dry.

In the warmth and steam of the kitchen, the cook was standing looking thoroughly angry, her ample fists on her aproned hips. The rest of the kitchen servants hovered in the background, looking worried.

"So, Wizard," said the cook. "Now maybe we can have the real story! Gwen has been trying to tell us you've taught her magic, and now she's accusing us of wanting the king dead!"

"I didn't say that!" Gwen cried. "I never thought it! I'm not accusing any of you, but someone's doing it!"

"Wait, wait," I said. "I never taught Gwen magic."

"Yes you did!" she countered. "That spell that turns food red! Only in this case it turned green."

There was a babble of voices, but I tried to stay calm. "Let's start at the beginning. What food are you talking about?"

"This, sir," said Gwen. From the table she picked up what appeared to be a bowl of chicken soup, except that it was a brilliant green—almost the same color, in fact, as the queen's eyes. "I was going to take it to the king; the queen thought a little soup would do him good. And then I remembered that you had taught me a spell to say to see if someone had slipped a potion in your food."

Jon was standing next to her, but she looked determinedly straight ahead. "You said if someone had, the food would turn red. And then I wondered, suppose someone had tried to slip a potion to the king? So I decided to say the spell over his soup. But it didn't turn red, it turned green. That's probably just because it's a different kind of potion, but I know someone wants to kill him!" At this she burst into tears. Jon tried to put his arms around her, but she pulled herself away.

I had no idea what it meant. All I knew was that the old wizard had told me this spell would detect a love potion. When I learned it and taught it to Gwen, it had never occurred to me that it might be a way to detect the spell that Dominic said someone had put on the king.

It still might not be the way, but I could not hesitate. "We've got to get the king out of the castle," I said.

They all looked at me as though I had lost my mind.

"But it's cold and it's raining! He can't travel in this weather! Where would he go?"

"Not far," I said, hoping what I was saying was true. "His rose garden should be far enough. Wrap him up well, and put hot irons in the wrappings to keep him warm. Pitch a tent in the garden, and set charcoal braziers in it. And you," to the cook, "will have to make him some more soup, but don't make it here. Make it outside the castle."

"What? You expect me to leave my warm kitchen and make a campfire in this rain and—"

"It may be the only way to save the king's life," I said. The cold touch of evil I had been feeling since summer was stronger in the kitchen than ever before, though I still could not tell where it was coming from. It might be Gwen, the cook, or one of the other servants, but I thought I would have been able to tell if it had been. "Come on!" I said. "There isn't enough time to waste any of it."

Almost to my surprise, they obeyed me. Within a very short time, the king, heavily wrapped and shielded from the rain, was being carried out into his rose garden. The few last blooms dripped wet.

Joachim came up to me, made as though to grab me by the arm but stopped himself in time, and instead drew me out of hearing range of the others with a jerk of his chin.

"Are you trying to kill the king?" he demanded, his black eyes glowing fiercely at me.

"I am not," I said back, just as fiercely. "I'm trying to save his life. I think there's an evil spell in the castle that's killing him, and I'm trying to see if he'll improve if he's outside."

"So now he'll die of pneumonia instead of magic? Is that your intention?"

"I hope he doesn't die," I said, fierce no longer. I had not seen the king in two weeks and had been shocked by his appearance. The shape of his skull was clear beneath the skin of his face, though he had tried to smile and speak normally.

"It will take a miracle to save him."

"I thought you said, if you need a miracle, see a priest," I retorted, and almost felt triumphant as he blinked and drew back.

When the king was settled in his tent, the queen sitting beside him, and when the cook, still grumbling but beneath her breath, had started a new batch of soup on a small fire lit with coals from the kitchen, just outside the garden walls, I drew Gwen to one side.

"I have to go somewhere," I told her. "Stay with the cook. Check the new batch of soup with the same spell. If it doesn't change color, the king should have some."

"But where are you going?"

"Not far. I'll be back soon."

Without giving her a chance to speak again, I rose from the ground and flew down the hill toward the forest, swifter than a horse could carry me.

I didn't know why I was embarrassed to tell her I needed to ask the old wizard for help, except that I never had told anyone I had been visiting him.

I was thinking very bitter thoughts about my own abilities and responsibilities. Although Dominic had told me he thought there was an evil spell on the king, and although I nearly believed him, I had done nothing to discover the source of that spell. For two weeks, while the king grew weaker and weaker, I had been concerned only with my own education, as though it was going to be useful to know wizardry even though I never practiced it in the service of the king who had hired me as his Royal Wizard. I had originally visited the old wizard to find out if he knew anything about this spell, but instead I had allowed myself to become distracted into learning the magic of herbs. It wouldn't be much good showing off my herbal magic to my friends in the City if I also had to tell them I had allowed my king to die of a magic spell when I hadn't bothered to find out its source.

The concentration needed for rapid flying beneath low-hanging branches made it difficult to carry this line of thought much further. I burst into sunshine as I entered the old wizard's valley. The lady and the unicorn were sitting by the little bridge, but today I saw no golden arrows.

I dropped to the ground outside the green door. The wizard was sitting in the doorway, the cat on his knee, enjoying the sunshine. He looked surprised to see me.

"Decided to skip the horse today, eh?" he said. "I just hope you weren't trying to impress me. We wizards trained in the old way have always been able to fly better than you young whippersnappers when we wanted to."

I swallowed my irritation. "I'm not trying to impress you, Master," I said. "I need your help." Quickly I explained to him about the soup that turned green when subjected to the spell to detect a love potion.

His brows furrowed, and he tossed the cat roughly from his lap as he stood up. "That spell just detects herbal potions," he said after a long pause, as though wondering what to tell me. "It turns food red if there's an herbal potion in it. There's no reason the spell should turn anything green. The girl probably got it wrong; maybe she said a spell of illusion by mistake."

"I don't think she got it wrong."

"Then it's detecting something else," he said abruptly, as though he had made a decision. "It might also detect the presence of the supernatural."

"You mean there's been black magic worked on the king's soup?"

"No, that's not what I mean, as you'd know if you listened properly! I meant that there's a supernatural presence in the castle. It might have nothing to do with the soup in particular, but in the right circumstances it might be detectable in food. No one need have put any potions in the soup for it to respond to that spell."

"Dominic said that he thought an evil spell had been cast on the king," I said. "Did he ever mention it to you, Master? Might this be the supernatural presence?"

"I don't know what Dominic's been telling you," said the old wizard, sitting down again. "There certainly weren't any supernatural presences in the castle when I was Royal Wizard."

"Then I'd better see if I can find the source," I said and flew back up the valley without even a proper farewell.

As soon as I left the wizard's valley, the rain started again. I was furious with myself as I realized that, if he could create an island of good weather, I ought to have been able to do the same for the king. And the thought kept on nagging that the green of the chicken soup really was the same color as the queen's eyes.

I had never flown so fast for so far before, and the concentration required left me no attention for a spell against the rain. I was wet through when I dropped to the ground outside the rose garden.

Gwen, standing under an umbrella, met me by the gate. "The cook finished the new soup, sir," she said eagerly, "and the spell didn't affect it at all. The queen's giving him some now."

"Good," I said, though I feared it would take more at this point than the cook's excellent chicken soup to heal the king. Hoping that drier weather might also help, I set to work at once on a weather spell.

But I realized immediately that I didn't know the spell against slow and steady rain. The spells I had prepared during the harvest were all against sudden storm. I could go back to my chambers and try to work it out, but I felt a desperate sense of urgency and decided to improvise. If I could turn this rain into a thunderstorm, I could then dissipate it quickly.

"You'd better go inside, my dear," I said to Gwen, as she stood, hesitating, beside me. "Don't get any wetter."

She went back into the castle, and it was just as well, because my first attempt to transform the rain into a real storm was so successful that a lightning bolt struck with a blazing flash and an acrid smell within ten feet of me, nearly taking off my eyelashes.

Peal after peal of thunder rolled around my head, and the air was blinding with repeated lightning flashes. I looked up and saw bolts of lightning dancing from turret to turret, hitting every tower in the castle and the spire on top of the chapel. I seemed to have created what must have been the worst thunderstorm in Yurt in a hundred years. My only hope was to make sure it was also the shortest. Setting my teeth grimly, I proceeded with the spells against thunderstorms, and abruptly the sky was clear. Both the thunder and the clouds rolled back, leaving a square mile of sunshine smiling down on the castle and the rose garden.

I checked my forehead to be sure I still had my eyebrows. Startled faces were looking at me over the garden gate, but I turned without saying anything and crossed the bridge into the castle. Since I had not in fact actually killed anyone with my lightning, it hardly seemed worth discussing the event at the moment.

As I crossed the courtyard, shivering in my wet clothes, I started toward my chambers to change, but decided instead to look for Joachim. I had been very rude to him and should probably show Christian tact by apologizing. He had been rude to me as well, but he had had more cause.

I hadn't seen him in the rose garden, but I hadn't actually gone into the garden. To save time, I probed with my mind to see where he might be in the castle. I couldn't find him.

Feeling uneasy, I started searching. It should be fairly straightforward for a wizard to touch the mind of someone he knows, as long as that person is not too far away. I went up to the chaplain's room, but it stood empty. I wandered around the castle aimlessly for a few minutes, not quite ready to go back out to the garden and face the inevitable questions about the thunderstorm, then realized I had not looked in the obvious place, the chapel.

I went up the stairs without the heart to turn on the lights, keeping my head low. So far I had been able to remove the king, at least temporarily, from whatever supernatural influence in the castle was harming him, and had been able to change the weather so he shouldn't get very damp out in his rose garden, but in my bones I feared it was too late.

Candles were burning on the chapel altar. A figure in black and white linen was stretched on his face on the floor in front of the altar, arms outstretched. I started to step forward, started to cry out, terrified that now Joachim had been struck dead—perhaps by lightning.

I stopped myself in time. He was praying. No wonder, I thought, I hadn't been able to touch his mind. Magic is, as I kept telling people, a natural force, and he was in company with the saints.

He was totally still, except for the slight rising and falling of his shoulders as he breathed. I tiptoed back out, though I doubted that even my thunderstorm had disturbed him.

I returned slowly to my rooms, physically and mentally exhausted, from flying, from working spells, and from fear for the king. I changed my clothes, intending to go back out to the rose garden to see if I could be of any assistance, but first I stretched out on my bed, just for a moment.

The next thing I knew, I woke up, ravenously hungry, confused at finding myself fully clothed. My magic lamps, which I had turned on yesterday afternoon, were still burning, though natural daylight made them seem pale. The angle of the sunlight through my window showed it was long after Gwen usually brought my breakfast.

I swung my feet to the floor, then remembered. If no one had come, then that meant—

I didn't know what it meant. I was afraid to probe for the king's mind because I might not find it. I brushed a hand across my hair and found my shoes, then opened the door to the courtyard.

Assembled in the courtyard, in a semicircle around my door, were most of the people from the castle. As my door swung open, a shout went up. "The Wizard! Hail the Royal Wizard! His magic has saved the king!"

I concentrated on the important point. "The king's alive?"

"Yes, and he's not just better, he's completely better! He's stronger than he's been in months, in years! You saved him! You saved him! Our Royal Wizard saved him!"

They had clearly been preparing themselves for hours while I slept. I didn't even begin to know what to say.

And then I saw King Haimeric himself, coming across the bridge to the courtyard, arm in arm with the queen. I had never seen him so vigorous, or her so beautiful.

I ran across the cobblestones to greet them. Not even bothering with the formal bow, I dropped to my knees before them.

The king took me by the shoulders to pull me up. "Let's not have any of your modesty, Wizard," he said with a laugh, "when you've just saved my life!"

I was still stronger than he was and remained determinedly kneeling. "I had nothing to do with saving your life."

"After your long night's vigil of magic? They told me your light was never extinguished all night."

Even though I knew that my orders that he be moved into the rose garden and be given fresh soup could not have saved him, it hardly seemed worth explaining that I had spent the night not in magic but in sleep.

"It was the chaplain," I said. "Even the best magic cannot save human life, when that life is truly draining away, as I fear yours was, sire. Only a miracle can save a man then."

"The chaplain?" said the king in some surprise. "I've spoken to him, of course, but he said nothing about a miracle."

"He's showing Christian humility," I responded, "but he spent the night in prayer, and he interceded for you with the saints."

The people around heard me and, after a murmur of surprise, seemed to believe me. However, it did not seem to make them feel any less favorable toward me.

"Then we have both the best Royal Wizard and the best Royal Chaplain a kingdom could have," said the queen. "We were all just going to go to the chapel for a service of thanksgiving to God. Won't you join us?"

"With greatest pleasure," I said, scrambling to my feet and brushing off my knees.

IV

I was sitting in my chambers, quizzing the Lady Maria on the first points of the Hidden Language, when a knock came at the door.

She was not doing well on the first-grammar. Her enthusiasm for learning magic was as high as ever, and I think she really wanted to study hard, but she seemed distracted.

Maybe, I thought, she was the only other person in the castle, besides me, still to be worrying about the king. A month after his recovery, he seemed to be growing even stronger. After a week in the rose garden, he had moved back into the castle, so far without any ill effects. But I still sometimes felt that lurking sense of evil and worried that he might weaken again. Or maybe the Lady Maria was not worrying about anyone else, but only about the three gray hairs I had spotted that morning among the golden curls.

"Come in!" I called, thinking it might be Gwen with tea. She often brought a pot if I had someone visiting in my chambers, but if she was jealous and checking up on what the Lady Maria and I were doing, she certainly gave no sign.

But it was the constable. I was surprised; he rarely came to my chambers.

"Excuse me, sir, I hate to interrupt you and the lady, but there's a ... person here who wants to see you at once."

Maria jumped up. "I can't concentrate this afternoon anyway," she said, before I could tell the constable to have this mysterious person wait a few minutes.

"Shall I see you later today?" I asked. But she had rushed out already. "Show him in," I said to the constable.

"Excuse me, sir, but he wants you to go outside."

Shaking my head, I went out, stopping only long enough to put the magic lock on my door, and followed the constable across the courtyard to the main gate and the bridge.

Waiting on the bridge was an unmistakable figure: tall, lean, with a tall red hat and a long white beard. It was Zahlfast.

I rushed forward, hands outstretched to greet him, and although he tried to give me a look of stern dignity I could see a smile already lurking at the corner of his lips. That was why I had chosen to write to *him*.

"Welcome to Yurt!" I said inanely. "Come in! Did

you have a good trip? Are you just stopping by, or can you stay for a while?"

He returned my handshake vigorously but resisted being drawn into the castle. "It's such a beautiful day," he said, "and there won't be many more this fall. Didn't I see a little garden over there where we could sit?"

We proceeded to the rose garden, where only the queen's rose bush, of all the bushes, was still blooming. I continued to chatter to hide my surprise at his arrival.

"I was glad to get your letter," said Zahlfast when we were seated on the bench where the king often sat. "Is your king still sick?"

"Oh, no. He was cured by a miracle a month ago."

Zahlfast shot me a sideways look, then looked away. "Good," he said and then added, "We never talk much about miracles at the wizards' school."

This of course I already knew. "The chaplain cured him. The chaplain's my friend," I added, feeling the same need to justify my friendship that I had felt with the old wizard. I started to say, "That is, I think he's my friend," but decided not to raise doubts.

But I should have remembered Zahlfast was the sharpest of my teachers. "You sound somewhat dubious about this friendship."

"Not dubious. But he had insulted me, and I insulted him, and I tried to apologize but, in a way, he wouldn't let me—especially since, I'll admit to you, I'm almost in awe of him after the miracle."

"Don't stand in awe of those who deal with the supernatural," said Zahlfast as though making a key point at the front of the lecture hall. "Wizards too can deal with forces beyond the natural, indeed have the special training to do it. And always remember, those who can heal with supernatural aid can always sicken."

Abruptly he changed the subject. "Anyway, it sounded from your letter as though you might be

lonely, so, as I was flying in this direction anyway . . ."
I was surprised to realize he was having almost as
much trouble feeling at ease as I was. He was still my
teacher, but this was my kingdom, and I was no longer
a student. "It really wasn't time yet for your first
checkup—"

"My first checkup!" I cried, devastated. "You mean
you go around checking on us after we leave the wizards' school? No one ever told me! Or is that just one
more thing I missed?"

"We don't tell the young wizards," said Zahlfast with
an amused smile he tried to suppress. "In fact, many
are checked and never even know it, at least for some
years. But I knew you were sharp enough to guess it
wasn't just friendly interest in seeing an old student
that brought me here, after I got your letter."

The compliment softened what would otherwise
have been another devastating blow. And I had even
hoped he remembered me fondly! But now I began
to wonder what ulterior motive he may have had in
passing me in that transformation practical—was this
an experiment to see just how badly a young wizard
could do?

"So what are you checking for?"

"In your case, I was interested in your progress.
In general, it's a continuation of the school's original
purpose, to organize and rationalize the practice of
wizardry, to be sure it doesn't go astray. That's why I
wanted to learn more about your study of herbal
magic and who has been teaching you."

"It's my predecessor. He lives not far from here,
and he's taught me the rudiments," I said, feeling
somewhat defensive, whereas I had expected to be
proudly demonstrating an unusual accomplishment
when I first met a wizard from the school again.

"He's your friend, too," said Zahlfast. It was a statement, not a question. "There aren't many young wiz-

ards who are even on speaking terms with their predecessors."

"Is that what you mean when you say I'm sharp?" I said, hoping for another compliment.

"Why do you think you were hired as Royal Wizard of Yurt?"

"I'd assumed I was the only person who applied."

"You may have been; I'm not sure. But when I heard you'd applied, I talked to the Master, and we agreed. I wrote to the constable of Yurt and told him not to hire anyone else."

"That was the constable who you met at the gate," I said, wondering again why Zahlfast had not wanted to come in. But another question took precedence. "Why did you want *me* in Yurt? Was it to keep me out of the way?"

"Not at all. We knew something was happening in Yurt, something odd, and it needed someone who combined your intuitive flair for magic with the potential, at least, to work hard and master academic magic. Neither careful mastery of spells nor innate ability would have been enough without the other. Also, of course, we hoped that here, away from the distractions of the City, you might meet enough challenges and find enough leisure that you really would set yourself to learning the magic we had tried to teach you."

There was not nearly enough of a compliment in this to mitigate the sting. "You mean you knew all along what was going on in Yurt? Why didn't you tell me?"

"Actually," said Zahlfast, with a snort that could have been amusement, "I have no idea what's going on in Yurt. I was hoping you would tell me."

"There's an evil presence in the castle," I said slowly, looking at my hands. "I don't know where it's coming from, and sometimes I can hardly even sense it. Most of the time I think it's a person, but I don't know how to find out which one. Once or twice I've thought it could be a demon, but the old wizard says there was never any evil presence in the castle before I arrived, and I don't think even I could have summoned a demon by mistake."

"An evil presence," said Zahlfast, as though this answered a question. "We've known in the City for several years that there was a supernatural focus here in Yurt, or at least nearby, but it was impossible to localize it precisely or even to say whether it was for good or evil. Several of the wizards at the school thought it might be a witch living in the forest who had taken the step into black magic."

"It's not in the forest," I said positively. "It's here in the castle. It was coming home to his kingdom that nearly killed the king."

"I knew it was here in the castle when I got your letter."

"But how could you know that? I didn't say anything about it."

"The very paper your letter was written on was permeated with the supernatural. Didn't you know that? That's why, when I arrived and discovered that the supernatural influence stopped at the moat, I asked you to meet me outside."

"But how could you tell anything from the paper?" I demanded, intensely frustrated, thinking the wizards of the school had been deliberately withholding information from me. But then I saw Zahlfast smiling and said in a lower voice, "Was that maybe in one of the lectures I missed?"

It turned out that it was. There was a rather simple spell to recognize the presence of a supernatural influence, a modern, more universal spell than the one the old wizard had taught me for detecting magic potions. I glanced over the garden walls at the turrets of the castle and felt my heart sink. I didn't want to try the spell. Yurt was my kingdom, and I loved it, and if I confirmed my fears I might never feel the same about it again.

"Do you think the king will become sick again?" I said.

"You think he was made ill by supernatural forces?"

"Dominic thought an evil spell had been put on him," I said, "even though I didn't believe him at first." I gave Zahlfast a quick summary of the king's three-year illness and miraculous recovery.

"If he really was healed miraculously," said Zahlfast somewhat dubiously, "he should be safe from black magic, or at least from the effects of the particular evil spell that was put on the castle."

"But will the spell now turn against someone else?" I said. "Such as the queen?" This was not a possibility I had contemplated until I said it, but it suddenly seemed fearfully likely. "Or do you think it's not merely a spell, but a demon loose in the castle?"

Zahlfast did not answer for a minute. "I'm not the person to ask," he said at last. "I specialize in transformations, not demonology." I remembered then a conversation I had had with him in the City several years ago, during which it had become clear that he was just as terrified of demons as I was. But he stood up. "I'll come into the castle with you and see what I can tell."

But the first thing he said, as we entered the courtyard with its whitewashed walls and green shutters, was, "What a lovely little castle! None of the other young wizards can have as charming a kingdom."

In my chambers, however, he looked around quickly, then said, "The supernatural influence is quite strong here."

I was about to demand to know whether he thought I was practicing black magic myself, but then I looked at his face and decided it was safer not to ask.

Instead I said, "Let me show you my glass telephones. They don't work, but they're very attractive."

At this he actually laughed. "Somehow, when you left the school, I never imagined that you were the type of wizard who becomes a telephone technician."

"Neither did I," I said cheerfully. "That's why they don't work. But the queen wanted me to try." I thought guiltily that it had been some time since I had tried anything new.

"I'll show you something, though," I said, reaching one of the telephones down from the shelf. "Watch the base." I set the instrument down, lifted the receiver, and spoke the name attached to the wizards' school.

"Pretty amusing, isn't it?" I said as the faint ringing came through the receiver and the base lit up to show the school's telephone on its table, with someone reaching to answer it. "Wait; it gets even funnier. Try to talk." I handed him the receiver.

Just as the Lady Maria and I had done, he shouted, "Hello? Can you hear me?" to an unhearing wizard at the other end, even though that wizard's voice came through faint but clear.

But when the other wizard hung up and the telephone base went dark, Zahlfast was not laughing. "You realize, of course," he said with what I might even have imagined was awe, "that no one's ever been able to do this before: attach a far-seeing spell to an object."

"But it doesn't work as a telephone. Sometimes I've even thought that whatever evil spell was put on the castle was hindering my magic."

"I think you'll be able to make it work," he said in his schoolteacher voice. "Keep working at it."

At that moment we were interrupted by a knock. I opened it, expecting the Lady Maria ready to resume her lesson, and was surprised to see Joachim.

I tried to draw him inside, to introduce him to Zahlfast, but he wouldn't let me.

"I'm going," he said, "and I wanted to let someone

know I probably won't be back for morning service. The king and queen aren't here."

"I think they went hunting. But where are you going?"

He paused as though unwilling to say, but his enormous black eyes steadily met mine. "A girl down in the village, five miles from here, was bitten by a viper last week," he said at last, as though there had been no pause. "The doctors have tried all their draughts and potions, but nothing has availed. She's near death. They want me to pray for her."

He turned and was gone before I could answer, striding across the courtyard to where one of the stable boys had a horse saddled and ready. A man in a brown tunic was mounted and waiting by the gate.

"Is that your friend the chaplain?" said Zahlfast behind me.

I nodded, watching the two ride through the gate and away. I knew, without the chaplain telling me, that the news of the king's miraculous recovery must have spread at once throughout the kingdom, and that anyone now who needed a miracle would not be satisfied with their local priest but would want the castle chaplain.

"So tell me more about herbal magic," said Zahlfast.

Although I had had some success teaching a little magic to the king and the Lady Maria, it was extremely odd to be suddenly explaining something to my former teacher. It was also difficult to do with no herbs at hand; the sense that the old wizard had taught me, of how to determine a plant's properties just by handling it, was difficult to put into words.

But I had been able to explain at least some of the basic principles when I heard voices, the sound of hooves, and the queen's laugh in the courtyard, and realized the hunting party had returned. "You'll have to stay for dinner," I said, "and I'd be delighted to have you stay with me if you are willing to spend the night. Even for you, a two-hundred-mile flight can't be easy."

To my surprise, he agreed. At dinner, he took the chaplain's chair across the table from me, which kept on startling me, as I would look up from my plate to see a face I had stopped being accustomed to see, in the context in which I had recently become accustomed to seeing another's. He kept our table highly entertained, with gossip from the City and stories about the northern land of dragons, which *he* had visited. I saw even the servants at the next table leaning to catch his words.

"I'll have to tell you something I tell all the young wizards after the first checkup," he said as he prepared to leave the next morning. We were standing outside the castle gate, looking down at the red and golden foliage of the forest. "I doubt this would be a problem for you anyway, but some of the young wizards, when they find that the school is still interested in what they're doing, feel they can ask for help for every little problem. We certainly want to make sure that magic is being practiced well throughout the western kingdoms, but we just don't have the time to keep helping out fully qualified wizards who should know how to do magic on their own."

But then his smile came out. "In your case, write me whenever you want. There were some of the teachers who had doubts you'd even learn enough magic to become a magician, but I knew from the beginning you'd someday be capable of becoming a good wizard."

This would have been more of a compliment if it hadn't been for the implication that "someday" had not yet arrived.

"Well, it was delightful to see you," I said, inane once more. Zahlfast rose from the ground and sped away, west over the treetops toward the City. It really had been very nice to see him, even though I continued to feel extremely irritated that he and the Master had apparently engineered my position at Yurt for me, for reasons he had perhaps still not told me completely.

As I watched his flying figure disappear in the distance, I wondered again if he had in fact even told me the real reason for his visit. I realized there were a number of questions I had not asked him, or if I had asked he had not answered. He had never said where he thought the evil spell on the castle might come from, and I had not had a chance to ask his opinion of the old wizard's empty tower room. Well, if I was supposed to be fully qualified to practice magic on my own, I would have to do so.

As I turned to start back into the castle, I saw a another distant figure, this one on horseback, coming up the road toward the castle. In a moment, I recognized Joachim and waited for him to reach me.

I became alarmed at his appearance when he came closer. His usually smooth hair was rumpled, his vestments wrinkled and stained, and his hand slack on the reins. The accentuated gauntness of his cheeks and his unseeing stare made me realize he was exhausted from more than riding five miles home after staying up all night.

I took the horse's bridle to lead it across the bridge and helped him dismount. He seemed to notice me for the first time.

"Do you think it's too late for me to hold chapel services this morning?" he asked, clearly concerned about this lapse.

"The king and queen have already left to go hunting again," I told him. "Tomorrow's Sunday; service can wait until then."

"All right," he said meekly and started moving slowly toward his room. He stopped then, looked back, and told me what I had already guessed. "The little girl died."

PART FOUR

The Duchess

I

The first snow had reached Yurt. It wasn't very much snow, a light dusting in the courtyard, but as evening came on it rose and whirled in the wind, and made all of us in the great hall linger around the fireplace after supper. Through the tall windows, I could see the moon, slightly orange and half obscured by whipping clouds—what Gwen told me they called in Yurt a witch's moon.

The Lady Maria had been talking about dragons at supper. The combination of Zahlfast's visit and the first volume of *Ancient and Modern Necromancy*, which I had given her to read when the first-grammar continued to prove frustrating, had given her enough information about the northern land of wild magic that she was talking as though she wanted to go there herself.

"But Maria, it's terribly cold even here!" said one of the other ladies with a laugh. "Think how much colder it would be so much farther north."

"Than maybe I'll try to go there in the summer," she said, undeterred. "Or maybe a dragon would come here."

The other ladies, who clearly did not believe in dragons, or if they did certainly believed they had nothing to do with Yurt, all laughed thoroughly at this.

I at least knew dragons were real, and maybe it was to support the Lady Maria that I decided to make an illusory dragon. I had never tried to match my predecessor by producing illusions over dessert, but while most of the castle was lingering by the fire it seemed a good time to start.

Illusions are among the first things they teach at the wizards' school, and they are so much fun that wizardry students tend to stay up late challenging each other with different effects, which is why even carnival magicians are proficient at them. At any rate, even though I knew I could never equal my predecessor's skill at lifelike creations, I started on a dragon.

It stayed rather flat-looking, and at certain angles one could see right through it, but that didn't deter me, as I set out to make a dragon that would fill our entire end of the hall. It certainly didn't hurt my efforts that the queen came over at once, eyes dancing, to watch the dragon being constructed.

First I did the tail, long and reptilian with a double row of spines down the center. When I had the tail lashing nicely, I started on the body, massive and scaled, with six legs and long, scaled wings. It was only coincidence, I told myself, that I made the iridescent scales emerald green. By now most of the castle was watching; even the servants who had taken the dishes down to the kitchen came back.

The head was the hardest part. I gave my dragon a gaping mouth with several hundred teeth, long fringed ears, and eyes of fire. It actually looked more like the dragon costume at the harvest carnival than like the rather small blue dragon in the basement of the wizards' school, the only real dragon I had actually seen. But since no one else there had ever seen a dragon at all, this did not matter. They stood well back from its slowly lashing tail and watched with growing excitement.

And I decided to make it especially exciting. As soon as I had finished the last detail, the long forked yellow tongue, I gave the whole dragon the order to move and stood back to catch my breath. It was a dozen times larger than any illusion I had ever made before.

It moved spectactularly. Eyes burning and mouth opening and closing in frenzied snaps, it whirled away from me and started toward my audience.

It moved totally silently, but that was all right, because the screaming of ladies, servants, and even knights made plenty of noise. People raced for the walls or fell down flat. Dominic stood for ten seconds alone, deserted by the rest of the knights and apparently paralyzed, before he gave a shriek like an injured rabbit and dived under the table. My dragon kept on going. Its long tail and heavy body naturally passed through real human bodies without having the slightest effect, but they did not notice this, as they were too busy trying to avoid the head.

Even the king took refuge behind his throne. But the Lady Maria, sheltering in the doorway that led to the kitchen, with half the castle staff behind her, was watching in what I could only describe as avid delight.

Almost frightened by what I had done, I said the words to slow the dragon down, intending to make it curl up placidly before the fire before I broke the spell of illusion.

And then I saw two people advancing on the dragon from opposite directions. One was the chaplain, who held a crucifix at arm's length before him, and whose eyes glowed with almost the same intensity as my dragon's. The other, armed with a poker from the fireplace, was the queen.

This had gone far enough. I said the two words to break the illusion, and the dragon was gone, leaving nothing but a shower of sparks that lingered for five seconds and then were gone as well.

The hall was suddenly very silent, and I held my breath, wondering how I had managed to make my magic go so thoroughly astray. But then the silence was broken by the king clapping.

"Marvelous, Wizard, marvelous!" he cried. "I've never seen anything to match that!"

After only a second's hesitation, the queen dropped the poker and began to applaud as well. The knights and ladies came slowly back toward the center of the room and joined in. Dominic came out from under the table as though trying to convey the impression he had never been there.

Everyone started talking at once, most apparently trying to persuade each other, themselves, and me that they had not in fact been in fear for their lives. The king did it most convincingly.

"Our old wizard used to do illusions all the time," he told me, "and they were beautiful. I thought when he retired that I'd never see anything like that again. But his, well, they never *moved* like that!"

There was a general laugh, and people started gathering up their hats and cloaks for the short trip from the great hall back to their chambers.

I looked around for Joachim. Although we had remained cordial since the king's recovery, we had somehow never shared a bottle of wine in the evening again. If I had owed him something of an apology before, I was afraid I owed him one even more now. But he had already gone.

I glanced across the hall toward Dominic. He was standing next to the fire, talking to one of the knights with great laughs and many hand gestures, on a completely different topic. I had originally been hoping to talk to him this evening, but now I decided it would be better to wait until the next day.

The next morning, when the sun was melting the light layer of snow, I went to find Dominic. I had decided I had to be systematic, and even though I didn't like the thought of talking to him just now, he had what I needed.

It seemed fairly clear that a spell had been put on Yurt. It was the spell that had nearly killed the king, and while the chaplain had broken its hold on him in particular, the spell was still there. I could still not sense the evil touch except obliquely, when least expecting it, but I was now armed with Zahlfast's magic formula for detecting the supernatural.

So far, I had found high concentrations of supernatural influence in my own chambers, the chapel, and the chaplain's room. I didn't like this at all until I decided that the spell was just detecting a saintly presence from the chaplain, who had after all spent a number of evenings during the summer in my chambers.

But no wonder, I thought, that Zahlfast had wanted to visit me. When he received a letter reeking of the supernatural, and knowing there was already something odd happening in Yurt, he must have wondered if I had plunged into black magic. I was irritated enough with him for this lack of trust that I had not written him again.

The two other places I had found the supernatural influence strongest were up in the north tower, in the old wizard's now empty and windswept chambers, and in the dank passage that led down to the rusty door of the cellars.

I found Dominic in the stables, checking on one of the geldings that had come back slightly lame from hunting. He was whistling as he and the stable boy lifted the animal's foot, which today seemed much better. But the whistling stopped as he saw me.

"Greetings, sire," I said with enough good humor for both of us. "I have a favor to ask you, about my mission here in Yurt."

He pulled his mouth into a tight line, then nodded. "We can talk in the courtyard," he said curtly and walked out, leaving me to follow behind. Neither one of us said anything about dragons.

"I thought the chaplain accomplished your mission for you," said Dominic, when we were standing in the center of the courtyard, well away from any windows. "The evil spell on the king's been broken." The implication seemed strong that now that my single mission had been taken care of, especially as it was done by someone else, it was almost superfluous for Yurt to have a wizard.

"But it's not gone," I said.

He had been glancing around, not meeting my eyes, but at this he turned toward me with a look that could either have been hatred or fear. "What do you mean, it's not gone?"

"Whoever or whatever put the spell on the king," I said, "made the spell strong enough that it remained in Yurt even when the king was miraculously freed from its influence. I haven't been able to determine yet *who* might have cast it, but I think I may be able to tell, if I can determine where it's strongest."

"And how are you going to do that?" he demanded.

"We wizards can detect the presence of the supernatural," I said with dignity. "Any evil spell will have been cast with evil intent, and possibly even demonic influence. We wizards can tell where demons have been."

"And where do you think they might have been?" His tone was enough to make the straightforward question an insult.

"I was wondering if they had been down in the cellars."

This clearly surprised him. The sour expression disappeared for a minute. "Why the cellars?"

"I have no idea. It's the only part of the castle I haven't been able to get into. The constable told me the cellars are damp and haven't been used for many years. I asked him for a key, but he said you had the only one."

"That's true," said Dominic in a puzzled voice. Although I didn't tell him, I had already tried to open the locked door using the same spell I had used on the bolt on the north tower, but a complicated lock had proved impervious to my magic, as a simple bolt had not.

Dominic took the heavy bunch of keys from his belt and flipped through them until he came to one stained with rust. "Here's the key. You'd better take a can of oil, as I doubt it's been opened in years." He paused then and glared at me again. "I hope you weren't planning to ask me for the key to the north tower, because I don't have it. When your predecessor retired, he bolted the doors and put on magic locks that he said even another wizard couldn't break."

It was my turn to be surprised. "But I don't need to go up in the north tower," I said blandly, neglecting to mention that I had already been there twice.

Dominic said something under his breath. When I asked him to repeat it, he denied having said anything, but it had sounded to me like, "Maybe you should."

With the key and a can of oil, I went down the narrow stairs behind the kitchen to the cellar door. It was iron and blotched with damp and rust. There was a small opening at eye level, too small for anything much larger than a cat to have climbed through, and a dank odor came out into the stairwell. Even with the oil and energetic turning, it took me almost five minutes to get the lock to open. Clearly no one had been in the cellars in years.

The door swung open with a protesting screech. I had tied a magic globe to my wrist with a piece of string. Its light bobbed eerily along the walls as I stepped inside.

It seemed to be nothing but abandoned storage cellars, damp because they had been dug too close to the castle well. The small rooms opening off the hall were littered with the unidentifiable remains of what might once have been stored there. Several of the rooms smelled as though used by cats or rats or both.

But permeating those innocuous dark stone rooms was an almost overwhelming sense of evil. I stopped and listened. I heard a very faint pattering noise, which could have been dripping water, could have been rats, and could have been nothing.

I tried to think clearly and calmly to combat the irrational fear that threatened to overwhelm me. Dominic had known there was an evil spell on the king, I told myself, forcing my feet to proceed down the passage. He didn't just think the king was sick, but thought magic must be implicated. Therefore, he knew more than he had told me about how that spell was cast.

I paused and listened again. There was no sound other than my own breathing. Even though Dominic knew something about the spell, I continued my reasoning, he still wanted it overcome. Therefore, he himself had not been responsible. I returned to a thought I had had long ago, that he was sheltering someone, most likely the queen. Could she have tried to put an evil spell on the king, which Dominic then wanted to overcome, even though he loved her too much to accuse her?

But Dominic might not know as much as he thought. He clearly believed, with the old wizard, that the north tower was still locked, and had no inkling of the evil now settled in the cellars.

I forced my feet to start moving again, although at this point I was starting to feel what could only be a terminal illness, caused by black magic, sweeping through my body. This of course is the weakness of being a wizard; we are much more susceptible to magic influences than ordinary people. Water splashed onto my socks with the next step; I had been following the passage slightly downhill, and the floor had gone from being damp to being flooded.

I murmured the spell that should have lifted me six inches above the water, to continue down the passage suspended in air. Nothing happened at all.

At this point, rationality lost. I turned and ran back toward daylight, the magic globe bouncing madly at the end of the string. At the door, I hesitated. I could not hear anything behind me, but I didn't want whatever was in there coming out. I made myself gather up some of the debris from the first storeroom and stuffed it into the small opening in the iron door. I held it in place with the best magic lock I could manage.

With the sight of daylight before me, I was able to control my heartbeat enough to wait one more minute. I called, "Kitty, kitty, kitty," not wanting to leave any cat trapped in the cellars. But when no cat appeared, I slammed the door, turned the iron key, and put an additional magic lock on the latch as well.

Back out in the narrow staircase, leaning against the stone wall, I slowly stopped feeling as though I were about to die. But in a minute even the staircase seemed oppressive, so I hurried back up the stairs. The smell of bread baking came to me from the kitchen like a benediction.

I didn't want to return to my chambers right away but instead went to the great hall, telling myself I needed to return the key to Dominic but really in search of human company. The king and queen, along with several of the ladies, were seated around the fire, talking animately.

"Wizard!" called the king when he saw me. "We've just been making plans. How would you like to go visit the duchess?"

After a second in which I couldn't imagine what he was talking about, I remembered the Lady Maria once telling me that Yurt had, besides that king's own castle, the castles of two counts and a duchess.

"I ought to visit my liege vassals more often," said the king.

"The king and I met at the duchess's castle," the queen told me, smiling at him.

"I would be very interested in visiting the duchess," I said. If Zahlfast was right (and I hoped he was, rather than believed he was), the king should now be safe from whatever black magic was lurking in the cellars. But no one else was safe. Until a supposedly fully qualified wizard, me, could find a way to overcome that spell, it might be better if we all went visiting.

II

The duchess's castle was closer than the city where we had gone to the harvest carnival, being only one long day's ride away. Therefore we didn't need the tents, and the pack horses were less burdened as we started out early on a frosty but sunny morning.

The king's party was also much smaller, as most of the servants were not accompanying us.

I had talked to the queen about this. "Don't you think it would be better if we brought everyone along?"

But she laughed. "The duchess won't have nearly enough room for all of us. Her castle is smaller than the royal castle, and she has her own staff, of course. If I didn't know better, I'd say you were getting too attached to that saucy girl who brings you breakfast!"

It was bad enough being hopelessly in love with the queen without having her tease me about Gwen. I tried the constable instead.

"Don't you think it might be better, while the king is gone, to send the servants away?"

He looked at me in amazement, as well he might, because the arrangement of the household staff was certainly no part of a Royal Wizard's duties. For a minute I could see that he was about to resent my interference, but then he remembered that it was, after all, me.

"Usually when the royal household is away, I give most of the staff their vacation," he said. "Some go to visit their families, although some of course stay here."

"But I don't want anyone to stay here."

This was clearly going too far, even for a wizard who had already proved himself to have an odd sense of humor. "My principal responsibility," the constable said with great dignity, "is the well-being of the royal castle of Yurt, including its people. My wife and I at any rate will not leave, certainly not on a wizard's whim."

It would have been hard to explain that I feared an evil influence was down in the cellars, especially as I had checked that morning and found my magic locks still in place. Since everyone in the castle, not just the king, seemed happy and well, I tried to tell myself that there was no danger. The night before we left, I spent hours with my books until I found what I hoped was a suitably strong protective spell. I put it on the castle and its inhabitants before we left.

The Lady Maria rode next to me. I had noticed that, in the last few weeks, she had stopped wearing as much lace and ribbon. This morning she was wearing a conservatively cut, dark-green riding habit, and her golden hair, rather than tumbling in ringlets around her shoulders, was tied up into a bun on the back of her head.

But her laugh and her conversation had not changed at all. "I think I explained to you once," she said, "that the queen's mother and the duchess's mother are cousins—or is it second cousins? When the old duke died in that terrible accident—I was just the tiniest girl then, but even so I remember it well—he left only a daughter to inherit. She grew into quite a beauty, I can tell you!"

"Does she look like the queen?" I asked, that being my standard for beauty.

"She does, a little," said Maria almost reluctantly, and I knew her well enough to realize that, while she loved to discuss charm and beauty in the abstract, she didn't like the implication that midnight hair could be more beautiful than golden.

"I'll bet she had a number of suitors!" I said, knowing that was what she wanted me to say.

"She certainly did!" she replied, her good humor restored. "But she wouldn't have any of them! She was too proud for any but the best, and maybe she hasn't met the best yet! She'll soon be getting old, however, so she may shortly have to lower her standards! Of course, she isn't as old as me."

I was flabbergasted. I had never before heard Maria admit that she might be old. Together with the pulled-back hair, this made me start to wonder if she had been affected by some variation of the spell that had nearly killed the king.

But her manner was unchanged. She continued all morning to tell me stories that I had already heard and to point out all the places in the landscape with any romantic associations.

"See that spire?" she said at one point. A sharply pointed spire rose from behind a snow-sprinkled hill, half a mile back from the road. The hill nearly obscured the low tiled roof of its church. "That's the Nunnery of Yurt. It's made up of widows who grieve for their dead husbands, and of young girls who have tragically renounced the world with broken hearts." I decided to try to ride with someone else that afternoon.

After our lunch break, which we took standing up because the half-frozen ground was too cold for sitting, I managed to position my horse next to Joachim's, at the end of the procession. This, I thought, might be the best chance I had had to talk to him in weeks.

"I owe you an apology," I said, starting there because this way he couldn't move away or change the subject before I'd had a chance to say it. "I was horribly rude to you when the king was ill."

I probably should also apologize for terrifying him with my dragon, but I was afraid of insulting him more by reminding him that he had believed in an illusion—even if he and the queen were the only people prepared to do something about it.

Joachim pulled up his horse slightly, so that we were soon riding fifty yards behind the rest of the party. Although he did not answer at once, he was clearly thinking over his response. Then he gave me a sideways glance from his enormous dark eyes that would in anyone else have been a look of amusement.

"You weren't rude," he said. "I needed someone to remind me of my responsibilities." We rode for several minutes in silence, then he spoke again as though there had been no pause. "I think I had still been feeling inadequate from my meeting with the bishop."

Since such a confession on his part seemed to call for something similar on mine, if I wanted to rebuild our friendship, I said, "Do you remember seeing the wizard in my chambers?"

He clearly did not.

"You might have seen him, just for a second, the

day you stopped to tell me you were going down to the village to see the little girl."

There was the slightest flicker of emotion across his face. "Yes. I remember seeing him now."

"That was Zahlfast, one of my old teachers. He'd come to give me what he said was my first checkup."

This time the chaplain actually did smile. "I thought you told me you wizards were left on your own, once you'd finished at the school."

"Well, that's what I'd thought. I guess it shows how mistaken a wizard can be. I think he meant to be encouraging, but by the time he left all my inadequacies had been made clear to me."

"And are you therefore feeling paralyzed, almost fearing to act because you don't want to turn to evil?" As he spoke, Joachim turned to face me so abruptly that he brought his horse's head around as well. We had to stop and disentangle the bells on my horse's harness from the harness on his. When we started again, the rest of the procession was far in front of us, and we pushed our mounts to start catching up.

At first I thought Joachim was accusing me of being paralyzed in the face of a threat to Yurt, but then I realized he was only speaking from his own experience. Someone whose own inadequacies had been pointed out very recently might indeed feel unworthy to plead with the saints.

"I told Zahlfast you'd saved the king's life," I said as we drew closer to the rest of the party and slowed down again.

"I myself didn't save him," he answered quickly, looking straight ahead. "My merits had nothing to do with it." I should have realized that he'd say this. Since the saints could not be manipulated, one's only hope was to have a pure and contrite heart, and a contrite heart wasn't proud of its merits.

But then he said something else that surprised me. "What did Zahlfast say when you told him that?"

I stammered, not sure how to answer, but almost immediately decided on the truth. "He reminded me that wizards don't talk very much about miracles, and that those who heal also have the power to sicken."

It sounded even worse than I had expected it to sound. While I was trying to frame a new apology, he kicked his horse forward, not even looking at me again, and pulled into line next to the Lady Maria. Since he, like me, had not been at Yurt yet when the king and queen happened to meet for the first time at the duchess's castle, she started to give him all the details. I was sure he had heard it all before; he had, after all, gone to visit the duchess with the royal party the first year he was in Yurt, while the king was still traveling at least short distances. But he listened intently, even smiling at the right places, and did not once look back at me.

The short early winter day had ended, and the sun was gone when we saw the lights blazing out from the duchess's castle in the valley before us. The knights had lit lanterns so that we could see the increasingly icy road, although I myself thought that the wildly flickering shadows from the swaying lamps made it even harder to guide one's way. We all kicked our horses and hurried down the last hill, bells ringing loudly. The bridge was down, and we surged across and into the courtyard.

Servants hurried forward to help us dismount, and the duchess's constable took the bridle of the king's horse. But the king waved away the servant at his stirrup and instead, with a look of intense concentration, rose slowly straight into the air, until he could swing his foot easily over the horse's back, then just as slowly descended to stand on the cobblestones.

Very few of the people from the royal castle of Yurt, and certainly no one from this castle, had seen the king flying before, so there was a stunned silence

before the applause broke out. The queen laughed
with delight as she dismounted in the more normal
manner and took his arm. His back straight and a not-
very-well-concealed grin of pride on his face, the king
walked toward the wide doorway leading into the great
hall.

I was about to follow him, extremely proud of my
pupil, when I caught a baleful glare. It was Dominic,
and he was glaring at me with eyes that were nearly
red with fury. I didn't know why, but I certainly didn't
need a second person furious at me today, so I turned
my face from him and hurried after the king and
queen.

They stopped just inside the hall, and I, following
closer than anyone else, nearly ran into them. Coming
to meet them was the duchess.

She did indeed look a lot like her cousin, the queen,
although the duchess was at least ten years older. Her
hair too was black and her features beautifully shaped,
but she did not have the queen's smile, which always
seemed to be hovering near her lips even when she
was sober or thoughtful.

The duchess did the full bow. "Welcome to my castle, which is your castle, my liege lord and king." And
it *was* the full bow, not the curtsy that women normally performed. The duchess, in spite of her femi-
nine features and the long hair braided into a graceful
coif, was dressed like a man, in a man's tunic and
boots.

"Rise, my faithful subject," said the king. He drew
her up, his hands on her shoulders, and kissed her on
both cheeks. The queen kissed her as well, but, I
noted, not nearly as enthusiastically.

"And who is this?" the duchess said, peeking at me
past their shoulders.

The queen brought me forward with a hand on my
elbow. I was glad I was wearing my new velvet jacket.

"This is our new Royal Wizard! He joined us this summer from the wizards' school in the City."

The duchess gave me a look of frank and highly interested appraisal, which startled me more than I wanted to admit; no woman had looked at me like that since—well, at all that I could remember. Fortunately, she appeared to like what she saw.

"I haven't had a wizard in my duchy in years," she said. "My father, the old duke, used to keep a wizard, but he had retired even before I inherited, and the old royal wizard of Yurt never deigned to visit me."

"That's why I wanted to bring him along," said the king. "Wait until you see his illusions!"

Although I was naturally crushed to discover that I had been brought along as an exhibit rather than as a necessary member of the king's personal retinue, I was too intrigued by the duchess to give this much thought. Back before I had entered the wizards' school, the women I had met in the City who dressed like men had for the most part, and ironically I always thought, not liked men. But the way this woman had looked at me suggested otherwise.

"Your rooms are all prepared, my lord and lady," she said. "My constable will show you and your companions. Dinner will be served as soon as you've had a chance to rest from your trip." As we all followed the constable out of the great hall, I glanced back to see her looking after us with a wide grin.

There were a number of different courses at dinner, all elaborate, but none, I thought, as good as those produced by the cook at Yurt. I also missed the brass choir before dinner. The chaplain sat across from me, as at home, next to the duchess's chaplain. But he did not meet my eye. I myself was surreptitiously watching the queen. I had wondered more than once why she, a woman of fire and air who should have been able to marry anyone in the western kingdoms, had married the king of Yurt.

Now that he was no longer ill, he did seem much younger than he had when I first met him, but he was still undeniably more than twice her age, and no taller than she. Here in the duchess's castle, as the Lady Maria had been reminding the chaplain this afternoon, was where the king and queen had first met, and I wondered if I might find some clue here.

We finished up with spicy cakes frosted in vivid colors, and while I was trying to decide if I liked them or not, the duchess called to me down the table. "Wizard! I hear you do excellent illusions. Would you care to entertain us?"

"He's tired, as we all are," said the queen quickly. "Maybe ask him another day."

I was surprised to find her suddenly so protective of me, and when I looked toward her I saw that she was not smiling. But the duchess's eyes met mine in an amused challenge.

"All right," I said, putting down the half-eaten cake which I had decided I did not like at all. "But I warn you, my illusions may be frightening."

"I don't frighten easily, Wizard."

But the lords and ladies from Yurt were nudging and smiling at each other, clearly hoping that the party here, who had not seen my dragon, would be frightened of it as they now pretended not to have been. Several of the duchess's attendants, seeing the winks, did indeed begin to look uneasy.

I went to stand by the fireplace, thinking quickly. I didn't want to become repetitive by doing another dragon, and although the magician at the carnival had not hesitated to make an illusory demon, I didn't want to terrify myself with my own magic. Besides, I only wanted to titillate the duchess and her lords and ladies, not send them screaming from the hall as I had almost done at Yurt.

I decided on a giant, one about twenty feet tall, which would leave his head (or heads—I rather liked the idea of a two-headed giant) only a short distance below the ceiling. I worked quickly, sketching in the different parts but not yet giving them substance, so that a ghostly pair of legs, a nearly invisible club, and a suggestion of massive arms took shape between me and the fire.

I glanced at my audience. The queen's eyes were dancing, and the duchess continued to look amused. The last detail was the double head, one smiling horribly, and one suffused with fury. The second head, even while half invisible, looked, I realized, a little like Dominic, but it was too late to try to change it. With a few quick words in the Hidden Language, I gave my giant visual solidity and put it into motion.

The giant spun around from the fire to face the table and raised its enormous club. The mouth of the furious face opened in a silent roar. The club swung downwards, and the king, showing an agility I had not realized he had, sprang from his chair just before the club passed down through the chair and the table.

There was a cacophony of noise, chairs scraping and falling backwards and the duchess's people shouting. The party from Yurt was doing fairly well, in that none of them were screaming, but they still sprang from the table as the giant started down it. The enormous hairy legs were buried almost knee-deep in the table, through which it seemed to wade like a man wading through water. The club descended again and again, passing without effect through glass, china, and wood, as one head roared and the other laughed. The only person who did not move was Dominic, who sat stonefaced, his arms folded, as one of the giant's thighs passed directly through him.

I stopped the giant just short of the duchess. She, like the others, had jumped up, but she was watching its approach with a broad smile. I had the giant stop roaring and grinning, drop its club, and go into the full bow before her. The effect was a little spoiled by the fact that, as it went down on its knees, much of it disappeared under the table, but the duchess still began applauding wildly as soon as the double head was lowered. I said the words to end the illusion.

The duchess ran to grab me by the hands. "Well, Wizard, I can see that, with you there, Yurt must be a much livelier place than it ever was before!"

People were straightening their hair and clothing and coming toward the fire with as casual an air as possible. The castle servants, who had been watching open-mouthed from the passage to the kitchen, disappeared again.

"I told you we had a fine wizard!" said the king. "Maybe you ought to send to the City for one yourself!"

"But I couldn't be sure of getting one like this one!" she said with a laugh. She was still holding both my hands, which was starting to make me feel uncomfortable. "Well, I don't think we'll have any more entertainment to top this tonight."

As though this were a signal, the lords and ladies of her party immediately started to leave. The king and queen glanced at each other. "If you don't mind," said the queen, "we'll retire now. We've had a long ride today."

"But you," said the duchess, looking at me, "you I'd like to take to my chambers for a final drink."

III

The queen turned sharply toward the duchess, as though about to say something, then changed her mind. "Good night, then," she said, leaving on the king's arm. For a moment I even hoped she was jealous.

The servants returned to clear the table as both

parties dispersed. The chaplain was almost the last to go, and before he went he fixed me with a burning stare that might have been a warning.

The duchess had released my hands, but I seemed to have no choice but to follow her, up the wide staircase at the end of the hall to the great ducal chamber.

To my relief, she stopped here and motioned me to a seat. A small fire was in the grate; she added first some sticks, then a log, and soon had it burning brightly. I felt I ought to help, but she seemed to want no help.

With the fire now burning, she went to a cabinet for two glasses and a bottle. She poured us each an inch of golden liquid and brought me mine, then sat down in the chair opposite me, one booted leg hooked over the arm.

I took a sip. "Excuse me, my lady, but this isn't wine. It's brandy."

"Yes," she said, as though wondering at my dimness.

"But brandy is a medicine."

"It's also an excellent after-dinner drink, as I discovered some time ago."

I took another sip. It was extremely powerful. "Very nice," I said.

Her face, which was close to being the queen's face, lit up with a smile that was not the queen's. "Enjoy it. There aren't many I invite to share a glass of brandy with me."

I started talking, in part to take control of the atmosphere, in part because that way I had an excuse for drinking more slowly. "This is the first time since I came to Yurt that I've accompanied the king on a visit to his subjects. It's hard to tell in the dark, of course, but as we came in it seemed that you had a beautiful little castle. I hear there are two counts in the kingdom as well. Are their castles as lovely?"

"The king's castle is of course considered the best in the kingdom of Yurt," she said, as though taking my inane comments seriously. "But the ducal castle, mine, is not rated far behind. Tomorrow I can show you all its features, inside and out. I don't have a rose garden like the king's, but if it were summer I could show you the flowers I do grow."

With any luck, I thought, we could talk about gardening until I could decently make my excuses and leave.

But she took control of the conversation back from me. "Wizard, I have a proposal to make to you."

I had been taking a sip from my glass and ended up swallowing suddenly much more than I meant to. "Indeed?" I said as blandly as I could, once I had stopped coughing. My eyes were drawn, against my will, to the door at the far end of the great chamber, which must lead to her bedroom.

"I know you wizards don't take oaths, but what I'm asking may still be hard for you." She was watching me, a look of amusement playing on her features.

"Indeed," I said with dignity. She seemed to be saying that we wizards did not take oaths of chastity, as did priests, which was true, but she also seemed to be insulting me.

"I know that, as short a time as you have lived in Yurt, your affections may already be fully engaged."

How did she know I was in love with the queen?

"Although," she said thoughtfully, "I would have thought a wizard with your flair wouldn't want to live his entire life ruled by someone with as soft a disposition as your queen."

Being too amazed to reply properly, I said nothing.

"Given a tempting opportunity, one's affections may change their focus," she continued with that same almost detached look of amusement.

"Possibly," I said, as noncommittally as I could.

"Therefore a woman may have to make her proposal as attractive as possible to woo a wizard," she continued, swinging her foot down and standing up.

I watched her approaching, almost in panic.

"That's why, Wizard, I need you to tell me what *you* like best."

She was standing directly in front of me, hands on her hips. I tried to buy time by seeming to drink my brandy, but it was gone.

"If I can offer you something the king does not offer you, then maybe I can woo you away from your affection for his castle and household and persuade you to give up being the Royal Wizard of Yurt and instead become my own ducal wizard."

In my relief at realizing that she was only offering me a position, not making an indecent proposal, at first I could only stammer. Then I caught her eye and realized she had been doing it deliberately.

"I am very happy as the Royal Wizard," I said, searching desperately for the remains of my dignity. Someone like the old wizard, someone who actually seemed to personify mystery and darkness, would not have been teased like this! "I'm not interested in alternate . . . *proposals*."

"But I'm quite serious, Wizard," she said, with a smile that was merely friendly. "I know it might seem like a step down to leave a king for a duchess, but I can offer you whatever you have now, and even more—your own tower, assistants to help gather herbs, freedom to come and go as you please."

For a brief moment I wondered what *would* happen if I left the king to become the duchess's wizard. Yurt would need a new Royal Wizard, of course, and this time they might be lucky and get someone competent. I would never have to deal with whatever evil force was lurking in the cellars.

Of course, they might get someone even less capable, and even a competent wizard wouldn't know about the empty north tower, about Dominic's veiled warning, or about the king's illness and recovery. The new wizard would resent anything that seemed like interference and certainly would not welcome hints from me.

Besides, Zahlfast would think I was running away. "I'm sorry, my lady," I said, "but even though I haven't taken an oath of loyalty to the king, I still feel that I am his man."

She nodded a little ruefully. "I'd been afraid you'd say that. I've been thinking for some time my duchy needed a wizard—my father's old wizard, whom I barely remember, was not, I believe, very highly qualified, but he had not been trained in the wizards' school. I was therefore very eager to meet a young wizard from the school, but as soon as I met you I realized there can't be many like you. Are there?"

She had, to my relief, gone back to her own chair. "Probably not," I said, "although the teachers at the school would tell you that's just as well."

"Maybe I should advertise and see who answers," she said thoughtfully. "But that was a wonderful giant! And was it deliberate that its second head looked just like Prince Dominic?"

I laughed and denied any such intention. After a few more minutes' conversation, I felt able to rise and tell her how tired I was after a long day.

She took my hands affectionately. "Thank you for sharing a glass of brandy with me. Think about my offer, if you grow tired of the royal court." Though not the queen, she certainly was an attractive woman. I wondered briefly what she would have done if I had taken what she seemed to be offering literally and had immediately begun to act on it.

"Thank you, and good evening, my lady," I said gravely, then left her great chamber to return to my own room. As I went, I wondered if the queen had, at least in part, decided to marry the king to keep him from marrying the duchess.

Since the duchess's castle really was smaller than the royal castle, and since it was already full of her own household, there had not been much room for the rest of us, after the king and queen and a handful of their closest companions had been lodged in a suite of rooms which apparently were always kept ready for them. As Royal Wizard, however, I had been given the dignity of a room of my own, the room the old ducal wizard had used thirty years earlier, which had apparently scarcely been used since then.

As I spiraled up the narrow tower stairs toward the room, ducking my head and wishing either for my predecessor's or my own magic lights, I thought I might look at the ducal wizard's old books for a minute before going to sleep. I had noticed a few books in the room before dinner and hoped that he might have written down some interesting spells that had never been known in the City.

As I came around the last turn, I was surprised to see the door of my room standing half open, and candlelight flickering within. I pushed the door slowly open and faced the deep black eyes of the chaplain.

He put down the Bible he had been reading and stood up. "Close the door," he said, as though this were his room, not mine.

I closed the door. "Look," I said. "What I said this afternoon. I realize I didn't make it clear enough"— this was an understatement!—"that I didn't think you were responsible for the king's illness." Most of the time this was even true. "I wish you'd given me a chance to explain. I really am sorry that I sounded as though I was accusing you."

But he didn't seem to be listening. "I don't enjoy doing this," he said, "but I have to. I'm afraid you're forgetting your duties, and I have to remind you of them."

"My duties?" I said in surprise. It would have seemed like a joke except that there was not even the hint of a smile on his face.

"Sit down," he said. "I didn't want to tell you this

when we spoke this afternoon, but the bishop was very unhappy about the possible influence on me from a wizard my own age."

I sat down obediently on my bed, as he had the chair.

"I told him what you had suggested to me in conversation, that the organization of the wizards' school is patterned on the organization of the church, and that, like the church, organized wizardry hopes ultimately for the salvation of mankind."

I knew I had never actually said this, but it was close enough to what I myself considered the goals of wizardry that I only nodded.

"That's why I have to speak to you now. I had to take responsibility with the bishop for your soul."

"I thought my soul was doing well," I said in a small voice, overawed by those burning eyes. I could not break my own glance away from them.

"If it were only playing with magic, I might not have to speak," he continued, unhearing. "Even when you used magic not to help but to terrify, as you did both at the royal court and again here tonight, tact kept me from speaking. But now!" He leaned sharply forward, as though wanting to make sure he had my full attention, although he had had it since I came in the room.

"I will not accuse you of immorality. Only the saints and God can truly judge a man's soul. But when you began to behave as though you have a licentious freedom, using casuistic reasoning to argue with yourself that a tradition against wizards' marrying is not enough to stop a man who has never had to take an oath of chastity, then I realized that you were in danger of applying this casuistry to other areas, to—"

At this point I had to interrupt him. "Stop. Wait. You don't understand."

"I fear I understand all too well."

"You don't. The duchess and I had a small drink together."

"And that was all?" he demanded.

"She told me that she admired my illusions so much that she wanted me to leave the royal court of Yurt and come be her ducal wizard. I turned her down."

Joachim sat back in the chair as though deflated. "And *that* was all?"

"That was all." I myself found the situation quite amusing. He must have sat in my room for close to an hour, waiting for my return, preparing both the accusations and the spiritual counsel he would give to me, and then he found out that, at least at the moment, I didn't actually need any spiritual guidance. But a look at his face told me he didn't find any amusement in the situation.

"Then I will apologize for disturbing you," he said stiffly. "I hope you sleep well." He rose and left the room, taking the candle with him.

I started to protest, then realized it was undoubtedly *his* candle, brought from his own room. I turned on my belt buckle to get enough light to find a candle of my own. I stared gloomily at the flame, once I had it lit, wondering how I was going to become friends again with the only person in Yurt who seemed to have the potential to be my close friend. At this rate, he'd soon be suspecting *me* of having poisoned the king.

But I still had to chuckle, thinking of him sitting here, imagining me embracing licentious freedom, at the exact same time as the duchess's teasing was almost driving me in panic from her chamber.

The next morning was Sunday, and I was in the ducal chapel early, sitting down in the front row while the duchess's chaplain and the royal chaplain conducted services together. Neither one of them seemed to notice my presence.

IV

We stayed at the duchess's castle for a week. Both because I feared being teased again and because I didn't want the chaplain worrying about my soul, I tried to avoid the duchess. Instead I devoted myself to the Lady Maria, always speaking to her at dinner, positioning my horse next to hers when we went out riding, standing as an attendant at her shoulder in the evening in the great hall. She was, I realized, the only person in Yurt to whom I spoke regularly with whom I did not always feel myself sparring.

But she could turn the conversation to her own purposes as deftly as anyone else if she wanted—something I had already known, and of which I was reminded when I tried to find out more about her previous experience with magic.

The king, the queen, and the duchess had all decided to go hunting—that is, the duchess asked the king if he would accompany her, and when he agreed the queen said that she wanted to hunt as well. They rode across the stubble of the duchess's fields and along the margins of the woods, hawks on their fists, hoping for a goose. Some of the rest of us, including the Lady Maria and I, went out with them primarily for fresh air.

The air was cold and slightly damp, although the gray sky did not immediately threaten rain. The Lady Maria seemed to enjoy my attentions and always raised her chin a little when the duchess glanced at the two of us together. Now, as we rode, I was amusing her by telling her again about the dragon in the cellar of the wizards' school.

"So, my predecessor agreed to teach you magic?" I asked suddenly, with no reference to what I had just been saying, hoping to catch her off-guard.

Her big blue eyes held mine for an instant, more

intently than they ever had before. Then she looked away with a small laugh. "I already told you; he refused to teach me anything because I'm a woman."

"Come now, you can reveal your little secrets to me!" I continued in a tone I hoped she would like. "You certainly learned to make magic requests somewhere!" When she did not answer, I added, "And have you requested the perpetual youth and beauty that adorn you, or was that given you at birth?"

She surprised me by seeming to take my fatuous comments entirely seriously. At any rate, her shoulders first stiffened, then sagged, and she looked straight ahead without any of the amusement I had expected.

"I asked for a while," she said in a very low voice. I could barely hear her, but I did not dare tell her to speak more loudly for fear she would say nothing at all. "But now all that I asked for has gone."

"My lady," I said in almost as soft a voice, "who did you ask?"

She suddenly became very involved with her horse's mane. We had reined in and were standing under a leafless tree, but a dead oak leaf had been carried on the wind and caught behind her horse's ears. She glanced at me once, a glance I was apparently not supposed to notice.

"You said you'd teach me magic," she said at last. "I don't need all that grammar. All I need is a simple spell, a spell to make me young."

"I'm afraid there isn't a simple spell like that," I said gravely, trying not to reveal how surprised I was at her admission that she needed a spell of youth—or apparently had once had one. "There's a difficult spell, which the young wizards don't even learn until we've been at the school for several years, that will slow down aging, but it won't make one any younger than one already is."

"Even if it's difficult, I know I could learn it," she

said with the trace of a smile. "After all, I learned
your telephone spell after hearing it once!"

"It's a different kind of spell, and much more difficult," I said, which was partly true, but in part I felt
a sense of panic that I had introduced her to magic
at all. Our duty as wizards is to help mankind, but
every spell, however small, has consequences far
beyond the spell itself. It was for this reason that all
the teachers at the school agreed, and impressed on
us strongly, that part of our responsibility as wizards
was *not* to freely extend the lives of everyone we met.

"You're teasing me because I'm a woman," said the
Lady Maria, facing me squarely. "I know I could learn
your spell, and I know that magic can make time run
backwards."

"Time can't run backwards. It's the most powerful
force in nature, and magic can never ultimately change
anything natural."

Tears of frustration appeared at the corners of her
eyes. "But it *can*! I've seen it work! Why won't you
tell me the truth?"

I was swept with a terror so sharp and sudden that
my lips were almost too paralyzed to speak. "My lady,
have you been dealing in black magic?"

"*No!* There's nothing evil in wanting to be young!
And all you do is laugh at me!"

She really was crying now. She kicked her horse
savagely and galloped away. My own mare turned her
head to look at me in inquiry, then, when I continued
to sit with the reins slack, started nosing again among
the half-frozen grass.

After a minute, I managed to gather up both the
reins and my mental strength enough to start back
toward the castle. I could see neither the Lady Maria
nor the rest of the hunting party, but I wanted to be
inside near a fire.

I wondered how it could have taken me so long to
realize that the Lady Maria had become involved with

black magic. First her extreme youthfulness, then the abrupt loss of that youthfulness, should have made me realize that she had found a magic that mixed truly supernatural power with magic's own natural power.

What I found difficult was to imagine her involved in evil herself. Could the supernatural that gave her magic the power to turn time backwards have been the supernatural power of the saints?

The difficulty here, I told myself, was that the saints seem to have little interest in magic. I wished I had paid more attention in my course on the supernatural to the part about the saints. There had been wizards in the past, as I dimly remembered hearing, who had tried to develop a "white magic" that would be as powerful as black magic, but those wizards must not have had sufficiently pure hearts and motives, for the saints had never listened to them.

Demons, on the other hand, love wicked hearts and perverted motives, and are, at least sometimes, even tractable if one knows precisely what to say. That was why black magic is not only possible but the single biggest danger, as they repeatedly warned us, for overly ambitious young wizards.

The answer must be that Maria had become involved in someone else's black magic, undoubtedly the same spell that had blighted the king and still suffused the cellars with a sense of evil. This put me back where I had been before, wondering who of the people of Yurt, all of whom I liked, could have been willing to give themselves to the devil.

"Let's be calm and rational," I told my horse, who had responded to a lack of commands from me by slowing first to a walk and then to a complete stop. Maria came to Yurt four years ago with the queen. She and Dominic, who some people thought might make a match, amused themselves during their courting by asking the old wizard to show them some magic tricks. Had he introduced them to black magic?

I didn't feel I knew my predecessor well, but I thought I had spent enough time with him to be able to say, fairly confidently, that he himself had not succumbed to evil. In some ways it was easier to tell with a wizard—I had spent eight years surrounded by nothing but wizards, and even someone trained in the old magic was not as strange to me as the duchess or the Lady Maria.

But who else could it be, if not the stray visitor to the castle that Dominic would have had me believe? I kept on coming back to the chaplain, who had come to the castle a year after the Lady Maria, just about the time that the black magic first had its effect, if I assumed the king's illness was indeed part of that effect.

"No," I said out loud. "Zahlfast is wrong." Maybe theoretically someone who healed could also sicken, but I refused to believe it here. I *had* paid very close attention in the part of the course that dealt with demons, and I knew that demons would not listen to a request to do good to someone else. A demon would happily do evil to others, but would only be helpful to the person whose soul he claimed.

Therefore, as I had thought all along, the supernatural power that had healed the king had been the power of the saints. Would the saints have listened to Joachim if his heart had been full of evil?

"Unless he'd since repented of that evil," I answered myself, "and his heart was truly contrite." I startled my mare by suddenly digging in my heels. I was not going to allow myself to take this reasoning any further. But then I was suddenly struck by the thought of the old chaplain, the one who had died unexpectedly. Could he have turned to evil, worshiping the devil in his heart while his lips addressed God?

This was a truly terrible thought, and I felt myself go cold and stiff again. If a castle's chaplain had invited in the powers of darkness, had died with his immortal soul in the devil's grasp, would a castle ever be able to recover?

I reassured myself with the thought that a chapel where a man could pray to the saints for a miracle was not a chapel where imps and demons frolicked unchecked. This left me Dominic as my final suspect. I wished I did not feel so much righteous pleasure in suspecting him.

In spite of the highly intermittent nature of my riding, I had at last arrived at the castle gates. I crossed the bridge into the courtyard, with more questions than I had had before but fewer answers. I needed to ask Dominic about his and Maria's attempts to learn magic from the old wizard, and I had no idea how I was going to ask him.

I was nearly as startled as I would have been to meet a demon to find Dominic's slightly red face looking at me as I entered the stables with my mare.

"Prince Dominic!" I stammered. "I thought you were out hunting!"

He frowned, clearly wondering what I could have been doing to make me react so guiltily to his presence. "I'm still worried about my horse's leg," he answered, "so I came in from the hunt."

The thought passed wildly through my mind that the horse's leg might recover more quickly with a lighter rider, but fortunately I was able to suppress any such comment. "I'm glad to see you here, as I'd wanted to ask you some questions," I managed to say instead, wondering what I *would* ask him.

"But first I have some questions for *you*," he said, standing up. He always seemed when I was close to him much larger than I remembered. "A royal wizard is supposed to use his powers to serve his king and kingdom, and I'd like to know what you think you're doing with yours."

"Serving the king and kingdom," I said promptly, with as much of a smile as I could manage.

He seemed to find neither humor nor reassurance in this. "All you've done," he said, scowling down at me and speaking slowly and distinctly as though I were slightly demented, "ever since you've come to Yurt, is to produce illusions that terrify the women—"

Fortunately I managed to keep a perfectly expressionless face.

"—and, I discover now, recklessly try to teach the king to fly."

"Didn't you know that?" I said inanely. "He asked me to months ago, back during the summer while the queen was visiting her parents. He wanted to surprise her when she came home."

"I most certainly did not know it," he said, his face growing darker red. This explained, then, the look of fury he had turned on me when we had first arrived here and the king had used his rather limited flying powers to dismount. Thinking quickly, I realized that Dominic had never been there before on any of the very few occasions when the king had shown off his ability.

"But what's the harm in it?"

"The harm," he said, still in that careful voice in which rage seemed to boil barely suppressed, "is that any *interference* in magic processes, as you tried to tell me once yourself, can lead to terrible consequences, and the king's too much of—too trusting to recognize the dangers. I shouldn't have to remind you of this, Wizard."

I was quite sure he had been going to say that the king was too much of a fool to realize magic's dangers. I wondered if some of Dominic's resentment of the king's flying was that it freed the king from the dependence on his nephew he had had when the queen was away. But now that the king was well—and Dominic had seemed as delighted as anyone else—this dependence would not be at issue anyway. Maybe Dominic himself had already experienced some of the terrible experiences of misused magic.

"And I shouldn't have to remind *you*," I said, making myself as tall as I could, "that you yourself once interfered in magic processes, and have refused to tell me about what happened then. It's my *duty* as Royal Wizard to know all the magic being done in the kingdom."

"I don't know what you're talking about," said Dominic, taking half a step backwards.

I hesitated. My immediate reaction was to push my advantage, to call him a liar to his face, but if he openly denied ever having been involved in magic I knew he never would tell me about it. "Then I'll bid you good day," I said calmly and left the stables.

So far, I thought, crossing the wet cobblestones of the courtyard, I knew no more than I had known that summer. The only advance I seemed to have made was in somehow leading the duchess to believe that I was a well-qualified wizard.

The Lady Maria was at dinner that night, which almost surprised me, but she seemed very cheerful. Since we had been sitting next to each other all week, it would have looked very odd if either of us sat elsewhere, and I also felt it necessary to reestablish our light banter.

"You know everyone's romantic secrets, my lady," I said in a low voice to her during the soup. The soup was made of fish and herbs, actually one of the better productions of the duchess's kitchens, but I could tell that it was ocean fish, not local river fish, and therefore must have been packed up from the City on ice at a remarkable cost.

"But I still don't think I know all *your* secrets," she replied with a smile, in the same tone, clearly eager to pretend that our afternoon's conversation had never taken place.

"There's one person's secret I hope you might tell me," I said coyly while the soup dishes were being cleared, taking advantage of the rattle of china to mask our conversation. "When the king and his party met you and the present queen's party for the first time, here at the duchess's castle, had there been a rumor that the king might be about to marry the duchess?"

"Oh, no," she said with a little tinkling laugh. "It wasn't like that at all." A servant leaned between us at that point to place the silverware for the next course, and I had a sudden fear that the rumor had in fact been that the king would marry the Lady Maria, and that I had just deeply insulted her by never before having considered this possibility.

But she bent toward me as soon as the servant stepped back and whispered in my ear. "The rumor had been that *Dominic* was going to marry the duchess."

I came within half a breath of saying, "Dominic?" out loud but stopped myself in time. He was sitting only four places down the table and would certainly have reacted to the sound of his own name.

"Yes," she continued in my ear, clearly enjoying the fact that everyone else at the table noticed we were whispering. "The duchess's servants told our servants that the king wanted to ensure the inheritance of Yurt past his own death, so he felt his nephew and heir had to marry. They had come here expressly to arrange a marriage, when our party fortuitously happened to arrive at the same time, and the king met the queen! I don't need to tell you what happened after that!"

"Wizard!" called the duchess from the end of the table. "Does a woman have to be blond for you to let her whisper sweet nothings in your ear?"

"As long as she's as lovely as all the ladies here present," I said gallantly, ignoring what I could tell was a warning stare from the chaplain, "I don't care what color is her hair."

This remark seemed to amuse most of the ladies, and the Lady Maria and I went back to eating. This meant, therefore, that the queen had not married the king to keep him from the duchess, my original and only half-serious thought, even though there was clearly no deep affection between the cousins.

From something that the Lady Maria had told me that summer, I could guess that Dominic had hoped, once he met her, that he and the queen would make a match, and that even the queen's father, Maria's brother, had made some plans in that direction. I didn't know for certain why the original plan for a marriage between Dominic and the duchess didn't go through, but I could guess: he had never been extremely enthusiastic about the plan in the first place, and then when he met the queen he had decided not to take the one cousin when he could not get the other. The king, hoping for a little son of his own, would have stopped worrying about finding a wife for his nephew.

So was that the answer to why the queen had married the king, that she wanted to get away from her father's plans to marry her to someone suitable, when some of these suitable persons might have been even worse than Dominic? It seemed a plausible answer, but it did not answer the real one: who in Yurt had been practicing black magic?

PART FIVE
The Stranger
I

I was relieved to be heading home again. The queen seemed also to be glad to go, although the king, bidding the duchess an affectionate farewell, appeared to have enjoyed his visit thoroughly. I guessed that he had no idea the cousins were not highly fond of each other. But while the queen was merely happy to be leaving the duchess behind, I was eager to get back to the castle of Yurt and reassure myself nothing had happened in our absence. We had received no messages via the pigeons, and had not expected to, but if the castle had been swallowed by a giant hole in the earth they might not have had time to release the pigeons.

Packed in my saddlebags were the books I had found in the room of the old ducal wizard. I had quite brazenly stolen them, reassuring myself that it was not theft to take something no one wanted. They had clearly been undisturbed for thirty years, and if the duchess did indeed hire someone from the wizards' school, as she had threatened to do, he would probably throw them out immediately.

At dusk we came out of the woods and up the hill toward the castle. A chill wind mixed with a little sleet whipped about our ears, and our horses were eager for the stables. I looked up, expecting to see welcoming lights shining out, and instead saw only the castle's dark shape against the dark sky.

"The constable knew we were coming home today," said the queen in surprise.

"Everyone may just be sitting warm in the kitchen," said the king.

A chill had gone through me far colder than the sleet. I looked toward Joachim and saw that a similar fear had gripped him, for he had reached into his saddlebag and taken out his crucifix. He too, I thought, must have been feeling that elusive sense of evil in the castle, and he must have been worried about it in ways that he never told me.

"At least the drawbridge is down," said one of the knights. The king's optimism was not shared by the rest of our party.

For a brief moment we hesitated by the bridge, looking in through the gates toward the dark and silent courtyard. Then the king said cheerfully, "They'll light the lights as soon as they hear us. Just don't let your horses slip going in!" He led the way, the rest of us following single-file behind.

No one spoke as we crossed the bridge and then the courtyard toward the lightless stables, but our horses' hooves on the cobblestones and the bells on their bridles made a sound that should have awakened any sleeper. There was an abrupt clattering sound from the direction of the great hall, then to my intense relief I heard the constable's voice. "On!" he shouted, and all the magic lamps in the hall blazed into light.

More lights came on then around the castle, and the constable ran out to meet us, disheveled and embarrassed. "Forgive me, sire," he said, holding the king's stirrup while he dismounted. "I don't know what happened to me. I must have fallen asleep. I didn't mean for you to come home to a dark castle."

Everyone else was now talking and dismounting, and a stable boy started taking the horses. The others seemed to have dismissed whatever fears they had felt looking up at the lightless bulk of the castle against the twilight sky. But the chill I had felt then was still with me. I caught Joachim's eye and knew that he too was not completely satisfied.

The cook came rushing into the hall from the kitchens, highly flustered, at the same time as we came in from the courtyard. She spoke quickly to the constable and rushed out again. "We'll have a hot dish for you very quickly, my lords and ladies," said the constable apologetically. "The cook somehow has let the fire go out, but she'll have it going again in just a minute."

The hall fire too was quickly built up again. We all stood around it, warming ourselves after the ride, waiting for supper. While we waited, I wondered what could have happened to cast everyone in the castle into slumber, and what had awakened them again. Only a small part of the staff was there, as the rest— including Gwen and Jon—would not be back from their vacations before tomorrow, but it was certainly not natural for all of the staff present to have been overcome with sleep at the same time.

And had it merely been the sound of our horses that awakened them? I put my coat back on and slipped away, taking one of the magic lamps with me. As I went by the kitchens, I could hear loud clattering and the cook giving rapid orders, and could smell supper cooking, a smell so delightful after a long day's cold ride that I had to stop myself from going in for a sample bite.

Instead I went down the dank staircase behind the kitchens, forcing my unwilling feet forward and doing

my best to ignore the plausible reasons that kept popping into my mind why it would be much better to
wait until morning.

It was as I feared. The rusty iron door was still shut,
but my magic locks were gone, and the debris with
which I had blocked the small window in the door
had all fallen to the ground.

I went back up the stairs much faster than I
intended and crossed the courtyard to my own chambers. To my intense relief, the magic lock on my door
was glowing softly, undisturbed. I went inside to be
out of the wind while I found my composure again.
If this lock too had been gone, I would have had to
believe there was a demon loose in the castle.

But a new thought also struck me. Someone who
knew very powerful magic had apparently been at
work while we were gone. This person had his or her
headquarters in the cellars, a place where spells were
cast and books and herbs kept. When I locked the
cellars with magic, he or she had had to break my
locks to get back in.

And this person, I reasoned, would have to be
someone on the castle staff: the constable and his wife,
the cook, the stable boy, or the kitchen maid, the only
people who had been here when we arrived. But why
would one of those five have put the others to sleep
and pretended sleep himself or herself? I shook my
head, realizing it could have been any other member
of the staff, who would have perhaps come back
"early" from vacation, entered the castle without any
challenge, put the rest into a sleep that would make
them forget he or she had been there, and left again.
In this case, the sleep could have been intended to
ensure there were no witnesses to whatever the person
was going to do—or people to hear the screeching of
the iron door being opened.

I left the lights on in my chambers and hurried back
to the hall, arriving just in time for a light supper of

soup and omelet, served with some of the cook's excellent bread. Hungry and tired, we all ate without more than the briefest snatches of conversation. As the food was being served, I had briefly considered trying the spell that had turned the king's soup green before his recovery, but I did not have the heart to do so, fearing what it might show. Besides, I was almost too hungry to care.

But in the morning, after chapel service, I went to talk to Joachim. He looked surprised to see me. We had barely spoken two words since he had nearly accused me of seducing the duchess. But that all seemed distant and trivial now.

He was sitting in his room, drinking tea and eating a cinnamon cruller. Since the kitchen maid had only brought me a cake donut this morning, I was wildly envious, but I forced myself to overlook it. I had something more important on my mind.

"You and I both know," I said, "that someone has put an evil spell on Yurt. It doesn't seem possible that such a charming castle should be touched by evil, but it is. I don't know who has cast the spell, but you and I have to do something about it. I don't think it was you, and I hope you don't think it was me."

"I try not to accuse anyone of evil, even in my thoughts."

"Tell me: How soon after you came to Yurt did you begin to feel the presence of an evil mind?"

He put down his teacup carefully. "I have never felt an evil presence here."

I didn't say anything for a moment but met his grave and slightly puzzled eyes in silence. Maybe only someone trained in wizardry would be susceptible to that oblique sense of evil magic. Or maybe, surrounded as he was by the aura of the saints, nothing wicked could approach him.

"But you too were worried last night when we arrived and found everyone asleep."

"Of course I was. There have been odd magical forces in Yurt as long as I have been here. At first I thought it must have something to do with your predecessor, since I knew he and my own predecessor had not gotten along well. But when he left and you came, the same disruptive magic forces were still there." He startled me by taking my arm in a sharp grip. "I decided you were not behind them—that was why I was willing to tell the bishop I would take the responsibility for your soul."

I eased my arm out of his fingers and did my best to smile. "It's ironic, isn't it? I feel something wrong in Yurt and assume it's part of the conflict between angels and demons. You feel the same thing and assume it's something to do with magic. But it's not just someone casting silly spells. There's an evil mind behind it."

"I try not to accuse anyone of evil," he said again.

I thought about this for a moment. "All right. I too don't want to think of anyone being absolutely evil. But I do think someone, deliberately or not, has involved the powers of darkness in his or her magic. Therefore, we—"

Joachim interrupted me, his intense black eyes blazing. "You speak much too lightly of someone 'being absolutely evil.' Don't you realize that, if you believe that, you are denying the power of redemption?"

"Well, I didn't really mean it in theological terms, so much as—"

But he was not listening to me. "All of us are God's creation. Therefore none of us can ever destroy the good within us, or not destroy it totally. We priests do our best to keep that spirit of good a living flame, but even those who are wicked and depraved in this life may still be redeemed in the next."

"But how about someone who gives his soul to the devil?"

As soon as I asked I wish I had not, because I didn't want to hear the answer.

Joachim's shoulders slumped slightly as he dropped his eyes. "Then that person is beyond the prayers of either mortals or the saints. He will still be redeemed when the devil himself is redeemed, but that will not be before the end of infinite time."

The bright sun on the ice and snow outside the chaplain's open window seemed dim for a moment, and the chill in my bones was not due to the air coming through that window.

If someone in the castle had made a pact with the devil, giving up his or her soul after death for advantages in this life, then that person's only chance was to trick or negotiate the devil into breaking the pact. His or her best hope was to have the negotiations done by someone else, someone who really understood the supernatural. The saints do not negotiate, which meant that a wizard—that is me, and not the chaplain who had already proved himself by healing the king—might have to deal with this.

All that any wizard in the City—or probably in the world—knew about dealing with the devil had been distilled into the *Diplomatica Diabolica*, which meant I was going to have to read it, even though every time I even looked at its spine I was struck with the same fear that had gripped me when I first bought it: that I might endanger my own soul by summoning a demon by mistake, when I had only intended to learn how to deal with one who was already there.

It was almost with a sense of light and ease that I thought again about the specific problem of who in Yurt might be practicing black magic. "I need your help," I told Joachim. "Someone's immortal soul may be in danger. I think that last night a sleeping spell had been put on the castle, though I don't know why. But if we can determine who did it, then we may be able to find out where the odd magic forces you mention are coming from."

"It cannot be your predecessor, because he's gone," said the chaplain thoughtfully, looking at his hands. "And I don't think it's you." He gave me one of his intense looks, then returned to his hands. "It must have been someone who was here in the castle while we were visiting the duchess." He clearly was not used to this way of reasoning, but I waited impatiently while he worked it through for himself.

Then he surprised me by asking, "From what distance can a spell be cast?"

I should have thought of this myself. "I really don't know," I said, "but I don't think it's very far. I at any rate have never been able to cast a spell farther than I could see." I stopped, thinking of my glass telephones, but decided not to confuse the issue by mentioning them. "Do you think it could be someone who lives down in the village?"

"Or even someone in our party."

I had been about to ask Joachim for his spiritual help against the constable, as the most likely of the people who had stayed in the castle, but now I was back to suspecting everyone in Yurt, perhaps everyone in the entire kingdom.

Then I remembered that the supernatural influence Zahlfast had first noted stopped at the moat. Someone in the castle itself must be casting the spells, as I had always assumed. This meant—

Joachim interrupted my thoughts. "Is it possible to cast a long-lasting spell, one that will continue to have effect when one is far away?" Apparently they taught them to ask sharp questions at the seminary.

"It depends on the spell," I said. "Some of the elementary spells, like illusions, will fade fairly shortly unless constantly renewed. But some of the complicated spells, like lamps or magic locks, should last indefinitely." I decided not to mention the broken locks on the cellar door.

"So someone who isn't even here anymore, such as your predecessor, could have put an evil spell on Yurt that is still having an effect."

I shook my head. "It's possible, but not very likely, even if the person is a master in wizardry." It was going to be hard to explain that the long-lasting spells, although the most complicated, were when completed often the simplest and most static. A spell that could sicken the king and make the apparently ageless Lady Maria start to age seemed too involved to be maintained from any distance, in space or time.

"Let's assume," I said, "that the magic is being practiced by someone here in the castle, someone here now. I need your help because it isn't just ordinary magic, which I could deal with myself. Someone is acting with evil intent, or the king would not have come so close to dying, and he or she may have involved the supernatural, for the Lady Maria told me she had seen time run backwards."

"I didn't think magic could make time run backwards."

"It can't. Only the truly supernatural can do that. That's why I'm so terrified." I hadn't meant to tell him I was terrified, but he did not seem to mark the comment.

"Where had she seen this happen?" he asked.

"She won't tell me."

"Did you want me to try asking her?"

I contemplated the chaplain trying to pry the Lady Maria's secrets out of her with what he would consider tact. "No," I said, "it might frighten her to know that two of us realized she was involved in some sort of magic gone astray. It would be just as well for only me, the wizard, to ask her about it."

"Are you suggesting that *she* is practicing magic with evil intent?"

"No, but somebody must be doing so."

"We'll have to think about this systematically," said Joachim. I noticed he was not meeting my eyes and wondered if he was starting to suspect *me* of evil intent. "Of those who stayed in the castle while we were gone, certainly the constable is the strongest individual. I have never thought of him as other than good."

"Neither had I," I said, "but he stays so much in the background that I realize I don't know him very well."

"But what possible motive could he have for putting the others to sleep?"

I was about to explain my theory of the person involved in black magic needing to get back in the cellar when there was a sudden knock at the door. "Come in!" called Joachim.

I must have jumped six inches when the constable himself opened it and addressed the chaplain. "Excuse me," he said, "but there's someone to see you."

II

Joachim stood up and followed the constable out at once. I sat for a moment, looking at the backs of his books on his shelf, then, feeling it was not polite to stay here while he was gone, wandered out into the hallway.

I had just had an idea about the constable. He had the keys to every room in the castle, yet he had told me that only Dominic, who had duplicate keys for most rooms, had the key to the cellar. Did this mean that he really did have the cellar key, but had wanted to deny it, knowing all too well what was down there?

The challenge of trying to figure out what was happening in Yurt would have been highly enjoyable if I had not kept being overwhelmed with terror. I was glad to think that Joachim and I were probably friends again, at least for the moment; he might have some good ideas. By the time he came back, I had a theory to account for the north tower.

The old wizard, I reasoned, liked to consider himself a wizard of light and air, but at some point he had dabbled in black magic. The old chaplain had suspected something of this, and so had the constable. The wizard had repented and gotten out with his soul intact, but when he retired he left all the paraphernalia of black magic behind him, locked up in his tower. The constable, however, who had somehow learned how to break magic locks, had gone in, taken everything down to his own den of evil in the cellar, and swept out the tower room to leave no traces.

This was quite an appealing theory, other than the gaps of where the constable might have learned how to break locks and what, exactly, the "paraphernalia of black magic" might be. Having tried to avoid such things, I actually had no idea, except perhaps some books of evil spells.

Joachim came swiftly back up the hallway and went into his room without speaking to me. But since he left the door open, I went in too after a minute. He had his saddlebag on the bed and was tossing a few things into it.

He looked up at me. "There's a sick boy in the village. They want me to pray for him."

I did not answer, feeling that "How nice," the all-purpose comment, was highly inappropriate.

"Fortunately, I don't think he's very sick, and the doctor is already with him." He threw his Bible in on top and strapped up the bag. "It's the brother of the little girl who was bitten by the viper."

"Dear God," I startled myself by saying.

"If I were the father, I wouldn't send for me," said Joachim with what would have been grim humor in anyone else. "But he did." He stood up, pulled on his jacket, and swung the saddlebag over his shoulder. I followed him as he strode through the castle to the courtyard. The same man in brown that I had seen before was waiting on his horse. In a moment, the chaplain was mounted and the two rode away together.

I went out onto the drawbridge, although I was cold without a coat. The morning sun glittered on the icy snow. I watched until the two riders disappeared into the edge of the forest and felt very glad that I was not a priest.

I hurried back inside and went in search of the constable. I found him in the kitchen talking to the cook. "Is something wrong?" she said, seeing me over his shoulder. "I know Gwen says that you always like crullers, but I'd only made a few this morning. She should be back from her vacation this afternoon."

"It's not about the crullers," I said, although another time it would have been. I didn't even mention how stale the donut I had gotten had tasted. "I wanted to talk to the constable."

"All right," he said, turning to smile at me. "Well, we can order whatever we don't have," he said over his shoulder to the cook. "Just start making a list of what you'll need. We can talk more later." Turning back to me, he said, "Shall we go to my chambers?"

I had never actually been in the constable's chambers, and I immediately agreed, although if I had expected to see the paraphernalia of evil I was sadly disappointed. His chambers, in fact, looked a lot like mine, without the rows of books on magic. Instead he had big leather-bound manuscript books that I guessed were the castle accounts and inventories. There were rows of plants inside on the windowsills, and the furniture was all painted blue and white.

The constable's wife was mopping the stone floor, the outer door open, as we came up. "Oh, excuse me, sir," she said, putting the bucket outside. She ran to close the bedroom door, but not before I had caught a glimpse of a wide, turned-back bed, the white pillows and comforter fluffed out to air. "I'll just go over to the kitchen for a moment, if you want to talk in private," she said.

I realized the chief difficulty with my theory of the constable having sold his soul to the devil was the constable's wife. It appeared on the face of it much more likely that he had given himself to her, heart and soul, many years ago, and had been happy enough with the arrangement that he wanted nothing else, or at least nothing else that a demon could promise.

"It makes such a happy difference having the king well again," he said. "But part of that difference is that we on the staff are kept much busier! The king told me this morning that he wants to have a big party here for Christmas. The cook will have to start planning immediately, as it's only three weeks away, and we'll have to send in our order by the pigeons in a day or two if we need to order anything special from the City. He wants the duchess and both counts to come, which means we'll have to clean out all the spare rooms and have them ready. I can't remember when he last had so many people at Christmas!"

This was the difficulty with all my theories about anyone in the castle. Everyone always seemed so good-hearted and happy—except for Dominic—that it was impossible to suspect them of practicing black magic. I would have concluded I was imagining the whole thing, except that both Zahlfast and the chaplain, in their own way, had sensed it too.

"The king must be feeling very social," I said, "to be planning to have a large party here when he's barely gotten back from visiting the duchess." Privately I wondered what the queen thought of this plan. "But I wanted to ask you something." It was probably pointless to ask, but since I had interrupted him anyway I might as well. "Are you sure you don't have a key to the cellars?"

He looked surprised, as well he might, and took the heavy bunch of keys from his belt. "I'm quite sure I don't," he said, flipping through them. "Dominic took the key some years ago, when we decided just to lock the cellars up rather than trying to use them anymore. They always were very damp. I'm not sure we ever had a duplicate key, because before then the door had always stood open." I certainly saw no key on his ring that matched the rusty iron one I had borrowed from Dominic. "Why do you ask?"

I had been afraid he would say that. "I'd been thinking it might be possible to dry the cellars out and use them for my own purposes," I improvised. "We wizards need rooms that won't be hurt if one of our experiments in fire and light goes a little astray. I understand the old wizard had the north tower, but that he didn't want the tower room used again, so I thought the cellars might be a possibility. I'd looked at them a little the other week, but I hated to bother Dominic for his key again, so I . . ."

The constable smiled knowingly. "I understand. You and Prince Dominic don't always see eye to eye, and you're almost afraid of him now. Don't be insulted!" seeing me about to interrupt. "It's not your fault. He's a hard man for anyone to get along with, as well I know."

I nodded, not wanting to say anything for fear I'd start laughing. It made a much better excuse for talking to the constable rather than Dominic about the cellar key than anything I could have invented. But this made me think again that I ought to suspect Dominic. Suspecting him of evil intent, however, seemed so easy that I was worried that my personal feelings might cloud my judgment.

"But are you sure you really want to try the cellars anyway?" said the constable. "We'd hoped you'd find the chambers we gave you satisfactory" ("The old nurse doubtless found them delightful!" I commented to myself), "but if you need something more we should at least be able to find you a room that's drier than the cellar. Could you wait, however, until after Christmas?"

The constable looked really troubled that he would be too busy to find me a good room for my experiments in light and fire during the next three weeks. Now I supposed I would have to find some such experiments to do. Remembering that I was keeping him from his work, I reassured him that January would be fine, and rose to my feet.

"Wait a minute, sir, if you don't mind," the constable said, and I sat down again. "There's something I wanted to ask you." He frowned and looked away. "When the king told me the people he wanted to invite for Christmas, he mentioned the duchess and the two counts, as I'd already said . . . but he also said he wanted to invite the old wizard."

"Yes?" I prompted when he fell silent.

"I wanted to ask if that was all right," the constable said, still not looking at me. "He lives very near here, down in the forest, and the king thought he would love coming up to the castle for Christmas, rather than spending it alone, that is, if you don't mind."

"Of course I won't mind."

The constable looked up then, smiling. "I'm sorry to bother you, then, but one hears rumors of how young and old royal wizards are always at odds, and even though I hinted to you when you first came that you might visit him, I knew you hadn't, so though I'd hoped that in your case . . ."

I interrupted before he could make his statement any more involved. "Actually, I *have* visited him two or three times. We've probably become as good friends as old and young wizards ever do."

The constable was positively beaming now. "Well!

That's very good news. I hadn't wanted to pry into what you'd done, knowing that a wizard needs his privacy, but I'm delighted to hear that! Now, if you'll excuse me." He was whistling as he took down an account book while I went back out.

I paused in the center of the courtyard, trying to think whom I should suspect next of having a den of evil magic in the cellar, since it was so difficult to suspect the constable. The constable's wife, the cook, the stable boy, and the kitchen maid, the only other people who had been in the castle when we arrived to find it dark, seemed even less viable alternatives. I briefly considered but rejected the possibility that Dominic had put everyone to sleep from far away. I didn't know of any spell that would do such a thing from a distance, and could think of no reason why he would want to do so. Besides, I always kept coming back to the fact that Dominic was the one who had first warned me against the evil spell on the castle.

I shivered and was starting back toward my chambers when I was startled by seeing a tall, thin form standing motionless just inside the castle gates. "Joachim's back already," I thought in surprise. Then the man turned to look at me and I saw it was not the chaplain. It was someone I had never seen before.

He did not in fact look like Joachim at all, except that he too had enormous black eyes, in a face that was almost inhuman in its pallor and expressionlessness. He stared at me without blinking.

"Excuse me," I said, "can I help you? Have you just arrived?" For a moment I thought it might be a new member of the caste staff, signed on by the constable while the royal party was away, and arriving to take up his duties this morning.

But the stranger turned away again without speaking and, with long strides, started toward the south tower.

I went after him, but he had a large lead, and he

disappeared around the tower's base. When I came up, there was no sign of him.

This, I thought, was very odd. There were several doors he could have gone into, so his disappearance was not very mysterious, but no stranger coming to a castle should flee before the Royal Wizard.

III

I went back to the constable's chambers and knocked. He was working on the accounts as his wife finished her mopping. Both looked surprised to see me again so soon.

"Did you hire a new member of the staff while we were gone?" I asked. "There's a stranger here, someone I've never seen before, and when I tried to talk to him he went across the courtyard and into a doorway."

"I certainly haven't hired anyone new," said the constable. "It must be a visitor. But I don't know why he wouldn't talk to you."

I had been concentrating so much on fears of black magic that I realized I had been overlooking something obvious: a thief sneaking into the castle. "Do you think it could be someone trying to steal something?"

"Let's hope not," said the constable, putting his account book back and jumping up. "We'd better find him."

We checked the doors leading off the corner of the courtyard behind the south tower. These were rooms that were rarely used, and only one of the doors was unlocked. The constable opened the others with his bunch of keys, to make sure the man had not gone in and locked the door behind him, but all the rooms were empty.

"I'll get Dominic," I said. "He should be able to help us."

While the constable headed toward the main storerooms to see if they had been disturbed, I located Dominic in the great hall, talking to the king and queen. "Can you help the constable and me?" I asked. "I've just seen a stranger in the courtyard, and we're worried it might be a thief. He ran away when I spoke to him."

There were advantages of having someone large and burly beside you when looking for someone who might be dangerous. Dominic came at once, but I felt uneasy as I saw the queen putting on her shawl with a smile of excitement. I knew she loved hunting, but I didn't think she should be hunting this person.

Nevertheless, she came with us. We met the constable in the middle of the courtyard. "I haven't seen any sign of break-in or tampering with the locks," said the constable. "Maybe the wizard frightened him off."

"There he is!" I said. At the far end of the courtyard, near the kitchens, the tall thin form appeared for a moment and then disappeared again into a doorway. We all ran that direction, but when we arrived he again was gone.

"He can't have gone far," said Dominic. "We'll have him in a minute."

But he was wrong. All morning we pursued the stranger, and all morning he eluded us. Sometimes we thought he was gone and sat down to rest, only to see him again, striding across the far end of the courtyard, or standing on the parapet far above us, or looking out a window with his enormous black eyes. Dominic recruited the rest of the knights, and as the servants came back to the castle some of them as well joined in the pursuit.

I was glad the others saw him too, or I would have begun to worry that I was losing my mind.

"Are you sure you aren't playing one of your tricks on us, Wizard?" a knight asked in one of the pauses in which we thought we had lost him. We were sitting in a row on a bench in the courtyard, panting in spite of the cold air. The queen was the only one who still looked eager for the chase.

"I'm certainly not responsible," I said. "And I don't think there are any other wizards near here who might try something like this." But I did consider the possibility that this person might only be an illusion.

A few minutes later, the queen spotted a dark head peering down at us from the parapet. I probed quickly with my mind to see if this person was indeed real, furious at whoever might have pulled such a trick.

A wizard can normally only meet directly the mind and thoughts of another wizard, one who is willing for such contact, even though the Lady Maria had once been able to hear my thoughts. But one should still be able to find and recognize another mind, to tell at least if it is the mind of a man or a woman, reality or illusion.

I found the stranger's mind and almost fell over backwards with the impact. This was no illusion. The man's mind was looking for my own, ready to meet it, and his was totally evil. The distant, oblique touch of evil I had been feeling for months was no longer distant; it was here.

The rest ran after him, but I broke my mind away from that contact and sank back on the bench. Where had he come from? Why had he appeared in the castle now? What did he want with us?

I heard a step immediately next to me and whirled around. But it was not the stranger, only Gwen and Jon, coming toward me hand in hand.

"We wanted to tell you first, sir," said Gwen. "We've gotten engaged!"

It took me several moments to recover my composure enough to be able to say, "Congratulations!" without fearing it would sound like the gaspings of a fish. I decided it would be tasteless to ask if Jon had resorted to the long-threatened love potion or if he had won her with his own unaided charms; I assumed the latter.

"I know you may be a little surprised, after a few things I've said," said Gwen with a smile up at Jon. "But when all of you left for the duchess's castle, Jon asked if I wanted to spend my vacation with him, visiting his mother, and I said I would. We worked everything out pretty quickly, then! Now, we'll have to tell the constable and get his permission to stay on once we're married. We'll want the chaplain to marry us in the castle chapel, of course."

"Of course," I said inanely.

"I just wanted to say something," Jon interjected. "A couple of times, sir, I was jealous of your attentions toward Gwen. I know it sounds silly, and I'm really embarrassed about it now, so I just wanted to apologize."

"That's quite all right," I said, feeling even more inane, and watching the courtyard beyond them for a tall, thin form.

"Well, I'm glad you don't hold it against me," said Jon with a grin. "I told my mother all about our glass telephones. I told her I'd let her know as soon as we had them working!"

"Yes, indeed," I said, standing up. I thought I saw a flicker of motion and wanted to investigate.

"We won't keep you, sir," said Gwen. "And I'll still be bringing you your breakfast in the morning."

"In that case," I said in my gravest voice, "I want you to know that the girl who brought me breakfast this morning brought me a stale donut. And the tea was cold."

This sent both Gwen and Jon into gales of laughter, and they went off, still holding hands, while I started walking as quietly as possible down the courtyard.

Here there were outside staircases leading up to some of the ladies' chambers. The angle of the sun was such that I was dazzled, looking up toward the chamber windows, shading my eyes and blinking. But between two blinks, I thought I saw the door of the Lady Maria's chamber opening and closing.

I ran up the stairs two at a time, rapped on the door, and opened it without waiting for an answer.

She was sitting by the window, sewing something lacy and pink. It appeared to be something a man shouldn't see, so I carefully kept my eyes from it.

She was, quite naturally, very startled. "What is it? What's happening?"

"Did someone just come in here?"

"No! Of course not," she said, staring at me with wide blue eyes.

I did not believe her. But I saw no one there now, and I couldn't call her a liar to her face. "Excuse me, then," I said and backed out the door.

I scanned the courtyard from the landing but saw nothing. I refused to believe that the Lady Maria was acting from evil intent. I had touched her mind when we were experimenting with the telephones, even if very briefly, and I thought I should be able to tell if she had embraced the powers of darkness. But how did she know the stranger, and why was she lying?

I went slowly down the outside stairs, shivering again; I never had gotten my coat. Maria might perhaps be trying to shield somebody. She had told me she had "requested" certain magic favors, and I presumed she had requested them from someone in the castle. It would be that person, then, who had enlisted the stranger's help in practicing black magic. I still had no idea who the stranger was, but I was suddenly convinced I knew who had wanted to cast the evil spell on the castle.

It had to be the queen. Ever since I had met her and had fallen in love with her, I had refused to harbor any suspicions against her, but there was no rational reason why I shouldn't. The Lady Maria, even if she guessed that her beloved niece was mixing dark supernatural powers with her magic spells, would never allow anyone *else* to suspect her. There still seemed to be no easy explanation why the queen had married the king, unless she hoped in a few years to be a widowed queen, able to rule Yurt as she wished, never again having to fear being married off to someone she detested.

There was a cry of, "There he is!" from the far side of the castle, and the group of pursuers shot into view. The queen was in the lead, her skirts and shawl billowing. Her long black hair had come unpinned and was flying out behind her. Dominic, the constable, and a group of knights ran close beside her. In another context, I would have found it hilarious.

I didn't see the stranger, although they had. He must have gotten by me, if indeed I had seen him here by the Lady Maria's door, and had not imagined it while dazzled by the sun. He clearly was able to make himself invisible if he wished, and he did not have my problem of invisibility stopping at the knees. *He* was certainly finding the chase hilarious.

It was well past time for it to stop. I saw him then, walking quickly but unconcernedly along the parapets. I set my teeth and began preparing a paralysis spell.

A paralysis spell is complicated, and I had only ever cast one successfully once, over a year ago, when I had frozen another young wizard in the middle of the classroom. Then it had worked spectacularly well, even though the instructor had spoken to me *very* firmly after class. I put the words of the Hidden Language together as rapidly as I could and cast it toward the stranger's retreating back.

This time the spell did not work at all. The stranger kept on walking, just as unconcernedly, and then either slipped into a doorway or made himself invisible again. I ran down into the courtyard to intercept the others.

They were all panting, even the queen, and quite willing to stop. "This person is a wizard," I said, even though I did not think of him as a wizard in the sense that I was one, or Zahlfast was, or the old Master in the City or my predecessor down in the forest. But it was too complicated at the moment to explain that this was someone able to walk through my best spells—and probably responsible for breaking my magic locks. "He's deliberately making us chase him, to tease us, because he knows he can always disappear when we get close."

"But can't you stop him with magic?" said the constable.

"His magic is nearly as strong as mine," I said. This was a wild understatement, but Dominic was glowering at me as though it were all my fault. "I'm trying to stop him, but it may take me a while. At the moment, I don't think he's doing any damage to the castle. But we don't want him to escape before I've had a chance to capture him and find out who he is and why he's come here."

I turned to Dominic. "Let me have the cellar key. If I catch him, I'll lock him down there. Meanwhile, rather than amusing him by running around the court-yard any longer, let's stop until I've found a way to break down his magic defenses. But put a guard on the gate, to be sure he doesn't sneak back out."

Privately, I was rather hoping he *would* sneak back out. If he made himself invisible, he would have no trouble slipping past guards at the gate, unless they put the drawbridge up, which I didn't think they would do. I had never seen the bridge raised since coming to Yurt, and the rest of the castle servants weren't all back yet. And even then, this stranger who was impervious to a paralysis spell, which had taken the instructor five minutes to break the last time I used it, would have no trouble flying over the walls.

The pursuers all agreed readily. Dominic handed me the rusty cellar key without comment. Even the queen had had enough of this fruitless chase. But as she stood next to me, her bosom rising and falling with her rapid breaths, I again found it impossible to suspect her. If she had married the king in the hopes of being a widow soon, why had she nursed him so tenderly when he was ill and been so grateful when he was healed?

The others went in search of lunch, but I got a coat from my chambers and sat down on a bench in the courtyard, where I could watch the gate. Dominic put two knights there to guard as well. I wished the chaplain would come back soon.

Several times during the afternoon I caught a glimpse of the stranger. New attempts at casting a paralysis spell on him had no more effect than had the first attempt. I did, however, miss with one of my efforts and catch one of the stable boys. He froze, as unmoving as wood, in the middle of the courtyard, and it took me ten minutes and a quick trip to my books to break the spell and free him. Fortunately, we were around the corner from the guards at the gate, and when motion suddenly returned to him he just shook his head, looked at me as though embarrassed to have gone into a sudden reverie in my presence, and hurried back to the stables.

At one point in the afternoon I became so desperate that I decided to try to telephone Zahlfast. I got down one of my glass telephones, added a few spells that I hoped might make it work this time, and spoke the number of the school telephone. But it worked no better than it had for Maria and me. I could see a young wizard answering it, but he could neither hear nor see me, and in a moment he hung up with a gesture of irritation.

All right, I thought. Zahlfast had told me that they didn't want the young wizards asking for help with every little problem anyway. I would have to solve this one myself.

I realized that, by refusing to chase the stranger, I

was giving him the opportunity to talk at leisure to the Lady Maria or anyone else he wished, but I was fairly sure he would be able to do whatever he wanted anyway, even with me close at his heels.

Several times, when he had not shown himself for twenty minutes or more, I hoped that he had gone, slipped back to wherever he had come from. But when, with trepidation, I tried probing for him, he was always there, a mind so evil that I was always shaken even when expecting it. He seemed deliberately to be mocking me. My spells did not have any effect on him, but his very presence nearly paralyzed *me*.

And then, very suddenly, he was gone. I did not see him, and I did not feel him. I probed delicately, then boldly, and found only the same oblique evil touch that I had long felt in the castle. Not knowing whether to be jubilant or wary at this abrupt departure, I looked up and saw Joachim crossing the bridge into the castle.

I ran to meet him, looking with some apprehension up into his face.

He was actually smiling. "The little boy is fine," he said as I helped him dismount. "I do not think he was ever dangerously ill. The doctor's draught had, I believe, already put him well toward recovery, and the village priest's prayers had assisted him long before I even arrived."

"That's wonderful," I said. It sounded inadequate, even in my own ears, but at least it was better than, "How nice," or, "Congratulations!"

"It looks like I'm even in time for supper," said Joachim, still smiling. "I don't know about you, but I'm in the mood for one of our cook's excellent dinners after the overspiced food we were served at the duchess's castle."

I carried his saddlebag up to his room for him, then left him to change and wash for supper while I returned to my chambers to do the same. At first I only felt an intense relief that he was back and the stranger gone. But while I was drying my face, I began to wonder how the two events were related. Perhaps his saintly presence was enough to drive away someone embroiled with evil, in which case I never wanted him to leave the castle again, no matter who might be sick in the village.

But perhaps in some way he *was* the stranger. This was such a terrifying thought that I froze with my face in the towel. I had never known of such a thing directly, but one heard stories and rumors. When he left, as the good, pious chaplain, perhaps he left behind his twin, evil self, who then was able to run wild through the castle until the good self returned and the two were again united.

I shook the towel out with much more than necessary energy. This was the kind of story the young wizards liked to tell the new students when they first arrived. In any event, I was going to do my best to see that the good, pious chaplain did not leave again.

IV

The morning of the day of Christmas Eve dawned snowy, but by the time I had eaten my cruller and drunk my tea—both brought to my door satisfyingly hot by Gwen, who had a sprig of holly in her hair—the sun had come out, and the snow in the courtyard sparkled like diamonds. It seemed almost a shame when the stable boys came out with big brooms to sweep it aside.

The duchess, the two counts, and the old wizard were coming that evening. Preparations for Christmas had kept everyone busy enough that they seemed to have forgotten about the elusive stranger and to be satisfied with my statement that he had vanished magically in the late afternoon, and that while I still did not know where he had come from, I was fairly confident he was not coming back.

An enormous fir had been cut in the forest the day before and set up in the corner of the great hall overnight, while the snow dried from its branches. Now, under the queen's supervision, the servants hoisted it upright at the head of the hall. Boxes of ornaments were brought out, and the queen and the Lady Maria spent much of the morning running up and down stepladders hanging the decorations. There were glistening silver stars, angels made of lace and velvet, colored balls that reflected the light, tiny wreaths made of straw, red velvet bows, and scores of tiny magic lights, made years ago by my predecessor. The king himself climbed on a ladder to help hang these deep in the branches of the tree, where they shone with a pure white gleam.

I brushed my best clothes and worked on the magic tricks I knew I would be called on to perform in the next few days. Since the old wizard was going to be there, with illusions much more solid and realistic than anything I could produce, I was going to have to find other ways to keep the royal party and their guests amused during the twelve days of Christmas.

I decided to try some transformations. I spent much of the day with *Basic Metamorphosis* and *Elements of Transmogrification,* actually realizing at last exactly where I had gone wrong with the frogs.

In the three weeks since the stranger's appearance and subsequent disappearance, I had been able to make no progress in determining who he was or where he had come from. I suspected everyone in the castle in turn, except for the king—even the boys being trained as knights in Yurt. I wished I dared tell Joachim my fears, but every time I decided that he was the presence of good that was keeping evil at bay, I found myself suspecting that the stranger might have been the manifestation of his own evil side.

I remembered when I had first come to Yurt I had wondered what I would be doing to fill my time away from the City. Somehow my days had become so busy that I had not even made any progress on the telephones, even though I had intermittently tried one or another new spell. At one point I had promised myself to complete them for the queen for a Christmas present, but that was impossible now.

In the late afternoon, we started looking out for our guests. The cook and the kitchen maids had been baking for days, and the smell of pies, cakes, crullers, and bread, mixed with the piny smell from the Christmas tree and the evergreen boughs hung throughout the castle, was almost overwhelming. I stood by the gate, looking out toward the sunset. The air was clear and still, and the sun was framed by the red and ice-blue of winter.

The stable boys went out with lanterns and poles, which they pushed into the ground at intervals along the road up the hill, so that the lanterns could light our guests' final approach. At the bottom of the hill, they met a figure on foot.

I recognized the old wizard, even at a distance, and went down to meet him. In his tall white hat, leaning on his oaken staff, he was unmistakable. As I came closer, I could see that he had brought the calico cat, perched on his shoulder.

"Welcome, Master," I said, doing the full bow in spite of the thin layer of ice on the road under my knees. I gave the stable boys a stern sideways look, and they ran back up to the castle, doubtless eager to tell the rest of the staff about the meeting between the old and new wizards.

"Greetings, young whippersnapper," he said in what was for him a cordial tone. "Getting too high and mighty in the castle to come see me much anymore, huh?"

"I've been busy all fall," I said. "I'm delighted to see you. We'll have plenty of time to talk while you're here." Although I did not mention it immediately, the principal topic on which I had to talk to him was the north tower. He would certainly find out very quickly that his magic locks were gone. Although he would have to admit, once I had told him about the stranger, that I had not been personally responsible, he would still certainly feel it had somehow been my fault for letting supernatural influences into the castle in the first place. He had told me unequivocally that there had been no supernatural powers in Yurt in his day, and although I didn't actually believe this, he might think it was true.

"I notice no one thought of sending a horse for me," he said, leaning on his staff going up the hill. "Just because I'm a wizard, no one remembers that I'm also an old man, and walking for miles in the winter is not easy."

I had already noticed that his white hair was windblown beneath his hat, in spite of the still air, and had concluded that he had flown most of the way, only setting down on the ground once he was within view of the castle. I decided not to mention this.

The constable and his wife met us at the bridge, with kind greetings to which the old wizard responded primarily with snorts, although I knew him well enough to see that he was actually extremely pleased to be remembered so fondly. "Let me show you the guest room we've prepared for you," said the constable, leading the way toward the rooms beyond the south tower.

"Perhaps I could have a word with you now, Master?" I said, hurrying beside him. It would be much better if I could tell him about the empty tower before rather than after he found out for himself.

"Later, young wizard, later," he said. "An old man gets tired after walking for miles, and I have to prepare for some really spectacular illusions over dessert. You probably haven't been able to equal anything of mine, have you?"

Since this didn't seem to call for an answer I didn't give one. Here, at the farthest point in the castle from the north tower, he would not accidentally notice the missing magic locks. Perhaps I could wait and tell him after dinner. My only fear was that he would slip out of his room to check them himself as soon as I was gone.

He turned on some of his own magic lamps in his room and closed the door behind him. As I was wondering whether I should leave him alone or knock in a few minutes, there was the sound of horses' hooves, jingling bridles, and voices calling from the gate. The rest of our guests had arrived.

The two counts and the duchess had apparently met on the road, and they all arrived together. For several minutes, there was a jumble of greetings, laughter, people running to and fro, and the constable taking the guests and their parties to the rooms prepared for them. The king and queen came out into the courtyard to welcome them. I stayed out of the way, wandering over to the north tower and its door locked only with a bolt, not with magic. I stayed there for half an hour while it grew darker and colder, but the old wizard never came.

After half an hour, I heard the brass choir start playing Christmas carols and knew that dinner would shortly be served. The secret of the tower was safe for now from the old wizard. I hurried to the great hall to be formally introduced to the counts.

One of the counts was fairly old, about the king's age, and his wife was a round and smiling middle-aged woman who looked as I had originally expected the queen to look. Their sons, they told me, were off adventuring in the eastern kingdoms and had not been able to come home for Christmas.

The other count was young, probably my age, and had come into his inheritance just last winter. He had beautiful alabaster skin, wavy chestnut hair (about the color mine would be if I hadn't dyed it gray), and gold rings on every long finger. Looking at me imperiously from wide-spaced brown eyes, he had the look of mystery and authority I had always hoped I projected but knew I did not.

I did the full bow to him as I had already done to the old count and his wife and to the duchess. The latter had actually put on a dress in honor of Christmas Eve. It was a lovely dark wine color that suited her well, but it was also exactly the same shade as what the queen was wearing, even though the two dresses were styled very differently. I noticed the cousins looking at each other sideways with little flarings of the nostrils. The duchess looked at me, however, with a small and somewhat ironical smile, as though interested in seeing my reaction to the counts.

"So you have a new wizard," said the young count to the king in what I was pleased to note was a high and rather nasal voice. "I myself would never have one. I'd been hoping that when your old one retired you'd have the sense not to get another."

Since I had just finished bowing to him, and my predecessor was standing only ten feet away, this struck me as unusually rude, even for a member of the aristocracy, but he kept on talking about us as though we weren't there. "My father kept a wizard— or he *said* he was a wizard, someone I think my father had picked up at a carnival somewhere—but as soon as I inherited, I sent him packing right away, you can be sure."

"We've always been very happy with our wizards," said the king stiffly.

"Is there anything in particular you object to about

wizards?" asked my predecessor with a calmness that he was having trouble maintaining.

"Everything about them is so, well, on the surface!" said the young count, waving his beautiful white hands. "Once you've seen an illusion or two, you have nothing left but vague talk about the powers of darkness and light, which someone like me sees through at once."

"I think you're underestimating real wizardry," continued my predecessor, with an evenness of tone I admired.

"You're the wizard who used to be here, aren't you? My father told me about your illusions over dessert, back when he used to visit the king. But really, when you go beyond illusions, what do you have?"

I turned him into a frog.

There was total, horrified silence in the great hall as everyone stopped breathing. The only sound was the crackling of the great logs in the fireplace. Where the young count had stood a minute ago, a large green bullfrog squatted on the flagstones, looking up at us with human eyes. The eyes seemed confused and rather alarmed.

The frog's wide, pale throat pumped with its breathing. It took one hop toward me, then paused to look around again.

The old wizard's cat broke the silence with a hiss. Immediately there was a babble of voices. The wizard took the cat firmly in his arms. "Hold on," I said cheerfully. "I'll have him turned back into a count in just a minute. I've been working on transformations all day, so this shouldn't give me any trouble. I chose a frog because frogs, who metamorphose naturally during their lifetimes, are very easy subjects for the magic of transformation."

No one seemed particularly interested in this insight into wizardry. They had all stepped backwards and were looking at me in trepidation.

But it did indeed take only a few seconds for me to return him to himself, once I had decided he had been a frog long enough to respect wizards more in the future. But as I said the words to restore him, I also added a few words to create an illusion of pale green color on his alabaster skin. It would fade shortly, but I thought it would be a healthy reminder of the powers of wizardry. If I had done this well in the transformation practical, there never would have been a question about Zahlfast passing me.

The count, restored, stared at me with eyes that seemed much more appropriate in a human's face than they had in a frog's, but he said nothing.

"Well," said the king in in his best jolly voice. "I can see the after-dinner entertainment has already begun, but shall we eat before we have any more? I know the cook has been busy today!"

The brass players had stopped playing to stare down from their greenery-hung balcony, but they quickly resumed as we all went toward the tables. Several extra tables had had to be set up, all glittering with the best silver and crystal.

As we jostled and found our places, I discovered the chaplain at my elbow. "Are you sure this wanton meddling with God's creation does not endanger your soul?" he said into my ear.

I laughed and shook my head. I personally thought the young count's soul might be improved by a wholesome lesson in humility, but decided not to mention this. I was suddenly very hungry.

V

I noticed at dinner that no one talked to me as freely as they normally did, not even the Lady Maria, who was, as usual, seated at my right hand, though one advantage of having guests was that Dominic had been positioned at a different table. Being freed from having to provide entertaining conversation gave me more attention to pay to one of the cook's finest efforts. By the time the mince pie was brought in, I was so full that I found I could only take two pieces.

When everyone was down to about half a piece of pie, from which they periodically extracted a raisin or a flaky piece of crust to munch with a sip of tea, the king said, "Well, Wizard!" to my predecessor. "Are you going to provide us some entertainments like you used to?" I noticed that the servants who had been taking empty dishes down to the kitchen had all returned to the seats at their table.

The wizard nodded, giving a rather smug smile. "I think I might be able to provide something to while away a few minutes."

He rose, leaving the calico cat sitting on his chair with its tail wrapped tidily around its paws. From his pocket the wizard took a dozen gold rings and arranged them carefully in front of the fire.

I realized what he was doing. Complicated illusions might take up to an hour or more to create, but it was possible to perform most of the spell, stopping short of the end, and then tie that spell to an object, where it would last a day or so. An unfinished spell would start to fade after that time, but if one did one's illusions fairly soon, one would have the advantage of being able to perform something highly spectacular with only a few words of the Hidden Language. The object to which the unfinished spell was attached could be almost anything, but the wizard's rings certainly added a nice touch. I never did illusions that way myself, except once for a class exercise, always being too impatient.

The old wizard picked up the first ring, held it toward the company, and said a few quick words. Immediately a light green sapling sprang up from the flagstone floor. It grew and grew, reaching branches now covered with pale pink blossoms toward the ceiling. For a second there was even a whiff of rose petals. I determined to ask him to teach me how to do that at the next possible opportunity; they had never taught us how to do illusory scents in the City.

Now the blossoms were changing, becoming long green leaves, as the tree was gently buffeted by a summer breeze, and for a second the hall was filled not with the smell of evergreen but with the scent of new-mown hay. Then the leaves darkened, became crimson and blood-red, and fell in silent showers, accompanied by a dark, woodsy smell of wood and earth. But the tree was not bare, for now white stars glistened in its branches. As the smell of the Christmas tree again returned, the stars cascaded to the earth, and the whole illusory tree quietly dissolved.

The company had been watching silently, except for a few murmurs of "Oooh" or "Ohh" from the ladies. But now loud applause burst out. I glanced toward the young count and saw that even he was applauding with great assiduousness. I was glad I was not going to try to match illusions with the old wizard.

He acknowledged the applause with only a bob of the head, but I could tell he was highly gratified. He positioned his next two rings, said the words to finish the spell, and stepped back.

This time two winged horses appeared, life-size and alabaster white—whiter than the young count's skin had ever been, even before I tinted it green. Flapping their enormous, feathered wings, they rose in absolute stillness, hovered over our heads for a moment while striking at each other with their hooves, then, side by side, soared the length of the hall and back again, to land lightly by the fire and dissolve in a shower of sparks.

Then the wizard changed the mood, making his next illusion a clown. It looked at first like a person, wearing baggy multicolored clothing, its face painted different colors. But then it began to dance, kicking enormous feet high into the air, and as it danced its neck suddenly grew to six feet long and shrank back again, its shoulders sprouted first wings and then rose-bushes, and an extra two legs grew from its hips and danced harder than ever. The eyes winked hugely, the wide mouth leered and grinned. The whole party was weak with laughter when the clown did a final bow and disappeared with a pop.

The old wizard kept us entertained for close to an hour. Some of his illusions were beautiful, some funny, and all finer than anything I had seen produced in the City. For his final one, he started with a small Christmas tree, which grew toward the ceiling and was suddenly transformed into a giant red Father Noel, who smiled and bowed to us all before dissolving away.

As the thunderous applause died down, the wizard returned to his place, doing a fairly good job of hiding his pleasure. "Any more of that pie left?" he said. "Illusions are hungry work."

People stood up then, stretching and talking. There were still nearly two hours until midnight service in the chapel. I wondered if the old wizard might take advantage of the interval to go check the north tower. But he seemed content, after a final piece of pie, to sit down in a rocking chair the queen brought out for him, and doze by the fire with the cat on his lap and a small smile on his face. He must have risen before dawn, I thought, to start preparing those illusions and have them attached to the rings before he started for the castle.

The rest of the royal party and the guest stood or sat near the fire, chatting while the servants cleared the tables. The king was talking to the two counts and the duchess with great animation, but I noticed the queen sitting by herself, near the base of the Christmas tree. I took a chair and went to sit next to her.

She looked up at me with a smile. "I hope you realize we are very happy with you as Royal Wizard," she said, "even if you don't do illusions like your predecessor!"

I personally thought that my dragon and giant had been at least as impressive in their own way, even though they had lacked the visual solidity of the old wizard's productions, especially since I had created them entirely on the spot. But I looked into the emerald eyes and knew that this comment had been meant to be reassuring.

"I'm very happy being at Yurt, so I'm glad you think that," I said. We were far enough from the rest of the party, and everybody else was talking loudly enough, that our conversation was highly private. I had drunk quite a bit of wine with dinner. "You know," I said, "I'm very much in love with you."

This confession was met with a pleased laugh. She clearly did not believe a word of it, but she did take and squeeze my hand. "When you turned the count into a frog," she said, "he really *was* a frog, wasn't he? That wasn't just an illusion."

"No, he really was a frog. If I hadn't changed him back, or another wizard changed him back, he would have stayed a frog for the rest of his life. Of course, inside, he would still be himself. He just wouldn't be able to talk or make insulting comments about wizards."

She laughed again. "You *are* a fine wizard, but it's probably just as well you changed him back."

"Could I ask you something, my lady?" I said. I actually wanted to ask if she could ever love me too, but I was fairly sure I already knew the answer to that. "I'm afraid it's a fairly personal question."

"Well, what is it?"

"I want to know why you decided to marry the king."

If it hadn't been for the wine, I would have been

quite shocked at my boldness. She did not seem shocked, however, but looked fondly toward him, as he talked to his subjects in front of the fire.

"Was it to keep him from marrying the duchess?"

She turned back toward me, laughing again. "Oh dear, is it that obvious? No, I don't think he was ever in danger of marrying her, so that wasn't the reason. I just fell in love with him."

I did not reply. This answer seemed quite inadequate.

But she had drunk quite a bit of wine at dinner as well. "You know I'm my parents' only child," she said at last. I nodded, waiting for her to continue. "They were of course eager to see me married. And of course, like parents everywhere, they wanted me to marry well, marry at least a castellan like my father, but preferably a count or duke."

I thought I could guess what was coming.

"They kept on introducing me to young men from throughout the western kingdoms. Maybe my Aunt Maria was the worst. She always tried to make the young men seem romantic, charming, wonderful, to the point that I already despised them before I met them. I actually enjoyed being introduced to lots of young men, because there were all sorts of opportunities for dances, for hunting parties, for buying new clothes, but I couldn't imagine actually marrying any of them. They were all, frankly, silly, vain, or shallow—or all three.

"We'd exhausted several kingdoms already before we came to Yurt. The last man they tried was the young count of Yurt." She nodded in his direction. The green had by now worn off his skin.

"He wasn't count yet, as his father was still alive four years ago, when my parents tried to persuade me to marry him. But his personality was already—shall we say—fully developed." She went into a series of giggles at this point that made several people look in our direction.

After a moment she regained her composure. "I told my parents I was going to become a nun, that I would enter the Nunnery of Yurt and spend the rest of my life in prayer and pious devotions. They were horrified, of course, and as I look back I'm quite horrified myself at my determination. I almost managed to do it."

"I have trouble seeing you as a nun, my lady."

"So do I, now. But I told them they had one final chance, to introduce me to a young man I would like before I took my vows of chastity. We were on our way to meet somebody, I don't even remember who, now, when we stopped at the duchess's castle—her mother and my mother were second cousins.

"As it turned out, the royal family of Yurt was visiting the duchess at the same time. I think my father had some idea of making a match between Prince Dominic and me, which would certainly have been more advantageous than whoever, in the next kingdom over, he had originally chosen for his final effort—Dominic is, after all, royal heir to Yurt.

"But my father reckoned without the king! He fell in love with me, and since nobody at all was trying to persuade me that he was young and gallant and charming, I fell in love with him! He actually *is* more gallant and charming than anyone I've ever met."

She looked toward him dreamily, even though he appeared at the moment to be telling an especially hilarious joke to the duchess. I was quite sure she would never call *me* charming and gallant.

"That's a wonderfully charming story," I said. This seemed to put a final end to the theory that she had put an evil spell on the king, and I was delighted to see the theory go.

"What are you two laughing about over there?" called the king. "Come here, my dear. The countess says she has some very interesting news you would like to hear, some gossip from the City."

The queen gave me a quick smile and sprang up, and in a moment she and the old count's wife were talking with their heads together. I guessed that the interesting news was about the new winter fashions, since the countess drew out a newspaper folded open to a page of sketches.

I sat back, my feet stretched in front of me, and did my best, in a spirit of Christmas-time charity, not to suspect Joachim of almost having killed the king. It seemed ironic that the queen and the chaplain, the two people in Yurt whom I liked the most, were the two people to whom my thoughts kept returning whenever I wondered who might have become involved with renegade magic.

Just before midnight, we all started up the narrow stairs to the chapel. I was worried that the old wizard would take the opportunity of being alone to slip off to the north tower, but to my surprise—and I think almost everyone else's—he said he would join us at service. "I've been wanting to see these lamps you told me about, young whippersnapper," he said affectionately.

For Christmas Eve, even the chapel was decorated with evergreen boughs, and some of the candles on the altar were red and green as well as white. Everyone in the castle was there, crowded together companionably on the benches. The chaplain's vestments were brand new, brought up from the City on the pack train with all the constable's orders just a few days ago. He read us the Christmas story, which while we all knew it well was always worth hearing again, before proceeding to the service itself.

The only way I could suspect him was to assume that he had done something truly evil, such as dealing with a demon, but that he had then just as truly repented, because otherwise his prayers would not have healed the king. But if he was truly repentant, he could have nothing to do with the stranger, and his presence could not be related to the sense of evil I still sometimes felt. I was left being forced to think that the stranger was someone totally foreign to the castle, who had come here to practice black magic—perhaps in our cellars—for his own purposes, but this was a very unsatisfactory explanation. The queen had come to Yurt, the king had grown ill, the old chaplain had died, and the present chaplain had arrived, all within a year, and there had to be some connection.

"Merry Christmas! Merry Christmas!" we all told each other as we separated after service. The stars were bright and incredibly distant in a black and icy sky. I watched as the old wizard, his face holding the same determinedly skeptical expression it had had throughout the service, went toward his room. He showed no sign of going to inspect the north tower. "Sweet dreams of presents!" somebody called, and there was a general laugh as the guests retired to their chambers and the castle party to theirs.

PART SIX
Christmas
I

Christmas morning dawned bright and clear. Since there were so many guests in the castle, rather than having the serving maids bring us our breakfasts individually we all assembled in the great hall. Here the cook had produced another masterpiece. Whole hams, platters of steaming sausages and eggs, donuts, crullers, and giant silver teapots were set out on the tables. Everyone was in a jolly Christmas mood; I even saw the chaplain smiling at a joke.

Once we had eaten, it was time for the presents. Packages wrapped in red and green paper, presents from the king and queen to everyone in the castle, were piled under the Christmas tree. The queen distributed these with smiles and laughter. Most of us received gifts of gold coins, or rings, or clothing. I received a new velvet suit, of midnight blue, which I wished I could try on at once. Even our guests received small presents, and the old wizard had to smile when he pulled out a gold ring shaped like an eagle in flight, holding a tiny diamond in its beak. The calico cat played in the scattered ribbon, chasing and biting it.

Then the husbands and wives and lovers gave each other gifts, some of them apparently jokes that they wouldn't let the rest of us see, although they giggled quite a bit. I tried unsuccessfully to spot what was in the box Jon gave Gwen, though it made her smile and blush a most becoming pink before she slammed the lid back on. Most of the ladies received such a present, though not the Lady Maria.

At this point on Christmas morning, it was usually time for Father Noel to come in with presents for the children, except that we had no children in the royal castle of Yurt. The serving girls and stable boys, even the boys being trained in knighthood, were all old enough that they would have been acutely embarrassed to receive a gift from Father Noel. But I knew someone who would love such a gift.

I slipped out while the knights and ladies were still teasing each other over their presents. In my room, I hastily put on my old red velvet pullover, stuffed the stomach round with socks, and draped a piece of rabbit fur I had gotten from the constable's wife around my neck. A little illusion made my eyebrows and beard bushy and white.

"Ho, ho, ho, boys and girls!" I cried as I reentered the hall. "And have you all been *good* little boys and girls this year?" They recognized me at once, in spite of the disguise, and everyone except one of the boys, who clearly thought he was about to be embarrassed publicly, laughed heartily.

"I've just got one present today, for an especially good little girl," I said, in my best jolly tone. "Let's see, there's a tag on this present, it will tell you who's the lucky girl!"

I made a major production of reaching into my sack and slowly pulling out a large box wrapped in red. "Let me see," reading the tag, "I think this says the present is for, let me be sure here, for someone named Maria. Is there a *very* good girl named Maria here today?"

She laughed with delight, as I knew she would, and came forward for the box. I let the white bushy beard fade back to my own beard as we watched her open it.

Inside the first box, which she opened with giggles of anticipation, was, not the present she was expecting, but another box, this one wrapped in green. Inside the second box was a much smaller one, this one golden. But inside the third box was the present.

She drew it out slowly, unfolding it to gasps of appreciation from the other ladies. It was a white silk shawl, printed with irises, which I had had packed up from the City earlier in the week. It was big enough to drape over her entire upper body, but delicate enough to be folded into a bundle smaller than her hand.

She put it over her shoulders at once. "Thank you, Father Noel! This is the nicest present this good little girl has ever gotten!"

With general laughter and more joking, people now stood up to go outside, to catch a little fresh air and try to find some sort of appetite for the noon dinner that the cook was already preparing. I hurried back to my chambers to take off the pullover and put on my new blue velvet suit. It fit perfectly. As I turned in front of the mirror, I thought that even if I didn't look mysterious in it, at least I looked dignified.

Back in the courtyard, several of the ladies had begun singing Christmas carols in three-part harmony. It would have been more effective if one of the knights hadn't been teasing them, which made them keep stopping, laughing, and losing their place, but the sound of their high, light voices in the frosty air was very pleasant. As I leaned on the parapet, high above the courtyard, looking out across the snowy hills of the western kingdoms, I thought this was a morning of perfect peace.

A gloved hand closed over mine on the railing, and I discovered the duchess beside me. I had not seen her come up. "Merry Christmas," she said. "I'd been thinking I ought to have a special present for you this morning, but after you gave that shawl to the Lady Maria I realized I'd be wasting my time."

She was teasing me, of course. "Oh, I can love any number of different ladies at the same time," I said airily, gesturing with my free hand. "After all—"

Her grip tightened, but I realized she was not listening to me. "Look, over there. What's that?" she said in an entirely different voice.

I looked. Beyond the forest, high above the hills, a dark cloud was coming rapidly toward us out of the north. But it was flying too low and moving too fast to be a cloud. For a moment I wondered if it might be the air cart, bringing someone to visit from the wizards' school, even though it was coming from the wrong direction. But as it approached, I realized it was much too big to be the air cart.

It was a dragon.

The duchess and I were not the only ones up walking on the parapet, and several other people had seen it too. One lady screamed, but several other people looked toward me questioningly, and one even laughed a little. They thought it might be another illusion.

This was, unfortunately, no illusion, but a real dragon. "Get down!" I yelled. "Get inside!" I grabbed the duchess in my arms and leaped off the edge of the walkway, flying us down and landing in the courtyard with hardly a bump. "Don't let it catch you outdoors!"

Although for a second I was afraid that blind panic would replace complacency, as all the ladies began screaming at once, I did manage to get them herded into the center of the hall. "Keep them calm," I told the duchess. "I've got to try to stop it."

I ran back to the high door out into the courtyard. The dragon had arrived.

It flew to the castle with extreme purposefulness, but now that it was here it seemed to be contemplating its next move with leisurely interest. It was perched on the top of the north tower, looking around with apparent curiosity. Then it looked down at me like a cat observing a mouse. It was too big to fit in the windows or even the door, but if it had wished it could easily reach in a clawed foot to grab us. I was almost gratified to see that it quite closely resembled the illusory dragon I had created last month, down to the emerald scales, even though mine had had six legs and this one four. But the red eyes did not glow with magic: rather, with active intelligence.

What was I going to do with a dragon? My mind seemed incapable of thought. For a moment the dragon and I locked glances, then it shot out a thin tongue of flame from its nostrils, and I had to jump back.

I found Joachim at my elbow. He had his crucifix before him and a grim expression on his face. "Don't go out," I said. "It's not evil; it's just a dragon."

"But it could kill us all!"

"Of course it could, and it probably will. It's doubtless very hungry after flying for thousands of miles, down from the northern land of magic. In a few minutes it may decide to start dismantling the castle with its claws. But it's still not evil incarnate, just the wild forces of natural magic, unchecked by any wizardry."

If Joachim was startled to hear this calm, academic statement he gave no sign. I was fairly startled myself to discover that my mind was compensating for a lack of good ideas by the repetition of a phrase from a half-forgotten lecture.

But *why* was there a dragon in Yurt? The dragons never, or almost never, left the northernmost land of wild magic. I caught a glimpse of the old wizard from the corner of my eye and remembered him saying that he thought that too many wizards practicing magic had worn the channels of magic so smooth that anything might come slipping in.

But surely my own magic was rough enough not to invite a dragon! The wizard at any rate did not say, "I told you so." He stood next to the chaplain and me, while we looked out at the dragon and it looked at us, and both sides tried to think what to do next. Until such time as it decided to start ripping the walls down, we were fairly safe, because I did not think it could reach all the way to the center of the great hall, in spite of its size.

The dragon was truly enormous. Its feet were planted on top of the north tower, its long scaly neck stretched far across the courtyard, and its spiny tail hung nearly to the ground. Its red eyes darted to and fro, and its wide mouth lolled open, revealing hundreds of teeth and a long forked tongue. It seemed to be wondering which ones of us to eat first.

The old wizard attacked. Suddenly, zipping around the dragon's head, there was a cloud of red bubbles, which darted, touched him, and sprang away again. But if this was intended to distract the dragon or even drive him away, it was ineffective. Clinging to the doorpost, thinking this had to be a bad dream and that Gwen would wake me soon, I watched as the dragon batted the bubbles of illusion away with one clawed foot and looked down at us with growing irritation.

There was a commotion behind us, and then Dominic and the duchess pushed past us, leading a group of knights. They were all armed with swords, spears, and shields, and several carried bows. Dominic may have bolted in terror from my illusory dragon, but he seemed to have no hesitation in facing a real one. I was ashamed that he, at least, seemed to have an excellent idea what to do.

With a roar from Dominic, the small war party charged. They ran up the stairs toward the parapet, trying to get closer, and the first archers set off a flurry of arrows.

But these bounced harmlessly from the emerald scales. The dragon turned sharply around, and as its tail swung it ripped roof slates loose. The knights and the duchess had their shields up just in time to protect themselves from a roaring burst of flame. As the dragon readied itself for another breath, they lowered the shields for a second and threw their spears.

Most of the spears bounced off as harmlessly as the arrows had done, but one lodged for a second in the dragon's throat. It reared back, clawing at this spear until it fell, but where it had pierced the skin was a tiny drop of black blood.

"The dragon's throat," said the old wizard in my ear. "It's the one vulnerable point on its body."

But the knights did not have a chance to try throwing their spears again. The dragon leaped at them, beating its scaled wings, and with a swipe of a claw knocked several into the courtyard, where they landed with metallic crashes. Then the dragon sprang upward and circled over the castle, its head back, roaring in pain. In the few seconds before it returned, we ran out into the courtyard, helped the knights gather up their companions, and dragged them into the relative safety of the hall.

All of them were scorched, and several were badly wounded. Dominic, who had been knocked off the wall, seemed to have several broken ribs. He was the worst, but all had suffered in one way or another. The duchess was not directly wounded, but all her hair, where it protruded from her helmet, had been burned off.

The dragon returned to the top of the north tower, where it lashed its tail and looked down at us with real fury. I glanced over my shoulder. The chaplain was helping deal with the wounded. Most of the women in the castle were clinging together in the center of the hall, all with white faces and many sobbing uncontrollably. The king and queen, their hands linked, were embracing as many as they could reach, ladies and servants alike, and trying to talk soothingly.

I was shocked to see a dancing pair of blue eyes among the stricken faces. The Lady Maria, with rapt attention, was thoroughly enjoying the dragon.

The duchess was exchanging her shield for another, less scorched, and picking up a spear as though planning to go out again. "Stay here," I told her. "You can't stop it with force." My slow mind had at last given me an idea.

I started to make myself invisible. I started with the feet, pronouncing the heavy syllables of the Hidden Language as quickly as I could. The feet disappeared, then the knees, then the thighs, and I was further than I had ever before gone with this spell. But at the waist I became stuck. The top half of my body remained obstinately visible.

"Cover me with illusion," I told the old wizard. "I've got to get close enough to the dragon's throat to pierce it." The duchess, realizing what I was doing, handed me her spear. Fortunately, I was able to make the spear itself invisible without difficulty, while still maintaining the invisibility spell on my lower body.

"All right," said the old wizard. "Go!" I stepped on invisible legs into the courtyard and launched myself into the air.

I looked down at my upper torso. The old wizard had made me into a particularly ugly bird, clearly too small to be a person, and, I hoped, too unappetizing for the dragon to eat at once.

The dragon was scratching with whimpers of pain at its throat. When it saw me, it lowered its claws, and opened its mouth. I darted upward as a tongue of fire shot under me. But, uninterested, the dragon returned at once to scratching. I considered chirping to give my birdlike form an air of verisimilitude but decided not to stretch my luck.

I circled delicately, trying to find a good angle for a spear thrust. I couldn't see the spear but I could feel it, gripped tight in my sweaty palms, and I hoped I had the point forward. Twice the dragon reached up to bat me away, and twice I had to duck as deadly razor-sharp claws passed within an inch of my invisible legs.

And then my chance came. Its head back, the dragon was roaring again, and I flew as fast as I could straight toward it, and thrust the spear with all my strength toward the base of the throat.

But just as I thought I had it, the dragon twisted its neck, and the spear, clanging uselessly against the heavy scales, was jerked from my hands.

I dropped to the ground outside the wall, waiting for the dragon to come after me. Maybe at least I could lure it away from the castle. But I knew it could fly far faster than I could.

But it did not pursue me. It sounded instead as though it had decided to start taking the roof off the great hall.

I flew back up in time to see the chimney topple. The screams from within seemed to excite the dragon. But as it saw me its scarlet nostrils flared, and again I was nearly burnt to cinders.

Then all around the dragon was a new cloud of red balls, bigger than before, swirling, popping, ducking and weaving. I dropped into the courtyard to pick up an abandoned spear and realized that I too had become an illusory red ball.

With my new spear newly invisible, I rose into the cloud of balls. Furiously angry, the dragon clawed at the balls and roasted them with fire, but both his talons and his breath passed harmlessly through them.

Camouflaged among them, ready to dart up or down, I waited for my opportunity.

When it came I almost missed it. Half obscured by the red balls, the dragon's throat appeared before me, the tiny wound in the center and all the scratches around it oozing black blood. Too close for a rapid approach and not daring to back up, I swung my feet up against the beast's neck and plunged the spear with all the force in my body into the space between them.

And the spear went home. A geyser of burning dragon blood covered me, blinded me, so that I was barely able to keep on flying. The roar of the dragon above me could have been my own scream. The tail in its writhing caught me, whirled me far out beyond the castle walls, so that my invisibility spell was knocked completely from my mind, and if I hadn't been able to free one eye in time to see the ground coming up toward me, the flying spell might have failed me as well.

I dropped gently to earth, looking back toward the castle. The dragon was in its death throes, still sprurting blood. It managed to pull out the spear, but too late, for it had penetrated its heart. Pieces of the castle went flying as it rolled in agony. Then, with a final roar, it slumped lifeless over the wall.

I took a deep breath and gathered up some snow to scrub my face. My hands were rubbed raw, all my ribs ached, and I had some lacerations and bruises, but other than that I thought I was unwounded. But my new Christmas suit was completely ruined by dragon's blood.

II

I walked back slowly toward the castle. It was incredible to me that only the evening before, after turning the young count into a frog, I had imagined myself a competent wizard. This was my worst failure ever. I had never before managed to destroy half a castle.

One would have expected, I thought, that a royal wizard would be able to deal with a product of wild magic without coming as close to getting himself and everyone else killed as I had done. For all I knew, there was a simple spell against dragons, taught in one of the lectures I had missed. I would certainly have to apologize abjectly to the king and queen. As I reached the castle and crossed the drawbridge, I wondered if I would have to resign as well.

I was highly startled when, as I stepped into the courtyard, the queen threw herself into my arms, heedless of the dragon's blood, and began showering me with kisses. I would have been able to respond more enthusiastically if I had not been so surprised.

In a few seconds she pulled herself away. "Oh, excuse me, I don't want to seem forward, but I'm so grateful! You're our hero! You saved Yurt!" Maybe, I thought, I would not have to resign after all.

The rest of the people in the castle who could still walk were mobbed around me, laughing and jumping to get a better look at me. "Our hero! The savior of Yurt! He killed the dragon!"

"Well, yes, but it took me an awfully long time to do it!" I protested. "Don't thank someone who almost let the castle be destroyed! The old wizard is the real hero."

They pulled the old wizard forward. "What are you talking about?" he said irritably. "Don't go putting your blame on me!"

"But you're the hero," I said. "You're the one who distracted the dragon long enough so that I could spear him! I never could have gotten close enough without your illusions."

"Took you long enough to do the business, too," he grunted, which was actually my assessment as well.

The king was checking the outer walls, but most of us went into the hall, where several of the wounded were already bandaged. Dominic was groaning steadily. "I wonder if the pigeons are still alive and flying, so that we could send for the doctor," said the constable, and hurried off to the south tower to see.

The hall had escaped much better than I had feared. The chimney had collapsed into the fireplace, and several of the windows were broken, but I was pleased to see that the Christmas tree was untouched.

"Well, I guess we'll just all have to squeeze into the kitchens for Christmas dinner!" said the queen.

"It's going to be hours late," said the cook.

"I must say," said the young count, who had not said anything since the dragon first appeared, "that I think this affair was all handled very sloppily. Castles should have established procedures to deal with emergencies." But no one paid him any attention—though I thought I heard one of the stable boys make a sound like a bullfrog just before he dissolved into hysterical giggles.

The queen stayed by my side. I was beginning to wish I had paid more attention while she was kissing me, but she showed no signs of starting again. "I'm afraid you've gotten dragon's blood on your dress," I said, as a hint that I had noticed how close she had been, only moments before. "And I feel terrible about my velvet suit, just after you and the king gave it to me."

She smiled. "I don't mind about my dress." I wondered if this was because it was the dress that was the same color as the duchess's dress. "We'll order you a new suit at once. I can see we'll have to order quite a few things in the next few days. Do you want midnight blue again, or would you prefer a different color?"

"One just like this would be exactly right."

I lowered myself into a chair, feeling more bruised

than I had originally thought. The king was back and talking to the constable about arranging for repairs.

"Come here, Master," I called to the old wizard, and he came toward me, frowning. He had the calico cat in his arms, but all the cat's fur was standing on end and its eyes were wild. "I want to thank you for saving my life. I can't thank you for saving the castle, but only because it's not my castle."

"At least you took advantage of what little magic you knew," he said grumpily.

"Also I wanted to ask you something," I said, starting to feel more cheerful. If the king did not think Yurt was irredeemably destroyed, maybe it had not been. After all, he had already been out to make sure his rose garden had not suffered. "I've heard that being bathed in dragon's blood makes one's skin harder than steel. Is this true?"

The queen excused herself to talk to the cook, who was showing no signs of starting dinner.

The wizard snorted. "I don't know what kind of old witch's story they tell you at that school, but all dragon blood does is make you stink. You'd better take a bath. And that reminds me. You there!" to the constable. "You'd better get the dragon's body cut up and dragged away from the castle right away. It will start rotting in a few hours, and the castle will become unbearable."

The constable sent out some of the young men with saws. I decided I was enough of a wounded hero not to have to join in. "I'm going to take a bath right away, Master," I said. "But before I do, I want to talk to you about that dragon."

"I'd warned you what all this loose wizardry would come to."

The hubbub of the hall was all down at the far end, and no one was near us. "That dragon didn't just come by itself. That dragon was summoned."

He thought about this for a moment in silence. "So

who do you think summoned it? You're not accusing me, are you?"

"No. But I think you know far more about what's happened in Yurt in the last three years than you've told me, and I think the dragon's coming is part of that. Did you know that your magic locks were gone from the north tower?"

"I found out this morning. Went out to inspect them while you were flirting with the duchess after breakfast."

So much for my efforts to keep an eye on the wizard!

"Why didn't you tell me, young whippersnapper? Were they just broken today?"

"They've been gone since I first arrived. I didn't dare tell you because I was afraid you'd blame me, and you'd said there was nothing up in the tower anyway. Master, you've got to tell me. What's escaped from the tower?"

For a minute I was afraid he would say nothing. He kept patting the cat, which was gradually calming down, although it clearly did not like the smell of blood on me. At last he said, "Well, you're Royal Wizard of Yurt now, and I'm retired, so it's your problem." And he told me.

Even though I had been expecting this, my veins turned to ice. I would have to get into a hot bath before I died, but I knew I would never have another chance to talk like this to the old wizard. "How long has it been here?"

"I first found it three years ago."

I decided it would be undiplomatic to remind the old wizard that he had categorically denied any supernatural presence in the castle while he was Royal Wizard.

"I don't know who summoned it to Yurt in the first place," he continued, "but finding it wasn't very difficult, once it arrived. The old chaplain, this one's predecessor, found it too. He blamed me for it, even though I'd never imagined to myself that the powers of darkness were romantic—not like you!"

I nodded, not daring to protest.

"Interfering old busybody! He tried to catch it himself, with his bell and candle. Pretty ineffective, I thought. No wonder it killed him."

He must have seen the horror on my face, even though his eyes were directed toward the cat, for he snorted. "I'm sure the old priest died with his soul 'intact,' if that's what you and your friend the young chaplain are worried about. He was chasing it around the parapets, and he fell off. Nobody knew how he'd fallen, except for me, and I didn't see any reason to say. Terrible accident, they all agreed. You can imagine I didn't tell that young priest anything about it!"

"But *you* caught it?" I said in a low voice, as he stopped and did not start again.

"It took me close to three years. It took all the magic I knew, and then some. But I finally cornered it in my study and put the binding spells on it. It had been out far too long for me to send it back, but at least I could bind it so it couldn't move."

Except that it *had* moved.

"I locked the tower so the person who had summoned it couldn't get in to free it, and, just in case it *did* break loose, I put separate spells around the outside of the castle, so it couldn't cross the moat."

"Did Dominic know about this?"

The old wizard glanced at me sideways. "How did you guess that? He did. I needed his help, near the end. He's not the person I would have chosen, but he'd somehow already found out about it. He was the one who did the drawing while I held it down with my spells."

The cat was almost asleep on the wizard's lap now. "We caught it just in time, too. I was afraid black magic was starting to kill the king, so I was pleased to see him so much better when I arrived yesterday. Maybe he's hoping for that baby boy again!"

The wizard stood up abruptly, scooped up the startled cat, and settled it on his shoulder. "Well, young wizard, it's your castle and your problem now. Capturing it once wore me out so thoroughly I decided to retire at once. Catching it again is the job for a youngster with fancy magic from the City."

He started stumping toward the door.

"Where are you going?" said the king. "You can't be leaving already! We haven't even had Christmas dinner!"

"I'd rather eat my vegetables at peace in the woods than eat a fancy dinner to the smell of dragon's blood!"

I turned toward my own chambers, in search of a bath, without waiting to see the end of the argument, for I already knew how it would end. At least I was pleased that the old wizard's hand, with which he was gesturing, wore the king's Christmas ring.

Lying in the bathtub, completely submerged except for my face, I could feel my bruised muscles starting to relax, but I did not dare relax too much. The old wizard had clearly guessed more than he had told me. But even he might not know why the dragon had appeared today.

As long as I stayed in the tub, I imagined, I would not have to deal with this. After all, evil had been loose in the castle for three years, without permanent damage to Yurt, so maybe another three years wouldn't matter much either.

But I could not persuade myself of this, because I knew it was not true. The old wizard had known that too, and that was why he had returned abruptly to the forest, before I could enlist his aid.

The bathwater was cold. I surged up and out of the tub, reaching for a towel. This was my kingdom and my problem.

III

The hall, with its fireplace destroyed, was unusable for dinner, but the kitchen was just about big enough to squeeze in the tables, and it was certainly warm enough. Pushed companionably close together, so that the smell of singed hair was all around us, we ate oyster stew, roast beef, and plum pudding.

Several of the kitchen maids had broken down completely and were unable to help, and the cook's own stability had lapses, so dinner was served in a leisurely manner, with pauses between courses while the next course was prepared. The queen, the Lady Maria, and several of the other ladies helped, all of them considering it quite a joke.

"Well, *this* will certainly be a Christmas we'll always remember!" said the old count.

Since everyone had survived, and even the worst of the wounded looked as though they would mend without grave danger, the mood had become cheerful. Several of the knights seem positively to have welcomed the rare chance to do something warlike, even though their swords and spears had been useless against the dragon. The terrors of the morning and the repair work of the weeks to come were primarily subjects for triumphant mirth.

While waiting for the courses, we sang Christmas carols. I did a few illusions, since the old wizard was no longer there with his much better ones. I made sure that all of mine were simple and pleasant, such as a shining golden egg that broke open to reveal an adult peacock. Even the young count managed to smile fairly amiably. I had never seen the Lady Maria so gay and lighthearted, even before the gray hairs had started to appear.

Only Dominic, heavily strapped around the body and needing help eating because his right wrist was broken, sat silent and glowering. He, at any rate, seemed unlikely to have summoned a dragon that had nearly killed him.

When the blazing plum pudding had been brought from the stove to the table, served and eaten with more cries of appreciation than normal, the duchess said, "Why don't all of you come to my castle for the rest of the twelve days of Christmas?"

"But we couldn't possibly leave the royal castle during the holidays!" protested the queen.

"You can't possibly enjoy a happy holiday in your castle the way it is now," said the duchess with a laugh. "Bring everybody along! I sent my whole staff home to their families for vacation, so there should be plenty of room in my castle if we double up in the chambers. It's going to take a while to repair this castle, and you're going to have trouble hiring any carpenters or masons for the next two weeks anyway. You don't want to have to start work just when everyone wants to relax and enjoy the festivities."

"But everything's here!" continued the queen. "The food, the decorations, even the tree!"

"Bring them all along!"

"And if you like," said the old count, "we can spend New Year's with the duchess and go on to spend Epiphany at our castle!"

I was delighted with this suggestion. Even though I knew now what had been in the old wizard's tower room, I still did not know who had summoned it. If we could get everybody, really everybody, out of the royal castle of Yurt while I tried to figure this out, we might all be much safer.

"What a wonderful offer, my lady!" I said, even though the decision was certainly not mine to make. "A week of relaxing is exactly what we all need!"

While the queen was turning to me in surprise, startled at the loss of someone she had expected to be her ally against the duchess, the king said, "The wizard's right. Thank you for a most generous offer! We'll go tomorrow!"

As it turned out, we did not leave until the second day. We all awoke late and irritable. Christmas was over, and the lighthearted mood of the night before was gone. The wounded complained about their cracks and bruises, and I was covered with blisters from the dragon's blood. Clearly my predecessor had no first-hand knowledge of dragons. The wounded knights, the doctor from the village told us, needed a day to rest and become at least a little less stiff before they could be loaded into horse litters.

The king directed the repairs that absolutely had to be done before we could leave: the boarding up of broken windows, the replacing of slates where the roof was only minimally damaged, the rigging of covers in those areas where it was clear that all the slates would have to be removed and some of the beams replaced.

I spent much of the day in the kitchen, my feet up before the main fireplace, while the cook and the kitchen maids packed up the two weeks' worth of food they had stocked for the holidays. The cook got into a prolonged quarrel with the constable's wife, insisting that she had to take along her own pans, not trusting the duchess's kitchen to have what she needed. Most of the staff in the kitchen were too busy to pay any attention to me, but Gwen put poultices on my face and changed them assiduously every hour. By evening, the blisters were almost gone, even though my ribs were aching worse than ever.

The queen reconciled herself to the trip to the duchess's castle by taking literally her suggestion to bring everything along. She and the Lady Maria spent much of the day on the stepladders, taking down all the ornaments they had put up just two days earlier, and packing them ready to go. Even the Christmas tree itself was gently lowered and strapped to a sledge with a tarpaulin over it.

Supper was a simple meal, except for the fruitcake. Everyone was too tired to talk very much. The chief conversation was between the queen and the constable.

"But, my lady, *someone* has to stay here in Yurt."

"No, I won't allow it. You deserve a cheerful holiday as much as the rest of us—more, in fact."

"If the castle stands empty, a thief might break in."

"This is a *castle*," she said with an exasperated laugh. "When we go, the last person out can raise the drawbridge and leave by the postern gate, and then not even an army will be able to break in. Even with the damage to some of the parapets, the walls are still sound. There used to be wars in the western king-doms, after all, and castles were built to withstand concerted siege! Certainly this castle will be inpenetra-ble to a common thief!"

"In the days of sieges, there were defenders in the castle to push back the scaling ladders from the walls."

I stayed out of the discussion. There was no way I could pretend to have the authority to decide this, and, besides, I was fairly sure the queen would prevail.

She did in the end, but only because the constable's wife finally said, "Please, dear, I'd like to have a few more days of merry holidays myself."

I felt relieved as I crossed the dark courtyard to my chambers, carrying a candle, even though I was aching in every bone. My breath in the candlelight made a frosty cloud around me. Zahlfast had first noticed that the supernatural influence stopped at the castle's moat, and the old wizard had told me he had put special binding spells at the castle's periphery. At the duchess's castle, we should at least be free of the direct influence of black magic, and maybe my mind would work better than it seemed to be doing today.

Beyond the castle walls, I could hear foxes barking over the dragon's carcass. I still did not know what to make of the stranger. He had refused to let me find out anything about him by turning that sensation of evil against me like a weapon. But I was beginning to wonder if the old wizard knew something about the stranger that he was not telling me.

The old apprenticeship system for learning wizardry had never actually been ended. It had merely withered away over the course of the last hundred and fifty years, as it became obvious that it was quicker and easier for a young man to study with the wizards in the City, where all of modern wizardry was arranged in books and coursework, than to put up with the crotchets of a single teacher. When I had asked the old wizard about studying herbal magic with him, he had referred extremely vaguely to his last apprentice.

I had thought at the time that he must know exactly who that last apprentice had been, and now I had a suspicion why he had not wanted to talk about him. That apprentice may have taken the plunge into black magic, and the old wizard knew it.

He must have been living in the woods near Yurt for years, maybe with the old wizard's knowledge, and maybe not. At any rate, I speculated, he had taken advantage of the few days between when the old wizard had retired from Yurt and I had arrived to move into the castle and establish himself in the cellars. When he realized I was a young, relatively incompetent wizard, he had become bold. He had broken the magic locks to get into the north tower, and had had to break my lock on the cellar door when I had inadvertently locked him out—or in.

I lit all the magic lamps from both of my rooms and arranged them near my shoulders. I did not like to think of a wizard who had given his soul to the devil standing there in the dark, waiting, perhaps avidly, as I had blundered down the wet cellar corridors.

But how had he squeezed in and out the small window in the iron door? In a moment, I realized this wouldn't be a problem for a highly competent wizard. He could temporarily transform himself into something much smaller, if necessary—even, *I* could probably do so now, though I preferred not to try. In the first transformation class they always told the story of the young wizard who had turned himself into a purple bird who couldn't form the words of the Hidden Language with its beak. It had therefore been unable to turn himself back, and it had flown away in panic before any other wizards could help.

Someone I knew, I thought, someone in the castle, must have become involved with the evil wizard. This was the point where my speculations became very difficult. This evil wizard, even if he had been living near the castle, could have no reason I could think of to put an evil spell on the king three years ago and summon the supernatural into the castle. Therefore, someone else must have wanted that spell, someone else must have asked for his help. I was brought back again, in spite of my best efforts, to the arrival of the queen in Yurt.

I stood up determinedly to start getting ready for bed. If the stranger *had* been a former apprentice of the old wizard, I was impressed with the power of his magic, stronger than anything I had seen, even at the school, in its imperviousness to my best spells. The old magic still had something to offer someone trained in the City.

With my red velvet jacket in my hands, I stopped to consider again. There ought to be some record of the old wizard's apprentices, who would after all have had to live in the castle. I pulled my jacket back on and hurried out into the night.

The constable and his wife were not yet in bed, but they were naturally surprised when I banged on the door of their chambers. "A list of the old wizard's apprentices? You need that *tonight*, sir?"

"Yes, I do. I'm sorry, but I can't tell you why, other than that it has to do with the dragon."

"It might take a while to find the information. He never had an apprentice in the time that I've been at Yurt. I'd have to go through my predecessor's records."

"I'm sorry, I know you're very tired, but I really need that information now."

"I'll help you find the right ledgers if you want," the constable's wife said to him. "Can't you see how worried the boy is?"

I was glad enough for her support not to mind being called a boy, although I did wonder if she would ever think of me as a man. The constable unlocked a cabinet, and he and his wife started taking out old ledger books.

Previous constables, it turned out, had kept very careful track of everyone who lived in the castle; the present constable, I assumed, had noted just as assiduously the day that I had first arrived. When my predecessor had first come to Yurt a hundred and eighty years earlier, he had quickly acquired apprentices. Usually he had only had one at a time, but there were periods in which he had had three or even four. Some left after only a short period; one stayed for a dozen years.

Then, a hundred and thirty or a hundred and forty years ago, the supply of apprentice wizards had dwindled. This would have been, I thought, at the time when the reputation of the wizards' school in the City had begun to spread. I bent close over the ledger, squinting to read the faded brown ink of the then constable's tidy handwriting. For a long time the wizard of Yurt had had no apprentices at all.

And then he had a final one, one who stayed in Yurt for nearly ten years. "That's right," said the constable. "He was the last. He left eighty-two years ago. The final indication we have was that he had taken up a post of his own."

This was it, I thought. It would be impossible to give the stranger a precise age, but, even though he must certainly have slowed down his own aging with powerful magic, I doubted he could be older than a hundred and twenty. "Where did he go?"

The wizard's last apprentice, according to the ledgers, had left Yurt to become the wizard in a count's castle in one of the larger of the western kingdoms, located a hundred and fifty miles away. Even that long ago, I thought, someone without a diploma from the school would have had to be satisfied with less than being a Royal Wizard.

I thanked the constable and his wife profusely and went back to my own chambers. My bones, I noticed, seemed less stiff. As soon as it was light enough for the pigeons to fly, I would send a message to that kingdom and begin to track down what had happened to the old wizard's last apprentice.

IV

We prepared to leave early in the morning. The sky was gray and the wind damp and chill. I sent my message by the pigeons, asking that an answer be sent to the duchess's castle. Since my message would have to be relayed through the City's postal system, I could not expect an answer for several days.

When we had all ridden out, the drawbridge was raised, the first time I had seen it done since coming to Yurt. The gears turned with a rusty screech. The two men who had raised the bridge then came out of the tiny postern gate, and last of all the constable came after them. He locked the postern carefully and balanced on the stepping stones across the moat to join us. The castle looked dark and forbidding under the dark sky; I doubted very much that any thief would try to cross the moat and scale those high walls.

If the old wizard's last apprentice was in the cellars, I thought, let him enjoy the empty castle. He'd certainly be able to break into the main storerooms if he needed food, but at least he wouldn't be able to enjoy any of the cook's fruitcake or Christmas candy, all of which was coming with us. I hadn't wanted to tell anyone else that someone who had sold his soul to the devil might be rummaging through their rooms while they were gone. But I myself, as well as putting magic locks on my door and all my windows as carefully as I knew how, had brought along several of my most important books, including the *Diplomatica Diabolica*. The stable boy who helped me load a pack horse had not commented; let him think that wizards needed mysterious heavy objects wherever they went.

We rode as quickly as we could go with the horse litters; no one wanted to linger in the bitter wind. I rode next to Joachim, but we barely exchanged a word. He, I suspected, was wondering if I had had anything to do with the dragon's appearance. I didn't know how to reassure him that I hadn't without also confessing that I had only a guess as to who had. At least, I thought, what the wizard had told me about the old chaplain's death made it clear that the beginnings of evil in Yurt must have preceded, rather than coincided with, Joachim's arrival.

Considering that I had been hired as the chief magic-worker in Yurt, I thought, there seemed to have been a very large number of people in the castle already who had become involved in magic. There was the stranger, who I was starting to assume was identical with the old wizard's last apprentice; there was whoever had first put the spell on the king, who I kept fearing might turn out to be the queen, in spite of what she had told me on Christmas Eve; and there was the Lady Maria, who had certainly seen or been involved in black magic at some point.

The Lady Maria managed to position her horse next

to mine after the brief lunch break. "I haven't had a chance to talk to you for two days," she said. "But I've been wanting to tell you how exciting and romantic it was to see you defeat the dragon."

Since there didn't seem to be any good answer to this, I merely nodded gravely.

"If the dragon had killed you," she said in great seriousness, "I would have always treated the shawl you gave me, such a short time earlier, as a sacred object."

If the dragon had killed me, I thought, it probably would have gone on to kill everybody else, unless one of the knights had been able to get in a lucky spear thrust. In this case Maria, being dead, would not have been able to treat the silk shawl or anything else as a special object. But all I said was, "Don't let the chaplain hear you referring to a simple shawl as sacred."

She laughed as though this were a highly witty remark and went on to tell me how excited and how terrified she had been by the dragon. Since I had seen her then, I thought excitement rather than terror had been the dominant emotion on her part, but I was not at all unwilling to confess how terrified I had been myself.

By riding rapidly and taking the shortest rests possible, we were able to reach the duchess's castle just before the early sunset of midwinter. Her constable and chaplain, the only members of her staff to stay at the castle over Christmas, had been warned we were coming and met us at the gate.

Our cook with her kitchen maids put together a quick supper, slowed down somewhat by her insistence that all the pans she found in the kitchen be packed up and the pans from Yurt unpacked and put in their places, before she could begin. Although every effort had been made to position the injured knights carefully in their litters, several were bleeding from wounds that had reopened during the ride, and Dominic was telling anyone who would listen that he was sure there were several fresh cracks in his ribs from the jostling.

But it was still a relief to be warm and snug in a castle without any damage done to it at all, and the next morning we all awoke more cheerful, in spite of a steady fall of sleet outside. Several of the younger ladies announced that they had been looking forward for months to a Christmas dance, and they intended to have one.

The morning was spent setting up the Christmas tree, rehanging it with all the ornaments, including my predecessor's miniature magic lights, and putting up the rest of the decorations. The brass players had brought their instruments and could be heard practicing snatches of dance carols.

In the middle of the afternoon, the dancing began. The ladies had unpacked their brightest dresses, curled their hair, and perfumed their shoulders. The unwounded knights were dressed more uniformly, in the formal blue and white livery of Yurt, and all seemed to be enjoying themselves hugely. I sat in a little balcony above the great hall, watching and wondering when I might expect to receive an answer to my message.

In spite of the liveliness of the music, which had the other watchers tapping their toes and swaying their shoulders, I scarcely paid attention to the brightly lit scene below. The best I could expect, I thought, was an answer from whoever was now count in the castle where the old wizard's last apprentice had gone, and perhaps some indication of when that apprentice had left. But the records in another castle might not be as good as the records of the royal castle of Yurt, and, besides, the count might see no reason to pull out dusty ledgers to answer the letter of a wizard of whom he'd never heard.

Even if I received a detailed answer, I was not sure what it would tell me, other than that the apprentice had left there, which I thought I already knew. Two nights ago, finding him in the constable's ledgers, I had thought I was well on the way to tracking down the mysterious stranger, but now I wasn't sure what good it could do me to follow his movements before he became established in Yurt's cellars.

In the first break in the dancing, while the dancers caught their breaths and the brass players shook the moisture from their instruments, the cook brought out punch and Christmas cookies. In the second break, however, they called for me.

"Come on down, Wizard!" called the young count, who had been leading the last set. "Show us some Christmas-time entertainments!"

Since this was asked almost politely, and he had suppressed any comments about entertainments being all wizards were suited for, I decided to oblige. For the most part, I made cascades of colored stars and a selection of red and green furry animals that scampered and played for a minute in the middle of the hall before disappearing with a pop. I also did a trick with two red balls, one real and one illusory, in which I mixed them up and made members of my audience guess which was which. Since they guessed wrong more than half the time, reaching out for what they thought was the real ball only to find that their hand passed right through it, this trick was considered a great success. To complete my entertainments, I made an illusory golden basket, piled high with colored fruit that shone like rubies and emeralds, and presented it to the Lady Maria.

She had been sitting by herself, not taking part in the dancing. Instead she smiled and nodded in an almost matronly manner, as though she were an old woman remembering the dances of her youth. Even when the old court tried to lead her out on the dance floor, she laughed and refused. When the dancing started again, I sat with her.

"Why don't you ask one of the young ladies to dance?" she inquired.

"I'm still too bruised from the dragon," I said, loud enough that the young ladies could hear me too. Since there was a shortage of men, I was worried about being pressed into service. "Besides, I'm just enjoying sitting here with you."

I expected her to smile, as she normally did at all my gallant and meaningless sallies, but she was looking at the illusory basket I had given her, which was perched on the table beside her and gradually fading. "Perhaps that's what I'm like," she said, but so softly I was fairly sure I was not supposed to overhear. As irritated as I had sometimes been at her fecklessness, I liked this even less.

Supper was announced after the next set of dances. As we were finishing eating, there was a clatter in the courtyard, and a group of people in disguises raced into the hall. "Good," said the duchess. "It's the mummers from the village. They must have heard I was back."

There were about a dozen of them, all wearing ordinary working clothes that had been transformed by the application of beads and sequins, or by combining different items of clothes in unusual ways. Their faces were painted, and they wore foil crowns, unusual hats, and, in one case, goat's horns.

They ran around the hall twice, gabbling and waving their arms. One of the girls was wearing a man's tunic and was apparently intended to represent the duchess herself. At first she stepped out boldly, but then on the second pass around the hall she became shy and tried to conceal herself behind her companions. The duchess seemed to find it hilarious.

Then the men in foil crowns and enough beads and sequins to suggest kings came forward, challenged each other, blew shrill blasts on tin horns, and began giving each other great blows with wooden swords.

Racing around them, prodding them into even fiercer
action, was the man in the goat's horns. He was
dressed entirely in red, and I had trouble laughing
and applauding after I realized he was supposed to
represent a demon.

The wounded "kings" fell back from the fight and
collapsed into the arms of the sequined women who
were supposed to be the queens. The girl who had
been wearing the man's tunic now pulled on a white
shift and foil halo to come forward as an angel, whose
touch caused the kings to jump up with a clapping of
hands and race once again around the hall. All of us
applauded and dropped a few coins in the chief king's
hat as he circled the tables.

"Now we're starting to have a properly Merry
Christmas," said the duchess after the mummers had
raced out. "Tomorrow, let's celebrate the Feast of
Fools!"

Good, I thought. A festival just for wizards like me.

V

I had of course heard of the Feast of Fools, even
though we had had nothing similar in the City when
I was young. At some big country houses, on a day
between Christmas and New Year's, for the whole day
the ordinary social structures were reversed, and a boy
became the lord and the lord a stable boy.

But while I knew what happened in a general way
on the Feast, I was still startled to wake and find the
queen in my bedroom, as a dark, sleeting morning
began outside the window. I pulled the blankets up
to my chin.

"Here's your breakfast, Chaplain," she said with a
laugh, presenting me with a breakfast tray.

I reached for it hesitantly. It contained a donut,

rather stale, but also a hot cup of tea. "Why are you calling me the chaplain?"

"We're all backwards today," she said with a smile. "I'm the kitchen maid; Gwen and Jon are the queen and king; and you and the chaplain are taking each other's positions. When you're ready to get dressed, get some of his vestments and give him some of your clothes to wear."

Neither of the chaplains, the duchess's nor Joachim, liked this plan at all. "Chaplains never take part in the Feast of Fools," said the duchess's chaplain loftily.

"But this is an unusual Christmas!" the queen insisted. She seemed to be taking direction of the Feast, perhaps, I thought, to wrest control from the duchess. "You won't have to do anything evil."

I ended up having to go into the chapel for morning service in the chaplains' place, wearing an old set of robes from the duchess's chaplain. If the members of the staff who came to the chapel, dressed in finery, had expected me to give a satirical version of the service, however, they were disappointed, for I merely laid the Bible on the altar, lit the candles, and went out again. Until I had decided what to do about Yurt, I did not dare risk offending the powers of the supernatural.

In the great hall, Gwen and Jon, wearing very fancy and very old draperies that I assumed had come from chests in the duchess's attic, sat on tall chairs next to the fireplace. Both held rods that apparently represented scepters, something I had never seen the real king and queen use, and both were shouting orders.

"Go weed my roses!" yelled Jon in a high, cracked voice that did not sound at all like the king's voice. "And do it right, this time! Don't start breaking off the branches like you did last time!" Since the king did almost all his own weeding, I was surprised at this, but the assembled staff seemed to find it hilarious.

"Why aren't you feeding my stallion?" cried Gwen

in a voice that actually did sound a lot like the queen's. "Why aren't you exercising him? Cook!" to one of the ladies. "We're going to have a hundred and fifty extra people for supper. I'm sorry I didn't tell you earlier, but you'd better get started. We have to eat in twenty minutes!"

I stood at the edge of the hall, leaning against the wall and watching. I found this disturbing, and was even more disturbed when one of the stable boys started shouting back at the "royal pair." "Why don't you let the cook alone? Why don't you and the hundred and fifty guests go dig in the fields for a while and work up an appetite?"

Gwen, as the queen, replied, "Don't bother me with your complaints! Can't you see the king and I are busy?" and threw herself into Jon's arms, to his evident approval.

The staff laughed uproariously. The real queen came to stand next to me. "Are you sure allowing this is wise, my lady?"

She smiled. "We did it every year when I was growing up, and I started the practice when I came to Yurt. The staff are somewhat limited, being away from home, but some years they have elaborate props and even whole episodes they act out."

"But aren't you encouraging them to think badly of you?"

"Not at all. That's why it's called the Feast of Fools; you have to remember not to take anything seriously."

"They're saying insulting things to you!"

"If they say insulting things to the false king and queen, they won't need to say those things to us. And sometimes we can pick up an indication of a real problem, something with which we had started burdening the staff without even realizing it. King Haimeric and I like to think that we treat our staff as well as anyone in the western kingdoms, but as long as they're in our pay they're always going to be a little inhibited about speaking up about their problems."

I nodded, somewhat dubiously. She seemed quite calm about the proceedings, even complacent, but if the queen thought this was all fun and harmless, maybe it was. I was still quite shocked when one of the trumpeters came running into the hall, wearing a ripped red velvet tunic. "The powers of darkness must obey me!" he shouted. "I am stronger than trees and rocks!"

There was a great deal of shouting. "No! You can't be the wizard!" "The chaplain has to be the wizard!" "But he said he doesn't want to be!" "Let him be the wizard if he wants to be!" I was especially mortified to see the queen herself struggling with only minimal success to keep from bursting into laughter.

"Maria and I are making lunch today," she said abruptly, straightening her face. "We'd better get started." I could tell from the back of her shoulders as she hurried away that she was laughing again.

The cook, who had found a blond wig and apparently represented the Lady Maria, came over to talk to me. "We want to have the 'wizard' do magic tricks at lunch. That boy is useless; we're going to have to have the chaplain do it. Can you teach him a good trick between now and lunch?"

"All right," I said. Maybe concentrating on the reckless activity of the Feast of Fools would keep me from worrying when, if ever, I would hear what had happened to the old wizard's last apprentice, much less how I was going to deal with him.

Both chaplains were sitting in their room, reading their Bibles as though determined not to hear the laughter and running feet in the castle all around them.

"They want you to do a magic trick at lunch," I said to Joachim, deciding that the older man who served the duchess was hopeless. "I'll make one you can do very easily."

"Don't you think the dangers of black magic are close enough to us already?"

"There's certainly nothing wicked in the spell I'll work for you. It would only become black magic if you approached it with evil intent." As soon as I said this I wished I had not, because it sounded like an accusation, but he just looked at me from his enormous eyes in silence.

I sat down next to him, to show that nothing I was doing was hidden or even morally questionable, and started preparing an illusion ahead of time, as the old wizard had done. I murmured the words of the Hidden Language just under my breath, while the two chaplains kept looking at me surreptitiously and tried to keep on reading.

"Do you have anything I can attach this spell to?" I asked brightly when I had it almost completed.

The duchess's chaplain snorted but found and handed me a button. I would have preferred something more inherently interesting than an old black button from a priest's vestments, but it would certainly do. I finished the spell and handed the button to Joachim.

"There. You won't actually have to do anything magical. Just wave this mysteriously, say a few things that sound arcane and deeply wise, and I can say the magic words to finish the spell. All you'll have to do then is drop the button and step back."

He took the button reluctantly, as though afraid it might come alive in his hand, and delicately slipped it into his pocket. This would have been much easier, I thought, with someone who had a sense of humor. "I'll see you at lunch," I said with a smile as I went out.

In the hall, one of the servants had heavily padded the stomach and arms of his tunic and was clearly meant to represent Dominic. "I'm the bravest man in the kingdom!" he announced in a roar. "Nothing can hurt me! Wait! What's that?" with a trembling of terror. "Oh, no! It's an illusion! It's got me!" He fell to the floor, fought off an imaginary attacker, rolled to the feet of the "king and queen," and stood up stiffly. "Oh, no! It's pain! I've been hurt a scratch! I can't bear a second of pain!"

I laughed as hard as anybody, but I was very glad that the real Dominic was not there.

The queen announced lunch not long afterwards. It was only heated-up soup that the cook had made the day before, cheese, bread, and Christmas cookies, but even if prepared by women who normally never cooked it was an excellent meal. "Wizard!" bellowed Jon to the chaplain as we finished the cookies. "I want to see some magic and I want to see it now! None of your normal foolish magic. Let's have something really spectacular!"

Joachim took a deep breath and stood up, with a look at me as though it were all my fault. At this point there was a pause as several people at the table noticed he was wearing his ordinary vestments; since I was still wearing the older priest's robes, we had three chaplains at the table and no wizard.

"He's got a have a costume." "He's got to look like the wizard." "What shall we do?"

"Here," I said and pulled off my belt, which I had been wearing around my trousers under the robes. "You can wear this. It's the chief insignia of wizardry."

While of course it was not, the moon and stars were impressive enough, once I set them glowing, that the rest of the table clapped and approved. Joachim buckled it around himself with the look of someone who just wanted this episode over.

But I was pleased to see that he had the sense not just to pull out the button and show everyone how ordinary it was. Instead he cupped it in his hands, looked down on it as though it were something exciting, and began to speak in a low tone. "Abracadabra," he said, which he must have known as well as I did was not a word of the Hidden Language, only the way the Language was represented in children's fairy stories. "Let the magic begin!"

He whirled around, holding the button over his head. I started putting the final pieces of the spell I wanted together, but he was not done yet.

"Magic is all powerful," he cried. "The supernatural is superfluous! Wizards are the kings of the universe!"

There was a good deal of laughter at this. While I was delighted that he still might be able to develop a sense of humor, I wished he had not started at my expense. He threw the button in the air, and as it came down it stopped being a button.

Instead it was a pack horse, slightly smaller than lifesize, a defect for which it made up by being brilliantly violet. On its back was a giant sack, from which brightly wrapped Christmas presents protruded. As Joachim unbuckled my belt and sat down again, the presents tumbled from the sack, their ribbons untying themselves, the gifts inside shooting out. There were diamond necklaces, a golden sword, silk dresses, whole hams, a book bound in red leather, cascades of coins, highly lifelike bluebirds, and, in the final box, a rosebush that grew, opened violet blooms, and faded away as the whole illusion disappeared into sparks.

There was a brief moment of appreciative silence, with no sound but the sleet against the windows. "Very good, Wizard!" Jon then called. "It's much better than our usual wizard's productions!"

I was actually very pleased myself. It was certainly the most elaborate and most realistic illusion I had ever done; maybe I would have to try more often the old wizard's method of starting an illusion ahead of time.

But my good humor was no more permanent than

the illusion and faded again in the afternoon. I was now convinced that I would never hear anything about the old wizard's apprentice. Although there was still over a week to run on the twelve days of Christmas, my time for deciding what to do about the stranger in the cellars was very limited. Since he had already called down a dragon on us, I hated to imagine what he would do for his next effort.

The rest of the party also seemed to grow tired of the game as the afternoon wore on. At one point Gwen took off her draperies and left the hall and did not come back. When, toward the end of the afternoon, someone from the village came to the door to announce that a boar had been spotted in the woods, conversation quickly shifted from a mockery of the royal castle's ordinary life to the question of a boar hunt.

"If the weather's clear by tomorrow," said the duchess, "we can start first thing in the morning. What do you say, Wizard?" addressing me. "Do you know some weather spells to make sure it's a good day for boar hunting?"

I had never seen a live boar and knew that I would normally have been very interested; now I just wished I had some ideas of how to proceed at home. How could I try to get the stranger and his evil out of Yurt when I did not know who he was, why he was in the castle, or who of the royal party was working with him?

"The Feast of Fools will be over at sunset!" announced the duchess. It seemed to be over in fact well before then. The young count, the unwounded knights, and the men servants were already checking the duchess's armory to see what she might have for boar spears.

At the very end of the afternoon, when the icy rain was clearing up even without a weather spell, the duchess's constable came into the hall and approached me. "A message just came into the pigeon loft," he said. "I think it's for you."

I snatched the tiny rectangle from him and unfolded it carefully, my heart pounding. Would this be the answer to the question of why the stranger had settled himself and his black magic in Yurt?

I had to read the message twice to understand it. "I was delighted to hear from the new Wizard of Yurt. I still remember my years in the kingdom fondly, even though it's been eighty-two years since I left. Let me wish you a happy New Year."

The message was from the old wizard's last apprentice. He had apparently spent his entire life in the count's castle where he had taken up his first post. If he was a hundred and fifty miles away, sending me messages, he could not possibly also be sitting in the cellars of the empty royal castle.

I was back where I had started from. If the stranger was not an apprentice wizard gone evil, who was he, and who in Yurt had invited him in?

PART SEVEN

Lady Maria

I

At supper that night, cooked again by the cook and served by the serving maids, the duchess stood up between courses and came to lean over the back of my chair. I was sitting next to the Lady Maria, eating glumly and scarcely tasting what I was eating.

"Could you come to my chambers after dinner for a glass of brandy?" the duchess said in a low voice.

Maria, who overheard, pursed her lips and shot the duchess's back a sharp look from narrowed eyes. This seemed to be the first time that I had made any woman in Yurt jealous on my behalf, and it was not the woman I would have selected for jealousy.

"I'd be glad to come, my lady," I said, "but your brandy is perhaps a little strong for a wizard. Could I join you in a glass of wine instead?"

"Of course," she said and returned to her seat. I just hoped she was not going to start teasing me again. I wasn't sure I could manage to be polite if she did.

But as she poured me some wine and herself an

inch of brandy, she showed no sign of making provocative suggestions. "There's something wrong, Wizard," she said, hooking her leg over the arm of the chair. "Even I know that dragons don't normally leave the northern land of magic to come attack one of the smallest of the western kingdoms. What's happening?"

"I wish I knew what was happening," I said ruefully. "You're probably glad I *didn't* agree to become ducal wizard, since I didn't even know what to do with a dragon. Does everybody here realize something's wrong?"

"I think the rest have been too busy thinking about the Christmas festivities," she said, "but that's part of the reason I felt I had to get everyone out of the royal castle of Yurt and bring them here. And it's clear to me, watching you, that you're deeply worried."

I looked at her face, serious and very attractive, even if after the dragonfire she had had to cut her hair as short as a boy's, and even if it was not the queen's face. I decided to confide in her. "I'm worried because the dragon was *summoned*. And the person who summoned it is involved in black magic."

"Black magic? You mean they're doing evil spells?"

"I mean they're working with a demon."

"A demon? You mean there's a demon in Yurt?" She looked at me incredulously and went to pour herself more brandy.

"The old wizard told me, but I'd already guessed. There's a demon in the castle, one who roamed the world freely for three years. The old wizard caught it and imprisoned it, but it's broken free, and now it's stronger than ever."

"How do you imprison a demon?"

"It's hard to do," I said slowly, feeling as pinned down by her rapid questions as I would have been by a boar spear. Everything she said brought home to me again what the old wizard had told me, that this was my kingdom now and my demon. "In this case, the old wizard held it down with magic spells while Dominic drew a pentagram around it."

"That may explain a lot," said the duchess. "I wouldn't trust Dominic to draw a good pentagram."

"Normally, neither would I," I said, trying to smile. "But I know my predecessor would have checked it over thoroughly."

"Pentagrams have to be drawn in chalk, don't they?" she said, putting down her glass. "I remember asking my father's old wizard about demons years and years ago, while I was still young enough to think they sounded exciting and mysterious."

"That's right."

"And chalk can dry up, blow away, wash away in the damp, be rubbed out by the bold foot of a demon who has already been free in the world for three years."

"It shouldn't be that simple." I looked down at my glass, realized I had not been drinking my wine, and took a sip. It seemed to have no flavor. "Even a partially worn-out pentagram should still keep a demon from moving—and it can't rub out the chalk itself."

"But could a demon who'd gathered strength from three years in the world still cast a magic spell if there was any flaw in the pentagram? Would it be able to call the person who had summoned it originally and ask him or her to free it?"

She was posing questions as though this were the oral exam at the end of the demonology course—and I hadn't known the answers then, either.

"Who *did* summon it, Wizard?"

Now she was sitting with her boots planted solidly on the floor, gripping the arms of her chair, ready to spring into action. But there was no one against whom I could tell her to spring. "I don't know, my lady. I wish to the saints that I did."

"But you'll have to imprison it again."

I didn't even try to smile. "Hard as it may be to

capture a demon that has been happily loose in the world for three years, it will be a thousand times harder to catch one who has already once escaped from a pentagram."

"Does this have anything to do with the message you got by the pigeons this afternoon? You looked terribly eager to get it, and then very disappointed."

"It was a theory I'd had, which might have accounted for a lot. I had suspected that the last young wizard to serve an apprenticeship under the old wizard, over eighty years ago, might have returned to Yurt to practice black magic. But from the letter I just got, he's been wizard in a count's castle for eighty-two years, a hundred and fifty miles away, and can have no relationship with what's happening in Yurt."

"What evil *is* happening in Yurt, aside from the dragon?"

"The king was very ill and almost died before the chaplain miraculously healed him."

She nodded. "I hadn't seen Haimeric for over a year, before all of you came this fall, but he looked better then than I'd seen him in ages. One of Yurt's servants told my lady's maid that a miracle had cured him, but I wasn't sure if I should credit that."

"There can be no doubt that the chaplain saved his life."

"But what else has been happening in Yurt, besides the king's illness and the dragon? As though that weren't enough!"

"Well," I said slowly, "we saw a mysterious stranger in the castle, right after we got back from here last month. He had apparently put the whole castle staff to sleep before we came, and the next day he kept slipping around the castle, appearing and disappearing, knocking me backwards with evil whenever I tried to touch him with magic. I don't think he did any damage, but he disrupted the castle and terrified me."

"And has this 'stranger' been seen again?"

"He disappeared that afternoon, when the chaplain returned from a trip to the village. I think he's afraid of the chaplain, but he's probably enjoying the empty castle now. I think he lives in the cellars. Since he's already summoned a dragon, I don't want to think what he'll decide to do next."

The duchess picked up her empty glass as though to refill it, then set it down again, still empty. Watching her, I thought that she did not want another drink so much as an opportunity to act, and listening to me talk about the stranger provided no good opportunities for her to begin her attack.

"So," she said, "the problem is primarily that you have a demon living in the cellars, and he may be afraid of the chaplain. That means—"

"But, my lady, just because I think the stranger is afraid of the chaplain doesn't mean the demon is."

"Oh," she said with a quizzical look. "I'd assumed the 'stranger' was just a physical manifestation of the demon."

I had not thought of this and was furious at myself for not doing so. If I had actually read the *Diplomatica Diabolica* more carefully, it might well have told me that demons did not need to keep the small size, the red skin, and the horns of the one demon I had ever seen, the one in the pentagram at the school.

"It may be," I said thoughtfully, my mind trying to race through the implications of this to make up for its previous slowness. "It would certainly explain a lot. I had been thinking there were actually two people practicing black magic in the castle, the stranger and someone else, and it would be much simpler if there were only one person."

"But who is that person? Why do you think it's someone in the castle?"

She wasn't going to let me get away from that question, the one I could not answer. Even though I was confiding in her, I didn't want to mention the coinci-

dence that the old wizard had first discovered the
demon not long after the queen arrived in Yurt.
"Demons don't normally appear by themselves," I
said, "at least not in this part of the world. They have
to be called."

"So you have to find out who called it and find a
way to imprison it, even with its new strength?"

She had summarized my problem very nicely. I was
thinking rapidly. If the stranger was, as the duchess
suggested, the physical manifestation of the demon,
then I should be able to find him in the cellars, and
I should be able to negotiate with him—I had, after
all, already spoken to him once, even if he had not
answered.

"But how *can* you imprison it? How can I help
you?"

"You've helped by getting everyone out of the castle," I said, smiling and answering the last half of her
question first. "I'll have to check my books, but I don't
think there's any way I can imprison it again. Instead
I'll have to treat with it, negotiate with it, persuade it
to return to hell."

"But isn't treating with a demon dangerous?
Couldn't you endanger yourself?"

She asked as though this wasn't something I had
already thought about, many, many times.

"If you negotiate, what will it demand?"

It crossed my mind that the duchess, with her rapid-
fire questions, might be able to pin the demon down
on a technicality and persuade it to leave empty-
handed. But this was only an idle hope. "Their chief
currency is human souls. When I thought that the old
wizard's last apprentice might have become a renegade, I'd even hoped I could persuade the demon to
take the soul it had already been given and be content
to leave with that. But now I don't know what I will
do."

She leaned her chin on her fist, faced, I assumed,

for one of the few times in her life, with a problem which her rapid mind and forceful nature could not readily solve. "Should you get some help from that school in the City?"

"No, I really can't. My old instructor visited me this fall to check on how I was doing and to remind me that, once we leave the school, we have to solve our own problems. My predecessor at Yurt told me it was my problem now, and he was right."

"How about the chaplain, if the demon is afraid of him?"

"That's part of the reason I couldn't ask for his help. We might be able to chase the demon around the castle forever, but at some point someone has to talk to it, someone trained in wizardry." I was amazed to hear the calm tone of my voice, as though I actually believed I was going to do it. "I don't think the demon is afraid of the chaplain personally, anyway, but only of the aura of the saints. If the chaplain was able to put off that aura long enough that the demon was willing to approach him, he would be destroyed—he doesn't know magic, and he wouldn't know the words to say."

"Are you sure, in that case, that another wizard couldn't help you?"

"When the chaplain saved the king's life, he didn't ask for help from the bishop. When I go against the demon, I have to be able to do it alone." I lowered my wineglass, which I had finally emptied, and stood up. "Thank you, my lady. I think, from talking to you, that my mind is clearer." Not that it could have been any more confused than it already was!

She rose as well. I put my hands on her shoulders, bent down, and kissed her gravely on the cheek.

As I went down the broad staircase from her chambers to the great hall, I noticed that almost everyone else had gone to bed. But Dominic and the young count were sitting in front of the fire, talking intently.

As they heard my step, they looked up hurriedly, even guiltily.

But I had too much on my mind to worry about them. All I had to do, before the twelve days of Christmas ended and everyone decided it was time to go home and start repairs on the castle, was to read the *Diplomatica Diabolica* properly at last, learn to deal with a demon as I had boasted to the chaplain when I first came to Yurt that I had been trained to do, find out somehow who had summoned the demon in the first place, and discover if that summons had involved asking the demon for the special advantages in this world which will destroy one's soul in the next.

II

The sunrise brought a clear and cold day, perfect, several of the knights assured me, for a boar hunt. The morning also brought the departure of the old count and his wife.

"At our age, all this excitement and upheaval become a little wearying," the countess explained to the duchess as they pulled on their gloves in the great hall.

"But we're still willing to have everyone come after New Year's, if you want!" the count assured the king. "Just send us a message so we'll expect you."

No one in fact believed this, and it was not meant to be believed. I was fairly confident that the duchess would be able to keep the party here for another week, through Epiphany, but at that point the king and queen would insist on returning home. Considering that I had been wondering since summer who had been practicing magic with evil intent, a week did not seem very long to discover who had summoned the demon and how to send it back again.

The old count's departure caused some shuffling in

rooms. The Lady Maria, as royal aunt, took the chamber the count and countess had shared for herself, while some of the ladies who had been squeezed in together took up the space that she vacated. The ladies insisted that they had to be along to see the boar captured, so the hunt did not actually leave until midmorning.

"Don't expect pork for supper even if you do catch it," the cook said darkly. "Game's got to be hung at least a few days, as I hope you know, or it will be too chewy to eat."

"We'll have it for New Year's, then," said the young count.

I rode out with the hunt because almost everyone healthy enough to ride was going, and I had some vague hope that someone might reveal his or her evil nature in the excitement of the chase. The duchess was wearing a disreputable man's cloak, already stained with the blood of scores of hunts. The queen, as if in response, mounted her stallion wearing an extremely elegant scarlet riding habit that I knew she had ordered packed in from the City.

We were joined by several men from the village, both mounted and on foot. The duchess's hounds were loosed and raced off across the stubble and into the woods, sniffing intently. I wondered absently if it would be possible to breed a hound who would have a nose to sniff out black magic.

For half an hour almost nothing happened. Then I discovered I was riding next to the young count, who was wearing a beautifully tailored riding jacket and whose very horse seemed to be looking at mine with scorn.

But he spoke without scorn. "Look, Wizard, we've been talking, and it's clear you need some help."

My first thought was that the duchess had betrayed me. "What kind of help?" I said as casually as I could.

I certainly did not want the young count trying to meddle with the demon.

"Sir Dominic told me your problem," he continued. At least, I thought, I could retract my bitter thoughts about the duchess. "He said there's a renegade wizard back in the royal castle."

I had, I remembered, told the knights of Yurt that the stranger was some type of wizard, but I had hardly expected Dominic to start telling the young count about it.

"He told me you'd been having some trouble with it, and we guessed that it might even have summoned the dragon."

I didn't like the way his guesses were getting closer and closer to the mark, and I especially didn't like the slightly patronizing air in which he said it, an air calculated to stop far short of the insult that might bring on another transformation but present nonetheless. I tried to adopt an air of mysterious wisdom and nodded in silence.

"Well, do you want my help, or don't you?" he said. My silence was beginning to irritate him.

"Wizards can only be combatted by other wizards. Surely Prince Dominic understands the powers of magic even if you don't."

"Well, I hope you don't mind my saying this," in a tone that implied that he certainly hoped I did mind, "but Prince Dominic suggested that you were still a fairly inexperienced wizard, which was why you hadn't been able to make any progress against this other wizard. So my plan was go to Yurt and catch him."

"Go to Yurt and catch him?" I repeated idiotically.

"Of course," he said, clearly thinking Dominic was right about me. "It was my idea. Even a wizard won't be able to stand up against an army of knights!"

"You'd be surprised at what a wizard can do. Did Dominic tell you that he and the other knights already spent most of one day chasing that 'wizard' without being able to catch him?"

He dismissed this with a wave of his elegant hand. "This time, *I'll* be leading. There's no need to thank me; as the king's loyal vassal, I'm always eager to assist." He kicked his horse and rode away, toward the baying of the hounds, before I could answer.

Last month, I thought, the demon had only showed itself to us because it wanted to taunt me. If a body of knights suddenly tried to roust it by force from the cellars, it would be furious, furious enough that I would never be able to negotiate with it, even assuming I knew what to say. And a noncooperative demon was going to be the least of my problems. If the count led a band of knights toward Yurt tomorrow morning, I was quite sure they would all be dead by night.

In desperation, I sought out the duchess. She was having an argument with her master of hounds, which argument she was apparently enjoying hugely, but when she saw my face she told him, "Then blow whenever you like," and pulled her horse over next to mine. The master blew his horn to summon the hounds, put them on their leashes, and led them over the next hill while we sat on our horses, talking.

The horses stamped and snorted clouds of white breath. "The count is planning to lead a body of knights to attack the demon," I said.

"Does he know it's a demon?"

"No, but I don't think he'd care. He has no respect for magic and probably has none for the supernatural either. What am I going to do?"

"Stop him, I presume," she said thoughtfully. "You know, you shouldn't really be surprised. There have scarcely been any wars in the western kingdoms since there started to be school-trained wizards in all the chief political courts. If you wizards want to stop all fighting, you certainly have my support; too many people without any sense end up leading the battles. But you've got to realize that the knights are starting to seem almost superfluous, even to themselves. They're trained as warriors, and the most warlike activity they normally have is escorting someone like me to the king's castle for Christmas. No wonder they're excited at finding someone to attack!"

I thought briefly that the same might be said about her. "The demon will destroy them."

"Of course," she said. "That's why you have to stop them. The king would miss his knights, and I'd miss mine, even if the young count isn't a favorite of any of us." She chuckled, but I was unable to join in.

I had thought I had a week to decide what to do. Now I had less than a day.

"They won't want to leave for Yurt until the boar hunt is over," said the duchess, echoing my thought but much calmer about it. "I wonder if we ever *are* going to flush this boar!"

As if in answer, there was a faraway blast of horns, and a much closer barking. We had been riding at the edge of the woods, and now there was a tremendous crashing in the blackberry thickets at the trees' margin. A hundred yards from us, a dark shape suddenly burst out into the fields, at least twice as big as I had expected. I had also not been counting on the vicious tusks.

I pulled my horse up so sharply it reared, but the duchess kicked hers forward. "Head it off!" she yelled. "Try to corner it down in the streambed!" At the moment, the demon was much less interesting to her than the boar.

I couldn't expect her to help me, I thought. Turning to her was only a last-ditch effort to find someone else to share the weight of the problem, when it was mine all along. I turned my horse to follow the hunt, turning over for the thousandth time in my mind the list of the people in Yurt. I kept coming up with the same answer as I had all the other times, that I could not imagine any of them deliberately bringing evil into the kingdom and putting a curse on the king.

Although the duchess tried to corner the boar in the streambed, it broke through the other side, rushing up the bank with the force of a winter storm and killing two hounds in the process.

Normally I would have been very interested in the hunt. Now I followed it because I did not know what else to do. I noted without much interest that the boar's bristles were soon streaked with blood, and that its sheer strength made it able to break away several times when someone thought he had a spear in it.

The king and queen stayed out of the center of the action, for which I was glad; it would be no use, I thought, having had the king miraculously cured if he was then attacked by an enraged beast.

The Lady Maria also stayed in the background, her eyes excited, but more timid of the boar than she had been of the dragon.

"I can't remember the last time we had boar meat for dinner in Yurt," she told me. "I'm quite sure it was before you came, maybe even before the chaplain arrived. I do know I thought it very exotic the first time I tasted it—my brother's castle is too close to the City for such wild animals!"

Since I had absolutely no interest in boar meat, in exotic flavors, or her brother's castle, I grunted, doubtless very rudely.

She noticed my lack of interest and apparently decided to draw me out. "You were born in the City, weren't you? This country life must all seem foreign to you."

I was touched enough by her interest to manage a smile. "I always thought of myself as a city boy until I came to Yurt, but I'm starting to think that I'm not one anymore."

"The queen herself isn't really a city girl now," said Maria agreeably.

"I at least grew up in the City," I said, "but I don't have any family there anymore."

"I knew you were an orphan," she said, turning wide blue eyes dramatically on me. "We orphans must keep together."

Even the hunt itself, the long spells of watchful inactivity, the sudden yelps and shouts, and the massive form of the boar shooting out of sight again seemed appealing in comparison to listening to her chatter. "Let's try to catch up with the others," I said. "They're sure to corner it soon, and we want to be there when they do."

We trotted along a streambed overhung by leafless branches, passing several men on foot from the village who were leaning on massive spears and looking disgruntled.

"Is the boar up ahead?" Maria asked them.

They shrugged. "Could be anywhere, my lady. It's the devil's own boar, that one."

Although I knew this was only a figure of speech, I didn't like it and kicked my horse. "Come on," I said. "The others should be just over this hill."

And then, with a roar, the boar burst out directly in front of me. With riding skills I did not know I had, I pulled my horse aside, managed to stay in the saddle, and used my hands and weight to help the horse keep its feet on the slippery stones.

The Lady Maria was not so lucky. As my horse came down, hers reared up, and the boar shot under its hooves. She gave a despairing scream and scrabbled uselessly at the reins. Her sidesaddle perch gave her no chance to save herself. She flew twenty feet and crashed into the blackberry bushes.

The boar was gone. I was off my horse and beside her in a moment. My heart was pounding so hard it seemed its sound ought to summon the others.

She was lying absolutely still. Her face was dead white, except for the drops of startlingly red blood beginning to ooze from the scratches where the thorns had caught her on the way down. Her arms and legs were spread out as limply as a doll's.

Furiously I unbuttoned her jacket and felt for her heartbeat. Blue eyes flipped open. "Fresh," she said.

The Lady Maria insisted on riding back to the castle. Although her horse had fallen after it threw her, it had leaped up again immediately, and it did not seem to be favoring any of its legs. The villagers helped me calm the horse, readjust the saddle, and scoop her back up and into it.

"Are you sure you wouldn't want to wait for a litter, my lady?" I tried to urge her.

"No," she said obstinately. "My father always said that if you're thrown you should get right back up, and he was right."

Since she seemed to have no broken bones, it was hard to argue with her. But she showed no interest in rejoining the hunt, and I was able to lead her back toward the castle.

By the time we got there, she was ready to admit that maybe she was slightly bruised, even though she insisted that she did not need a doctor. The duchess's lady's maid went up to help her get ready for a nap, while I sat down in front of the fireplace in the empty great hall. For much of the afternoon I sat there, doing nothing more useful than keeping the fire burning.

Just before sunset, I heard the sounds of the returning hunting party. Even before I could hear the words, I could tell from the sound of their voices that it had been a success. With the boar dead, I feared, there would be nothing to prevent the young count from starting for the royal castle first thing in the morning.

The duchess came in, fresh bloodstains on her

cloak. "I heard the Lady Maria was thrown. Is she all right?"

"She says she is. She's been resting this afternoon."

"I'll go up to see her." I accompanied the duchess as she strode toward the stairs: I wanted to be sure myself. "You missed a great hunt, Wizard!"

The Lady Maria was awake, sitting up in bed and wearing what I was fairly sure was the frilly pink item I had seen her sewing last month. She blushed when I came in.

"This wizard worries too much," she told the duchess with a pretty laugh. "It was just the merest fall, as both you and I have had many times."

"I hear the boar almost smashed into you."

"I know," she said. "I've especially noticed these last few months, maybe you'll laugh at me but it's true, I just seem *unluckier* away from home. Nothing bad like this ever seems to happen to me in the castle of Yurt."

"Probably because there are very few wild boars in the castle," said the duchess.

But this went beyond joking. For a moment I was unable to move or even breathe. I had been incredibly foolish, but I thought at last I understood it all.

"Are you going to want to come to dinner," said the duchess, "or will you want a tray sent up?"

"Oh, I'll come to dinner, of course!" She glanced in my direction. "In a minute, when you're gone, I'll get dressed and come down. I certainly will want to hear all the details of the hunt. The strategems, the beast's last stand, who finally thrust the spear home, the heroism of the villagers—I'm sure it will all be terribly exciting."

"I have to wash and change myself," said the duchess gaily. I guessed that she might have thrust in the final spear herself, but at this point I scarcely cared. "Come on, Wizard."

As I carefully dressed in the red and black velvet

suit that had been my best suit until a short period
on Christmas morning, I realized that I was looking
forward to dinner in the assumption it was the last
meal I would ever eat on earth.

III

There were indeed tales of the hunt at dinner,
which I scarcely heard. At the servants' table, two of
the kitchen maids were giggling and one was almost
in tears because the cook, faced with five hundred
pounds of pork to deal with, had discovered that her
own best butcher knives had not come from Yurt, and
she was not at all sure that the duchess's would do.

The Lady Maria had come down with a slight limp
and had a small bandage placed artfully on one cheek.
She told the story of her fall several times, with embel-
lishments, including the despair of "her knight," who
was apparently me, when he had thought she might
have been killed. When the fruitcake had been served,
I whispered in her ear, "Could I come see you in your
chambers, my lady?"

She laughed and even blushed, though after all this
time I would have expected her to realize that my
intentions were strictly honorable. As the dessert tray
went around a second time, she and I slipped away.
I helped nurse the fire in her room back to life, and
we were soon cozily settled in soft chairs.

"I don't want you to go riding again," I told her.

She smiled. "You're a dear man, but you really do
worry too much. Everyone who rides gets thrown
sooner or later."

"But I think you're in special danger."

"You're thinking of what I told the duchess? Well,
we'll be back in the royal castle soon, and then I'll be
lucky again."

I was afraid I knew where her "luck" came from.

Since I was also fairly sure she would not answer a straightforward question, I started telling her my best guesses, in the hope that she would confirm them. "You told me once, my lady, that you'd seen time run backwards. Was that when you had recently come to Yurt, and you and Prince Dominic tried to get the old wizard to teach you some magic?"

"How did you know?" she said with a laugh.

"Oh, I just guessed," I said cheerfully. "You know I told you time can't run backwards, normally, so it must have been pretty powerful magic, so I'd like to hear how it worked."

She looked at my face, to see if I was going to accuse her of anything or scold her, but she saw only an interested smile. I did not say that I had at last realized, long after I should have, that the key event that touched off the situation in Yurt four years ago was not the arrival of the queen so much as the arrival of the Lady Maria with her.

"Well, the old wizard told us to come up to his room in the tower," she said. "It was *very* exciting and mysterious, because normally he would never let anyone in his chambers. He wasn't like you that way at all."

I decided to let this pass. It was far too late for me to become exciting and mysterious.

"And then he said a spell, a really long spell—and I knew it must be important to get every word right, because he had it written out on a piece of parchment that he looked at just before he said it."

The wizard might want to be sure such a critical spell was said correctly, I thought, but the Lady Maria, with her ear for the Hidden Language and her total ignorance of the dangers, would have needed no such prompting.

"And you'll never guess what happened!"

"A demon appeared."

"No, silly!" She slapped at me playfully with a cushion. "First everything grew very dark, and then a man appeared, but a very tiny man, maybe only six inches tall. And you'll never guess! His skin was bright red."

A demon, I thought, but said nothing.

"The old wizard had drawn a complicated star on the floor, and the little man appeared right in the middle of the star."

No wonder, I thought, that the old wizard had at first denied that the supernatural had ever been active in the castle. He would not have wanted to admit, even to me, that he had been showing off for Dominic and the Lady Maria. After all those years without an apprentice, and nothing more than dessert illusions to occupy him . . .

"And then the little man asked if we wanted anything! The old wizard said we wanted a demonstration of time running backwards."

"And did you get it?"

"Well, I thought his was a pretty silly demonstration, but he did it! We each drank a glass of water, and then, it was the strangest thing, the water was coming back up our throats and into our glasses, and then we had to drink it again. And even when we poured the water on the floor, the little man made it run back up into the glass!"

A demon, firmly within the pentagram, will, if asked correctly, perform a few very basic tricks. I personally thought even the trick with the glass of water might have been skirting the danger-line; at school they had sent the demon back as soon as it appeared, without asking anything at all. A demon may be willing to make a brief demonstration of its power for free, but very soon it will be demanding payment in human souls.

"And what happened next?"

"That was actually it. I'd been hoping that maybe *I* could ask it for something, and I was certainly planning to ask for something better than a trick with glasses! But the old wizard said some words, really quickly, and it was gone, and he rubbed out the star."

"And what happened *next?*"

"Nothing at all," she said complacently.

Since I knew this wasn't true, I took a teasing tone. "Well, *I* know something else happened. You decided to try the spell yourself, didn't you! You can't hide your secrets from wizards!"

Making jokes and coy statements was the last thing I felt like at the moment, but it worked. She laughed. "I should have known you'd guess it sooner or later. After all, you saw me repeat your spell with the telephones! By the way—did you ever get them working?"

"No," I said, refusing to let her distract me. "Go on about how you summoned the little man yourself."

She giggled. "Do I really have to tell you? Well, since you've already guessed most of it, maybe I do, though it's actually rather silly. I'd asked Dominic, of course, if he wanted to help me, but he seems to have turned against magic for some foolish reason, and he didn't want anything more to do with it."

Dominic, I thought, had had the good sense to be terrified of a demon. It was at last clear to me why the hoped-for match between Dominic and the Lady Maria had never come about. Aside from the differences in their personalities, he would never have allied himself with someone he feared might at any time foolishly summon a demon.

"So I had to do it myself. I made the star, just like the wizard had, and I repeated the spell."

"And the little man appeared," I said through frozen lips.

"And I told him I wanted to see time run backwards, but not just as a silly trick. That is, I—"

"You asked to become younger," I said, because she seemed to be having trouble saying it herself.

She nodded, grateful for my understanding. "And the man explained that I didn't *really* want time to run backwards, as that would just make everything exactly as it had been years ago, but that instead I wanted to get some extra youth.'

"And he said he could do it.'

"First, though, he said I had to rub out the star, so he could move about more easily. When I did it, he grew so that he was the size of a normal man, and his skin wasn't red anymore. He said he had to find the extra years for me.'

"And he found them.'

When the old wizard had discovered the demon, I thought, Dominic had offered to help him catch it. He had managed to keep secret the Lady Maria's responsibility for summoning it, but he had more of a problem with me, since I was too obtuse even to realize what was happening in Yurt. The old wizard had retired, convinced that the demon was locked safely away, and Dominic had no reason to think it had escaped, but he could tell the king was continuing to grow weaker. He would have had to admit his own original involvement to tell me openly that there was a demon in the castle, but he certainly hoped I would be able to overcome its evil magic, prompted by his hints.

The Lady Maria looked at me with eyes that were suddenly brimming with tears. "He found some extra youth for me for a few years. But when I talked to him most recently, he said that it was too late for that—"

I had been a fool since the day I arrived at Yurt. It should have been obvious at once where the demon had gotten the extra years he had given the Lady Maria. He had taken them from the king.

When the saints had intervened and saved the king from death, her years had been reclaimed from her, and the demon couldn't get them back again. This was when she had decided to ask for something entirely different. This was when she had told the demon she wanted to see a dragon.

"You fibbed to me," I said, shaking my finger at her until she giggled. "You told me no one had been in your chambers that day, when actually you were requesting things from your magic man."

Did she realize that her "request" had nearly destroyed the castle? Since the dragon's presence had been extremely exciting, even romantic, and since, as it turned out, no one had been killed and the damage to the castle all seemed reparable, she was just delighted to have been able to see a real dragon.

"Maybe he couldn't make me younger anymore after he had been back in that star," she said thoughtfully.

"Was that just before I arrived?"

"It was, actually," she said, surprised. "The old wizard had left two days earlier, and the constable told us you were coming at the end of the week. It was a very strange experience. I hope you won't think I imagined it."

"Wizards are used to strange experiences," I said encouragingly.

"It was late at night, and I'd been in bed, so at first I thought it must be a dream, except that my bathrobe was all damp from the rain, so I knew it couldn't be a dream."

"Go on," I urged her when she seemed to be stopping.

"As I say, I was lying in bed. And then I heard this voice, almost inside my brain. He was calling me. You reminded me of it, that time you spoke inside my brain with the telephones. He told me to come stand at the base of the north tower, and so I put on my bathrobe and I did."

"But the door was locked," I provided.

"That's when the second strange thing happened," she said. "I started rising into the air. At first I was terribly frightened, but then I decided it was only a dream and that I should enjoy it. When I got up to the top, I was able to look in the window and see my man in there. He'd been shrunk back down, and he was caught in the star."

"So what did you do?"

"I kicked out the glass in the window—I'd put on my riding boots when I left my room, because of the rain."

So much, I thought, for the magic locks on the casement latches.

"And I went inside and talked to him. There was one little flow of rainwater that had cut across the chalk lines, but he said he needed me to rub it all out so he could help me again. So I did, and then, maybe he put me to sleep, but the next thing I remember it was morning and I was back in my own bed. That's why I thought it was a dream at first."

"You've only had the one magic man here in the castle, haven't you?" I said as casually as I could.

"Well, yes." There was something in the way she said it that made me break out all over in a cold sweat.

"You didn't send for any others who might be able to find some extra years for you?"

"Well, I tried, early this fall," she said, looking at me accusingly. "At first when I freed him from the star everything seemed fine, but then it seemed he couldn't make me young anymore. You'd promised to teach me magic spells, so I'd hoped I wouldn't have to rely on that man—and, frankly, sometimes he made me feel a little, well, funny. But then you just gave me all that grammar. That's why I decided I would have to call on a different magic man."

"And did you?" I managed to croak, even though my tongue felt paralyzed. If there were two—or even more—demons in Yurt, we were all moving to the City and never going back.

"No," she said, with the tears of frustration at the

edge of her eyes. "I tried, but it's been three years since I said the spell, and I could only get partway through it."

I said the best prayer of thanksgiving that I knew.

But there was something else, even more important, that she probably did not know and which I myself had only just admitted. Sweet, silly, pretty Lady Maria, sitting comfortably in her chair by the fire, wearing the white silk shawl I had given her for Christmas, had sold her soul to the devil.

It felt like the middle of the night, though I knew it was much earlier, as I staggered from the Lady Maria's chambers toward my own. If she had died in her fall this afternoon, if we all had died in the dragon's attack, she would have gone straight to hell. If the dragon had destroyed Yurt, probably some of the rest of us would have joined her in hell, including me for all I knew, but for her there could be no doubt.

In my room, with the fire blazing, I pulled out the *Diplomatica Diabolica* with nerveless fingers. As I read, the duchess's castle grew silent around me. The only sounds were the crackling of the fire and my own heartbeat, which grew louder and louder in my ears as night wore on. As the first morning light came in the window, I closed the book and tried to stretch the knots from my shoulders. I knew what I had to do and just hoped I knew how to do it.

IV

I swung the door of the chaplains' room open with a bang. The duchess's chaplain, whose room this actually was, had been on the point of opening it from the inside, and he jumped back, startled.

"Excuse me," I said, as calmly as I could. He went

past me with a concerned look and hurried down the corridor.

The royal chaplain, Joachim, reached down to pick up his Bible, which he had dropped at my abrupt entry. The remains of the priests' breakfasts were on the table, and he had been reading after service.

"There's a demon in the cellars of Yurt," I said.

"Dear God," he said without any expression at all.

"I'm going back to negotiate with it, to persuade it to return to hell. But in return it's going to demand a human life. Now you and I have to decide who we'd be happiest to sacrifice. The young count? One of the ladies? Would anyone ever miss Dominic?"

He rose, shaking his head. "You really frightened me there for a minute. I think you'd joke if your immortal soul was in danger."

"I think it is."

At this point reaction set in, and I collapsed on his bed, trembling so hard from fear and exhaustion that I was nearly blind.

Joachim kicked the door shut and knelt beside me. "You mean it, don't you," he said quietly. "There really is a demon in the cellars of Yurt."

"And it's got the Lady Maria's soul." I heard his sharply indrawn breath and with difficulty opened one eye to look up into his own blazing black eyes. I told him the story in a few halting sentences.

"I think I'll be able to negotiate for her soul, because she never intended to sell it. She *has* in fact done so, in return for a few years of youth and a chance to see a dragon, but because her intention was never evil I have a bargaining loophole. But somebody will have to die."

Joachim rose purposefully. "Don't go away!" I called weakly. "Hold my hands."

He returned at once. Though it would have been far better to have the queen holding my hands, I was very glad for the human contact.

"So when will this person have to die?" he asked quietly.

"Right away. Immediately. As soon as I've completed the negotiations."

"It should take me no more than a few minutes to prepare to go."

I managed to struggle to a sitting position. "Not you! It's going to have to be me. You can pray for my soul, but the saints would never listen if I tried to pray for yours."

"But I can't let you do it."

"Please don't argue," I said, blinking and feeling ashamed of my fear when he was so calm. "If you give up your life, who will minister to the people of Yurt? Since you've taken responsibility for my soul, you have to be alive to pray for it."

He said nothing, which I hoped meant he agreed. "I read the whole *Diplomatica Diabolica*," I said, "and I think I know how to do all the negotiations. But just in case I can't, and the demon kills me but refuses to go back to hell, you'll have to be here to stop it. The demon's already afraid of you. Beg the old wizard for his help. He caught the demon once, even though it was much weaker then. Send a message to the wizards' school in the City. They might be willing to assist you, since with me dead you'd have no qualified wizard here trained in the modern methods."

"This all sounds as though it would be better to have a live wizard and a dead priest."

"Please, don't think I'm insulting your abilities. Call for the bishop instead of the Master of the wizards' school if you want. But my life will be the life it will want."

Neither of us said anything for several minutes. "It seems so silly, in a way," I said. "When I was young, back before I became a wizard, I always thought it would be romantic to die for the woman I loved. Now I'm going to have to die for the Lady Maria."

"Christ died for all of us, most of whom have much worse sins than folly and vanity."

"Yes, but I'm not Christ."

"I'd already noticed that." Maybe, I thought, my dying would at last give the chaplain a sense of humor.

"There's something I have to ask you. I must go soon, very soon, because the Lady Maria has insisted she's going to go riding again, and the young count is going to lead the knights back to Yurt, and all of them will be in horrible danger. But you have to tell me. I shall offer the demon a *life* for Maria's soul, not another soul. But when it kills me, will it take my soul as well?"

"I don't think so," said Joachim slowly, and much more hesitantly than I would have wished. "Usually, if a person disinterestedly gives his life to save another, his soul is saved. But in this particular case, I would have to ask the bishop. I could send him a message by the pigeons."

"There's not enough time. I'll just have to risk it."

We sat in silence for several minutes more. I kept hoping that if I waited I would either start feeling brave or think of an alternate plan. "It's probably too late for proper spiritual instruction now," I said with an attempt at a smile. "I just wish I wasn't so scared."

"Courage is doing what you have to do, no matter how frightened you are."

"Even *I* know that. But I still wish I wasn't so scared."

Outside the chaplains' window, we could hear voices and clattering as the castle began to go about the day's business. I waited for but did not yet hear the sound of a mounted party preparing to head out.

"I suspected you of evil once," I said. "Will you forgive me?"

"Yes, of course. I suspected you of evil more than once. Please forgive me as well."

I stood up at last. "I have to go now. I'll leave it to

your judgment what to tell the others. Just please don't let the Lady Maria know I had to die because of her; it would upset her too much. But do try to warn her against future experiments with pentagrams. Let Zahlfast—he's the teacher at the wizards' school I told you about—hear the whole story, whatever happens. And tell the queen I love her."

"I'm going with you," said Joachim, suddenly and intensely.

"You can't. It's thirty miles, and it would take you most of the day on horseback. I can make it flying in half an hour."

"But I could—"

There was a sharp rap on the door, causing us both to jump. It swung open, and Gwen came in for the chaplains' breakfast tray.

"I'm so sorry," she said, "but with everything so different in this castle, I lost track. I should have gotten it an hour ago."

"It's all right," Joachim said gently. She hurried away, closing the door behind her.

The interruption made me realize that the precious moments were draining away. I tried taking deep breaths. "Good-bye," I said. "I have no right to imperil anyone except myself. Pray for me."

Joachim was about to say something else, but he did not have a chance. I leaped out the window and was gone, flying back home.

I dropped from a gray sky in front of the castle. A cold rain was starting to fall. After leaving the duchess's castle with burning determination half an hour earlier, I now felt reluctant to go inside. The cracked parapets where the dragon had writhed in death looked like a row of broken teeth.

I wandered toward the king's rose garden, arguing unsuccessfully with myself that I needed to go inside at once. The individual rosebushes were all mulched and carefully covered, but the lawn was dead and sodden. I donned a protective spell against the rain.

My eye caught a glimpse of something just beyond the garden. I went around to investigate and found a pile of white stones, rounded pieces of chalk, emerging from the last of the snow. The stones were positioned half under a shrub, where they would never be noticed in the summer.

I continued on around the castle. There were four more of the piles of white stones. This, then, was the giant pentagram the old wizard had erected around the castle. The demon had escaped from the tower room, but it had been unable to escape from the castle.

The thought passed wildly through my mind for the second time in twelve hours that perhaps I could leave the demon in the castle and find some reason to persuade the king and queen never to return home again, but to start a new life with their household somewhere else.

I shook my head hard to dismiss this thought. Besides the unlikelihood that I could persuade them of any such thing, I knew that the piles of stones could be disturbed some day, whether anyone was living here or not, releasing the demon from its temporary prison. And the Lady Maria's soul was in jeopardy no matter where she was. I shivered, set my jaw, and rose to fly over the castle walls.

I dropped into the courtyard and stood still for a moment, listening. There was no sound but the dripping of water. But the cobblestones in the courtyard seemed unnaturally warm, like the surface of a stove. Something whizzed silently by my face. I jumped back, throwing up my arms, and realized it was a bat. More bats wheeled around the castle towers. What were bats doing out in the middle of the day?

For several minutes I walked through the empty castle. Giant gray toads squatted in several of the rooms, and heavy flies buzzed against the windows. Small dark shapes that I recognized as rats scattered as I opened doors. The door to my own chambers was closed, but the magic lock was gone.

I opened the door and stepped inside. Nothing looked disturbed, although the supernatural influence was very strong. I had worried about a stranger reading my books of magic, but a demon, whose own power could cut right through the natural powers of magic, would have no need to do so.

It occurred to me that perhaps what I needed to do was to light a fire in my fireplace, sit down and get warm for an hour or two, and make sure I actually knew what I was going to say to the demon. Almost by force I dragged myself from the fireplace, where I was already reaching for the kindling.

I knew perfectly well what I was going to say to the demon. The negotiations were straightforward. If what the world's demonology experts had to say in the *Diplomatica Diabolica* was correct, at the end the demon would agree to release the Lady Maria's soul, would agree to return to hell, and would look around for the life it had been promised. And the life would be there.

I went back out into the courtyard, closing my door and putting on a magic lock. They would remember me in future years by the rooms that no one could enter.

I started walking toward the great hall, thinking vaguely that I might meet the demon there, but stopped myself. I knew perfectly well where I would find it.

But I wanted to do one final thing. I went to the little room by the main gate and worked the winch to lower the drawbridge. Even if the royal party did not return until the end of the twelve days of Christmas, someone from the village would see the bridge down and come in to investigate. The constable might be worried about the storerooms, in spite of the heavy locks on the doors, but I was more worried about my body. I hoped someone would find it before it was too badly nibbled by the rats.

The bridge went down with a clang that vibrated through the whole castle. I opened the main gate wide enough to admit a man and forced my feet to cross the courtyard.

Thin swirls of foul smoke were wafting up the cellar stairs. More bats flew up as I reached the top of the stairs. They flew back and forth, blind and disoriented. I took a final breath of clean air and went slowly down.

The key I had taken from Dominic a month ago, when we had been chasing the stranger, turned with a rusty screech in the lock. I propped the door open and started down the long, black corridor.

PART EIGHT
The Cellars
I

The faint daylight faded away behind me, and I paused to turn on the magic light on my belt buckle. It cast just enough light for me to see a few yards ahead. Motes in the coils of foul smoke danced in the light of the moon and stars. I pushed aside the thought that I should go back for a lantern or a magic globe and walked determinedly onward.

But my determination lasted only for a few steps. The cellars were absolutely silent except for the sound of my feet. Instead of being half a dozen yards underground, I could have been half a dozen miles. I did not even hear the dripping and scurrying sounds I had heard when last here. All I could hear was the sound of my own blood rushing in my ears.

"Maybe the demon's gone," the thought popped into my head. "In that case it's silly for me to be down here." But I dismissed the thought and continued slowly on. I might not be able to hear him, but I was pushing against a wave of evil like walking into a headwind.

The hall turned, and I put my hand on the wall while trying to peer around the corner. The stone was wet under my hand, and the wet was stickier than water. I held my hand at the level of my waist to look at it in the faint light of the moon and stars. It was dripping red.

I gritted my teeth and forced myself onward against a terror that threatened to overwhelm me. Soon I had proceeded farther than I had gone before, past the spot where the floor had been flooded. Now it was dry and ominously warm.

My knees began to tremble so hard that each step became an effort of will. My steps came slower and slower until I found I had stopped completely. The smoke made me cough, as my lungs desperately sought purer air, and the sound of my coughing seemed to echo throughout the cellars. "Where are you?" I almost shouted but bit my lip just in time.

"You know that's not the way to open a conversation with a demon," I told myself firmly. This was not a time for improvisation, for using good ideas and flashes of inspiration to cover up for a lack of preparation. If I was going to save my kingdom, I would have to be the wizard I never had been and proceed absolutely according to the rules.

But I wished I would find the demon before I lost my nerve. I made my feet start moving again. "Merciful saints," I breathed, then shook my head. The Lady Maria's soul was beyond the prayers of even the saints. Her only hope of any kind, and the only hope for the life and happiness of all the people living in the castle of Yurt, was for a negotiated compromise with the demon. And as I had reminded myself once before, the saints do not negotiate.

The corridor turned again and continued downwards. I glanced sideways at some of the rooms I was passing, afraid of what I might see in them. They no longer looked like storerooms. They looked like prison cells.

Once again, I had to keep myself from shouting, "Come out! Let's get this over with!" If the demon wanted to drive me back out of the cellars with terror, he was close to succeeding.

I stopped, trying to steady my ragged breathing. I had no idea how much farther the cellars went. The absolute stillness seemed to bear me down as though under a physical weight. But barely had I thought that any noise would be better than this silence when I discovered just how wrong I was.

A cloud of bats, squeaking frantically, rushed up the corridor toward me. Their wings flapped all around my head, and I felt the brush of tiny, hairy bodies against my face. At that I *would* have fled, heedless of the consequences, but my foot slipped and I crashed to the floor. Here the paving stones were damp, and as I sat up I could hear for the first time the dripping of water.

The bats were gone. I stood up, rubbing my bruises. It didn't matter if I had cracked any bones, because I would soon be dead anyway. All I had to do was keep moving until the demon showed himself. Now the air was thick with scurrying noises, with unidentifiable reptilian calls, and with distant and ominous moans. Emboldened by any change from the deadly silence, I walked on as quickly as I could make my feet move.

Rats scampered down the corridor in front of me, and several times I nearly stepped on a scorpion or a snake that slithered across my path. Another cloud of bats burst out of a side room, but this time I was ready for them. But I did not like the moaning sound, and I was drawing closer to its source.

A flutter of movement caught my eye, just on the edge of my peripheral vision. I jerked around so fast I nearly lost my footing. It disappeared as I turned, but I had had a faint glimpse of an apparition with a human face.

I braced my back against the stone wall and felt more dank blood seeping through my clothes. Giant roaches scuttled by my ears. The light from my belt was very faint, but I managed, after a few panic-stricken moments, to increase the brightness momentarily.

I was standing at a widening of the corridor where many doorways opened on either side. In each doorway was a barred gate, rusted open. There was no possibility of imagining that these were storerooms. These *were* prison cells.

A white form moved in the cell I was facing and started toward me. It wailed as it came, with a cry that melted my bones. It was a skeleton. It rattled with every step, and its eye sockets were gleaming. I tried the two words of the Hidden Language to break an illusion, and it kept on coming.

Fingers made of dozens of tiny bones reached toward me. My arms went up over my face, and I pressed back hard against the wall, waiting for the skeleton's deathly touch.

The touch did not come. I opened my eyes again. The skeleton was gone. I did not know if it was an illusion, given voice and propelled by stronger magic than mine, or if it was a real skeleton, given life by black magic. All I knew was that the demon apparently did not intend to kill me by proxy. Either he still hoped to frighten me away, or he was saving me to kill himself.

This thought gave me the confidence to glance around at all the other barred cells. Skeletons or ghostly apparitions were in most of them. I had never known much of the history of Yurt and was unlikely now to learn more, but I remembered that, generations ago, there had been wars in the western kingdoms. These then would be manifestations of the souls of traitors, of prisoners, of men broken under torture. I shuddered as a ghostly hand passed through me, insubstantial but leaving a chill as an illusion never did. These apparitions might not be planning to kill me, but they could be drawing my soul toward hell with theirs.

I pushed away from the wall and staggered onward. Maybe I was being presumptuous, I thought, to try to save the Lady Maria's soul when she herself had willingly sold it away. Maybe I could keep the cellars locked up, since I had the only key, and talk the young count and the knights out of their mad plan to attack the "renegade wizard." Maybe, having nearly killed the king and then nearly killed us all with the dragon, the demon would now be satisfied and cause no more trouble.

But these thoughts scarcely slowed my steps. I had already had all these arguments with myself many times and had won—or lost, depending on whether or not one thought my own life worth preserving.

The dripping was steadier, and I had to step carefully, because a thin film of water was coursing over the floor. I had no idea how far I had come or how long it had been since I left the courtyard. It briefly occurred to me that I might be dead already.

The corridor turned again, and I paused, for ahead I thought I could see a light burning. Again, I barely stopped myself from calling out, "Who's there?" I knew perfectly well who was there. The floor grew warmer and drier with every step I took, and the noxious fumes grew thicker.

I turned another corner and found myself looking into a wide chamber, at the very end of the cellars. I walked warily into the room. The walls were glowing red, and the heat was nearly unbearable. The room seemed empty.

A voice spoke behind me. "Were you looking for me?"

•   •   •

I made myself turn around slowly and deliberately. The demon was standing in the doorway. I was struck dumb. He was only about a foot high, bright red, and had horns and burning eyes. If he hoped to lull me into complacency by appearing small, he was mistaken. He smiled, which gave his face the final touch of absolute evil.

"Greetings, Daimbert," he said in a high voice. Since everyone in the castle called me Wizard, it was extremely startling to have someone use my name again, especially a demon.

I found my voice and closed my eyes against his face so that I could concentrate on the words of the Hidden Language. "By Satan, by Beelzebub, by Lucifer and Mephistopheles," I said, as this was the correct way to begin a conversation with a demon. "I have come to offer you a bargain." I spoke rapidly, before the pervasive evil could drain from my mind the memory of the words I had to say, before I could change my mind. "In return for a soul to which you may not be fully entitled, I offer you a life."

A laugh forced me to open my eyes again. The demon was taller now, and he was not so red. "Come, Daimbert," he said in the language of men, not in the Hidden Language. "Before you say anything you may regret, shall we talk for a moment?"

"Non-binding conversation," I said, choosing the correct words of the Hidden Language carefully. I made it a demand, not a request. One is less likely to be tricked by a demon if what one says has been declared non-binding, but the *Diplomatica Diabolica* was very clear that one should never request anything from a demon.

"Non-binding conversation," the demon agreed formally. He had continued to grow as we spoke, and he was now the tall, gaunt-faced stranger I had first seen when we returned from the duchess's castle.

Now that it had at last begun, I was almost relieved, though rivulets of sweat were running down my face from the heat. The demon stepped into the room, conjured up two chairs with a wave of his hand, and offered one to me. "Then let us talk!"

II

"You want me out of your castle, Daimbert," said the demon conversationally, crossing his long legs. I reminded myself not to trust his friendly demeanor for a second and repeated over in my mind the phrases I had selected from the *Diplomatica Diabolica*.

"I myself rather like Yurt," he continued. "But I'd be willing to consider another castle. You know I won't go back to hell empty-handed if I can help it, and I presume you didn't even bring the chalk to try to capture me. Am I right? I knew you'd have too much sense even to try."

"In return for a soul to which you may not be fully entitled," I tried again. "I offer you a life."

"We're having a non-binding conversation, remember?" he said with a laugh. I could almost have borne it had it not been for the laugh. "Why do you have to be so melodramatic? Do you think anyone will appreciate it if you kill yourself senselessly? How much more sensible to move the chalk from outside the castle."

"Move the chalk," I repeated, not understanding. In a moment, I thought, my mind would go, and then he would be able to do whatever he wanted with me.

"You've seen, surely, the five piles of white stones outside the moat, forming a pentagram to keep me in the royal castle of Yurt. If you move the stones, I'll leave Yurt and never bother you again."

"But where will you go?"

"Does it matter?" he said with a wave of his hand.

He fixed me with his enormous eyes. It looked as though he had tiny flames where a human should have pupils. "I'll be gone, and I won't try to capture anyone else's soul. I promise!"

I reminded myself that this was a non-binding conversation. Besides, his words were not even close to the words which, according to the *Diplomatica Diabolica*, would actually engage a demon.

"A demon loose in the world is too dangerous," I said. "And the Lady Maria's soul would still be forfeit."

The demon leaned forward and touched me on the knee. I had somehow expected his touch to be insubstantial, that of an apparition, but it was solid as iron and hot as fire. If he had touched my bare skin, I think it would have blistered.

"Why are you so worried about the Lady Maria?" he asked in tones of reasonableness. "If she didn't know the consequences of asking favors of a demon, she certainly should have. She may have 'imperiled' her soul by talking to me, as you might put it, but there's something you ought to know."

"What's that?" I said as he paused.

"I can see the future. Even if you romantically throw your life away for her, in two years she will commit a mortal sin so great that even the saints will turn their backs on her."

"And what's that?" I burst out.

"Are you asking for information?"

"No," I cried, adding quickly in the Hidden Language, "I seek no help or information from you!" This was too close an escape for comfort.

He fell silent for a moment, watching my face. I tried ineffectively to wipe my forehead with a wet sleeve. If he tricked me into asking for knowledge beyond that possible in the natural world, I would be well on the way to selling my own soul.

But could he be right about the Lady Maria? There

was no way to know, but I had to act as though he were wrong. "You're lying," I said firmly. "I don't want to have a conversation with a lying demon."

"I'm telling the perfect truth," he said easily. "Even if you don't believe me, you certainly should realize I have the power to discover such things."

"You can't know the future, even you," I said, trying desperately to remember a fragment of a conversation I had once had with the chaplain. "Only the past is knowable and repeatable. If the future were fixed, that would deny free will."

The demon dismissed this. "If you'd rather believe a priest than someone who has actually seen what will happen— But think, Daimbert. Even if you could 'save' the Lady Maria's soul, why throw away your life for someone you don't even particularly like?"

"I'm responsible for her and for everyone else in my kingdom," I said stubbornly, "and you imperil them all."

"But you've asked yourself the same thing, haven't you, Daimbert?"

I didn't dare answer.

The demon leaned back in his chair. "You're surprisingly obstinate," he said in a macabre parody of good-fellowship. "I gave you a good excuse with my apparitions to go back without having to meet me, but you kept coming anyway."

"I should have known all along you were here," I said. "From the moment you first broke the magic lock on my chambers, you've been teasing me, eluding me. I'm not going to let you do it anymore."

The demon shrugged. "Why don't we leave for the moment the question of 'saving' a soul that will fall into mortal sin in a short time anyway. Instead, if you're determined to die, maybe you and I can agree on something that will make your final days of life more pleasant."

"I'm not agreeing to anything," I said cautiously.

"Let me offer it before you agree!" he said pleasantly.

"I came to make a different bargain!" Although I had long since despaired of my life, and my body would not stop trembling, my mind was momentarily clear. I was almost beyond terror. The demon had first tried to frighten me away before I had even reached him, I told myself, and now was trying to distract me with pointless conversation, because he knew that my bargaining position was sound.

The demon seemed to be growing again, and the chair he was sitting on with him. "Suppose I accept your bargain, Daimbert," he said, "your life for Lady Maria's soul. That *is* what you're offering? Good. Now, why should you have to die today? I'd be happy to put off your death if *you* would."

Against my will, I felt hope surging up.

"Think what you could do if you and I just added a few details to our bargain. It would be easy enough for me to offer you whatever you want."

"I don't want anything."

He laughed again. "You know that's not true. You're just being stubborn. I know perfectly well what you want, Daimbert. You want to be a master wizard."

He had me there. I closed my eyes and clamped my jaw shut.

"Why should you and I be enemies? You and I are so similar in so many ways. We've both failed: you in being a competent wizard, and me in being an angel. You knew, didn't you, that demons are fallen angels?"

"I have nothing in common with you," I said through clenched teeth.

"You've had to get by with halfway knowledge and the occasional brilliant improvisation," the demon continued, his high voice almost gentle. "Think about it: with me working with you, you could have magic powers beyond the imaginings of any of the other students of your wizards' school, even beyond that of the teachers."

I kept my eyes closed, but a series of images raced across my unwilling mind. I could see myself returning to the school in triumph, performing magic that would stun Zahlfast and the other teachers. "No," I said to these images, and "No," I managed to say out loud. "I'm *not* becoming involved in black magic. I want to save the Lady Maria's soul, but I'm not going to lose my own."

"And why are you so sure about that?" asked the demon, softer than ever. "Did you ever think that you might belong to the devil already?"

At this I had to open my eyes, although I immediately wished I hadn't, for the demon smiled at my expression, and his mouth was full of dozens of razor-sharp teeth. As he grew, he looked less and less human.

"Yes, Daimbert," he said companionably, "your soul is already 'lost.' You can't give me an argument about free will there. I know your soul, and I know the sins you have already committed."

"You're lying." I felt I was rapidly losing whatever advantage I might once have had, but there seemed no way to stop this conversation.

"Not at all. Think about it for yourself: have you always had the impossibly 'pure' mind and heart that your religion laughingly makes the condition for what it calls salvation? As long as you belong to the devil anyway, why not take advantage of it during the next two hundred years?"

I almost believed him. But the *Diplomatica Diabolica* made it clear how full of trickery a demon could be. I had no more competence or good ideas; all I had left was stubbornness. "No," I said again. "You wouldn't now be offering me anything for my soul if you already had it."

"So you aren't interested in the powers black magic

could give you," the demon said thoughtfully. "Maybe *this* will interest you. I can offer you the queen."

I gasped so suddenly that my mouth was full of the evil fumes I had been trying hard not to breathe. By the time I had finished coughing, I was able to make my lips say, "No," although at the last moment they almost said, "Yes."

"But think about it!" I *was* thinking about it. "That head of midnight hair lying on the pillow next to yours, those emerald eyes and that smile greeting you every morning, those soft arms greeting you every night—"

"You can't know what I think!" I cried.

"And you could prolong her life to match your own. Two hundred years of bliss together! And for what? Agreeing to give up a soul you've already thrown away years ago. I'd even let the Lady Maria go."

"But—what about the king?"

"He's an old man already. He won't be a problem."

I breathed very shallowly, feeling I was choking. "You've made a mistake there, Demon. I'm not going to do anything that would hurt the king. You lost your chance that the Lady Maria gave you, to take the rest of his years from him, and you're not going to get a second chance from me."

"So wait a little while, and the problem will solve itself anyway," said the demon casually. "When he dies naturally, as you know he will within a few years, I can make sure the queen's affections turn at once toward you."

"No," I repeated, looking at the floor because I did not dare look at him. A viper was crawling near my foot but I didn't even bother to move. "I would not consider two hundred years with her as two hundred years of bliss if I knew I owed her love to you."

The demon laughed, a deep laugh now that seemed to resonate in his belly. "If I didn't know better, I'd think you liked the Lady Maria better than the queen!"

The viper moved away. I forced myself to look up again. His mention of Lady Maria brought me back to the knowledge of why I was here in the first place. "I'm only making one bargain with you," I said. I had to drag this discussion back to the reason I had originally come, before the demon tricked me out of my soul without conceding anything, or he simply killed me with fear.

He was now more than twice as large as I was. An enormous belly hung over his knees, and he leered down at me from near the ceiling. "You can't bargain for the Lady Maria. She sold herself to the devil."

"One can *always* bargain with the devil," I said with as much confidence as I could. I was moving back now toward the points set out in the *Diplomatica Diabolica*. But I wondered how I could ever have imagined the negotiations would be straightforward.

"A soul for a soul, of course," said the demon in deep, resonant tones. "But why should the devil make any bargains for your soul when it already belongs to him?"

"I do not offer my soul," I said formally in the Hidden Language. "Besides," I added firmly, "my soul does *not* belong to the devil." The black despair in the pit of my stomach did not believe that, but maybe the demon did. "I offer only my life."

"A life for a soul is not a good bargain."

"It is if the soul isn't really yours to begin with!" I stopped myself. This was not the prescribed negotiating language, but I did not think I had made any serious mistakes so far. "Binding negotiations!" I remembered then to say.

The demon nodded his enormous head. He once again had grown horns.

I put my hand over my eyes, visualizing the page in the book. "First and most importantly, her intention was never evil. A soul is judged on intent, and if you took her soul you took it on the flimsiest grounds.

Secondly!" as the demon seemed about to interrupt. "She may have gained some advantages for herself, but she brought no evil to anyone else."

"She nearly killed the king," said the demon with another leer.

"No, *you* nearly killed the king. She has never wished any harm to anyone."

The demon did not answer. Taking his silence for agreement, I pushed desperately on. "Her soul may be yours, but only on the slimmest technicality. Therefore!" I paused to make sure I had the words absolutely right before I spoke. "I have come to offer you the following bargain. You shall release the Lady Maria's soul and return at once without it to hell. Before you go, you can take my life, but my soul must be judged on its own merits."

"But I like it here in Yurt," said the demon with what would have been petulance in a smaller being.

The last of my strength gathered itself into fury. If the demon was able to delay for only a few more moments, I would throw myself at his feet and promise anything in return for my life, and he knew it. "Binding negotiations!" I cried. "You *have* to answer!"

"All right," he said with a slow smile. "I would be delighted to take your life. I agree."

"Formally!" I shouted as the enormous mouth opened, revealing more teeth than ever. "You must agree formally!"

The mouth closed slowly, and long flames darted from the demon's eyes. "By Satan, by Beelzebub, by Lucifer and Mephistopheles," he said finally.

This at last was the beginning of the correct terms of a binding engagement. I concentrated as hard as I could through the roaring in my ears, watching for the slightest deviant word.

"In the space of what you in the natural world call one minute, I shall return to hell, not to return to this world unless deliberately summoned by woman or man."

Joachim had told me, I reminded myself, that he thought that someone who gave his life for another would save his own soul. But I also remembered that he would have to ask the bishop to be sure in a case like this.

"I release, give up, and free the soul of the Lady Maria."

So far, so good.

"But before I go, you shall die." The demon's last semblance of a human form was going fast, but he still had a face that grinned at me. "Agreed and accepted?"

I started to speak, could not, swallowed twice, and tried again. "Agreed and accepted."

My eyes went black as the enormous mouth full of razor-sharp teeth bent toward my neck. The last thing I heard was the demon's booming voice. "See you in the afterlife, Daimbert!" The last thing I felt, even before the jaws reached me, was his iron forefinger burning against my chest. It passed effortlessly through skin, muscle, and bone, until it touched my heart, which leaped once more and was still.

III

The afterlife was wet and extremely cold. For a long time, which could have been hours and could have been months—although I expected they reckoned time differently here—there had been nothing but confusion, of colors, black, white, and red, of giant wings, of spaces in which I knew nothing and spaces in which I could hear myself screaming. But now everything was calm and completely dark.

I wondered with mild curiosity where I was. Purgatory, probably, which meant that they hadn't yet decided what to do with me. At least hell would have to be warmer than lying in purgatory in half an inch of icy water.

Very far away, I heard a door creaking. Maybe they had made up their minds. Steps were coming toward me, deliberate and slow. I turned my head stiffly, interested enough to want to know if it was an angel coming for me or the devil. To my surprise, it was carrying a candle. Somehow I had not expected them to need candles in the afterlife.

I couldn't see the angel's or devil's face behind the candle, although the fact that I couldn't keep my eyes open properly may have had much to do with it. I lay back and awaited my fate.

The candle was put down by my head. I could see its light, pink through my closed eyelids. There was a slight creak of joints as the angel or the devil knelt beside me.

He put his hand lightly over my heart, and then I could feel his hair tickle my nose as he put his ear to my mouth. He was so gentle that I decided he had to be an angel.

"Thank God," said the angel in Joachim's voice. "He is alive."

I tried to speak but managed only a faint croak. I moved one of my arms experimentally and was able slowly to reach up to feel a pair of clasped hands and a cheek wet with tears.

Joachim put his arms around me, under my shoulders, and drew me partly up and out of the water. "Can you hear me?" he asked quietly. "I've got to get you out of here."

I tried again to speak. This time I was more successful. "I thought I was dead."

"I think you were. But it's no good your coming back from the dead if you then die of pneumonia."

"Did you ever contact the bishop?" I croaked. It had been my final thought.

"Yes; I asked him to send me an answer here in

Yurt, and it was here when I arrived." He tried to ease me into a sitting position. "He said that if some-one lets himself be killed, even killed by a demon, for completely pure reasons, his soul will go straight to heaven."

Just my luck. Probably the only time in my entire adult life my soul would ever be completely pure, and I'd wasted my chance by coming back to life.

"But how did you get here?" I asked, realizing I had last seen him thirty miles away, in the duchess's castle.

"When you flew away, I knew at once I had to follow you. As soon as I'd sent the message to the bishop, I went to the stable and took the queen's stallion—I didn't give the stable boys a chance to argue. I was here by midafternoon." There was a sound that would have been a chuckle from anyone else. "I've never been on a horse that went that fast. I found the drawbridge down when I arrived."

"I'd lowered it."

"I had intended to rush down into the cellars after you. But great choking clouds of yellow brimstone were billowing out, and vipers and scorpions were crawling up the stairs. It was clear that no one could walk a dozen yards into the cellars and live. I got as far as the door and couldn't go any farther. I knew then the only way I could help you was through prayer.

"So I rubbed down the stallion, went to the dove-cote in the south tower for the bishop's answer, and then to the chapel, and I've been there ever since."

He tried to pull me farther out of the water. "Do you think you could walk if I supported you? I could probably carry you, but I'm afraid of dropping you with the floor so slippery."

"Help me up." Although all my joints ached excruci-atingly, I could actually stand. I checked my throat for fang marks and my chest for a hole and found nothing.

But my red velvet jacket streamed with water, now as thoroughly ruined as my new suit.

"But why did you come down now?"

"Just now, fifteen minutes ago, I felt a sudden certainty that whatever was going to happen was *over*. Whether the demon would go or stay, or you would live or die—and when I reached the cellars, most of the brimstone was gone."

We proceeded slowly up a long slope, out of the standing water, me half collapsed against Joachim and both his arms around me. Abruptly I stopped, and he stopped with me. "Oh, no," I said. "I've broken the agreement by coming back to life. The demon must still be here."

"*Is* he?" asked Joachim, very low in my ear.

I took a breath and managed to find enough words of the Hidden Language to probe for evil. There was none. When I had walked down this corridor into the cellars, the air had been so permeated with evil I had barely been able to move. Now there was nothing but abandoned storerooms whose floors flowed with icy water. I probed further. There was no evil mind in the castle, not even the oblique touch of the demon when he had been hiding from me. He was indeed gone.

"It's all right," I said, fairly complacently considering that I was now shivering so hard I had trouble speaking through chattering teeth. "I *thought* I'd done the negotiations right. The demon killed me and went back to hell without either the Lady Maria's soul or mine."

"Let's keep moving, then," said Joachim gently.

We staggered on to the front of the stairs. A big silver crucifix leaned against the open cellar door. Here Joachim did have to carry me, lifting me with a grunt over his shoulder. "Thank you for bringing me back to life," I gasped.

"I had nothing to do with it. The saints had mercy on you and interceded with God for a miracle."

I had my own ideas about who had enough influence with the saints to bring that about, but it was too hard to argue. Joachim carried me up the cellar stairs to the courtyard.

The sky was dark, except for some faint streaks of light in the east. Swung across Joachim's shoulder, I took as deep a breath as I could of the cold winter air.

As we came into the courtyard, I saw a swirl of faces, of people I had believed thirty miles away, and heard a sudden incoherent murmur of voices. This was all too confusing to me in my present state, so I let my eyes fall shut again. Joachim paused, and the voices were all around us.

"He's alive!" he said in a tone of command that carried over all the rest. "Now, in the name of God, step back and let us pass!"

They fell silent, and Joachim strode on, while I wondered without much curiosity what had happened.

But when we reached my chambers, he had to turn and bend down so that I could reach out and touch the magic lock with my palm to free the spell. With the demon gone, my locks should be safe after this, and I would be able to write letters without the paper being permeated with the supernatural influence of a demon who had been rummaging through my possessions.

Inside, Joachim pulled my drenched clothes off and wrapped me in blankets while he found me some pajamas. He pulled my bed close to the fire and knelt to rekindle the blaze. As I fell among the pillows, I saw that his clothes too were filthy and soaking.

"I'm afraid you've ruined your new vestments coming for me," I said. At the moment it seemed inexpressibly sad that he had done so.

But he shook his head and smiled. "I'll go change

and come right back to sit with you. I want to make sure you don't develop pneumonia."

"What day is it?"

"It's dawn of New Year's day, the morning after you went to meet the demon."

"I think I'll go to sleep now," I said indistinctly, feeling warm waves of sleep breaking over me as I slowly stopped shivering. "But I think when I wake up I'm going to be very hungry."

IV

I had of course done everything wrong. I thought about this with pleasant detachment some twenty-four hours later, from what seemed a great distance, lying comfortably propped up in a warm bed with the sun pouring through my windows, eating cinnamon crullers and drinking scalding tea. My breakfast tray was decorated with holly.

Joachim had gone to celebrate morning service in the chapel, but I had managed to wake up enough to speak briefly to him before he left and to order my breakfast. Everyone, it turned out, was home again.

The first place I had gone wrong was in being too frightened for months to admit the obvious to myself, that a demon was loose in Yurt. Nothing else, not even a master wizard, could have repeatedly broken my magic locks as though they were cobwebs, or filled the cellars with such a powerful sense of evil that even a first-year wizardry student would have felt it. I should have realized at once what was happening, rather than waiting until it brought a dragon down on us.

My second mistake was going down alone to face the demon, when I could no longer ignore its presence. With the duchess's assistance, I doubtless could have persuaded the Lady Maria to stay safely inside, at least for a few days, and the knights to delay their attack. That should have given me enough time to send a message to the City, to ask for help from one of the experts in demonology. Someone else might have been able to persuade the demon to leave in return for far less than a human life. In retrospect, this had probably *not* been one of the "little problems" that Zahlfast had said I would have to solve on my own.

Finally, even if it *was* going to take a human life to return the demon to hell, I should have demanded at least a short period of grace. If I had had a day or two before what had almost been my death, I might have been able to use my own natural charms to win many more kisses from the queen.

Gwen came in at this point in my deliberations. She did not meet my eyes. "I'd like about that much again," I said, handing her the empty breakfast tray.

She took it with a little duck of the head, not with a saucy look, not even with the smile an elderly uncle might deserve. I realized she had not said anything or even looked at me directly when she brought me my food originally. She was treating me with the same reserve she showed the king.

"You can talk to me, Gwen," I said, holding on to my end of the tray until she had to look up. "I'm not so weak that I must have absolute silence."

Her eyes were very wide when they finally met mine. "Excuse me, sir, I don't want to seem rude," she said hesitantly. "But—I never knew anyone who miraculously returned from the dead before."

I hadn't either, of course, but I saw no reason that she should treat me with awe on that account. "That has nothing to do with me personally," I said hurriedly. "It was the chaplain's prayers that worked the miracle." I realized I was as anxious as Joachim to disavow any personal merit—with the important distinction that he was wrong to do so and I was right.

"But how did you know I was dead?" I asked when

she remained silent. "Were you out there in the court-yard last night—or I guess it was night before last?" She stared at me without speaking, so I smiled and said, "All right, Gwen, I'll ask you something simpler. Sit down—you can bring the chair closer than that! How about if you tell me why all of you left the duch-ess's castle to come back here?"

She examined one of her thumbnails with apparent fascination but spoke clearly. "We realized something was wrong when our chaplain took the queen's stallion from the duchess's stables. The stable boys couldn't stop him. They ran to tell the constable, and he told the king. Nobody could imagine why he'd done it. They asked me if I knew anything, since I had just been up for the chaplains' tray a few minutes earlier, and when I said that you'd been with him, they real-ized that you were gone too."

"But how did you know we'd come back to the royal castle?" I prompted when she fell silent.

"Prince Dominic and the young count guessed it," she continued with a quick glance at me. "They said there was an 'evil wizard' here in the castle, who had summoned the dragon. And they said that you must have gone back to fight him all by yourself, even though they'd offered to help you. And the count said— I really would just as soon not repeat it, sir."

"It's all right, Gwen. Go on."

"He said"—she paused, then went on defiantly—"he said that you would make matters with the evil wizard even worse through your 'incompetence'! I knew you weren't incompetent, sir. But they wouldn't listen to me. The count started to gather the knights at once."

"But they listened to the duchess?"

"That's right," she said in surprise. "How did you know? She told them it wasn't another wizard at all, but a demon in the cellars! She said that you and the chaplain must have gone without telling anyone because you were afraid that the knights would imperil their souls by trying to fight it without realizing what it was."

I considered this for a moment. "Did she say where the demon had come from?" I asked casually.

"Well, from hell, I assume," Gwen said in confusion and fell silent.

So the duchess had not revealed everything I had told her. With luck, no one else had guessed that demons were unlikely to appear without reason in one of the smallest of the western kingdoms. I thought very affectionately of the duchess. Someone would have to have a long and private conversation with Lady Maria; I would ask Joachim to do so. Maria might guess her own role in bringing both the demon and the dragon to Yurt, I thought, but I did not want to say anything to her myself. Besides, matters of the soul's salvation were the chaplain's responsibility.

"It's back in hell now," I said to Gwen, who was giving me a wide-eyed stare again, "and I'm alive and still own my soul. But you haven't told me yet why you're all here."

"It was the king and queen. They said that if the two of you were fighting a demon to save their kingdom, it was their responsibility to be here with you. In the end, everyone came, though we had to leave the boar and the Christmas tree in the duchess's castle. It was late evening when we got here."

"And what happened then?" I asked when she fell silent.

She shook her head as though to shake off a strong emotion. "The castle was dark and empty, and strange—the stones were all oddly warm, and there were rats and bats and roaches all over the place—"

She gave a shiver of disgust. I nodded; I knew exactly what it had been like.

"I think the count would have gone straight into the cellars after the demon if he could have, but he couldn't even get down the stairs. There were big yellow clouds pouring out of the cellar door; the duchess's chaplain told us it was brimstone, from the demon."

I didn't know whether to admire the young count's courage or wonder at his foolhardiness—he had prudently stayed inside during the dragon's attack.

"Jon and I found our royal chaplain. He was lying in front of the altar in the chapel, and for a minute we were afraid *he'd* been killed! But when Jon touched him on the shoulder, he sat up suddenly—I'll never forget the way his eyes looked."

It sounded as though the castle had been an exciting place while I was dead. I was sorry to have missed it.

"He said—" Her voice dropped so low I could hardly hear it. "He said that you were dead, sir. And then he said that, in the name of Christ, we had to leave him alone to pray for you, and not to go into the cellars if we valued our immortal souls!

"Jon and I told the king and queen at once. The duchess's chaplain wanted us all to leave the castle immediately, but they said they wouldn't run away, and besides it was too dark and too cold to go anywhere else. We didn't even know if the demon was still in the cellars, or if you had been able to defeat it before it killed you, but there wasn't much we could do but wait.

"Nothing happened for most of the night. We were all too sad and frightened to go to bed. We sat in the kitchens or else went out in the courtyard to see if anything had changed. Even when the clouds of brimstone started to clear, we didn't dare do anything. Then suddenly, toward dawn, our chaplain appeared in the courtyard. He was carrying the big silver crucifix from the chapel altar, and he went right by us as though we weren't even there. When he came back from the cellars, an hour later, he was carrying you."

She fell silent, and I lay back in bed. This explained

the faces and voices I had half perceived in the courtyard.

"We knew then that his prayers had been answered," she continued quietly after a moment, "and that you had been returned to life. All day yesterday, he sat with you and wouldn't tell us anything, except that thanks to God you were alive. I think the duchess may have tried to speak to him briefly, but everyone else, even the king, stayed away from your room. But this morning, before service, the chaplain stopped at the kitchens to say you were better."

Gwen suddenly jumped up. "I'm sorry to keep you talking, sir. I'll get your food right away."

"Maybe ask the cook for a cheese omelet this time, to go with the crullers," I said. "And bring another pot of tea. By the way, are you ever going to tell me what Jon gave you for Christmas?"

She shook her head, blushing, and hurried out.

Joachim came in as she was leaving, taking the door from her. "There were a lot of people at chapel service this morning," he commented.

"I'm not surprised," I said. "I'll go tomorrow myself if I can walk that far, or the next morning for sure."

He sat down on the bed next to me and gave me a long look from under his eyebrows. "Whenever you can come to chapel, I'll celebrate a special thanksgiving service for your return to life. You already look better."

"I feel better. Could you hand me the washbasin and a comb?"

I scrubbed my face, getting the last of the aura of brimstone off, and looked critically at the roots of my beard and hair while I was combing them. Three days ago, at the duchess's castle, I had seen chestnut-colored roots starting to appear and had thought I would have to apply the gray dye again once I was home. But I had no dark roots now. My hair and beard were coming in white.

"But how about you?" I asked Joachim. "Haven't you let anyone else sit with me?

He shook his head. "I'm responsible for you."

"Have you even gotten any sleep in the last two days?" Several times, during the day and the night that I had slept, I had awakened, but always to see him sitting nearby, to hear his voice saying something, although I had always been asleep again before he had completed the sentence. Now his eyes looked as peaceful as I had ever seen them, but the skin was drawn tight over his cheekbones.

"A little. I dozed in your chair last night. But I didn't want to leave you."

"You should go get some rest now," I said. "I'll be all right by myself."

He stood up, yawning. "Maybe I will."

"But there's one thing I want to ask you, before Gwen comes back. Since I've already died once, with a pure heart, does that count? When I die again, will they have to assess my soul again, or will the previous assessment still stand?"

He smiled, even though I had been perfectly serious. "Maybe someday I really will understand your sense of humor. To answer your question, I don't think enough people have ever come back from the dead to make this point theologically clear. There are things that none of us will ever know on this earth. But if you're asking for my opinion, not the theologians' position, as long as you live you can do good and you can sin, and your soul will be judged accordingly."

"Or will I maybe never die again? Doesn't the Bible say that, after Lazarus was brought back to life, he became immortal?"

This time he laughed. "You're not Lazarus. Besides, that story isn't in the Bible, which only tells us that Christ raised him. It's the kind of story young priests like to tell but it's not true. All of us are going to die, and you're not an exception."

He smiled cheerfully, as though he had just said something very comforting; and in a way he had. He went out as Gwen came in with my second breakfast.

She hurried away without a word, and when I heard a step outside a few minutes later, I assumed Joachim was returning, having forgotten something. "Come in!" I called, when the step seemed to hesitate.

My door swung open, but it was not the chaplain. It was two wizards, one in a tall red hat and the other with piercing blue eyes and an enormous white beard: Zahlfast and the Master of the wizards' school. "May we indeed come in?"

V

"Yes, yes, come in," I said, flabbergasted. I struggled to raise myself from the bed, to make the wizards the full bow, but fell back without success. "What are you two doing here?"

They entered in a stately manner, closed the door, and found chairs. "The supernatural influence is gone, I note," said Zahlfast. "We saw the remains of the dragon's carcass down by the edge of the forest as we flew in, and then your constable told us you'd overcome a demon! He took us for an escorted tour of the cellars, including the hole he said the demon made when it returned to hell."

"The hole?" I had no idea what he was talking about.

"It's at the very end of the cellars," said Zahlfast soberly, "a black hole about two feet across, and it's still smoking. When you look down, you can't see anything, only darkness so black it's almost solid, and when you drop something down, you can hear it hit. We put a triple pentagram around it. As you know, nothing should come back up unless summoned, but it seemed to make your constable feel better, and we wanted to save you the trouble. He plans to cover everything over."

That sounded like an excellent plan to me.

"Now," said the Master, "could you tell us exactly what's been happening?"

I told them, although when I had left the City for Yurt and imagined someday telling the Master of my triumphs, I had not imagined doing so sitting up in bed in yellow pajamas. Besides, it wasn't a triumph I was describing.

"So I guess it's all right now," I finished, "even though I'll know, if it ever happens again, to get a demonology expert right away. Someone else, more expert, might have been able to negotiate a settlement with the demon without having to offer it his own life. But what are you doing here? Did the chaplain send you a message?"

"No," said Zahlfast, "we got no message, unless that was you calling a month ago. The phone rang at the school, yet there was no one on the line. When I heard about it, at first I just thought someone had called us by mistake, or was doing so for a joke, but then I remembered you and your far-seeing but inaudible telephones."

"That was me," I said. "The demon had grown bold and was teasing us by running around the castle in daylight, while the chaplain was away. It was afraid of the chaplain."

Zahlfast and the Master looked at each other, the same slightly skeptical look they had given each other when I told them Joachim had miraculously brought me back from the dead. "I want to show you these telephones, Master," said Zahlfast. He reached one of them down from their shelf and spoke the name attached to the wizards' school instrument.

This time it worked perfectly. The base lit up, as it always had, but when the tiny figure of a young wizard picked up the receiver, he could hear Zahlfast.

They spoke for several minutes. "Yes, that's right," said Zahlfast. "So we'll probably be home tomorrow or maybe the day after. No, there's no problem now."

"Congratulations, young wizard," said the Master, his frost blue eyes sparkling. "You've made an original contribution to wizardry and will probably have your name in the new edition of *Ancient and Modern Necromancy*. Not bad, for someone not yet thirty."

"It works!" I gasped. "I'd told the constable an anti-telephonic demonic influence was affecting my phones, and I was actually right!"

"You'll have to teach us that spell," said Zahlfast.

I thought ruefully that they seemed more impressed by my telephones than my return to life. "But what are you two doing here?" I asked, returning to my original question, wondering if I could possibly reconstruct the sequence of spells I had tried on the telephones over the past few months. "Were you just so busy it took you a month to get here after my call?"

"Well," said Zahlfast, looking surprisingly embarrassed, "at first I didn't think anything of it, though I should have realized immediately it was you asking for help. It wasn't until we heard about the dragon going over on Christmas day that I began to think there might be something seriously wrong in Yurt.

"First we got telephone calls from the wizards in courts with telephones, and then the next day the messages started coming in from the pigeon relay station. When we plotted them on a map, it became clear that the dragon had been heading for Yurt, for no one south of Yurt had seen it."

"And even then," said the Master with a chuckle, "we had an idea that you might be a competent enough wizard to handle a dragon, although we probably should have considered the likelihood of a demon as well."

"Didn't you," I said accusingly, "even for a minute,

suspect that I was practicing black magic and might have brought the dragon down for my own purposes?"

Zahlfast blushed, which I had never seen him do before.

"Not at all," said the Master. "At most, one or two people had momentary doubts. Besides, we knew there was another wizard here, the retired wizard of Yurt, who could help you."

"He did help me with the dragon. I never could have killed it without him. But what do you know about the old wizard?"

"I've only met him once," said the Master, "this summer. That's when he came to the City to try to find out about you."

"He came to the City?" I cried in amazement. "You didn't tell me this, Zahlfast."

"That's because I only found out about it myself the other day."

The Master laughed. "He said when he arrived that he would talk to the head of the school or to no one, so he had to talk to me."

"But I always thought he didn't want to have anything to do with the wizards' school."

"I don't think he ever does. But he wanted to know about *you*. He said he'd left you sleeping among his herbs for the whole day, while he flew down to the City. Said he'd never been to the school before, hoped he'd never come there again, but he thought this was the fastest way to find out about someone he called a 'young whippersnapper.' Took me a few minutes to realize he meant you."

"So what did you tell him?" I asked, feeling highly inadequate. Once again, everyone else seemed to know my business much better than I did.

"I told him you had flair and promise, if you ever applied yourself. And from the look of the telephones, it's clear that you have. To say nothing of killing a dragon and defeating a demon, even if you nearly got yourself killed in the process."

"Did get myself killed," I corrected, but they pretended not to notice.

Zahlfast stood up. "You look tired. I think we should let you rest."

"Just don't leave Yurt yet," I said. "Most of the guest chambers are still sound, in spite of the dragon. And you'll want to try our cook's excellent holiday meals. I hear they had to leave the boar at the duchess's castle, but I'm quite sure she wouldn't have left the Christmas cookies."

"We'll stay tonight at least," said the Master. "Sleep now, and we'll talk more later."

I still did not feel strong enough to climb the chapel stairs the next morning, but the following morning, leaning on the constable's arm, I ascended by the light of my own magic lamps. The others respectfully stood aside for me and made sure I was comfortably seated in the front pew. Joachim led the thanksgiving service, and while I had good reason to be highly thankful myself, I was rather surprised to see that everyone else in the castle was also delighted to have me alive. Even Dominic smiled at me, and the queen gave me a radiant look that made my heart turn over.

The winter sun burned red through the chapel's stained glass. Listening to Joachim read from the Bible, I decided I was not worthy either of a miracle on my behalf or of the friendship of all these excellent people. When the congregation sang the final hymn, I did not trust my voice and stood silent.

Once Joachim had pronounced the final benediction, every person there, from King Haimeric down to the stable boys, came up to me. Most said a few words, of how glad and grateful they were to have me again with them, though a few just touched my arm hesitantly and turned away as though overcome with profound awe and wonder. Not daring to speak, I nodded at all of them and tried to smile.

But my foray into sentimentality was cut short by talking to Zahlfast and the Master of the school. They had ended up staying two nights in Yurt, but this morning they were ready to go, waiting only until I returned from the chapel to say good-bye. We stood by the castle gate, talking for a minute, with me well wrapped up in two coats and a muffler. The two wizards were the only people in the castle who had not been at chapel service.

"We're delighted you're feeling better," said Zahlfast briskly. "Now that your telephones are working, I hope you realize you *should* call us if you run into any other problems this serious. I hadn't realized you'd take my warning against calling the school for every little problem so literally!"

I nodded glumly.

"Though I must say I should have credited you with more courage than I did," Zahlfast continued. "Most wizards wouldn't have gone down alone to face a demon, even those who did a lot better on the demonology exam than I happen to know you did. I hope you aren't going to turn into one of those rash young wizards who think of themselves as indestructible."

There didn't seem to be much danger of that. I had never expected to have a second chance at life, and I knew I would never get a third.

"Just remember you're a wizard," said the old Master. "Don't start relying too much on the priests."

"This makes it all very symmetrical," I said. "The bishop is worried about my possible evil influence on the chaplain."

The two glanced at each other. "Coming close to death doesn't seem to have changed you very much," said Zahlfast.

I had noticed the same thing myself. One might have hoped that if I came back from the dead I'd come back better, but I was too happy to be back at all to care.

The old Master looked at me with a twinkle in his eye. "I hope you realize we *are* very glad to have you still alive. In a few weeks, after all of you here have had a chance to repair some of the damage to the castle, we'll send up some wizards from the technical division. They'll take down the details of how you put the spells on your telephones so we can start putting far-seeing attachments on other instruments."

After watching them fly away, I sat on the bench in the courtyard for a few minutes to catch my breath, wondering how soon the new edition of *Ancient and Modern Necromancy* would come out and what it would say about me. I hoped it wouldn't say that I had made a brilliant invention but that no one could ever duplicate it because I hadn't kept good notes. The sunlight was almost warm here in the shelter of the castle wall, even though there was still a dusting of snow on the ground, left behind by the stable boys' brooms. But in ten minutes, as soon as my strength returned enough to walk again, I went inside in search of Joachim.

He was sitting in his room, finishing breakfast. "Thank you again for interceding with the saints for me," I said, sitting down and breathing hard. "I've just been seeing off the wizards; they're on their way back to the school. But I wanted to find out if you'd spoken to the Lady Maria."

"Yes, I spoke to her yesterday. I told you I would."

When he seemed unwilling to continue, I said with an exasperated laugh, "What is this, Joachim, the secrets of the human soul that a priest can never reveal? Since I realized she'd sold her soul to the devil long before either you or she did, and then got myself killed negotiating for her soul, I should at least be able to find out what she's going to do now that her soul is safe again."

Joachim looked at me gravely a moment, then slowly started to smile. "You're right this time; but I may have difficulty explaining this to the bishop.

"She had worked much of it out for herself already," he continued after a brief pause. "So when I sent her a message to come to my room, she had a good guess what I was going to say. She seemed to have the strangest idea, however, of how to act in such a situation. She came in as though she were a naughty schoolgirl caught in some mischief."

I could have told her this would never work with Joachim. It wouldn't even work with me.

"But it all seemed to be a façade, behind which she was genuinely terrified and repentant at what she had done. Even though she kept referring to the demon as a 'little magic man,' she realized how close she had come to damning her soul for eternity. She agreed at once when I explained to her that a few years of vain youth and beauty in this world could never be worth an eternity in hell. She had also had a chance to realize that asking to 'see a dragon' was not the innocuous request she had originally imagined.

"In fact," continued Joachim, looking somewhat uncomfortable, "once she stopped pretending she thought of it as a naughty joke gone wrong, she broke down and sobbed. I was trying to impress on her the need to beg God's forgiveness, and she kept on asking if I thought *you* would ever forgive her."

"I hope you told her I would."

"I told her that you were not angry with her personally, that you had been willing to die to save both her and the kingdom because you were following the high purposes of God."

Joachim's black eyes were completely sober, and I began to wonder uneasily if he was going to start treating me with the awe and reserve that everyone else in the castle seemed to be demonstrating. Of course, in his case it was harder to tell. But it was no use coming back from the dead if I then spent the next two hundred years being treated like some saint. In the next few days, I would have to think of something outrageous to do to remind everyone that it was, after all, only me.

"I did warn her very sternly against further experiments with pentagrams."

"I'm sure you did," I said, "and I'm sure you imposed some suitable penance on her. You don't need to tell me about that—that really should be a matter kept secret between a sinner and her priest." I changed the subject abruptly because I did not want to talk about the Lady Maria anymore; I was just glad that he had spoken with her, so I didn't have to. "But tell me, Joachim, how did you do it?"

He lifted his eyebrows at me.

"First you saved the king's life and then you saved mine. I want to know how you do it. It can't be a very common ability. Everybody seems in awe of me for being alive, whereas they really ought to be in awe of you for having worked a miracle."

"Prayer is available to anyone," he said, more soberly than ever, "who calls on God with a contrite heart. I already told you that the saints had pity and mercy on you for your sacrifice. It had nothing to do with me."

I considered suggesting that in that case maybe I had been sent back to this world because neither heaven nor hell wanted me in the next, but I decided not to. Joachim had limits.

He was still looking at me, as though in assessment. "You yourself don't seem to be taking spiritual issues as seriously as one might expect."

I was glad I had not spoken. "But I am serious," I assured him, which was true. "It's just that I'm joyful as well. Isn't someone who's come back from the dead allowed to be joyful?"

Joachim took a slow, deep breath. He had leaned his chin on his hand, so I couldn't see his mouth, but I could swear from his eyes that he was smiling.

VI

Gwen came in at that point to get Joachim's breakfast tray, and she gave a little jump, as though remembering the last time she had found us together like this.

"It's all right, Gwen," I reassured her. "Neither of us is going anywhere." She rushed back out, clutching the tray, without a word.

Since we had been interrupted anyway, I stood up to thank Joachim again and to go back to my chambers. I was still weak, and my head was beginning to ache badly. But I wanted to go to lunch with everyone else today—the cook had been sending very small meals to my room, apparently not realizing that someone who has been miraculously restored to life needs to eat a lot, and she hadn't even given me any Christmas cookies. A little nap before lunch, I thought, was just what I needed.

But as I reached for the handle to my chambers, I felt a hand on my arm and turned around to face the duchess. "Can I come in for a moment?"

"Well, my lady, I was just going to lie down—"

"I won't keep you a minute," she said, stepping inside before I could protest further. I wondered what had become of awe and respect just when I needed them. "But I'm about to go home, and I couldn't leave without finding out what really happened."

I noticed then that she was dressed for travel, in tall boots and a heavy cloak, and as she shut the door behind her I could see the stable boys starting to bring out the horses.

"If I leave now, I can celebrate Epiphany comfortably at home," she said. "The household here doesn't need any more people underfoot, now that the holidays are almost over and you're going to start repairs to the castle. Besides, my own staff will be returning from vacation, and I need to be there to explain to my cook why she can't find anything in her own kitchen and why she has five hundred pounds of boar that need immediate processing."

I stretched out on my bed and she sat beside me. "I gather you suggested to the others," I said, "that the demon had decided on its own to come live in our cellars. Thank you for doing so; I wouldn't want everybody to start suspecting each other of black magic."

"But that's why I had to talk to you," she said. "You told me that someone here had summoned a demon, and I've been wild with curiosity the last three days to work out who it could be."

I hesitated. Having decided that I would have to do my best from this point on to keep my soul pure, I didn't want to start lying. On the other hand, I did not want to give away the fact that Lady Maria had heedlessly sold her soul without even realizing she was doing so. Repenting of her actions would be painful enough to her, without feeling that everyone in the castle knew her for a sinner and a fool. I was glad again that Joachin had spoken to her, instead of me.

"I talked to your chaplain right away, of course," she continued, "just after he'd brought you back from the cellars. I wanted to be sure that *he* knew someone here had been working with a demon. He gave me the strangest look—he's so dour, you can't tell half the time what he's thinking."

I let this slur on Joachim pass without comment.

"All he'd say was that the person who had summoned the demon had done so unintentionally, without evil purpose, and that that person's soul was now safe. So I've had to work it out for myself. I remembered that King Haimeric first became ill within a year of his marriage, about the same time his old chaplain died. So my first thought was that the new royal chaplain must have been responsible. But then I realized that since he'd been able first to heal the king and then bring you back to life, he couldn't possibly be in league with the devil."

I was interested to see how the duchess's reasoning had paralleled my own. It had taken her much less time than it had taken me, but then she had the advantage of knowing from the beginning that there was a demon involved.

"So I started thinking who else it might be, and it didn't take me long to realize that it had to be the queen!"

"No!" I said involuntarily.

The duchess looked at me appraisingly. "Not my cousin, eh? You're certainly quick enough to defend her." I wondered how much she guessed of my feelings for the queen. "But the problems all started not long after she moved to Yurt. And it occurred to me that the demon might not have summoned the dragon all by itself, but rather that someone here might have been silly enough to think that a dragon would be fun. She's become more level-headed since becoming queen, I'll give her that, but she always did do just what she wanted to do."

She paused and looked thoughtfully out the window. Then slowly she started to smile, as though seeing something that made everything clear. "Of course! It wasn't the queen at all. I should have realized at once! It was the Lady Maria."

I didn't answer, but the duchess took my silence for assent. "Good. I couldn't have gone home without knowing. Don't worry—I won't say anything to Maria, or to anyone else. At least I can be sure, knowing her, that she didn't do it out of evil intent. It was only because she didn't know any better!"

The duchess slapped her knees in satisfaction. "Now I'll leave you alone, as soon as you tell me one more thing. Did the demon kill you while you were fighting with it, or did you have to offer it your life to save Maria?"

There didn't seem to be any way to get rid of her without answering. "You can't fight demons, my lady," I said. "All you can do is negotiate."

She stood up. "Now I really *will* let you rest. It looks like my knights and chaplain are ready to go. But if you ever decide you'd rather be ducal wizard than stay on here, let me know immediately."

The door slammed behind her as she left, and in a minute I could hear a clatter of hooves and farewells being called as the duchess's party left.

But just as I was fluffing my pillows to settle down properly, there was a knock at the door.

"Come in," I said wearily. At this point more awe and respect seemed highly desirable.

My door opened to admit the Lady Maria.

Except for my white silk shawl, she was dressed entirely in black. I remembered now that she had been in black for church service. She was not a naughty schoolgirl now, but rather a melancholy and penitent matron, looking back in sorrow at a life ill-led. Her golden hair was pulled tight into a severe bun; there were quite a few gray hairs at the temples.

But even though I was sure she had enjoyed picking out a suitably repentant outfit to wear, there were quite genuine tears at the corners of her eyes. She sat down next to my bed, pulling off her black gloves, apparently unable to speak at once. I sat up, rubbing my aching forehead with my knuckles, and waited.

"I wanted," she said at last, a catch in her voice, "I wanted to thank you, and I wanted to ask you if you could ever forgive me."

"Certainly I forgive you," I said, speaking very seriously and holding her eyes. "I didn't go to deal with the demon either hoping for thanks from anyone or feeling the need to forgive anyone. I went because it was my duty as a wizard."

It sounded horribly self-righteous in my own ears, but it seemed to be what she wanted to hear. It was also true. She wiped her eyes with a black-trimmed handkerchief and attempted a smile. "Then you and I can still be friends?"

"Of course we can." With any luck I could have her out of here in a few more minutes.

But she had much more on her mind. "Then if you're my friend," she said intently, "I need you to tell me something. Are they— Is everyone— Is everyone laughing at me?"

"Laughing at you?" She was entirely serious.

"Maybe it's just part of the penance I need to bear, but I have to know! Is everybody chuckling behind my back at the silly Lady Maria, who didn't even recognize a demon when she summoned one, and who happily sold her soul just so she could act girlish for a few more years?"

"Certainly not," I said without hesitation. Joachim did indeed seem to have explained matters to her most clearly. "The chaplain and I are the only people in the castle who know that *you* summoned the demon, that it didn't just appear in Yurt by itself." I told my conscience that this was, strictly speaking, true; the duchess was by now well out of the castle.

"Then you didn't have to tell the king and queen—"

Dominic, I remembered, had known all along that she had summoned the demon originally, even though he had not wanted to give her away, and even though he did not realize the demon had broken out of the pentagram that he and the old wizard had drawn to imprison it. But since he was highly unlikely to say something now, I felt safe in not mentioning him. So much for my pure soul!

"I didn't say a word to the king and queen about you. Everyone was just too delighted to have the demon sent back to hell to worry very much about how it got here in the first place."

The tears appeared at the corners of her blue eyes again. I pretended to be looking out my window; I had quite a nice view of much of the courtyard. If the Lady Maria had been standing in a doorway, waiting for the duchess to leave before she came to talk to me, the duchess would have had no trouble spotting her. Perhaps her clever guess had not been as clever as I had thought.

"I tried to explain something to the chaplain," Maria said after a moment, bringing out the black-trimmed handkerchief again, "but I think he's too high-minded to understand something so foolish, so I'd like to try to tell you instead."

Oh, well, I thought. It was too late to become awe-inspiring anyway.

"Of course it was silly to want to be young again— even I knew that. But it was *fun*—fun to think about what I might do if I were to be young, even more fun actually to find myself growing younger. Of course, Yurt doesn't offer much scope, but when the queen and I went to the City I was able to go to the dances as a participant, not as a chaperone. I had more fun three winters ago at the City balls than I've ever had before or since in my life! And then *you* came to Yurt."

"I?"

"Of course you, my gallant knight! Not that I had any real intention of making you fall in love with me!" she added hastily, as an expression I tried to suppress must still have appeared on my face. "I knew wizards never marry, and you knew that I was quite a bit older, even though I liked to imagine we looked about the same age."

Apparently the gray beard had fooled no one at any time. Maybe I could do better now that my beard was coming in white.

"And then, of course, it quickly became clear that you had given your heart to my niece. But still I—"

I interrupted her. "You knew I was in love with the queen? Was it that obvious? Does everybody in Yurt know?"

She looked at me with her head cocked to one side, then a surprising and quite genuine smile appeared on her face. "You're as worried about everybody laughing behind your back as I am!"

"I'm afraid so, my lady," I said ruefully. "But *do* they all know?"

She gave a tinkling little laugh. At least I had been able to cheer her up. "No, they don't all know. Certainly my niece has no idea—she's never had eyes for anyone but Haimeric. And I don't think anyone else has guessed, either. There *are* advantages of being single and forty-eight—one has had plenty of practice in spotting both romance and unrequited love."

I said nothing but felt very sheepish.

Maria returned to her thread, much more cheerfully. "Even though I knew you would never fall in love with me, I truly enjoyed the opportunity of having someone to flirt with, and of looking young enough that my flirtations would not simply seem pathetic. I've been in Yurt for four years now, and I presume I'll live here for the rest of my life, and I'm not going to get very many more opportunities for maidenly amusements.

"I know it was wrong to deal with a demon, even if I didn't realize then that was what I was doing. And I know it was wrong, as the chaplain told me in great detail, to want to get extra years rather than being profoundly grateful for those years God does give us. But—maybe you can tell me—it's not wrong, is it, just to want to have fun sometimes?"

I took both her hands in mine. It was no use referring her back to Joachim on this issue. "Maria, I've always been extremely fond of you, ever since I came to Yurt, and, no, it's not wrong sometimes to want to have fun."

She smiled rather complacently. "I *knew* you liked me. I knew you didn't just think of me as a silly old woman. Otherwise you wouldn't have let me help with your telephones, wouldn't have tried to teach me that hard old Hidden Language, wouldn't have given me this beautiful shawl for Christmas, and wouldn't have been willing to lay down your life for me."

I kept hold of her hands and looked deeply into her eyes as I spoke. I wanted to make sure that she understood exactly what I was saying, that she recognized my genuine sympathy while having absolutely no seeds of possible future romance planted in her mind.

"You're right that I'm in love with the queen, even though I know perfectly well she'll never look at me, and you're right that wizards never marry anyway. But I hope that you and I can continue to be good friends over the years. After all, I'm going to be living in Yurt too, and I like to have fun sometimes myself."

"I will try to act more mature and wise," she said thoughtfully. "In fact, I may not have to try very hard. Coming this close to losing my soul has made me—well, think about things I never used to worry about. I think I'll start going to chapel every day."

I remembered the demon saying that in two years she would fall into horrible and mortal sin. Even in the cellars, it had seemed a probable lie. Sitting in my warm room, I wondered how I could have even half believed it.

"If you notice me falling into sin again," she said, "do let me know."

"I will if I notice," I said, sitting back and releasing her hands. "But this time I had no inkling, until just a few days ago. I suspected almost everybody in the castle at one time or another of working black magic, but I never suspected you."

I smiled then and stood up. As I hoped, she stood up too. "Over the months to come, some people in the castle might wonder if you had something to do with the dragon, but no one will ever suspect you of evil intent. You're just going to be the mature, wise—though fun-loving—Lady Maria."

I bent to give her cheek a very chaste kiss and opened the door for her. She waved with her black-trimmed handkerchief as she hurried away.

I turned back to my room, reaching for my curtain to draw it shut so I could take a nap at last, but instead I stood at the window for several minutes, looking after her even when she was out of sight.